Another Kind of Love

WITHDRAWN

Paula Christian

KENSINGTON BOOKS
http://www.kensingtonbooks.com

KENSINGTON BOOKS are published by

Kensington Publishing Corp.
850 Third Avenue
New York, NY 10022

All Kensington titles, imprints, and distributed lines are available at special quantity discounts for bulk purchases for sales promotion, premiums, fund-raising, educational or institutional use.

Special book excerpts or customized printings can also be created to fit specific needs. For details, write or phone the office of the Kensington Special Sales Manager: Kensington Publishing Corp., 850 Third Avenue, New York, NY 10022. Attn. Special Sales Department. Phone: 1-800-221-2647.

Kensington and the K logo Reg. U.S. Pat. & TM Off.

ISBN 0-7582-0314-4

First Kensington Trade Paperback Printing: November 2003
10   9   8   7   6   5   4   3   2   1

Printed in the United States of America

With grateful thanks to our beloved sister;
she knows who she is.

Contents

Another Kind of Love

Chapter 1

Laura stood at the massive front door, her slim fingers twisting the polished knob, not daring that final quick turn, which would open the door and betray her eagerness to leave. She had been poised for flight for the last ten minutes.

But Saundra, serenely oblivious, held her in a conversation that showed no signs of waning.

Desperately Laura tried to concentrate: it was not prudent for anyone in her position to reveal impatience with an important personality like Saundra Simons. Movie stars were the bread and butter of the fan magazine writer, and a notorious, glamorous actress like Saundra was a frosted seven-layer cake. So Laura straightened up and arranged her face in a fresh smile of attention. Fortunately, Saundra was *far* too mesmerized by the sound of her own voice to notice Laura's impatience.

The sound of a car coming up the drive was a merciful interruption.

Saundra glanced quickly at her watch. "Oh, dear. It is getting late. I'm sorry you have to leave so soon, Miss Garraway . . . Laura. We seem to have so much to talk about." Saundra flashed her famous smile in Laura's direction.

Laura smiled back in bright response. "I'm sure we will be talking again soon," she told Saundra smoothly. "I wish we could go on right now, but Walter's waiting to go over these changes with me. And you know Walter."

Saundra's laugh was more in revelation than appreciation. "Indeed I do. A dear boy. But a slave driver."

"I've got the lash marks on my back to prove it," quipped Laura, moving carefully but steadily through the now open door onto the flagstone steps.

A car door slammed and footsteps sounded on the walk. "That will be Ginny," exclaimed Saundra. "I'm so glad you're still here. I want you to meet Ginny. She's really a terribly sweet person and may one day turn out to be a truly great actress."

Laura winced internally.

However, she smiled and nodded. She couldn't be rude. But damn it, she really had no interest in meeting Saundra's protégé. Hollywood sprouted starlets the way Florida exported oranges. By the carload. Except that oranges stood a much better chance for survival. Only yesterday at the studio commissary she had run into a starlet. Odd kid.

The steps came nearer, and all at once the figure of a young girl materialized from the shrubbery that hid the path.

The girl's eyes met Laura's, and there was the sudden shock of recognition. Why . . . this was the same girl. The one she had met at the studio cafeteria.

"Well . . ." Ginny began uncertainly. "It certainly is a small world."

"Isn't it?" smiled Laura, touched by Ginny's awkward cliché.

"I didn't know you two knew each other." There was a distinct note of resentment in Saundra's voice. It surprised Laura. She glanced from Saundra to Ginny, uneasily aware of a strong tension between them.

"We only met by chance yesterday," Ginny replied softly, almost apologetically. "I don't think I even told her my name."

Saundra placed a well-tanned arm around Ginny's shoulder. "Ginny Adams. Don't forget that, Laura. You'll be begging her for an interview one of these days." The famous melodic laugh embroidered the hint.

4

Ginny blushed very slightly. "I'm a long way from that," she said quietly to Laura. Still, it wasn't hard to see that she was just waiting for her "big break."

Laura wondered why Saundra had singled out this fresh-faced, shy-looking young girl to be her protégé. Ginny didn't look like the typical Hollywood starlet, and she wasn't wan enough to be a product of one of the more popular acting schools in New York.

"Well," Laura began, feeling trapped, "why don't we have lunch one day soon and discuss your future?"

"Marvelous idea," Saundra chimed. "That darling boss of yours might even let you do a feature write-up on Ginny."

Laura forced a laugh. "That's a possibility, but of course, so much depends on our schedule." She wondered if Saundra expected a promise.

"Wouldn't she be marvelous in Technicolor?" Saundra lifted a strand of Ginny's deep-red hair between her manicured fingers. "And look at her bone structure!"

Ginny was obviously uncomfortable, and Laura found herself in sympathy with the girl. She took a step toward the porch steps and let her car keys jingle in her hand.

Saundra said, "But we're keeping you, dear. Give my love to Walter. And tell him that if he prints a word of truth about me, I'll sue him."

"All right," Laura answered automatically. "Thank you again for letting me come by tonight. I'll pick up the photos tomorrow morning. Just mark the ones you want us to use. Good night," she said and nodded silently to Ginny.

"Good night, darling," Saundra called as Laura walked down the stairs. The rich, expertly modulated voice trilled after her with startling fidelity in the stillness. Even the elegantly indifferent Bel Air trees seemed to respond to the unexpected sound; their leaves suddenly shivered in the still California night air.

Laura half turned and waved briefly. Then the huge front door shut with abrupt violence, and the veranda lights switched off into blackness. She almost stumbled on the flagstone path and muttered a soft curse.

Driving down the winding tree-lined streets to Beverly Hills, Laura's mind chewed away at the strangeness of the interview.

Saundra's almost devouring intensity . . . the coincidence of the meeting with Ginny . . . the whole weird mood of the evening.

"Saundra is an experience that should be required of all writers," had been Walter's teasing remark just as she'd left the office.

Saundra was an experience, all right. No wonder he'd pushed the assignment off on her. Usually Walter liked to do the lead stories himself. Well, Laura really couldn't blame him. If Saundra was exhausting with a woman, she must really devastate a man.

Laura turned the car onto Sunset Boulevard and glanced quickly over the lights of west Los Angeles, glistening like drops of moisture on a huge spider web. A perfect habitat for Saundra, she thought wryly—a spider web. Come into my parlor . . .

She recalled the strangely intent look in Saundra's eyes when she first introduced herself.

"You're very lovely," Saundra had remarked with the smile that had thrilled a million hearts. "I'm sure we'll get along just wonderfully, darling."

And the way Saundra had leaned over to give her a light for her cigarette. It was, of course, done in the grand manner, exhibitionistic . . . and yet there was something deliberately seductive about it, too.

Well, women like Saundra have to conquer everybody, she decided. Her graciousness had a distinctly predatory quality. The charm was too supple, too practiced. *Exercised*—that was the word.

Laura had a vision of Saundra giving her charm a daily workout along with her knee-bends and push-ups.

Yet, Laura had to admit the woman was damned impressive. And despite Saundra's bursts of intensity and her rambling irrelevancies, things had gone smoothly.

Laura had gotten some really interesting stuff—some fascinating anecdotes. That should make Walter happy. Yes, from Laura's point of view it was a very successful interview. Actually, it was only that last bit with Ginny that threw her.

Ginny's presence in that house just didn't seem right. . . . Oh, hell, it wasn't any business of hers. But the memory of yesterday's meeting came flooding back with startling clarity.

She had spent the morning getting a final okay on some special features from Excelsior's publicity department. By one o'clock she had completed her business on the studio lot and decided to have lunch there.

As she made her way slowly down the studio cafeteria line, Laura wanted nothing more than to just sit down and unwind. She wasn't really aware what dishes she was pointing at, and cared even less.

Laura waited quietly for the cashier to figure her tab. She paid it quickly and moved out of the way. Holding her tray, she scanned the tables to find a place to sit.

There were no empty tables in sight, but there were two tables where only one person sat. Not much choice, she thought: it's either the poor girl's Marlon Brando or that young girl reading.

She decided the young girl offered her the best chance of having a quiet lunch. Getting a firm grip on her tray, Laura walked to the table, mentally cursing the overfilled coffee mug that slopped coffee onto her tray.

"Mind if I share your table?"

"No."

Laura smiled. A simple reply to a simple question. She looks familiar, Laura thought, but on a movie lot who doesn't?

Absently Laura ate the tasteless low-calorie food, her mind busy with the changes she would have to make in the Saundra Simons story. It had been a touchy matter getting a release from the studio about Saundra's latest marital fiasco, and Saundra had been in one of her prima donna moods.

But I guess I would be too, Laura conceded, if I had to be on a set at six in the morning looking beautiful. Still, Saundra had agreed to give Laura an interview at her home the next night.

"You're going to drip coffee on your nice suit. Better put a napkin under the cup," the soft voice broke unexpectedly through her thoughts, and Laura looked up, somewhat startled.

Laura put the cup down again and reached for the paper napkin dispenser. "Thanks."

"You're welcome," the girl said. She raised her head and pushed back her untamed red hair. A shy smile crossed her face and brightened her large gray-green eyes. Laura smiled back, trying to decide if she had met this girl.

"It humiliates me to ask this," Laura began with a friendly laugh, "but don't I know you from someplace?"

"I'm on the lot quite a bit," the girl said. "But I don't think we've met—I'd remember if we had." She blushed and looked down at the table.

Gloriola, but it's Orphan Annie, Laura thought. And then contritely told herself not to be hard on the girl. Just the same, Laura was uncomfortable; it seemed such an obvious attempt at flattery.

A short silence ensued. Laura felt impelled to make some small gesture of conversation but didn't quite know how to begin. Finally, she said, "Shame to waste such a nice day indoors, isn't it?" Snappy, Laura, real snappy dialogue . . . Uncle Sam Goldwyn wants you!

"It's funny," the girl replied. "I was sitting here—before you sat down—thinking just that. But now I don't feel that way," she said in a slightly embarrassed tone. "I was studying you and hoped you wouldn't notice."

Laura gave her a startled look. "Me? Good God, why?"

"Well, not really studying. I don't mean to sound like I was staring or spying." She placed her hands on the script opened before her. "It's just that you're so self-assured, and I wanted to analyze your gestures, see how you get the effect."

Laura felt a twinge of annoyance. And yet, the remark was too corny to be anything but sincere. Besides, why should anyone need to flatter her? She wasn't a "somebody."

"Guess my elocution lessons are showing," Laura said wryly. "You an actress?" Deliberately she avoided using the term "starlet."

The girl smiled. "Some day I hope to be."

Laura found herself liking the girl. In spite of the ambition visible behind the girl's soft, quiet manner, a quality of gentleness in her piqued Laura's curiosity. She was a welcome change from the run-of-the-mill, over-polished studio hopefuls.

She wondered how long this young redheaded girl had been in Hollywood. Despite her fresh appearance something about the girl didn't read right: she wasn't quite sure what it was or why she should get that impression . . . yet there it was. Laura wished she had time to find out more about her. Might even make a good human interest filler for *Fanfare*.

Oh, well. Enough of this nonsense. It was getting late, and she still had to stop by the press and pick up this month's galleys.

She pushed her chair back slowly, not wanting to seem as if she were anxious to get away.

"Well," Laura said softly, "thanks for sharing the table. And . . . good luck."

"It was nice meeting you," the girl murmured. And that was all.

Thinking about it again, Laura realized that there had been something unusual about the girl . . . that even if she never saw her again she would go on wondering about her—and wondering why she herself had felt so oddly moved.

Now she noticed she was almost back at the office. She could put Ginny out of her mind. Walter and a couple of martinis would melt away the shadowy anxieties that plagued her. They always did.

She pulled up in front of the familiar two-story building and honked the horn. Then she slid over, leaving the driver's seat for Walter. She smiled to herself as she sat back in the uncomfortable bucket seat. He can be so terribly conventional, she thought. Never once had he let her drive the car if he was in it—he claimed a man lost some of his superiority over women that way.

She heard him run down the stairs.

When he got into the car, he said, "I see you lived through it." He grinned impishly.

"You coward," Laura replied, "you owe me a Purple Heart for that little mission."

"Will you settle for a drink?"

"Two!" Laura sighed and put her head back against the seat.

"Did Saundra bite?"

"No. But she chewed my ear off. . . ."

Walter chuckled. "Poor darling." He leaned over possessively and kissed Laura's nose. "Lovely monster, isn't she?" he said with amused appreciation, and drove slowly toward La Cienega Boulevard.

"She loves you, too," said Laura. "Called you a slave driver among other things. She sends her best regards, anyway. In fact, I think she's putting you on the candidate list for husbands. Built-in publicity and all that."

Walter shook his head. "I'll admit she isn't reticent about her personal life . . ."

"Amen! You should have heard her version of this divorce." Laura smiled, grimly imagining the millions of shocked gasps that a verbatim quote would elicit from her unsuspecting fans.

"Don't let Saundra make you bitter about marriage," Walter said softly, and rested his free hand on her thigh.

Laura turned and looked at his profile in surprised appreciation: how sweet he could be when he wanted to. She gave his hand a squeeze.

It was a beautiful night. Laura closed her eyes and let the crisp smell of dew-covered grass and cool night air relax her.

Walter placed a warm hand on her cheek and gently brought her head over to his shoulder. If he's being this sweet, Laura thought, I'm not going home alone after the martinis. . . .

That's a cruel thought, she scolded herself. I'm beginning to sound as blasé as Saundra. After all, I let this affair happen and wanted it as much as he did.

"Nick's all right for a martini?"

"Of course."

"We'll be there in a moment." His voice was tender and low.

Unexpectedly, Ginny popped back into Laura's mind, and she was tempted to ask Walter what he might know about her—but for some reason she didn't think it would be wise right now.

Snap out of it, she told herself. She sat up and took two cigarettes from the pack in Walter's custom-tailored Ivy League jacket. Lighting them, she wondered how often she had made this simple gesture. Thousands of times, she decided.

Walter glanced at her quickly, then looked back at the restaurant-lined street with its flashing neon signs. "Still thinking about Saundra?"

"Yes," she lied. "I was." She looked at his strong, masculine hands with mild awe and studied his body. Laura admired the way Walter kept himself fit, never allowing middle age to get the edge on him if possible.

"I've got a great lead for you," Walter said gaily, imitating the well-known nasal whine of a highly overrated Hollywood columnist. *"Inspiringly valiant in her desperate search for love, Saundra Simons explained to this reporter in an exclusive interview . . ."*

Laura laughed. "Well, after four divorces what *can* she say?"

"What difference does it make as long as it sells *Fanfare*?"

Laura shrugged and stared out at the hillside homes ahead and wondered how many of them were mortgaged to the hilt. Talk about the almighty dollar, she thought. She laughed silently.

What difference does anything make, she echoed to herself, as long as everybody *thinks* you've got money and thinks you love your spouse? What difference . . . who cares . . . make-believe emotions for make-believe lives. She suddenly felt very depressed and lonely.

Walter pulled into the parking lot at Nick's, and they entered the bar. The place was nearly empty, and somebody had let the fire burn down in the mammoth brick fireplace. It was too early for the nightclub crowds to stop by after the last show and too late for the dinner crowd.

Walter excused himself and walked over to a table where a group of men sat. They looked bored with each other.

Lively Hollywood atmosphere, huh? Laura sighed inwardly and walked alone to the bar and sat down, barely conscious of the admiring glances at her long legs, provocatively outlined by her tight linen sheath dress.

"Hi, José."

"Ah, Miss Garraway. A pleasure to see you. But you are not alone?" José was an institution at Nick's, famous all over town for martinis that slipped down your throat caressingly—but smothered your gray matter within minutes.

"No. Mr. Hobson is with me, but he has business. . . ." She said it in an offhand way to show there was no resentment and nothing for her to mind. "I'll have one of your 'Sneaky Josés' while I'm waiting for him."

"Immediately."

Walter came up to her and placed his hand on her shoulder. "Sorry, Laura." He gave her an apologetic peck on the cheek.

"Oh, that's all right." It's amazing, she thought, how he always smells of just the right mixture of tobacco and shaving lotion. "But you'll miss me when you go back east. When are you leaving, by the way?"

"Next week."

"So soon?"

Walter ordered a double martini. Then he raised a thick eyebrow, a quizzical expression in his deep-set blue eyes. "Sure you wouldn't like to come along? A few days in New York would be good for you."

Laura deliberately delayed her reply while José placed their drinks in front of them. The old question caught her off guard. She had known for almost a month he was going, but she had been too busy to think about it. Thinking about it now and with a definite departure date, she was startled to realize that she was almost frightened at the thought of being without him for so long.

"Well?"

"You know I'd love to go, Walter," Laura began in a voice that clearly showed she wasn't going, "but I've no desire to be named a correspondent in a divorce case. We've been all through this, Walter. Unless you can come up with a legitimate reason—business reason—it's rather foolish to keep rehashing it."

She couldn't look at him. She could sense his expression and share his frustration. She wondered now what she would have done without Walter those first few months after Karl had left her . . . Karl. Big, hulking, crazy, adorable Karl. She had loved everything about him from his blond crew-cut hair down to his size fourteen shoe. God! What big feet he had, even if he was 6'3". Karl could always make her laugh—he could make her do almost anything he wanted. It seemed as if the only time she was wholly alive was when she was with him . . . could touch him. Everything took on a new color, a new vibrancy, when he was with her. Karl.

But it didn't really hurt so much anymore. In fact, she was sure it was just her pride that was still hurt. After all, she had been around a lot more now—knew how to take life . . . and men.

Walter's hand on hers brought her sharply back to the present . . . sharply aware of her new situation and her upper hand. The contact with him was warm and reassuring; it offered a comfort that words would have destroyed.

"You're right about not going, of course," he said slowly in his deliberate manner. "If I could only . . ."

His words trailed off. But he didn't have to finish his sentence. Laura knew what he was thinking immediately: if only he could get a divorce.

She suddenly found herself wanting to be in his arms, to press her cheek against the roughness of his jacket and feel secure and protected. But she fought down the feeling—fought it with all the hurt memories of Karl. She wouldn't be caught again; she wouldn't be hurt again. Oh, no. What was that old line? Better to have loved and lost . . . Laura mirthlessly decided that it was usually recited by those who had never gone through the pain of losing love. No. Her relationship with Walter was safer. He *loved* her, and she was "fond" of him—she liked him, respected him, and enjoyed his company—but her world would not fall apart again if he walked out of her life. She'd miss him, of course. . . . But then, he's only going away for two weeks . . . He'll be back. Nothing was going to change, not for a while anyway . . . unless . . .

"Hey," Walter's deep voice interrupted her thoughts, "where are you?"

"Here, darling," she answered, and looked again at his face as if she had lost something and was trying now to find it.

His hand tightened on hers. "You know you drive me nuts when you call me that. About the only time you ever use it is when we're . . ."

"Never mind," she laughed.

She raised the frost-covered glass to her lips. "Cheers," she said. Then she laced her fingers with Walter's. "Don't mind me. I suppose talking to Saundra tonight left me feeling a little ashamed of my own transgressions—silly as it may sound."

Walter grinned slowly and put his arm around her shoulder in fraternal tenderness. "It's not silly, Laura. At least, not in you. One of your best qualities is that touch of old-fashioned morality. It's nice. I like it in a woman if it's sincere."

She wondered if he'd still like it if he knew how really sincere it was. Basically, she was old-fashioned—she knew it. And she had taken great pains to hide it as a young girl in college. Even in New

Hampshire, the times had changed and Laura had accepted the challenge. It hadn't been so difficult. All she had to do was juggle a few childhood taboos, tie them up into a tidy bundle, and store them away. Poor Mom, she thought. She tried so hard . . .

Walter gestured to José for another round and sat quietly for a moment. "Laura," he asked softly.

She lifted her face toward him but said nothing.

"You would marry me if I were free, wouldn't you?"

"Yes," she whispered. But she couldn't suppress a feeling of guilt—a feeling that she had no right to marry a man she didn't really adore. Childish romanticism, she scolded herself.

He blew her a discreet kiss. Then he looked miserable.

"Oh, Walter," she said gently. "Don't torture yourself. Lots of men are unhappily married."

"Yeah . . . but they can get divorces," he replied bitterly.

"All right, but you have me, anyway. Would it be worth giving Edna everything just for a divorce?"

"It just makes me so goddamn mad," he cursed under his breath. "If she'd just settle for plain alimony and child support! But no. Oh, no. She wants the magazine, and the house, and anything else that's not nailed down. I can't begin all over again at my age. . . ."

They both sat silently and stared into their drinks. It did appear to be a pretty hopeless situation. It seemed odd to Laura, but she realized she was almost glad that he couldn't get a divorce—almost glad that she would never have to go through with marrying him. But that was silly. Of course I'd marry him, she told herself.

"Let's change the subject, shall we?" Laura suggested finally.

Cupping his hand under her chin, Walter turned her face toward him. "All right," he said, and brushed his lips against her cheek. "No morbid thoughts tonight. I'll go on to New York alone as originally planned . . . and we'll go along together as originally understood." He smiled and stretched, then relaxed his arms. "Just as well. Who'd look after the shop if we were both gone?"

A few minutes later, finishing their drinks, they left the bar with a friendly wave to José.

Chapter 2

On the way to Laura's apartment, Walter discussed his plans for New York. For months now he had been looking for a way to open a New York office of *Fanfare* magazine with financial aid from someone who wouldn't interfere with the way he ran it. Laura was well aware how big the magazine could grow if Walter had a chance. It was making a profit now, of course, but he would have to expand to make it really pay. He would look for a backer in New York.

They turned down Crenshaw Boulevard and, lost in discussion, found themselves at Rodeo Drive before they knew it.

Laura looked straight ahead, ignoring the ultramodern shops with the inevitable palm trees in front. All she could think of was that they were only three blocks from her apartment, and she knew that Walter expected to be invited up. It irked her that she should feel so torn about it—she knew damn well she wanted him to come up.

Bet Saundra never had this problem. Laura speculated thoughtfully, and Ginny's image crept back into Laura's mind. She tried to envision Ginny saying good night to a boyfriend, putting her arms around him and kissing him.

What's gotten into me? Laura asked herself guiltily. Do I have a secret yen to become a Peeping Tom—or would it be a Peeping

Jane? She chuckled to herself. But there was something uneasy and slightly bitter about her humor.

Walter pulled up in front of the buff-colored stucco apartment building almost lost in the long row of other modern buildings. Each of the buildings had colored spotlights illuminating the entrances, and more of the palm trees.

Nostalgically, Laura asked, "Do you ever miss the drab, funny-looking houses of twenty years ago, Walter? All the fancy wood-work and slats?"

Walter smiled at her. "No," he said.

"I mean," she continued, "doesn't all this modern, straight-line, prefabricated, built-in-a-day trend sort of frighten you?"

"It's life," he said. "Progress."

"Progress, hell! Sterility. That's what I think."

"Stop thinking, then," Walter grinned, knowing this sort of teasing annoyed her. "You're too attractive to think. . . ."

"I thought you liked my mind."

"Only at the office." He slipped his arms around her waist slowly.

"You're not objective at all," Laura scolded.

"Disgusting, isn't it?" Walter kissed the tip of her ear.

"I suppose you'd like a nightcap," Laura suggested softly.

"You inviting?"

"I'm inviting."

"Thank God!" Walter laughed. "For a horrible moment I thought you were going to send me away."

They entered Laura's apartment in conspiratorial silence.

"Home again," sighed Walter, sinking down on the couch.

"Help yourself, darling . . ." Laura gestured to the paint-it-your-self bar she had bought one day in an impetuous mood. "I'll just be a minute."

She undressed and showered quickly, somewhat amused at the deliberate but detached quality of her preparations. Then she put on her only feminine dressing gown.

Who's seducing whom? she asked the tanned, slender reflection in the mirror, studying her smooth shoulders, the well-shaped breasts so invitingly contoured under the flimsy gown. Flimsy? It was practically transparent!

"Diaphanous," the sales girl had called it. Some handy word, that. Covered a multitude of sinful intents. My God! If she didn't look like one of those classic wantons on a paperback historical . . . Well, it was eye-catching, anyway. Or rather, she amended wryly, man-catching.

Returning to the living room through the bedroom, she picked up her hairbrush and brushed her long light-brown hair with vigorous strokes. She enjoyed being one of the few women brave enough to flaunt long hair despite the dictates of fashion.

Walter, now jacketless, crossed the room carrying two tumblers and sat down next to Laura on the studio couch.

"Here, darling." He placed the glasses on the low table in front of them carefully, almost awkwardly, then reached over and took the brush from her hand.

Abruptly he pushed her back on the couch, and she could feel the warmth of his body against her own . . . could feel his need for her as he kissed her.

"There's something about soap and water that affects me more than the best perfumes in the world," Walter said with his lips against her throat. He bit her lightly and then pulled away.

Laura remained lying against the cushions, her eyes only half open and her lips still stinging from the hardness of his kiss.

She felt cheated—even a little insulted.

"Walter," she said softly, "come here and do exactly as I say." She smiled into his questioning eyes, feeling powerful as she saw the dark blue they turned when he was aroused.

He leaned forward hesitantly, and she slowly raised her arms, then folded them around his neck, bringing his face to within an inch of hers. "Now, just kiss me quietly and slowly . . . as though I might break otherwise." It was something she had always wanted him to do but had never before had the courage to ask. . . .

Laura molded her mouth around his softly, hardly touching his lips at first; then, as his tongue tried to seek hers in sudden harshness, she lightly traced her fingers around his lips until he became more gentle.

Finally, he pulled away just far enough to ask, "Is that what you want?"

Laura gazed at him for a moment and then, without realizing why, felt hurt. As hurt as she would be if he had laughed at her. She didn't bother to answer him directly.

Instead, she laughed lightly and, with a slight wave of her hand, said, "Oh, it was just an experiment. Don't you like to try new things occasionally?"

She accepted the drink he offered her, sipping the bitter Scotch and letting its strong flavor remind her that men are strong, masterful. That's what a woman wants from a man . . . the rough possessive touch, isn't it? Only, she knew it wasn't true. Karl, she remembered, had always sensed her moods, her needs. Without a word he had always known just what she wanted. But how many men can do that? she asked herself silently.

Or is it me? she wondered. How can Walter sense what I want if I'm not in love with him? It was a disturbing thought.

Walter took her free hand in his and gently touched her arm with his lips. "I want you," he said hoarsely. His eyes met hers with unguarded sincerity. "It's not that crude," he explained hastily. "I don't want you to think that I consider you just another Hollywood party girl; you know I don't. Besides loving you, I really like you . . . before, and even more important, afterwards. It's not easy to find someone you can truthfully say that about."

"I know; I know," Laura said almost harshly. She realized that he was sincere, but somehow she found herself detached from the moment—detached from herself. The feeling of his lips and the visualization of how the scene would look to someone walking into the room . . . the entire situation was too much for her. She began to laugh but caught herself up short when Walter looked up at her, his face darkened with confusion bordering on anger.

"I'm sorry, Walter. I wasn't laughing *at* you. It was just . . . well, it seemed so much like a silent movie—the picture of us I had in mind as we sat here." Well, she hadn't meant to hurt his feelings—at least, she didn't think she had.

He snorted lightly. "I see what you mean. The big embrace."

He stood up slowly and ruffled her hair to show there were no hard feelings.

"Pour me another drink, will you?" She heard herself ask. It was as if her own mind was foiling any attempts she might make to consider matrimony or the possibility of letting down her barriers to share herself with a man for the rest of her life.

"Sure, darling," Walter answered, and brought the half-empty bottle from the bar. "Here you go."

Laura stared at him as he poured, and thought almost maternally that he was really an awfully nice guy.

"What's your interpretation of love, Walter?"

He laughed. "Hollywood propaganda to sell more movies . . ." He tucked the tip of his tie into his shirt and pulled Laura over onto his lap.

"I can see this is not the night to discuss anything serious with you."

They sat quietly for a moment, each deep in thought.

"Walter?"

"Hmm?" His thick eyebrows raised slightly, making deep frown lines on his forehead.

"Kiss me. Kiss me hard so that I ache and cry for you to stop."

"A minute ago you wanted to be kissed softly," he chided lightly, and leaned over her. His nostrils were dilating, and there was a gleam of urgency in his eyes.

Laura's breath came heavy now; her eyelids felt thick and her temples throbbed. "That was a minute ago. A woman can always change her mind."

He let his large hands wander over her roughly and took her mouth hungrily, as if his very existence depended upon his ability to envelop her mouth and reach into her with his tongue.

She could feel her lips being crushed under his teeth, and it was good.

It hurt like hell, but it was good.

Chapter 3

Laura awoke in the morning to a bright sun in a smog-free day. As she threw back the covers, she was startled to feel her arm and leg muscles aching uncomfortably. Then last night returned to her quickly, and she smiled slowly to herself. "Little Miss Passion Flower," she said aloud.

She showered quickly, her mind working on what she would have to do today: finish up that article about Ron Ramsey and his horse. And, oh God, I have to stop over at Saundra's and pick up the glossies I left with her—she wondered briefly if Ginny would be there too—and I'll probably have to grin politely again, and that'll be a bore. . . .

I need to fall in love again; that's what I need.

No. No point in falling in love, she decided. Only means I neglect my work, and I never pick out a man who's really marriage material. It's too much of a risk, and I can't afford to lose again. What I really need is a few friends so I won't be so dependent upon Walter.

Better find a new man to date, she advised herself again. But she knew it was more trouble than it was worth—the countless dates to weed out one or two men who didn't really bore her. No. She was just as well off with Walter— it was safer. And friends—a couple of old maids like herself were the obvious solution. Maybe she could begin getting together with Helen, Walter's secretary, after office hours . . . but she decided against it. Office friendships sometimes proved very awkward or unbearably tiresome.

Her makeup completed, she gulped down a hasty cup of coffee and called the office to let Helen know she would be a little late because she had to stop off at Saundra's.

The huge Bel Air house was awesomely majestic even in the harsh daytime glare. She rang the bell impatiently. As she waited, the morning atmosphere reminded her of days when she was a little girl, especially those last few weeks of school before summer vacation. There was that moist, clean smell and the light breeze just barely touching her hair. She remembered the hush of the classroom while everyone studied and only the old wall clock broke the silence with its tired tick-tock. Somewhere in the room someone would shift his position, with the sound of feet shuffling on the worn wooden floor, and invariably someone would sneeze, warning them all of summer colds.

Laura sighed in wistful reminiscence and turned her mind back to the present. She hoped today wouldn't get too much warmer. She wished now she hadn't brought her jacket.

As if of its own accord—no one was in sight—the front door opened slowly. Then she recognized Ginny, half hidden behind the door, dressed in blue jeans and a bright green cashmere sweater.

"Hello, Ginny," Laura said warmly. "Is Saundra home?" She took a step forward.

The girl stood back and opened the door wider to let Laura pass. "No. But she left a package for you and said that the pictures she wanted are marked on the back." Ginny walked ahead of Laura into the cool living room. "She also asked if you could possibly wait for her. . . . She should be home any minute."

There was an odd, cloying deference about the way Ginny asked her to stay. It was almost the you-great-big-wonderful-you type of phrasing so popular in Cinemaville. Laura didn't like it . . . not at all. It smacked of that obsequiousness she had observed in so many shallow Hollywood hopefuls.

But she tried to push it out of her mind and told herself that she was becoming a cynic and a self-righteous prude. What if Ginny was an opportunist . . . so what? Wasn't everyone—in one way or another?

Laura watched her leafing through the secretary desk, and the incongruity of Ginny in Saundra's home still troubled her. Yet, the way she had said that Saundra would "be home" instead of "be back" had a note of authority—even possession—about it.

"Here it is," Ginny exclaimed finally, with a nervous laugh. She pushed her thick red hair back from her face. There was something in her manner that gave Laura the impression of flight, almost fear of being "caught." At what? Laura was puzzled and watched the girl move a few objects on the desk as if she didn't know what to do with herself or her hands. Suddenly, Ginny asked, "*Can* you wait for Saundra? Can I get you a cup of coffee?"

Laura couldn't imagine what Saundra wanted her to hang around for, and she really had no time. But Ginny's hospitality was a trifle too anxious for comfort, and she couldn't flatly refuse without sounding rude . . . and Walter would not like it if she didn't go out of her way to please Saundra.

"Well." Laura hesitated, looking at her watch, then laughed with practiced good nature. "I'm expected at the office, but they know where I am if they need me. I'll take you up on that coffee invitation."

"Fine! I'm sure Saundra will be glad, and she really shouldn't be too long." Ginny smiled brilliantly at Laura, then left the room, almost running.

Laura was grateful for a few moments to shift into gear for this change in plans. She disliked finding herself in uncertain situations like this—this one didn't feel like an adventure. More like a trap. Her original, dubious reaction to Ginny suddenly swept through her. She wasn't too sure she liked Ginny—but she had to admit she was fascinated by her, by the odd mixture of shyness and opportunism.

Once again she looked around the big living room with its rococo furniture and ornately framed Flemish paintings. Laura decided that the room looked like a movie set: artificial. The only time it had life was when Ginny was in it.

At least she's alive, Laura told herself. Wonder how she endures

Saundra? And what the hell is taking her so long for a cup of coffee?

Curious, Laura walked out into the hallway and followed the faint aroma of fresh coffee.

In the kitchen, at a table, Ginny stood pouring the coffee. Her back was to the door.

"Hi," Laura said as casually as she could. "Need any help?"

Ginny turned slightly. "Oh, hi." She smiled and held up the pot. "Just coming in. Sorry to be so long."

Laura smiled and sat down at the table.

"Long as we're here, we may as well stay. Or do you like all those fifteenth-century ghouls peering down at you?"

Ginny laughed and sat down lithely.

The kitchen was almost as sterile in its perfection as the rest of the house—the smell of coffee saved it.

There was a short silence, and Laura felt that if she didn't break it now, this brief moment of friendly casualness would be lost. She asked Ginny several questions about her career and her friendship with Saundra. Ginny was thoughtful, courteous, and artfully non-committal, her answers both too pat and too evasive.

Conversation lingered uncertainly and then came to an abrupt halt as they heard the front door slam and Saundra's unmistakable voice call, "Hello there? Anyone home? Ginny?"

Then Saundra pushed open the kitchen door exuberantly.

"Well!" she said, glancing sharply at Ginny, then at Laura. "Here we are. Enjoying yourself?"

Saundra threw her few parcels on the drainboard and sat down with swooping grace. "And how are you, Laura? So glad you waited for me."

"I'm . . ." Laura began.

"Well, Ginny? Don't I get any coffee?" Saundra smiled, but the coolness in her tone was unmistakable.

"Oh, sure. I'll get you a cup."

"We don't say, 'Oh, sure'; we say, 'Surely.'" It was a cruelly deliberate burlesque of the old "impatient but amused mother" routine. "It's a foregone conclusion that if you agree to serve me coffee, it will be in a cup."

Ginny said nothing, but it didn't take much to know she was exerting self-control. She rose and brought back Saundra's coffee.

Laura couldn't help wondering if Saundra often treated Ginny this way, or if it was a performance strictly for her benefit.

"How's the shooting going on the new picture, Saundra?" Laura asked, deftly shifting the dangerous mood of the moment. "Wilson sober long enough to finish his scenes?"

Saundra laughed sarcastically. "I wouldn't know, since I've never seen him sober. But his agent will give you a better story for the public. After all"—Saundra smiled knowingly at Ginny—"a few sordid tales could be spread about me, too."

"Or any of us, for that matter," Laura offered. It seemed a benign comment to make in view of Saundra's notorious reputation.

"I like you, Laura." Saundra said it as if the walls should crumble and the waves should part at this earth-shattering pronouncement.

"Thank you. . . ."

"As a matter of fact"—the older woman reached over and patted Ginny's hand affectionately—"I was planning on taking Ginny to Tijuana for her first bullfight a week from Sunday. Would you like to come along? We'd love to have you as our guest."

Ginny slowly pulled her hand away from under Saundra's. Her face was immobile, and she avoided Laura's glance.

"Wouldn't we, Ginny?" Saundra commanded.

Ginny looked up obediently. "Oh, yes. Of course."

"Silly child hardly ever listens to people. Be a dear, Ginny, and get my purse."

Laura watched Ginny stiffen slightly then get up to bring back Saundra's huge straw bag. Laura wondered when Saundra was going to tell Ginny to go out and play in the yard and not bother the grown-ups.

"Have you ever been to Tijuana, Ginny?" Laura asked as casually as she could manage.

Saundra didn't even bother to wait for Ginny's reply.

"Of course she hasn't. I don't know how she's lived this long and managed to remain so ignorant." Saundra laughed at her little joke.

"I don't know about that." Laura matched Saundra's smile. "I've never been to a bullfight."

"Really?" Saundra asked absently, and took from her purse her famous special cigarettes that were almost twice the length of any American brand. "Do you have a light, Laura?"

She leaned forward to accept Laura's match, steadying Laura's hand, which didn't need steadying. "I seem to have lost my lighter. It never worked properly, anyway."

"The one I gave you for Christmas, Saundra?" Ginny asked.

"Oh. So you did." Saundra laughed gaily. "But then, it is the sentiment that counts, isn't it?"

Laura wanted to say something—anything—to break the tension. But she didn't dare. Instead, she sat quietly in her chair, pretending an air of amiable detachment. She could just see Ginny's hands out of the corner of her eye and noticed that they were nervously clenching and releasing her coffee cup. Somebody say something, Laura thought as she felt the silence grow.

Finally, Saundra's well-controlled laugh shook the air like a volley of pebbles against plate glass. "You two may sit here and meditate if you wish," she said gaily, "but I have more important things to do."

She rose busily from her chair, gathering her purse and cigarettes from the table. "We'll call you a few days before the bullfight and remind you, Laura."

Laura looked up at the actress's smiling face and was torn between a feeling of sudden hatred for Saundra and overwhelming pity for Ginny. Before she could realize what she was saying—much less why—Laura nodded. "Fine. Do we wear anything special?"

"No. Just be comfortable. Slacks or something." Saundra gazed musingly at Ginny's bent head for a moment. Then turning her head toward Laura, she looked at her long and steadily. "Ginny's a sweet child," she remarked as though the girl weren't even in the room. "Don't keep her too long," she added tensely. "We've lots to do this afternoon."

Laura laughed. "I wouldn't have kept her at all, except that I thought you wanted to talk to me about something."

Ginny's head came up abruptly, and Laura thought she caught an expression of defiance in her large gray-green eyes. "You did say you wanted to talk to Laura . . ."

"Don't be ridiculous, Virginia. I would have called Laura at the office if there had been anything to discuss. I certainly wouldn't waste her time by asking her to wait for me. I thought she'd stayed on to talk to you."

Saundra smiled sweetly at Laura and left the room like a vindicated politician.

Laura watched Ginny's rigid position at the table for a few seconds and finally said, "Don't worry, Ginny. She doubtlessly just forgot about it. Anyway," she said more lightly, "it gave me a chance to get to know you better."

"She really did tell me to ask you to wait . . . really."

Laura stared into Ginny's eyes. Her first reaction was that Ginny was lying, but she shoved it aside quickly.

"I never doubted you."

"Thanks." Ginny smiled a little uncertainly. Then she stood up and took the cups to the sink. There was a sort of resignation in her walk.

Laura had to get out of here. It was uncomfortable. She patted Ginny's arm gently and walked out into the warm sunshine. Exhaling a deep sigh of relief, she got into her car. She sat there for a moment, resting her head against the seat. What a morning! Well, at least it wasn't boring.

But as she drove to work she couldn't throw off a feeling of anxiousness about her Sunday date with them. And the more she tried to understand why she was anxious, the more confused she became.

"Oh, the hell with it," she said aloud.

Chapter 4

Thursday and Friday passed for Laura with the usual routine and nonroutine events. But she was aware that something had changed inside her. Only, she couldn't figure out what it was. In one way, she seemed to be unusually lighthearted, filled with a vague but pleasant sense of anticipation. On the other hand, she was strangely irascible—more quick-tempered about the daily annoyances.

"Schizoid," she told herself. "The split in my personality is definitely showing." But her mocking self-abuse didn't alter the situation. Even with this awareness of her contrary emotions, she continued to seesaw from one extreme to another.

Returning to the office late Friday afternoon in her new mood, the old Spanish-style office building took on a fresh appearance for her, with its black wrought-iron gates and patio in the center of the squared structure. It didn't seem quite so much in need of paint, nor did it any longer look like a rather poor imitation of the colonial California days. As a matter of fact, Laura decided as she reached the top of the stairs, it was really rather quaint and charming.

"Hi, Laura. Coffee's on." Helen, Walter's secretary, poured another cup from the battered coffeemaker.

Laura accepted it gratefully and sat down at her desk, feeling companionable.

"What's the matter, Helen? Bad day?" Laura asked with friendly concern as she opened her purse and took out her cigarettes and reading glasses.

"No. Nothing that simple," Helen laughed bitterly. "Just one of those old-maid blue days."

"We all get them, so don't feel alone." It occurred to Laura that she was an old maid, too. Last week she had felt just as miserable and numb. Last week, hell! Two days ago.

Her thoughts were broken as Helen tilted her head toward Walter's office, whispering, "He's in a work-work-work mood today. Otherwise, the place has been pretty quiet, considering it's press time."

Laura watched her as she neatly arrayed her day's work. She admired Helen's quiet efficiency. But she also knew that Helen was unable to think for herself and took as little responsibility as possible. That had often annoyed Laura.

"Any calls while I was out, Helen?"

"Nothing in particular. Fishburn called about the copy on Mario. And Excelsior called to find out when the Dalton Scott story will hit the stands. Oh, and a Ginny Adams called. Said it wasn't urgent and she would call back."

Laura tried to control her swift reaction. She was almost shocked that Ginny had called. Even perhaps guilty, as if Ginny shouldn't have called at the office—strangely illicit. She considered quickly why Ginny might have called—perhaps for Saundra, or perhaps they were not going to Tijuana after all.

Then, seeing Helen's questioning gaze, she covered up by asking for more coffee.

Afterward, Laura busily leafed through papers on her desk and read the afternoon mail. Just like Ensignia Studios to veto the press release on their lawsuit against their top box-office star! Neurotic Hollywood characters, Laura thought.

Saundra Simons is a good example, she told herself. What the hell is she trying to do to Ginny? Wonder what Ginny wants . . .

The door opened behind them loudly as Walter called out, "Laura. Can you come into my office a minute?"

Laura gulped down the rest of her coffee. "Sure, Walter." She rose and walked into his large office, sank onto the overstuffed leather chair in front of his desk.

She waited for him to begin and wondered if she should expect one of his "Chairman of the Board" orations or if this was just a social confab. Should I let my nails grow really long and paint them a bright red? Walter does have a nice strong back . . .

"Now, if the phone will stop ringing long enough for me to discuss a couple of things with you, then it shouldn't take too long and we can both go home." Walter rapped lightly on his desk with one of the ballpoint pens given to the staff by their printing house.

The word "home" from Walter always jarred Laura. She never really thought of him having a home, or being any different from the way he was at the office or when out with her. She tried to visualize his "home personality" and finally gave it up. Why should he have a different personality at home?

She followed his pen's tapping for a few seconds, then stretched languidly in the chair to get his attention. With an inward smile of satisfaction, she watched his eyes pass from her face to her breasts, and on down to her legs.

She crossed them casually—but artfully—for his benefit and began to keep time to imagined music with one foot swinging loosely. I've become a terrible flirt, she scolded herself. But the observation really delighted her.

Walter was still staring at her legs.

"What's on *your* mind?" she asked pointedly.

He looked up, obviously a little taken aback. She returned his gaze steadily.

Walter abruptly shifted his expression into neutral and cleared his throat, as if to signal her that this was not the time or the place for reminding him of their personal relationship.

"I called you in," he began in his most businesslike voice, "to tell you that I'll be leaving for New York sooner than I expected, and that I'm going to leave you in charge."

"Oh?" For some reason Laura felt cheated at his change in plans.

"Yes. I'm leaving tonight instead of next week. I had a wire from Willy last night. He thinks he has the backer we need to foot the bill for a New York office."

"Walter, that's wonderful!"

"A very sane divorcee he met—Madeline Van Norden. Wealthy and looking for a good investment."

Laura sat quietly while her mind was racing with possibilities. "I must admit it sounds like this is it."

"It hasn't come through yet. I rather imagine Willy wants me to talk to her in person before she gets away and some other guy relieves her of the money."

"Darling," Laura laughed, "if she's a divorcée, you won't have any trouble competing for the investment—not after she gets a look at that gorgeous exterior of yours."

She knew she was being feline rather than jealous.

"Cut the jokes, Laura." He said it with a smile. However, his tone gave away how much he wanted to put over this transaction. Circling the desk, Walter placed his arms on Laura's shoulders.

"I want you to finish up anything you've got on your desk—for a very good reason."

"What reason?" Laura asked suspiciously.

He cupped his hand under her chin and looked down into her eyes affectionately. "If this goes through—the financing—I want you to take over the Special Features Department of the New York office. Make the rounds with Willy for the right contacts, and help get it going. Sound interesting?"

Laura was a bit stunned. "The New York office!"

"That's right. I'll even throw in a retroactive raise if everything works out as I think it will."

She pulled away from his grasp gently and ground out her cigarette in the enormous ashtray by the framed photograph of Edna and the children. "I don't know, Walter. Helping to organize something like that is a pretty big job to take on. I'm a writer, not a—"

"Don't be ridiculous," Walter interrupted. "You know you can do it. I can trust you, Laura, and I'll need someone I can rely on to do a good job. Frankly, I think it would be the best thing that's happened to you since you came to work for me. There's no future for you as a staff writer on a fan magazine—no real future, anyway. But in New York you'll have a good chance to get a production background, work into real editing. Not the piddly stuff you're doing here. Writers are a dime a ream, but a good writer with editorial production experience . . ."

Laura stopped listening as she turned over the possibilities in her mind. It was a big jump. She'd been to New York on a vacation once, but that was hardly enough to make her feel she would know her way around. She would have to set up an apartment from scratch—no point in moving her things until she saw how the department shaped up.

Am I crazy? she wondered. It was the perfect rescue mission for an aching libido—a real shot in the psyche for someone on the verge of stagnation. It was a gift from the gods. And she was certainly able to take care of herself. With Willy there, too, she wouldn't have any real trouble setting up the department—she had enough experience to handle that.

"Well? What do you say, Laura? Is it a deal?"

She looked up quickly, her decision made. "Deal."

"That's my girl." He placed his arm around her shoulder and escorted her to the door.

Laura felt a sudden surge of maternal sympathy for Walter. He is sweet, and I certainly can't complain, she said silently. If only I could fall in love with him—but she knew she wouldn't. She felt his warm hand on her and looked up at him with an unexpected choked feeling in her throat. "Well, have a good trip, Walter."

His face was serious. "Thanks. For many things that I never thanked you for before."

She wanted to kiss him but knew that if she did she would probably cry, and then everything would be ruined.

"Walter," she said quietly.

His answer was a light laugh, a little too forced. "Never mind, Laura." Walter opened the door and swatted her affectionately. "Just get out of here and let me get some work done. Go on, beat it!"

She reached up and pulled his face to her lips quickly. They heard

Helen drop some papers and laughed together when they realized that she was doubtlessly shocked to the core. But now the strain of the moment was gone.

"Helen," Walter called in his business voice, "will you come in for a moment? Bring your pad and the New York file."

"Yes. Yes, sir," Helen answered, fumbling in the gray file cabinet behind her desk for a moment, then stiffly walked into Walter's office.

Laura went over to the coffeemaker and refilled her cup with tepid coffee. Dear world, she thought with mixed feelings of sadness and elation, today ends a chapter of my life.

From this moment on things will be different.

How do I know?

I just know . . .

Chapter 5

Laura lay in bed, leisurely smoking a cigarette. It was the one luxury she really enjoyed on weekends. Just to lie there with no feeling of having to rush and dress for work.

Noises of the outside world—other tenants talking, somebody washing his car, a lawn mower with its clipping whine, children in the street, and the sound of splashing water from the pool in the courtyard of her apartment house—floated up into her shade-dimmed room like ragged echoes of a familiar chorus.

She gazed thoughtfully at the drawn shades. Funny, she mused, the little unnoticed routines we set for ourselves. Simple things like leaving the shades up during the week so that the morning sun will help wake you and then putting them down for two days because it's the weekend. Saturday and Sunday . . . lovely names. She laughed and wondered what would happen if the names of the days were switched around—would people go into a confused panic?

"Saturday," she said aloud. It sounded funny. Language is strange—meanings even stranger. One word can have so many interpretations.

Laura put out her cigarette and dimly wondered what she should do today. There was always the marketing and the laundry, but she wanted to do something special.

She took a long, cool shower and dried herself slowly, peering intently into the mirror at her reflection. No real signs of age yet, she reassured herself. Then she combed her hair in various ways to see if she could manage something to make her feel different or more daring.

She wondered how soon she would have to go to New York if Walter's plans worked out. She decided the new receptionist at the office would probably take her apartment if Laura would let her pay for the furniture on time. The girl had mentioned several times that she wanted to move into a nicer place but didn't have any furniture.

Maybe I should ask her about it Monday just to be on the safe side. Safe side. As if she'd ever played on any other side. She threw a scornful look at herself in the mirror. Laura Garraway, the greatest little safe-side player in the world. Bah!

She walked into the bedroom, enjoying the breeze that had come in. Mechanically she put on an old pair of dungarees and a sleeveless blouse. Her mind grazed over the problem of what to do—something impetuous, something exciting for a change.

Maybe I should borrow a motor scooter and ride it down Hollywood Boulevard naked—that would shake things up a bit.

Slowly she finished her second cup of coffee. She wished she had someone to talk to. Someone to share her little daily tidbits with. She looked around her room, from the burnt-orange pillow on the charcoal-gray couch to the low modern bench with the black television set squatting delicately on it like a fat woman on a bar stool.

It's a nice apartment, she considered—studio-ish. But I'm lonely . . . so goddam lonely!

She felt like a little girl again when she had been bad . . . sent away without punishment but secretly wishing somebody had spanked her. Laura recalled the hidden spot by the stream, where she would spend long, secret hours in the summer. Then, for some strange reason, she suddenly thought of the English teacher in the sixth grade—what was her name? She couldn't remember now, even though she had idolized her, had even written poems, silly poems about her. All she could remember now was that the teacher was young and had red hair that she kept in a knot at the back of her head . . . and how Laura had always wanted to see her hair all undone, just let it be in the magic of its wild, red freedom.

Ginny's hair was the same kind of dark red, Laura remembered with a start. So what? she asked herself. Strange that I should think of Ginny . . .

She could almost feel her mother's disapproval of her thoughts . . . feel her tense, puritanical glare. Sinful! Everything was sinful! Even love . . .

Even now she could hear her mother's high-pitched whine accusing Laura of some perverted act with her best friend in college, and still, after all these years, the color rose in Laura's face. Her mother had been unable to understand that two girls can be really close friends without "something" going on . . . and it had been the following semester that Laura had met Karl, a medical student who worked weekends at the gas station to help pay his tuition. She remembered how Karl had looked at her that first day during registration . . . and her mother's reaction when she had inadvertently mentioned his interest—yelling at her again that medical students had no morals, because they were used to looking at "naked women," and that Karl was just after "what he could get."

It was too much to think about right now, Laura decided. Too much—and too unpleasant. "People-starved," Laura said aloud, "that's what I was. Just plain people-starved."

She turned the phrase over in her mind and savored it as something significant. . . .

Suddenly hungry for the sound of human voices, Laura switched on the radio. She was paradoxically annoyed when the phone rang simultaneously. "Who can that be?" she muttered as if it was an intrusion.

"Hello?" She turned down the radio.

"Laura? This is Ginny."

She had a swift, strange feeling of being caught unaware, of being cornered. But it disappeared just as quickly and was replaced with sincere gladness that Ginny had called.

"I called you yesterday at the office, but I didn't get a chance to call back."

"That's all right," Laura said, and wondered where Ginny was now and why she had not been able to call.

"I wanted to talk to you when Saundra wasn't around," Ginny began falteringly. "I wanted you to know that this wasn't my idea and that I would never have asked you . . . but she'll check up on me somehow."

"Asked me what?" Laura inquired with interest.

Ginny hesitated. "Remember that remark of Saundra's about you interviewing me? And how you said—although I know you just said it to be nice—that you would talk to me about it one of these days over lunch?"

"Vaguely," Laura replied, not really remembering.

"Well," Ginny went on with a heavy sigh, "now you can tell me that you're too busy, and that will get her off my back."

Laura could just picture Saundra telling Ginny to call and see to it that Laura didn't forget. How like Saundra, she thought.

"Actually," Laura said aloud, "I've been sitting here wondering what to do with myself today. But even if I did interview you, I couldn't promise you any results. Walter's out of town right now, and it looks as though I soon will be, too."

There was a strange silence on the other end, and Laura wondered if Ginny was listening. She could hear muffled voices now and what sounded like a cash register. Obviously, Ginny was not calling from Saundra's home.

"Are you going on vacation?" Ginny asked finally. There was a curiously hurt tone in her voice, Laura noted and wondered why. She thought of commenting on it but decided against it. If she had misinterpreted it, Ginny might think she was prying.

"No. Nothing's definite yet, so I can't tell you about it."

"Of course," Ginny answered flatly. Again that faint tone of accusation.

Inexplicably, Laura felt guilty, as if she had let Ginny down or had disappointed her in some way.

"Look, Ginny," she said without thinking twice, "are you busy this afternoon? I have a few routine chores to do about the place, but if you like, we could meet for cocktails and maybe have dinner together. Do you have a date for tonight?" Laura didn't know why, but for some reason she was certain that Ginny did not have a date.

"I . . . I'm not sure," Ginny said after a moment. "So much depends on what Saundra has planned."

"Oh?" Laura asked in surprise. "Surely you don't study Saturday nights, too!"

"Oh, no," Ginny said quickly. "I mean, well, sometimes she takes me to certain movies or plays and points out techniques . . ." Ginny's voice had that rehearsed quality again.

Laura sensed she should not pursue this aspect of the conversation. "I understand," she conceded carefully. "But you could ask her, couldn't you?"

There was a slight hesitation. "Yes. Of course."

"Do you know where she can be reached now?"

"Yes."

"Call her, then," Laura commanded briskly. "Make sure you can meet me. After all, it was her suggestion. I don't think Saundra would turn down an interview for you. Play it up a bit; tell her I've agreed to push it for the fall schedule, or something."

Another silence, and Laura heard music and someone laughing in the background.

"I'll call you back in a few minutes and let you know."

"Of course, we don't have to do it today," Laura volunteered hastily, giving Ginny a chance to back out. "If you have something else to do, just say so. You're probably sick of talking shop, anyway."

"No, no, I'm not. I'd really *like* to talk with you tonight. I . . . I don't have anything else to do."

"All right, Ginny. I'll wait for your call."

Laura hung up and lit a cigarette. She was relieved that Ginny had said she did want to see her, but she didn't really know why. Probably a sense of competition with Saundra. Or some other sneaky trick of her subconscious.

Laura had accepted the fact that she must have a subconscious like everybody else—but she wasn't gracious about it. Slimy, conniving little bastard, she reflected bitterly. I hope I never have to meet you face to face.

She waited by the phone patiently, staring out the window to the street below. She was aware that the radio was still on, turned low, but she couldn't make herself walk away from the phone to turn the volume up.

The minutes dragged on, and Laura grew restless. She watched the mailman approach the apartment with disinterest. The only mail she received was circulars and bills. Her school friends were all married now, and their lives had gone in such separate directions that keeping up a correspondence seemed rather useless. She had never been good at writing newsy, detailed long letters and had admitted to herself long ago that she was really not interested in how her friends' children were growing.

Although her mother was still alive, Laura had long ago let communication with her drop—they'd never had much in common, anyway. It was different with her father. . . . Laura had adored her father. But he had left them when Laura was only nine. How she had pleaded to go with him. She knew he wanted her. How she had hated the idea of staying alone with her nagging, bitter mother. Of course, in the end, Laura's mother had won out and Laura never heard from her father again until the state notified them of his death—she had been nineteen then.

Her mother had complained often that her father had been an irresponsible weakling. Often she said Laura was becoming just like him. . . .

She found herself wondering now what it would have been like to have a normal home; then she tried to picture what Ginny's family was like. Ginny had mentioned that she was from out of state, but not much else.

Somehow Ginny made Laura think of summer fields and light breezes. . . . She had to be from the Midwest. Laura could just see her at a county fair with a young freckle-faced boyfriend whose arms were too long and whose pants were too short. A real cornball. In fact, the whole idea was corny as hell.

Ginny might be just a simple girl from New York City. Sure, like a simple nightclub singer maybe, with a string of playboys or rich gangsters at her beck and call.

Brother! I'm really getting high on clichés, Laura scolded herself, then started walking up and down. Ten minutes had passed since she had hung up.

Maybe Saundra was en route somewhere and Ginny hadn't been able to reach her . . . or they were having an argument about tonight. But that would be silly, Laura thought. Why should they? Two women don't argue over something like that. Yet what was taking her so—

The phone rang sharply, and although she had been expecting it, Laura jumped.

"Yes?"

"It's all right," Ginny said. "Where shall we meet?"

"Where are you now?"

"Googie's."

Laura calculated her time swiftly and decided to ignore her chores. "Okay. I'll meet you there in half an hour."

Before Laura entered the glass-walled café, she saw Ginny sitting inside by herself in a booth. She smiled to herself for no particular reason and went in.

"Hello."

Ginny looked up and smiled. "Hi."

There was a moment of uneasy silence.

"Shall we get started? You don't want to spend the day in here, do you?" Laura asked cheerfully. Surprising herself, she picked up Ginny's check and paid it while Ginny slid out of the modern, plastic-covered bench.

She silenced Ginny's attempt to object and led the way to the car. Laura had changed into a flowered skirt, topped by a black sleeveless blouse that showed to advantage her firm, slim arms. She looked sophisticated and coolly chic. It was gratifying to notice Ginny's unconcealed expression of admiration.

In the car, she felt positively brazen as she drove down Sunset Boulevard toward the beach . . . almost as if she hoped Saundra might drive by and see them together. How adolescent, she chided herself, but she did not change course.

As they drove, Laura began to ask Ginny questions about herself and her career. Not exactly a routine interview, but who was counting?

Ginny, however, didn't seem to want to talk about herself: unusual for anyone in Hollywood. Laura was about to write off the whole deal when Ginny said, "You're really very nice, Laura. I mean, asking me out today and being friendly even when you don't have to. You must know lots more fascinating people than me."

"Oh, I wouldn't say that." Laura grinned at her. "Besides, being 'fascinating' is an occupational disease in this town, and I'm rapidly developing an immunity. I just wanted some plain old-fashioned friendly conversation."

Ginny laughed. "That's heresy. But it sounds wonderful."

The brief bit of banter broke the tension between them, and Laura found it very easy to talk with Ginny. And she had the pleased feeling that Ginny was enjoying herself, too.

They arrived at Hermosa Beach a little after four. There wasn't much to see in the town—it was just another small California beach community with as many acres of oil wells as there were of sand. They drove up and down the little streets slowly. "Anything you'd like to get out and see?" she asked Ginny.

"Not particularly," Ginny answered.

Laura nodded without comment. The afternoon sun made the town look like a stage set now that the midday clouds had disappeared and the rich colors around them took on an unnatural vividness.

"I'm glad I came today," Ginny said suddenly. "I like you even better than I thought I would."

Laura laughed.

"No. I'm serious. You seemed so above it all and almost disdainful the other day. I was impressed because you were a writer and sophisticated and attractive. But now I'm not really what you'd call impressed. I just like you. You're the kind of person I want to know and . . . and be good friends with."

"Thanks." Laura felt a strange chill of excitement. Still, she couldn't quite shake the feeling that Ginny was playing up to her.

"Just where are we heading for, by the way?" Ginny asked looking around.

"Like Mexican food?"

"I don't know."

"It's a little early—are you hungry?"

"Starved. I didn't have lunch." She reached over and placed her hand on Laura's arm. "Let's try the Mexican food."

Laura had not expected Ginny's touch, and it came as a surprise. She felt her breath quicken. It was the first time Ginny had touched her, and for some strange reason it was disturbing.

She thought about it as she turned off at the next intersection and headed back toward Redondo Beach and a little place called Consuelo's.

All through dinner Laura could not forget Ginny's touch, that light touch on her arm. Yet it was such a small thing. It didn't matter. Not really.

Or did it?

Chapter 6

Without any consciously deliberate effort Ginny and Laura either met or called each other at least once a day the following week.

Laura had been surprised and delighted to see Ginny in the Excelsior Studio Commissary one afternoon that week, and later that day they had gone to the movies together on Hollywood Boulevard. Friday, someone had left two passes for Laura for one of the famous Greek Theater outdoor operettas. It had seemed only natural to call Ginny to go with her . . . nor did it seem odd that Ginny had had no date on a Friday night.

Neither girl mentioned Saundra other than to swiftly send regards, usually in a mumble. It was tacitly understood that conversation about her was, if not taboo, at least unnecessary.

Consequently, when Sunday morning came around, Laura was full of doubts and misgivings about the trip to Tijuana. Saundra had not forgotten about it: she had left word at *Fanfare* late Thursday afternoon as a reminder.

Now Laura, driving slowly through the quiet Sunday morning, felt her anxiety growing with each mile.

"Damn it," she said aloud as she pulled into Saundra's driveway and parked. "Why should I feel guilty? It isn't as if I were seducing anybody's husband!"

With a sudden burst of irritation she slammed the car door and strode up the steps. She felt herself rigidly awaiting the opening of the door. It stayed closed. After a few seconds she thought: they left without me.

Laura fidgeted a moment, almost ready to retreat. Then she heard footsteps inside the house. Saundra flung the door open.

"Laura, darling," she purred. "I'm so glad you remembered our trip and could make it."

Oh, man! Laura thought. Has this one got a bug! "I wouldn't have missed it for a scoop on Louella Parsons," she replied. Smooth.

"Well, come in, come in. Ginny's been worried about you all weekend . . . and so have I." Saundra placed an arm around Laura's waist as she closed the door. "You look beautiful. You've a perfect figure for slacks with those long legs of yours." A hand slipped down the side of Laura's thigh and pinched her lightly. "Cup of coffee before we leave?" Saundra asked cheerfully, leading Laura toward the kitchen.

Ginny came out of the kitchen looking like a scrubbed waif. "I've already poured three cups, so come on in." Her face was bright with welcome. Somehow Ginny made everything seem more normal and more relaxed.

But as they sat down at the now-familiar table, Saundra said, "Ginny's quite taken with you, Laura. I'm glad she's showing such good taste."

It was an odd remark—a baited one. And though it disturbed her, Laura pretended to ignore it . . . and Ginny pretended not to hear.

A few minutes later they settled into Saundra's Cadillac convertible. Laura sat in the middle, and Ginny and Saundra debated spiritedly over whether to put the top down.

Laura began to relax.

The drive south to Tijuana was filled with laughter, and an atmosphere of genial companionship prevailed. Saundra told them some funny and fantastic anecdotes about her rise to stardom. There seemed to be no trace of her cutting sarcasm, and Laura found herself becoming utterly charmed.

43

Saundra took the longer route via the Palos Verdes Estates and pointed out the beautiful homes, and they admired the unbelievably impressive coastline. A short way beyond Laguna they stopped for breakfast and then continued down to San Diego. Instead of going around Coronado, they took the ferry across the narrow bay. About two o'clock they arrived at the Mexican border.

"Look at the line of cars!" Ginny gasped. Cars were backed up for about five hundred yards, waiting to drive through the border inspection post. There was more honking and yelling than if the president had decided to fight the bulls himself that day.

"Park here, ladies! Fifty cents all day."

"Win lots of money. Reliable scratch sheets."

"Over here. Over here. We watch your car! Fifty cents. All day."

People walked by dressed in what in had come to be known as the California fashion in clothing; cameras dangling, sunglasses, straw hats, cigars, and shorts with tossed-salad-patterned shirts.

Saundra drove into a parking lot, and she explained, "It doesn't pay to take the car across; it's better to walk." She accepted the lot ticket from a frowning youth.

"Hey. Ain't you Lana Turner?" he asked in awe.

"Darling," Saundra drawled, "she's my mother."

The girls burst into laughter.

"My admiring public," Saundra commented dryly. They joined the crowd that walked toward the border inspection officers, joking and talking animatedly even under the hot early-afternoon sun.

Laura felt enthusiastic about everything. She was aware that Saundra had contributed most of the wit to the day, but Laura knew without even thinking that it was Ginny who gave her the real pleasure. . . . She wondered briefly if just the two of them would have had as good a time. But she knew the answer to that, too.

They could already hear the inspectors' voices, touched by a trace of Spanish accent, "Anything to declare? How long is your stay?"

As they reached the arches, Ginny grabbed Laura's hand and squeezed it enthusiastically. "Look." She pointed to the sign near the top.

Laura looked up and then laughed. "It says *Mexico*. Where'd you think we were?"

"I know. I know. But it really is."

Laura laughed again and returned the squeeze of Ginny's hand. She felt very young and very carefree. She glanced at Saundra to share her good mood and was surprised to see Saundra's tight expression.

Laura felt uneasy immediately. But she just smiled at Saundra and decided not to analyze so damn much. Live it up, she told herself. It's been a long time since you've felt as relaxed with anyone as you have with Ginny—so very long.

They cleared the inspectors quickly and, after an unbelievably hectic taxi ride, arrived in front of Caesar's Hotel on the main street of downtown Tijuana.

Saundra led the way across the hotel veranda into the lobby. People were everywhere, making conversation virtually impossible. The crowd was dressed in a variety of styles that went from native Jamaican casualness to cocktail dress. The hotel was a meeting place, a clearing house, a point of origin for most tourists whether they were registered there or not.

Languages mixed; arms gestured; faces grimaced. The spell of the bullfight was everywhere and coursed through the crowds in waves of animated chatter; bits of predictions, reminiscences, comparisons floated through the air like confetti. Laura's eyes shone with happy excitement.

Saundra waved gaily to various friends as she led her little troupe across the sweltering room.

Ginny walked close to Laura. "Don't lose me."

"Don't worry," Laura said. She took Ginny's hand and held it tight.

"Here we are." Saundra offered a bright smile to the bowing manager of the hotel as they entered the dark and even more crowded bar.

She led them to a booth in the far corner where it appeared the occupants were about to vacate.

"Only cats and lushes can see in these places," Saundra laughed, "and I'm both. Sit down quick."

"Are we going to stay here long?" Laura asked quietly. "I hate to be a tourist, but I would like to browse around the shops before it gets dark."

"So would I," said Ginny, "if—if it's all right with you, Saundra."

Saundra glanced at her; then she smiled, but there was a cold glint in her eyes. "Of course. But it would be a bore for me, dear. Why don't you and Laura go alone?"

She watched Saundra pull out a crisp fifty-dollar bill and place it on the table in front of Ginny. "Get the tickets for the fight while you're in the lobby," Saundra said. "Whatever's left you can use for trinkets—but buy the best seats you can get."

The way Saundra laid the money on the table instead of handing it to Ginny struck Laura as a subtle insult to both of them. But as Ginny mechanically picked up the bill, folded it neatly, and placed it in her purse, Laura told herself that she was being absurd, reading meanings into anything.

Then some of Saundra's friends appeared.

They ordered a round of margaritas. And Laura and Ginny decided it was time to see the town. Although Saundra had ostensibly been absorbed in her friends, she noted the girls' departure with distinct irritation. She gave an annoyed little cluck as they stood up and then, as if not wanting to show her feelings, said a little too loudly, "Be back by quarter of four, you two."

"Darling!" An effeminate young man came bounding over to Saundra's table as they walked away. Laura couldn't help overhearing him ask Saundra, "Cutting your time?" and Saundra's reply, which sounded like "Not likely!"

Once in the lobby, Laura breathed a little more freely. She turned around and looked at Ginny, who stood rigidly next to her. "Relax, Ginny," Laura said, and realized that she had not let go of Ginny's hand. "It's me—not Saundra."

Ginny looked up abruptly, pulling her hand away. "What made you say that?"

"I don't know." Laura shrugged. "Maybe because I can see a few of your problems . . . in being Saundra's protégé."

"Never mind," Ginny said wearily. "Let's buy the tickets and get it over with." At the cigar counter in the hotel lobby an attractive young Mexican girl pulled out a handful of colorful tickets. "Sun or shade?"

"Which is better?" Laura asked.

"Shade. But it is more expensive. We have very few left and only because of a cancellation by a party of six."

"Three of the best seats," Laura said.

"Tres, primera fila sombra," the girl wrote down in some sort of log. It seemed an exorbitant price to Laura. She had insisted on paying for her own ticket. She did not want Saundra to pay her way.

"It will be a good *corrida*. You will not be sorry," the girl said with an apologetic smile, and handed the three narrow and long paper tickets to Laura.

It better be, Laura thought as she stood waiting for Ginny to get her change.

Outside they strolled up the busy street, investigating the more interesting shops, ignoring the street barkers in front of the run-down cabarets, buying tacos at the little pushcarts. On Ginny's insistence they had their picture taken on top of a wagon pulled by a humiliated burro painted to look like a zebra.

Laura didn't have to ask Ginny if she was having a good time. Her enthusiasm about everything was more exciting than anything else on the trip so far. Each time Ginny took her hand or touched her arm to emphasize a conversational point, Laura felt her senses quicken with awareness. It was a feeling of closeness—and something else. Even as she reflected on it, her feeling of guilt grew. But why?

It was odd, too, that although Ginny seemed to lean on her and relied on her to take care of everything from getting the tickets to deciding what street to walk on, Laura had the feeling that she was the one who was being led. There was something arch about Ginny's helplessness, a sly quality that was disturbing.

"It's three-thirty, Ginny," Laura said finally. "We'd better be on our way back to the hotel."

"My watch says two-thirty." She put down the earthen jug.

"They don't go on daylight saving time here. We can walk around some more afterwards."

Ginny said quickly, "I doubt it!" Then, with a forced laugh, "Saundra wouldn't like it." She paused as if trying to think of some way to clarify her already simple statement. "I mean, well, we did come with her, and it's only polite . . ."

"I get the picture, Ginny." Laura put down a pair of Mexican wall masks and started for the street.

"You're not angry, are you?" Ginny asked, a slight frown on her face.

"No. Of course not," Laura answered. But she was angry, and it made her angrier to realize it.

They walked back to the hotel in silence, and into the dark bar. Saundra hadn't budged from her table and her friends. From the loudness of her voice, even Laura could tell she was feeling her liquor.

Ginny stopped. "Wait here," she commanded Laura, and walked over to Saundra.

Laura couldn't hear what she said; the bar was too noisy with the addition of strolling musicians serenading the patrons. But she saw Saundra place her arm around Ginny's waist, hug her, and then wave her away. Laura felt a cold knot in her stomach as Ginny returned: was Saundra going to sit out the afternoon in the bar?

"Let's go," Ginny said tightly. "Madam Queen is too busy with her friends to join us at the bullfight."

After another madcap taxi ride Ginny locked arms with Laura as they fought the crowd to the entrance turnstile marked *Sombra-Shade*.

Laura was disconcertingly aware that she could feel Ginny's soft breast with her forearm, could feel her body warmth. Self-conscious, she released Ginny quickly.

They climbed the worn and rickety wooden stairs under the bleachers and were grateful for the shade. Finally, at the top, they followed the crowd into the shock of open sunlight. The sense of excitement was almost overpowering. Brightness, color, and movement flooded their vision. The bleachers swarmed with people talking, yelling, and laughing. Climbing down the bleachers as stairs, they made their way to the first row and found the painted numbers corresponding to their tickets.

Suddenly the trumpets sounded. A hush fell over the entire arena. Two enormous wooden gates opened at the east end of the circle, and a beautiful horse came thundering out, straight to the opposite side of the arena, ridden by a *charro* on an elaborate silver-and-black saddle. The rider stopped abruptly at the wooden wall of the bleachers, took off his sombrero to the judges and officials of today's sport, and slowly rode the carefully trained horse backward to the entrance.

Then the trumpets blasted with renewed vigor. The bullfighters and their assistants saluted the aficionados on the shady side, their ornate "suits of lights" catching the afternoon sun.

The formalities out of the way, Ginny leaned on the rail to see better as a voice announced over the loudspeaker that Carlos Arruza would fight the first *corrida* on horseback.

Laura found herself leaning forward, too, and her elbows touched Ginny. She felt that she should pull away, and then that it was silly to feel that way, and then felt silly for feeling anything at all. She left it where it was, but awareness of the contact kept creeping into her brain.

The first bull had been killed with pageantry and—even to the novice spectator—obvious skill and respect by the matador.

But it was too much for Ginny. She wanted to leave. She had been all right throughout the initial plays, and even the *picadores* and *banderilleros*, but the kill had done something.

They walked back down the stairs under the bleachers silently.

Laura felt pity well up in her as the feet overhead stomped and shuffled. She heard the people shifting on the hard benches, avidly squirming for action. It wasn't pity for the bull that she felt—she accepted his fate. She knew there was no "contest" in the accepted sense—the animal was going to die. Only the *how* of its death was important to the audience.

She hated that. If she could have, Laura would have lifted the whole arena and shaken it violently—the bullfighters, the crowd, and the bull too.

"I'm sorry I made you leave," Ginny apologized as they walked out of the darkness toward the parking area. They stepped into a waiting cab.

"Hotel Caesar," Laura told the driver; then, without looking at Ginny she said, "Don't be sorry. In a way, I was glad to go anyhow."

"It wasn't that the blood made me sick. I can't quite explain it to you. The matador and the bull seemed the least important—it was the crowd that bothered me."

Laura was surprised that Ginny had described her own reactions so accurately.

Once again they entered the bar. It was relatively empty at that hour. The patrons were either at the bullfights, the dog races, or the jai alai games.

Saundra sat in the same booth. She was very drunk. Two men were seated with her.

As Ginny and Laura approached, Sandra slurred, "There's my baby! Back so soon, baby? Didn't you like all the blood and screaming?"

Laura wanted to turn around and walk out. She felt embarrassed for Saundra and sick for Ginny. The two men made token attempts to stand up.

Saundra flung out her arm dramatically. "You don't have to stand up for her; she's my baby! Have a nice time, baby? Did old Laura hold your hand crossing the big street? What d'ya want to drink?" Saundra leered drunkenly at the two men. "My baby's old enough to drink. What d'ya think of that!"

Ginny's face flushed, and she sat down quietly.

"This is William," Saundra introduced them, "and that's Martin." She grinned lecherously at Ginny. "Which one do you want, baby? I'll give him to you."

Laura decided that someone had to break up this conversation. "What's your drink, Saundra," she asked casually. "We'd like to get in on your kick."

Martin snorted. He looked as drunk as Saundra.

Laura ignored him. Instead she stared at Saundra and waited for her reply.

"You're cute," Martin went on, undaunted. "Younger, too. Saundra's slipping. Too much competition."

William reached out and gripped his friend's arm violently; then he smiled at Laura.

"How's that for an old friend of Saundra's? They've known each other for years, you know." He looked at Laura apologetically. "Of course, he takes a lot of liberties."

The atmosphere around the small table was electric. Laura could feel the violence closing in.

"Friends!" Saundra sneered. "Buddies, that's us." She grimaced and raised her eyes to look contemptuously at Laura. "I detest him. But you want to know something? He's a man. . . . Do you know what that means? No," Saundra went on with a cold, sick smile. "No. You wouldn't. You don't know even what it means to want a man, do you? Your kind never knows!"

"Come on, now, Saundra," William interrupted.

"Shut up!" Saundra commanded without even looking at him. "Wearing pants doesn't make you a man, and lipstick doesn't make her a woman." She glared at Laura. Then she giggled.

Laura sat helplessly. She knew that any second Saundra would say something that Laura would not want to face. Something she knew already but had not admitted.

Saundra continued slowly, maliciously. "The only one at this table who's got any real sex is Martin." She raised her head with obvious effort. "But that's all he's got!"

"Saundra, please . . ." Ginny whispered.

"Oh, so you do have a tongue," Saundra laughed cruelly. "What's the matter, sweetie? Don't you like the way I talk about sex? Want me to show a little respect for your stock in trade?"

"Don't make a scene, Saundra . . ." Ginny pleaded. "Everyone is watching."

"Scene? Me?" Saundra glared at Ginny. "Next to your daily performances I'm practically an amateur. I may be the star, Ginny," she continued in a hoarse, drunken voice, "but you are the actress. Of course, I'll admit you have to resort to props . . ."

Saundra's eyes dropped slyly to Ginny's breasts, and her mouth slackened into a mirthless grin.

Panic ripped through Laura, and everything around her faded into a kind of haze. A stinging metallic clatter brought her back to reality. She stared at the car keys Saundra had hurled on the table. Then she heard Saundra's voice again, rasping and infuriated.

"Take the car, Ginny. Go ahead." She laughed again with a frightening choke in her throat. "You don't have to act with me, you know. I know you've got a new audience. . . . She'll be a little diversion for a while, anyway."

"*Don't.* Please!" Ginny was close to tears.

But Saundra disregarded her. "It's all right with me. I have my own plans for tonight!" She ran an unsteady hand over Martin's chest. "Besides," she said, turning back to Ginny, "I'm not worried about you, sweetie. You'll come back to me . . . to what nobody else can do for you."

Ginny's face filled with rage and despair. She started to answer, then got up and walked unsteadily out of the room. It was obvious that she was crying.

Laura stood up, feeling surprised that there was no weight to her body. She felt numb. With detached fascination she saw Saundra lift the keys from the table and throw them in the air with alcoholic passion.

Automatically, Laura reached and caught them.

"Go to hell!" Saundra screamed.

Laura wheeled around quickly and walked out of the room without looking where she was going.

Walking into the lobby brought her back to reality. The late-afternoon sun poured into the large room, and suddenly it looked dirty and old. The quaintness and charm she had seen on her arrival were gone. In their place was an ordinary, dingy hotel lobby and all the things her mind suddenly recoiled at: illicit love, prepaid orgies, drunken parties, empty promises, loneliness.

Then, she saw Ginny sitting on the far side of the lobby. She sat in a straight-back chair, the bleak wall of the room behind her. She was staring blankly at nothing.

Laura felt her throat constrict with sympathy. My God, that poor kid. She felt an overwhelming need to help Ginny, to offer her friendship, to take care of her.

As Laura walked slowly toward Ginny, her body tingled strangely and her mind seemed very sharp and clear.

"Come on, Ginny," she said with a new, quiet tenderness. "Let's get out of here."

Ginny sat still as if unable to move or to speak. Her face was rigid.

Laura put out her hand, helped the girl to her feet, and led her out of the hotel. The street looked like a ghost town now; everyone was gone, it seemed, except for a few scattered people. Even the cabaret barkers had gone indoors out of the hot sun. Laura became aware of the dirt of the town, the gaudiness of it.

She led the silent Ginny halfway down the block to a small restaurant she had seen earlier, and walked in behind her.

Chapter 7

They sat down at a table against the imitation-adobe wall, their chairs scraping noisily on the floor in the nearly empty restaurant. The restaurant boasted checked tablecloths, painted gourds, hanging wall plants and fake balconies with awnings. All trite, Laura thought. And shabby.

Ginny still said nothing.

The waiter came up to their table, surprised to have customers at this time of day.

Laura ordered two ponies of brandy and advised him they would not have dinner. As he walked away, she asked, "All right with you, Ginny?"

Ginny nodded and suddenly burst into tears. She covered her face with her hands and turned toward the wall. "I'm so ashamed," she gasped softly. Then, incongruously: "That whore!"

It was almost more than Laura could bear, just watching her cry. She said, "You don't have to say anything, Ginny." But Laura knew she didn't mean it; she did want an explanation. She waited for Ginny to regain control of herself.

The waiter placed their drinks in front of them and walked away, apparently unconcerned with these crazy Americans.

Ginny straightened up slowly and sighed almost perceptibly. She dried her eyes. Then she raised her glass with an unsteady but manageable hand. "Here's to self-pity and psychiatrists," she said quietly, with a trace of bitterness in her voice.

Laura smiled and met Ginny's eyes with her own, hoping she looked as casually friendly as she wanted.

"And—honesty," Ginny added in a whisper.

"Feel like telling me about it?"

Ginny gave a short little laugh. "Saundra seems to have covered the most important facts. . . ."

"I was asking for *your* version." It was terribly important now to Laura, as if by knowing what had happened to Ginny she could avert . . . *avert*. Now there's a good word.

"Could we leave here?" Ginny asked suddenly.

"Where do you want to go?" Laura felt her stomach tense strangely.

Ginny shrugged hopelessly. "Home, I guess."

"No," Laura said decisively. "I don't think you should be alone tonight. You can stay at my place until we figure out what to do with you."

Ginny made no protest, and Laura paid the check. They took a cab to the border and walked across to Saundra's car. Automatically, Laura slid into the driver's seat.

She had just assumed that she would drive, and it didn't occur to her to ask Ginny; she was taking care of Ginny; it was her obligation to help Ginny. The silence between them was now becoming unbearable.

As if Ginny sensed Laura's need to know her story, she lit a cigarette for Laura, then, faltering a moment, began, "Still want to know?"

That so much time had passed since Laura had asked her didn't seem at all important—they both had only one thing on their minds right now.

"You don't have to tell me anything, Ginny," Laura said after a moment.

"It's no big confession," Ginny laughed a little stiffly. "You'd probably get a better 'story' out of hundreds of other women."

"But I'm not interested in other women right now." Even as she said it, Laura felt that she should not have phrased it quite that way. But Ginny had not seemed to notice.

"I came to Hollywood a little over a year ago on contract to Excelsior. But there was nothing for me to do. Oh, I'd get a bit part here and there, but nothing worth mentioning. I found one of those cheap, stamp-size apartments on Melrose and tried to make the best of it." She paused. Laura waited.

"After about two months of crumbs, I got another bit part. Only this time in a picture starring Saundra. I'd heard a great deal about her, of course." Ginny exhaled, then said, wryly, "But not enough!"

Laura kept her eyes on the road. The evening sun was just horizon level, casting long dark shadows across the road, yet bright enough to sparkle on the glass and chrome of other cars. "Anyhow," Ginny went on in a soft voice, "Saundra seemed to pick me out from the others. She began by asking me to do things for her: she forgot something in her dressing room, a cup of coffee between takes, cue her for a scene—that sort of thing." Her voice sounded weary and hard.

Laura nodded.

"The next thing I knew, she was telling me that she believed in me—thought I had what she called an outstanding talent. But I needed coaching, she said. I was too immature, stiff, and needed rounding out. Not just with my acting, she explained, but as a person, too. An actress of stature could not separate her personality from her career and remain on top—much less reach the top."

"Of course, you were impressed," Laura said with a trace of sarcasm.

"Impressed?" Ginny laughed. "I was walking on air!"

"Go on," Laura said.

"Saundra was going to teach me the ropes, and I was spellbound. She can be pretty spellbinding, you know. Why, according to her I'd be a star in no time at all."

Laura nodded grimly, and Ginny went on. "She began by having me over to her house on Saturday mornings—her last husband played golf then. Diction, posture, dress, just about everything.

"One day I showed up and she was still in her dressing gown . . . said that her husband had gone out of town and that her house-keeper had gone to Oakland to be with her sister and that she was all alone and terribly bored, and . . ."

"And would you stay overnight with her?" Laura supplied know-ingly.

"Yes."

"And you accepted?"

"Yes." Ginny twisted in her seat. "It never occurred to me that . . . that . . ."

"All right, I get the idea." Laura felt a little sick to her stomach. She was torn between hating Ginny for being such a dumb little kid, and marvelling at her spirit. You don't hate people for being dumb, she told herself; you hate them for pinpointing your own weaknesses. Oh, sure, Laura sneered silently to herself, now I sup-pose you think you're a pervert like Ginny.

It was an unkind—and uncomfortable—thought.

"But why did you stick it out all this time? That's what I really would like to understand."

Ginny didn't answer immediately. Then, "I suppose you're think-ing that I'm over twenty-one and could have walked out, that no-body was holding me prisoner."

"Something like that."

"I'm not sure I can explain it to you," Ginny said.

Laura waited for her to try but was beginning to feel uneasy with the whole conversation. She wanted to know about Ginny's prob-lems, yet she didn't like hearing about her being a . . . abnormal. Yet at the same time Laura was fascinated.

"I'm not sure even that I understand it myself," Ginny contin-ued. "I guess it was sort of the easiest way."

"Easiest!"

"In a way, I had no decisions to make, I didn't have to be alone and wonder what to do with myself. But most of all, my career was—important to me. And Saundra is helping me."

"You would have made friends on your own."

"How many friends do you have, Laura?"

The question took Laura by surprise. She remembered her own thoughts recently about finding friends—and she had lived in Los Angeles a long time.

"I see what you mean," she acknowledged grudgingly.

"Sure. Make friends, everybody tells you that. But call them up to go to a movie, and they're busy or too tired or some other reason. This is the most unfriendly town I've ever been in!" Ginny's voice rose.

Laura had never actually thought about that aspect before. She had her work, her business associates, and Walter. She had always believed that Los Angeles was a nice Western homespun, friendly little town simply because the publicity-happy chamber of commerce said so.

"How about dates? Don't you ever go out with men?"

"Oh, I dated several guys back home. But I was just drying my ears out here when I ran into Saundra. Those first few weeks were pretty busy, finding a place to live, getting used to the change."

"Uh-huh." Odd how fictional life sounded, but Laura believed Ginny. Her own life, as a matter of fact, wouldn't sound very plausible.

"I'd never been with anyone like Saundra before, and, well, I felt kind of tainted—oh, that's the wrong word. I just didn't want to see anybody who wasn't . . ."

The unhappiness on Ginny's face, the misery in her choked tone, touched Laura deeply. Still, she could not dispel the momentary feeling that Ginny was "playing to the gallery." After Saundra's scene it would be more than difficult to play it straight.

It seemed as if they would never get off the Santa Ana Freeway. It was a maze of steel and concrete—once on it you were trapped. Following meekly in your little lane as other cars whizzed by, not daring to honk at the older cars in front of you . . . Goddamn it, Laura cursed mentally, I've a right in this world! I pay my taxes!

She switched on the lights and pulled out into the left lane with a burst of speed. "Why didn't you tell me to turn on the lights?"

Ginny looked up with a trace of a smile. "I did, but you weren't listening."

Laura slowed up and reentered the middle lane.

"You started out to comfort me and listen to my sad story," Ginny said with almost her old spirit. "What happened?"

Laura laughed self-consciously. "Guess the whole subject is a little out of my depth." She reached for Ginny's hand. "Have you any plans now? I mean, after this afternoon you aren't going to keep living with Saundra, are you?"

"I don't know," Ginny answered. "I don't know what I'll do. I just feel so disjointed." Ginny hesitated as if there was something more she wanted to say. But she didn't say it.

Laura automatically took the Harbor Freeway turnoff and was headed toward her own apartment.

Ginny frowned slightly. "You don't have to put me up, you know. I could drive the car myself after you pick up yours. . . ."

"Don't be silly, Ginny," Laura interrupted. "Unless you'd rather be alone . . ."

"No. No, I'd rather not," said Ginny hastily.

"Then it's settled. We'll go get my car on my way to work in the morning, and then you'll be more in the mood to go home."

Ginny attempted a smile. "You're very sweet to do this for me, Laura."

"I like you—I just wanted to help, that's all."

"I know."

There was something odd about the way Ginny said that, but Laura wasn't sure why it was odd—and at this point she didn't care. She just wanted to get home.

Chapter 8

"Hang your coat in that closet, Ginny," Laura said, walking into the kitchen and turning on the light. There had been a telegram under the front door, which she had placed in her purse before Ginny saw it. Probably from Walter, Laura thought, and didn't open it. . . . I'll read it later.

"I need a drink. How about you?"

In a way Laura felt relieved that Ginny had agreed to stay. But now, with Ginny actually walking around in her apartment, she felt uneasy. She pulled out ice cubes mechanically and wondered if she was right in reacting to Ginny's problem with such apparent nonchalance—or if she should have drawn back in disgust and sent the dirty little girl away.

No—she knew she was right in accepting Ginny. Actually, she didn't have much of an alternative. Almost as though in accepting Ginny she was accepting herself—but that was idiotic, of course, she amended hastily. What did she have to accept herself for? Here I am—what else can I do?

Listening to Ginny walk around the apartment, Laura became aware of a kind of strange peace; a curious hush settled over the room as if no one else were alive in the world. All she knew right now or wanted to know was that she was going to help Ginny all she could. And that at last she felt like a living person instead of some electronically operated observer from outer space—which was how she felt much too often these days. Walter had filled some of her needs, and her work had kept her going . . . but lately, neither Walter nor her work had been sufficient. Unless that New York offer of Walter's . . .

I wonder what is in that wire—or if Walter is having any success with his divorcée. Walter. Wouldn't he be shocked if he knew what I was up to!

But what am I up to?

"I like your apartment, Laura," Ginny said, entering the kitchen.

"Thanks." Laura handed a drink to Ginny. "Let's go in the living room and sit down."

She raised her free arm to put around Ginny's shoulder, then thought better of it—what if Ginny misunderstood? Thought I was making a pass? Well . . . what if she did! Ridiculous.

"A stiff drink, a hot bath, and a good night's sleep will help both of us," she said as they sat on the couch.

Ginny looked up at her slowly. "Why did you ask me to stay, Laura?"

A wave of apprehension gripped Laura as she wondered how to answer the question. "Why? Sorry you came?"

"In a way . . ."

"Oh?" Laura had not expected that. It threw her off balance for a moment. "In what way are you sorry?"

Ginny took a long swallow of her drink and turned her large eyes—now suddenly sophisticated, knowing—toward Laura. Ginny smiled. "Are you so sure you don't know?"

Laura shook her head impatiently. "Let's cut the runaround. What are you driving at?"

"You asked me because you're curious about it, aren't you?"

"Curious about what?"

"About lesbians!"

The word spilled out so abruptly, so starkly, that Laura wondered if she had heard correctly. It puzzled her that Ginny had brought it up, and so unexpectedly. And there was a hint of theatrics in Ginny's gestures—like a veteran politician feeling out the mood of his audience.

Ginny waved her hand into the air as if to gesture away side issues. "I like you, Laura," Ginny said with just a trace of intoxication in her voice. "But you're a phony!"

In spite of herself, Laura had to laugh. "Why?" The more Ginny talked, the more Laura became convinced that Ginny was getting tight. But talking to her now was almost like talking to herself—to all the things that had flashed through her mind before, taunting her but not staying long enough for her to fully grasp at them.

"Because you won't admit you want to kiss me. That's why."

Laura's face grew hot. She wanted to deny it. But she couldn't.

"Well?" Ginny's eyes probed hers. "It's true, isn't it?"

"I don't know," Laura answered miserably. "Maybe it is. I don't know."

"But I know, Laura." Ginny's voice was a tense whisper. "I know because it's the way I feel about you. I want you!" Her eyes filled with tears; she turned away. Laura stared helplessly at the girl's rigid back.

"Are you crying, Ginny?"

The girl shook her head, but Laura knew that she was. A stab of resentment ripped through her. She hated being trapped in emotional situations; the scene in Tijuana had been enough of a shock for one day. But as quickly as the feeling came, it dissipated, routed by Laura's natural compassion—and the excitement that Ginny's admission had aroused.

She put a consoling arm around Ginny's shoulder. Somehow the mere contact of the girl's body unleashed something, and all the plaguing doubts flew from Laura. All she knew now was what she felt, could feel . . . Laura turned the girl to face her. Her voice didn't seem her own. "I'm glad. I think . . . I think I feel the same way about you."

Ginny didn't stir, seemed almost not to breathe.

Very slowly, Laura leaned forward and hesitantly kissed Ginny on the lips.

She felt Ginny's body tighten, but her lips were soft and warm . . .

and waiting. Then Ginny's lips parted, and her arms rose up and encircled Laura's neck, pulling her slowly, so slowly closer. All other thoughts were blotted out.

It was so unbelievably sweet—the faint aroma of sun and soap on Ginny's smooth face, the down-soft lips that now parted more so that their tongues touched . . . at first strangely, exploring, then completely, familiar.

It was delicious to Laura. No rough beard scratching her face, no large hands asserting their masculinity, no feeling of being cornered into an affair—just a soft kiss with small, gentle hands and smooth arms caressing her . . .

Laura was lost in the ease and tenderness of this moment. No other thought but now, no other sensation than that of total surrender to Ginny's touch . . .

Effortlessly their lips separated, but Laura didn't move away, nor did Ginny. Their faces so close that Laura could feel Ginny's breath, she raised her hand to Ginny's flushed cheek, enjoying the very contact with her, the feeling of possession of the very bones beneath her young face.

Ginny smiled and, turning her face into Laura's hand, kissed her palm. She leaned back on the couch, pulling Laura over her. Her eyes were dark, challenging, probing, suggestive.

Ginny's hands reached up to Laura's throat, stroking, caressing, and traced down smoothly to her breasts. It was so strange to Laura—exciting, intense, yet oddly gentle. It didn't seem as if they were "making love" in any way Laura had known before. It wasn't lust competing with frenzy.

The last thing Laura remembered was that every inch of her body seemed to leap, struggle, surge to meet with Ginny's.

Laura lay quietly on her side, staring at the sunlight on Ginny's hair as she slept in Laura's arms. She had been awake for almost an hour, just watching Ginny, incredibly content just to have her sweet body next to hers.

She wanted to wake Ginny and share her pleasure with her, share this first delicious morning together. If anyone had told her six months ago that she could feel so completely fulfilled, so perfectly at peace, she would have laughed. The sentimental trash in every corny poem, every romantic novel she had ever read, now had a vitality she had missed before, almost a special message just for her.

Ginny stirred and cupped her hand around Laura's breast gently, nuzzling her face against the other.

"Ginny?" Laura asked softly.

"Hmm?"

"You awake?"

"Uh-hm." She pressed closer to Laura.

Laura smiled and held her more tightly, resting her lips against Ginny's hair. If she felt any more alive, she was sure she would burst.

"Talk to me," she coaxed Ginny.

"This is no time for talking."

"Sure, it is," Laura answered with a light laugh. "I've been thinking about us. Thinking about you here in the apartment with your shoes under the bed, a sweater hanging out of a drawer, the arguments we'll probably have . . ."

"Why should I have my sweater in your drawer?" Ginny asked sleepily.

"When you move in, I mean," Laura explained.

Ginny said nothing but pulled away from her slowly. Then she sat up on one elbow, a clouded expression on her face. "Hand me a cigarette, will you?"

Laura looked at her carefully; she tried to make out what Ginny's expression meant, but couldn't.

"I said I'd like a cigarette, please," Ginny repeated with a tight smile on her lips.

"Is something wrong?" Laura asked, a cold knot forming in the pit of her stomach.

Ginny hesitated as she lit the cigarette Laura had given her. "Not wrong . . . exactly." She inhaled deeply of the cigarette. "Just mistaken."

She rolled over on her back and watched the smoke curl up. Laura didn't want to look at her now; she was even a little afraid to look at her.

"Mistaken?" she managed to say.

"I can't just move in, Laura."

"Oh, not right away. I know that," Laura said hastily. "You'll have to clear up a few things first, and talk to Saundra . . ."

Ginny shook her head. "No."

Laura turned and stared at her in confusion. "I don't understand."

Ginny heaved a long sigh. "I love you, Laura. You know that. But let's be practical about this, shall we?"

"All right, Ginny," she said casually despite the constriction in her throat, "let's be practical. By all means. Where would you like to start?"

Ginny turned and faced Laura, petulantly at first; then her expression softened. "Please, Laura. Try to understand. It's not as if this kind of love ever led to a home and family . . . I mean, well, it's not acceptable to the world, so why not face it and do the best you can with it? If you get married to a guy, you're prepared to endure certain hardships, like working while he goes to school or something. But if the marriage doesn't work out, at least you can get alimony. What does a gay marriage get if it doesn't work out? Nothing. So you have to get the most you can while you're together."

"That's a stirring speech," Laura managed to say.

"Laura! Listen to me!" Ginny ground out her cigarette and put her arms around Laura with unsuspected strength. "I love you. I really do."

"But?"

"No buts . . . It's only that we have to face life the way it is. I'm no file clerk or laundry marker. I have a career ahead of me if I play it smart. Saundra can do things for me . . . things you could not do. If we moved in together it would mean the end of my career— Saundra would see to that—and I'd grow to hate you."

"Did it ever occur to you to try to make it on your own?" Laura's tone was scorched with bitterness.

Ginny released her abruptly. "Of course it has," she snapped. "But you know damn well what kind of a chance a nobody like me would have on my own. Come off it, Laura. You know the score.

Without somebody like Saundra underwriting me, I'd be lucky to get an extra job in a remake of *The Ten Commandments* twenty years from now." She put a tentative hand on Laura's arm.

"I couldn't stand it, Laura," she told her urgently. "I need success—like a dope addict. I have to make the grade and I . . . I guess I don't even care too much about how I do it."

"I guess you don't," Laura agreed coldly. She couldn't tell if she was angrier because she had allowed all this to happen, or because she had been naive enough to think that once it had happened something good would come of it. Well, she'd learned her lesson the hard way as usual. The only thing left was to forget about it, pretend it never happened. She turned and crushed out her cigarette in the bedside ashtray, turning back on Ginny as she did so.

"Please, Laura," Ginny begged, "don't shut me out."

"It seems to me," she answered evenly, "that you're the one who's doing the shutting out."

Tears began to gather in Ginny's eyes. "I see now that it was very selfish of me. . . ."

"What was?"

"I . . . I expected you to just let everything go on as it is. Saundra is busy so often that we could easily see each other. . . ."

Oh, Christ! Laura thought, torn between self-pity and disgust. It was bad enough that the world condemned their kind of love. That they would have to hide it. Now Ginny planned to sneak around even more, so that they would have nowhere to go without constant fear, drawn shades, secret phone calls . . .

Queer I might be, Laura told herself, but I'm no goddamn backstreet gigolo! She looked at Ginny with almost cold detachment. Just looked at her. Ginny wasn't one of those hard-faced, coldblooded females determined to destroy. But success was what she really wanted, really needed. Everything else was expendable.

"*Please* don't look at me like that, Laura." Without waiting for an answer, Ginny gently pulled her close.

Laura stiffened, but the girl's soft, determined touch made her feel suddenly weak—unable to resist. And the anger she had so solidly walled up inside only a moment before began to drain away.

Ginny brushed warm lips against her ear, and such a rush of desire swept over Laura that it frightened her. It was almost as if her body no longer belonged to her—as if it were possessed of a will of its own.

"Damn it, Ginny," she said twisting away from the mesmerizing embrace, "that's no fair."

The girl looked up at her, a faint grin teasing at the corners of her mouth. "All's fair in love and war," she said softly. "And this seems to be both."

Laura chuckled in spite of herself.

Ginny hoisted herself on one elbow. "You're really an awful prig, Laura. Know that?"

Laura nodded and stared thoughtfully at the girl beside her. It was true. She was a prig. And selfish, too. She had no right to expect other people to rearrange their lives at a moment's notice just because it was what she wanted. Besides, how did she really know how long she would go on wanting this. Maybe it was just a form of temporary insanity—or a kind of psychic rash that would disappear like measles after the fever passed. Hell of a thing to ask anyone—to revamp a whole future on the basis of one wild night. Looking at it this way, she certainly had no right to ask Ginny to give up everything on just the transient kind of love two women have for each other.

Everyone knew these "affairs" never lasted. And of all the people to choose, she had to pick an actress—where success meant being under constant public scrutiny. Oh, no, Laura, me girl, it would never have lasted anyhow.

All right. Now that my mind knows all this, she asked herself, when does my heart catch on? Why do I still love her? Can two people walk out of my life like that? Can I go through this all over again?

She's not walking out on you, Laura told herself resignedly—she's willing to just go on this way.

But I'm not! Damn it, I'm not!

"Laura?" Ginny asked quietly.

Laura wished she could cry then but knew she wouldn't. What for? "Yes," she replied heavily.

"Do you hate me?" Ginny burst into tears, burying her face in Laura's breasts. "I didn't mean to hurt you . . . honest."

It was almost more than Laura could take at that moment. She stroked Ginny's head and held her close with a slight rocking movement. "No, Ginny. I don't hate you."

She had to take a deep breath before continuing. She hurt inside. In fact, the only way to think of the pain was that her guts were killing her.

Ginny kept repeating that she had not wanted to hurt Laura, that if she could she would undo the whole thing.

But it was too late now . . . too late for undoing. And she wanted Ginny too much to sit on the sideline waiting for bones. She wanted everything or nothing—and it looked as though it would be nothing.

Maybe she was being bourgeois and immature, but her pride—and her heart—simply would not let her conduct an *illicit*-illicit affair. She had not been playing with Ginny. . . . It had not been just a game to fill the hours. . . .

She would have to get up now and go through the day somehow. She would have to take Ginny home, pick up her own car, and go to work. She would have to stay away from Ginny. . . .

She would have to.

Chapter 9

It was a strained and awkward ride to Saundra's house. Ginny had become increasingly defensive, but Laura refused to rise to the bait. Talk would lead to charges and countercharges. Better to leave it alone. She would call Ginny later, Laura decided, when both of them had had a chance to put things in their proper perspective. She recalled briefly the wire she had opened while Ginny showered.

It had been from Walter, as she had suspected: he wanted her to come to New York as soon as possible.

She wouldn't answer him just yet—she had to decide what to do with herself first, then Ginny, and then and only then, Walter. It would be pointless for her to go to New York until this was settled. She wanted time—time to think, time for Ginny to reconsider, and time to make her own decisions. How much time? She didn't know.

At the office she went through the day in a frenzy of application to her work. She tried not to think about Ginny or last night or the conversation this morning. Each time her mind wandered back to Ginny, hot chords vibrated throughout her body, and her hands became cold. It seemed that she really didn't think of Ginny as a person but as a fleshly embodiment of her own passionate fantasies—

something responsive to hold and kiss, to let out a torrent of emotions and love upon.

Finally, the unending day became evening, and at last Laura looked around the office and was surprised to see that she was alone. She knew she must have talked to people during the day—Helen, at least. But she couldn't remember anything that had happened, not even if she had had lunch or where, or what she had done.

Go home, Laura, she told herself, before you crack up. Home. It was an empty word when there was no love.

She let herself into the apartment and found that it was near agony to remember that Ginny had sat in that chair, had crossed the room here holding a glass in her hand, and that it had been on that couch where they had first kissed. . . . She had to see Ginny here again.

"Call her," she said aloud. "Call her and tell her you're sorry about the way you behaved."

She walked over to the telephone, feeling her hands grow cold, and a thick heavyness touched the base of her skull.

Rrupp! Tic-a-tic-a-tic. Operation Apology under way.

The line rang exactly three and one-quarter times.

A short silence.

"Ye-es?" A very hesitant and falsely bright Ginny answered.

What will I say? Laura wondered frantically.

"Ginny?"

Silence, then, "Where are you calling from?" Laura heard Ginny's breathing, short and quick. "You shouldn't have called me here."

"I wanted to talk to you. . . ."

"But Saundra's back. I mean, she's just taking a shower upstairs. She'll be out in a minute, and I don't want her to know you've called. We've had a furious fight."

That wretched hurt again, that miserable sick pain in the pit of her stomach. How can one person hurt you so much with a few simple words? Laura pushed her fist hard against the edge of the table to steady herself, to keep the choke out of her voice.

"I'm . . . I'm sorry, Ginny. I didn't mean to interrupt. I just wanted to talk to you. . . ."

"Not now, Laura, please. I'll call you. Later on, maybe, if I can think of an excuse to get out of the house. But not now. Please don't call here again. I've just gotten her calmed down. She'd be in an awful rage if she thought . . ."

Laura hung up quietly. She wanted to cry, to scream, to throw something. So this would be their life—don't call me; I'll call you.

And what happens when you run out of excuses, Ginny? Or if we get caught, Ginny . . . Who wins you in a hands-down fight?

My God, everything would have to be geared to keeping Saundra pacified. No. Damn it. No!

Laura walked into the kitchen and put some ice in a glass and brought the half-full bottle of Scotch to the living room. She sat down on the couch and filled the glass to the brim. Slowly she raised the glass to her lips and smiled at the television set across from her: dead, imageless—a prideless, sightless stand-in for life. Ersatz pleasure.

That's what I would be, she said inwardly . . . an instrument of amusement to be turned on and off, filling a need of sorts but not enough to be an entity. No. Not amusement, not even amusement. That's too healthy a word. Diversion. Yes. That's it.

Laura drained the glass without stopping for air. She threw off her shoes and stretched out on the couch, facing the TV set.

Then, she fell asleep while holding a silent conversation with the blank set, mulling over the things they had in common.

As she drove to work the next day, she decided, today I must make up my mind.

Somebody honked when she failed to move on a green light. Always pushing . . . Some bastard's always there to keep you moving, she cursed under her breath with unusual vehemence.

If Walter wants me in New York right away . . . if I could catch a plane this afternoon . . . if I could leave today . . . I wouldn't have time to change my mind or worry about the consequences.

She sighed as she pulled the car into the office parking area, and sat a moment after she turned off the ignition. Then, slowly, she climbed the stairs to her office.

If I can get reservations today, that will be it. No arguments, no decisions. Just Kismet.

As Laura entered the office, the receptionist gave her a bright "Good morning, Miss Garraway."

Laura mumbled something and headed for her desk. She wished she could talk to Helen about this but imagined the shock on Helen's face if she did.

"Morning, Laura. Coffee?" Helen said cheerfully. "Must say, you've looked a wreck these past few days," she chuckled good-naturedly. "*Tours l'amour?*"

One more word, Laura thought with exasperation. Just one more word and I'll punch her in the nose! Wouldn't that be ladylike, she told herself sarcastically. Calm down, Laura, old girl. Helen is your friend—she can't know your problems. Take it easy or the only place you'll go to is an institution. Lesbians Anonymous, she joked bitterly, a quaint Village home for shook-up broads.

She saw Helen's hand place a cup of steaming coffee on her desk, then felt Helen's other hand on her shoulder.

"What's the matter, Laura?" she asked with serious concern. "Are you feeling all right?"

"Oh, yes, Helen," she answered guiltily. "Got a wire from Mr. Hobson." She gave the news as a peace offering. "Wants me to leave for New York right away and I'm trying to figure out how I'll do it." With an effort Laura smiled. "Would you be a doll, Helen, and call the airport? Find out if I can get on a plane this afternoon . . . non-stop. Buy a ticket and charge it to *Fanfare*."

"Sure, Laura. Sure." Helen returned to her desk, leaving Laura alone to think things out. She'd just have to let Walter handle the loose ends around here when he got back. Walter, she thought. Her own part in his life seemed like an adolescent fling now.

Compared to what she and Ginny had shared . . . Ginny, Ginny.

Kismet. Reservations were available. Helen got her a seat on a 4:10 plane leaving from International Airport. With all the hectic arranging for her departure, the morning passed quickly.

At last Laura picked up her purse, looked over her desk to be sure she had forgotten nothing, and in an unexpected moment of fear of what she was venturing upon, hugged Helen quickly. "Thanks for everything, Helen. Take care of the boss for me when he comes back."

She turned quickly to hide the unwanted tears coming into her eyes and walked swiftly out of the office. She hardly heard Helen's call of good luck.

She was leaving behind everything that she knew, everything familiar . . . for what? This wasn't the way to go, was it? But she knew the tears were mostly for Ginny. Never to see Ginny again . . . never touch her soft cheek with her own, never feel the young breasts with her own . . .

It had been so strange and so wonderful.

Laura drove home like a madwoman, packing hastily in constant fear that her phone would ring—or that like an alcoholic, she would weaken and make that "one call" just to say good-bye.

But nothing happened.

Ready at last, Laura ran out of the apartment.

Chapter 10

"Eleven," Laura told the bored-looking hotel elevator operator. The car was crowded with people who looked even more bored.

Laura leaned against the back of the elevator with a soft sigh of relief. The worst was over—at least for the moment. She'd made the break, and the trip itself had been quite painless. As soon as she had boarded the plane, she had taken a sleeping pill so that she wouldn't have those idle hours to think. . . .

So far, so good.

She wondered if Ginny had ever called her.

"Nine," the operator called out in a dry little voice.

Ginny. Forget Ginny, damn it. That's why you're here, isn't it?

"Eleven."

Laura took a deep breath and stepped out of the car, grateful for the freedom. There was something about elevators that was too confining.

She stood a moment in the hallway, breathing the musty air and staring blankly at the opposing arrows indicating the division of rooms. Forcing herself to focus on the numbers, she turned left down the corridor, her footsteps making a muffled sound on the thick, worn carpet.

From the fire escape window at the end of the hall she could hear faint strands of dance music from the cocktail lounge in the hotel.

Funny, she thought, how most hotel dance bands sound the same . . . But the couples on the floor don't notice it. If I were dancing with Ginny, I wouldn't notice it.

And then that terrible stab of loss, of injustice. She could never go dancing with Ginny in public, never look at her with love in her eyes across a public dining table, never do any of the little things that people in love do.

Well, she barely whispered, that's why you're here, old girl, and not with her. . . .

She stopped at room 1107. Her knock sounded loud enough in the silence to wake the whole floor. No answer. Suddenly she was very impatient. The clerk had said Walter was in—why didn't he answer? Where else could he be at this ungodly hour?

"Laura!" The door opened, and Walter stood there, smiling broadly. He put his arms around her and hugged her fraternally. No kiss.

He has company, she guessed. She could *feel* it in his reception. Besides, he never played a radio when he was alone—always said it made him nervous.

"Come in, Laura. Come in." Walter helped her off with her coat swiftly.

He gave her another little affectionate hug, then whispered in her ear, "We have a guest . . ." and led her into the suite.

"Madeline," Walter said enthusiastically, "I want you to meet the best little feature writer this side of Hedda Hopper." He grinned. "Madeline Van Norden. Laura Garraway."

Laura saw a strikingly handsome woman seated on the divan. Her clothes were exquisitely simple. Her poised, easy manner, her pleasantly attentive glance—everything about her suggested wealth . . . and taste. Intelligence, too. Laura guessed her to be in her mid-thirties.

So this is our backer, she mused. Our gay divorcée. Even sight unseen Walter could pick 'em.

"Welcome to New York, Laura." Madeline raised a half-empty cocktail glass in salute. The soft, cultivated tones were exactly what Laura expected. "I can see you'll get along well here."

She smiled and winked at Walter with a sort of mutual-appreciation expression.

Shades of Saundra Simons, Laura thought.

But she managed a polite smile and mumbled acknowledgment.

Walter fussed over her and praised her to Madeline.

"If you're going to talk about me as if I weren't here, Walter," Laura said dryly but keeping a twinkle in her eyes, "I'll need a drink."

Madeline laughed heartily. "Get the poor girl a drink!" The explosiveness of her laugh struck Laura as oddly out of keeping with the rest of her. Walter walked over to the small improvised bar on the writing desk.

"Scotch, Laura?"

"Fine. I haven't checked in yet. My baggage is in the lobby; wanted to be sure you were still here and"—Laura glanced confidentially at Madeline, "that you hadn't made reservations for me at some hotel on the other side of town."

Walter brought her the drink and sat down on the arm of her chair. "No, I didn't register you anywhere, but getting a room at this time of the year isn't any problem. I thought it would be easier for you if you stayed in this hotel, but decided to consult you first." His tone was elaborately businesslike, but Laura could sense an undercurrent of uneasiness in his manner.

Laura watched him with amusement. She was thoroughly enjoying his predicament: he wanted to keep his tomcat privacy for himself, play the faithful lover for her, and yet hide all this from Madeline.

As always, Walter's juggling was very adept, but this time he had failed. She had the feeling that Madeline was not missing a thing.

Laura feigned a look of indecision.

"Well . . ." she began.

"Had *you* any special hotel in mind?" he asked hesitantly.

Laura grinned mischievously. "Expense account?"

Walter stood up and laughed. "If you're a good girl."

He reached over and took Madeline's glass. "Freshener?"

"Please." Madeline reached across the small round table between their chairs and took out a cigarette, then handed the pack to Laura.

"This hotel would be convenient for you, Laura," she said evenly.

"Yeah," Walter added enthusiastically. "*Fanfare* on Madison Avenue. How do you like that for dreams coming true?"

"Sounds elegant," Laura replied, feeling oddly disturbed by Madeline's curious glances.

"Tell you what," Walter continued as if in one breath, "I'll call downstairs and have them register you and send your bags up."

Laura sat quietly while Walter called. She listened with detached interest as he made the arrangements. She didn't want to look over at Madeline, and she felt strangely on guard.

"Is it difficult to find an apartment?" she asked Madeline finally.

Madeline laughed, and Laura decided that her laugh was not really loud or boisterous—just sincere, and full of a pleasant childlike gusto. There was no obvious attempt on Madeline's part to play the urban sophisticate. Laura thought that her naturalness made Madeline all the more genuinely sophisticated.

"A nice apartment is very hard to find," she explained without snobbery, "even if price is no object."

The conversation glided effortlessly from general observations to specifics about *Fanfare* and the new job. It seemed to Laura that Madeline and Walter had her future very neatly in tow. It felt good not to have to decide anything. Good—and safe.

At last the bellhop arrived with the key to Laura's room and the registration card for her to sign. Her luggage had been placed in her room.

"I don't wish to seem rude," Laura said after a short silence, "but I think I'll turn in. It's been a long day."

"Certainly, certainly," Walter agreed. There was a touch of concern in his voice. "Anyway, you'll be seeing a lot of Madeline these next few days. There'll be a lot of things she can help you with in getting started—especially when Willy isn't around."

"Stop yakking, Walter, and let the girl go to bed," Madeline smiled. She extended her hand to Laura casually. "I'm going to enjoy working with you, Laura, even if it is only for a few days. Do you want me to call you in the morning?"

Laura wished everyone would leave her alone, but she knew that they were simply trying to be helpful. "No. No, thanks. I'll leave a call at the desk. See you at the office around nine?" she asked with equal casualness.

"Yes."

"Well, good night, then."

Walter walked her to the door. "Good girl," he whispered. "She likes you."

"Did you think she wouldn't?" Laura asked wearily, but she didn't wait for him to answer. "Good night, Walter. See you tomorrow."

She closed the door behind her. She was grateful to be alone—and yet afraid of it, too. The best-loved person in the world can feel lonely in a hotel . . . and if you're already lonely . . .

Her room was a room; it was a "nice" room. It had four walls, a clean bathroom, and only slightly faded curtains. It had a view—an office building on the opposite side of the street. Laura looked for a radio but found none. Just a free TV set. Her luggage had been piled neatly at the foot of the bed.

She opened the suitcases and began hanging her clothes. The bureau drawer contained the usual card listing the hotel's regulations, and the Gideon Bible. Strange how she only needed three drawers now. In her apartment there had never seemed to be enough room.

Entering the bathroom, she let the water run for a hot bath. She stared for a moment at her reflection in the mirror. She wondered vaguely what other people thought when they looked in a mirror. . . . Did they think they were pretty or ugly? Did they try to hypnotise themselves by staring into their own eyes with noses pressed against the glass, or strike poses alien to their daily habits?

"What difference does it make . . . as long as it sells?" Laura said aloud to her reflection, and speculated briefly on why that phrase of Walter's had remained so tenaciously with her.

She tried to relax and soak in the tub but found that she couldn't; she was too keyed up and overtired. So she just bathed quickly and returned to the bedroom and turned down the bed.

As if the management wanted to be certain she would not forget that she was not at home, not where she belonged, the hotel name was printed on the sheets and pillowcases. Laura took this as an insult and turned on the television set as a small revenge. Only one station was still on. In between the commercials there was a badly edited and rather awful old horror movie.

But it was better than the silence that surrounded her. Better than this impossible aloneness. She sat cross-legged on the bed and stared at the screen with all the concentration of a sinner at a revival meeting.

A knock at the door startled her enough so that she gave a small cry, and then she laughed nervously at the state of her nerves. She crossed the room to the closed door.

"Who is it?" she asked.

"Walter."

She unlocked the door and stood back for him to enter.

He walked in almost sheepishly and closed the door quietly behind him. "Anything good on TV?" he asked inanely.

She laughed. "No. I'm just trying to unwind before going to sleep. What brings you out?" She walked over and turned off the set.

He followed her and put his arms around her.

"I've good news for us," he whispered.

Laura could feel herself tense up in his arms but tried not to let him realize it. "Wonderful," she said, disentangling herself as nonchalantly as she could. "What is it?"

Walter chuckled with self-approving mirth. "I can finally get a divorce. . . ."

"Oh. Walter," she answered immediately, "that's wonderful." Then she realized all that this meant. She was frightened suddenly. Walter would now want to marry *her*—and she couldn't do it. Not now . . . maybe never . . .

". . . That detective agency we thought was doing nothing finally came up with proof that Edna *has* been fooling around. Now let her try to contest a divorce. Let her try to take the magazine away from me!" he gloated.

"But the children . . ." Laura asked before she knew she was thinking it.

"I'll get the usual custody now—or at least, I'll stand a good chance. Don't you see what this means, darling? After the year is up, you and I can get married. But till then we'll have to be very careful. I don't want you to be involved as a corespondent. I'm sure Edna has had her little spies out, too."

Laura sat on the edge of the bed. She wondered what she ought to do now. Just tell him she couldn't marry him until she got a woman out of her mind and heart? She had a big mental picture of a declaration like this. She shuddered.

Walter sat down beside her and pushed her back on the bed, very gently. He put his arm under her head and lay next to her, playing idly with her long hair, kissing her softly on her forehead and eyes. In between he went on with a narrative about their future.

She wished he would go away and not touch her. Then she felt unbearably cruel and guilty. It's not his fault, she told herself over and over; it's *me*. He loves me—how can he know . . . ? He mustn't know that I'm in love with someone else . . . a woman. Oh, God! she cursed silently. What a mess!

". . . you'll love the kids, Laura. And they're no problem since both of them are in private schools anyway and only home during the holidays. You'll see."

Oh, Walter, she asked voicelessly, what can I do? How can I tell you?

". . . and that's why I didn't register you. I didn't want it to look premeditated, I didn't want Edna to have a shred of evidence that could be misused." He sat up and laughed exuberantly. "I could hardly keep still while Madeline was there. I just wanted to take you in my arms and hold you and know that for the first time my being with you held a future instead of a checkmate."

"Are you going to file as soon as you get back?" Laura asked, hoping she sounded happy and knowing she was failing.

"I've already wired my attorney. He can file without me."

"I can't tell you how happy I am for you, Walter."

He turned and faced her slowly, his expression suddenly perplexed and serious. "For me?"

"Yes. Of course."

"What about *us*?"

"Oh, Walter . . ." Laura cried and covered her face with her arms. Suddenly she was weeping.

"Honey!" Walter said, shocked. "What is it? What's wrong?" He took her into his arms and rocked her gently, whispering reassurances. Finally, she stopped crying and regained her control.

As she dried her eyes, she scolded herself. Stupid! What's wrong with you that you keep acting like some neurotic female just one step out of an institution?

"Feel like telling me now?" Walter asked softly. He got up from the bed and went to the chair next to it.

"I . . . I can't, Walter. At least, not all of it. Not now." She managed to say that much and was grateful that at least her voice was even.

"I gather that it has something to do with us."

She nodded. She searched for some story that would satisfy him and keep the degree of injury to a minimum.

He said, "You don't want to marry me. No. I'll amend that for you—don't say anything. You don't want to make a decision right now about it. . . . Isn't that it?"

To her surprise, he smiled. "But, Walter, this is so sudden," he mimicked good-naturedly. "Old maid jitters, Laura?"

She laughed with him and nodded. "Something like that."

"Just answer me this, Laura. Is there another guy?"

"No. Not exactly," she replied cautiously.

"But you have met someone . . ."

"I'm not sure," she answered with the half guilt of a half lie. He was making it very easy for her, being much more fair than she thought she deserved. She was so grateful to him that she felt like sitting in his lap and telling him that she *would* marry him, would be proud to marry him—but she couldn't do it.

"All right, darling," he said. "We won't talk about it anymore. Not tonight. I have a whole year to wait, anyhow, so no one's rushing you. Besides," he laughed, "I'm a pretty egotistical bastard. Somehow I feel sure you'll end up realizing what a good deal you'd have with me. Some other guy might be younger—but he wouldn't appreciate you as much or love you as much."

It was almost more than she could take. If only he'd scream at her, or snarl in bitter hurt! Anything but this trust and kindness. She gazed at him affectionately, then averted her eyes. If Karl had been just half the man that Walter is, she thought reminiscently, maybe a lot of my present problems wouldn't be plaguing me.

Walter's voice broke into her thoughts. "One more thing before I go back to my room."

She looked up at him, afraid that he might have guessed more than he was revealing to her.

"No matter what you decide—now or later—I think you should plan on moving from this hotel as soon as possible."

Thank God! Laura exclaimed to herself.

"If possible, find a roommate. I don't want Edna to have any suspicions about you . . . or me. Not until the divorce is final. Stay here for a few days, but look around. A young single girl in the big city living in a hotel doesn't sound as respectable in court as it should. If it comes to court. Will you do that for me? This isn't the time to start being careless."

"Of course, Walter," Laura said with relief and genuine warmth.

He stood up slowly, walked to her, and bent down to kiss her softly on the lips. "Good night, then. Get some sleep, darling, and don't worry about us."

She couldn't answer him. She sat silent and motionless as he went to the door, blew her a kiss, and left.

After several minutes it took all her control to relax and lie down. She didn't seem to have the energy even to blink; she was exhausted. Then she felt herself falling softly into sleep almost immediately and was glad for the release.

Good girl, she likes you, Walter had said about Madeline Van Norden. And Laura envisioned an enormous Madeline nodding and smiling approval. Something like the official laughers at the funhouse.

Oh, I get along fine with women . . .

Ginny . . .

Chapter 11

The next few days Laura worked very closely with Madeline and hardly saw either Willy, who was going to be in charge in New York, or Walter. The offices that Walter had rented were being painted. He left it up to the two women to make all the other decorating decisions and purchases, and with the narrow budget he had imposed, it was taking every bit of ingenuity they could muster. Luckily, Madeline seemed to know the best places to find everything—from drapery outlets to warehouses of repossessed office furniture. She kept Laura constantly on the go.

Laura had quickly sensed that she had an ally in Madeline—someone she could trust and be friendly with. Madeline had an offhand way of completely ingratiating herself without even trying, and it seemed impossible to Laura that anyone might not like her. Once or twice the old guarded feeling returned to Laura, but most of the time she felt very much at ease. The older woman's responsiveness to Laura's ideas was wonderfully reassuring. It became a positive delight to discuss the problems of writing for a fan magazine, or reminisce about her experiences with movie stars and studio executives. In fact, the amiability and informality of it all made work seem so much like play, Laura felt almost guilty.

At last the office was painted, and they could begin to put things

in shape. As a sort of celebration they all agreed to meet at Walter's
suite for a drink—a toast to their mutual success.

Laura was quite apprehensive about this celebration. She dreaded
any opportunity Walter might take to ask her if she'd decided.

She met Madeline in the hallway in front of Walter's door.
Without a greeting, Madeline said hurriedly, "Now that all the
work is done, I suppose I won't be seeing so much of you."

"Of course you will," Laura said. As she knocked on the door,
she realized it would feel strange not to have Madeline around.

Walter opened the door, a half-sheepish grin on his face.

"Hello, hello, you two. Come in and relieve this working man
from his boredom."

They entered, and Laura suspected immediately that Walter had
begun the party without them.

He poured them each a drink and sat down rather unsteadily
next to Madeline. "How's the New York *Fanfare* Office? Beautiful?"

Madeline looked over at Laura and with a swift glance silently
conveyed a confirmation of Laura's suspicions: Walter was drunk.

"Of course it's beautiful!" she returned, smiling. "Look who took
care of the decorating for you!"

"Haven't you been by to see it?" Laura asked him.

"No time, no time," Walter said. He was very serious.

Laura suppressed a laugh. "We only need one more desk and
several filing cabinets. Everything else is ready for even a competi-
tor's inspection."

"Put a lock on the door!" Walter commanded with mock horror.
Then he began a long monologue about his activities in the past
few days. At any other time Laura would have listened, amused.
Tonight Walter's monologue didn't seem very clever. She sensed
that Madeline was anxious to break away. Once she caught Madeline
looking at her watch.

Finally, Madeline gave her a perfect opening to change the subject without appearing rude. It was nearly teamwork.

"We've been rather busy ourselves," Madeline commented.

"That's true enough," Laura laughed. "This perpetual motion
machine you attached to me hasn't left me enough time even to
look for an apartment."

"Say," Walter said, rising slowly, "I've been worried about that. What are we going to do with you?"

He frowned slightly. For a moment there was silence; then Madeline said, "I may be talking out of turn, Walter, but may I make a suggestion?"

An odd quality in her voice alerted Laura: she became tensely watchful.

"Shoot," Walter called from the bar.

Madeline smiled. "I was just wondering if Laura couldn't stay at my place for a while? Then she could take her time looking for an apartment."

Madeline took out a cigarette and lit it before she went on casually, "I'd hate to be in a strange city and have to stay alone in an impersonal, unfriendly hotel."

Laura could see she was going to be cornered into this. Actually, after a moment, it didn't sound like such a bad idea. She did like Madeline, and it was made to order for Walter's divorce problems, since it would give her a respectable roommate and apartment, at least for a while.

"That's very sweet of you Madeline," Walter began, "but are you sure you have room? I mean, you don't have to take *Fanfare* boarders . . . I mean . . ."

"Oh shut up, Walter," Madeline commanded jokingly, "you don't know what you mean." She smiled at Laura. "How do you feel about it?" she asked. "I've plenty of room, and I don't think we'd get in each other's way. I'd appreciate some company."

"Well . . ." Laura hesitated.

Walter looked at her with an expression of helplessness: it was an indirect prompting to accept. Laura resigned herself to the situation. She glanced quickly at Madeline, whose face showed a friendly amusement—as if she knew Laura's position but also knew that if Laura accepted she wouldn't be sorry.

"It's very kind of you," Laura said levelly. "I accept."

"Good! If it doesn't work out, I'm the kind of bitch who's unnecessarily honest and I'll tell you." She laughed with tolerance of her own declared shortcomings.

Laura thought it was best that she had accepted Madeline's invitation. She could just see herself staying alone in this hotel, trying to sleep but tormented with thoughts of Ginny, remembering the feel of her, how sweet her touch. No. At least being with Madeline would keep her busy, would give her someone to talk to when the going got rough.

". . . who knows, we might even get along famously and have a ball. Right, Laura?"

"We've done all right so far."

"How about moving in tonight," Madeline suggested. "I was never one for putting things off."

"It's a little late . . ."

"Don't be such an old maid," Walter chided. "After all, you only have to pack a few things back into the suitcases. Shouldn't take you twenty minutes."

Laura looked from Walter to Madeline. "Guess I'm outvoted," she said slowly. "All right. Give me half an hour, though."

She excused herself and left the room, wondering how it had all come about. Not quite twenty-five minutes later she returned with her makeup kit in her hand.

"What about your suitcases?" Walter asked. There was a strained quality in his voice now. It was understandable—at least to Laura. Moving away meant he'd see even less of her, have less opportunity to win her back. "Shall I send for them?"

"I had the bellboy get them." She glanced at Madeline, who was finishing off her drink quickly, then back to Walter, who had a forlorn expression on his face. Madeline noticed it, too.

"She's not going to Siberia, Walter," Madeline said with a laugh.

Laura allowed herself to be bundled into her coat, said good night to Walter, and swiftly followed Madeline out the door. She suddenly felt exhausted, unable to cope with anything but her next breath. . . .

She thought about facing tomorrow, next month, her life, without Ginny. The thought left her in a vacuous state of disinterest for everything about her. She appreciated Madeline's tactful silence, appreciated her taking charge. Without question she walked beside Madeline.

They collected Laura's luggage at the hotel desk, where Madeline told the clerk to add her bill to *Fanfare*'s. Then, outside the hotel, she hailed a cab.

It seemed to take forever to arrive at Madeline's place, especially since Laura could not positively identify any of the landmarks other than that she was on Fifth Avenue, and that when the cab pulled up to the curb she could see Washington Square just one and a half blocks away.

Laura felt obligated to say something. "I feel like an intruder. . . . It's not too late if you want to change your mind, Madeline."

Madeline laughed and reached for a suitcase. "Don't worry. You're really doing me the favor. I usually just rattle around in the place and get frightfully bored listening to my echo."

The modern apartment house lobby advertised its chi-chi atmosphere by having no decoration except an indoor rock garden, and its discreetness by employing no doorman and no elevator operators.

"Home sweet home," Madeline sighed as they entered. She deposited the suitcase on the nearest chair.

Laura looked around the enormous living room with respectful awe. Although the ceiling was high, not a single object or painting rose above eye level; the walls and carpet were of the same pale blue, with only intricately woven oriental throw rugs on the floor— over the carpeting—for color. The effect was one of unhindered spaciousness.

This was Danish modern furniture, the like of which Laura had never seen. Not the usual spindly-stick sort of thing that was so popular—it had substance and visible comfort, plus the simplicity of line commonly associated with Danish work. Doubtless custom-made, Laura concluded. The room was an extraordinary blend of the new styles and the charm and delicacy of the traditional—nothing stood out, yet everything held interest.

Laura said, in rapturous admiration, "Magnifique! I'd almost forgotten you weren't a rank-and-file member of the working class. Comes the revolution . . ."

Madeline smiled, took off her shoes, and sank gracefully into the nearest sectional divan. "Shall we have a good-luck toast, or do you want to go right to bed?"

"I'm too tired to sleep, and a drink would be just fine. Thanks."

Madeline stood up and crossed the long room to the bar. "Scotch?"

"Sure." Laura looked out the balcony window and, for the first time since she'd arrived, had a feeling of excitement about living in New York. From the big window she had a wonderful view of Washington Square, and Laura asked, "What section of town are we in? The Village?"

"Yes. Nice view of the arch, isn't it? Makes you almost think you're in Paris."

"I've never been to Paris, but it does look like what I imagine it to be." Accepting the glass Madeline offered, Laura sat down in a low turquoise-upholstered chair and watched absently as Madeline made herself comfortable again on the divan. For a moment she let her mind conjure up the image of Ginny, but the bittersweet sting of tears just under her eyelids was a sharp reminder of the dangers of such fantasy.

Swallowing hard, Laura brushed her fingers across her eyes. Then she took a long drink of the Scotch.

The brief telltale gestures had not escaped the penetrating eye of her hostess. "Homesick?" Madeline asked gently.

Laura shook her head, not yet trusting her voice.

"I'm sorry," Madeline said softly. "I'm not being nosy. But when you spend as much time in bars as I do, you develop an eye for unhappiness—you start playing sidewalk psychiatrist and making bets with yourself about the whys—like money, worries, love affairs, divorce blues, and so on."

"Do you ever find out if you're right?"

"Sometimes." Madeline looked at her candidly.

"And what's your diagnosis in my case, Doctor?" Laura had a feeling she shouldn't have asked, but it was too late now.

Madeline seemed to hesitate. "I'm not quite sure yet . . ." She gazed thoughtfully at Laura. *"Similia similibus curantur,"* she laughed self-consciously. "Only thing I learned at finishing school."

"What's that mean?"

"Oh, something like it takes a thief to catch a thief."

Laura looked at her, puzzled. "You're getting away from the subject a bit, aren't you?"

Madeline smiled. "No. Quite the contrary. Love. That's the subject, isn't it? Love in all its multisided glory—and misery."

She sipped her drink and glanced speculatively at Laura. "But the kind of love-misery I'm talking about is something rather special—worse than an affair that hasn't worked out," she continued.

"Go on," Laura urged.

"This is the suffering that comes not from loving and losing, but from losing love before you've even been able to have it . . . because you don't *dare* have it."

Madeline's gaze held Laura's meaningfully.

Laura realized with a start that Madeline's words and tone seemed deliberately pointed, but she couldn't be sure.

Her heart began to pound, and her body quickened in a strange mixture of fright and anticipation. Had Madeline really understood? Or was she just fishing? Or was Laura reading something into Madeline's words? It was all very upsetting—and exciting.

Chapter 12

She wanted to tell her . . . tell someone. This hell inside her, this burning and aching, was slowly suffocating her.

But this wasn't the kind of thing you told someone you had met just a few days ago. No!

Madeline remained very still, saying nothing. She just waited.

"I'd give anything to be able to confess that I'm in love with a married man . . . or that I'm pregnant. . . ." Laura said with difficulty. The absolute quiet in the room seemed to hammer at her relentlessly.

Still Madeline said nothing. She crossed the room without making a sound and placed the bottle of Scotch on the cocktail table in front of Laura. She smiled knowingly as she said, "Have another. Tomorrow you can blame the fact that you talked too much on the Scotch."

Laura hardly heard her. Suddenly she knew she was going to confide in Madeline. She *had* to . . . or lose her mind.

She was dimly aware that she should be curious about the source of Madeline's perceptiveness, but she was too absorbed with her own turmoil, and too overwhelmed by this luxury of having a confidante, to explore the matter further.

At this moment it made no difference what Madeline might think of her—or even if Madeline would be repelled and throw her out afterward. All she knew was that she couldn't bear the hurt alone anymore . . . or the guilt. Right now, logic, intellect, objectivity, and reason played no part in her emotions—if they ever had. Her brain seemed to have shrugged off all responsibility for her reactions.

Whether she could trust Madeline, whether Madeline might tell Walter, did not then occur to Laura.

"I don't know," Laura began slowly, "if I can even put what happened into words." She glanced at Madeline as if expecting a cue. "Do you understand?"

Madeline walked over to Laura and stood very still. "I think so." She studied the girl for a long moment. "If it weren't so apparent that you're about to crack up, I wouldn't dream of doing this."

"Doing what?"

Madeline ignored the question and went on as if talking to herself. ". . . But I'm an old timer with the ins and outs of love—I've seen hundreds of tormented expressions like yours . . ."

Laura felt her body tense.

". . . and neither of us have anything to lose, if it helps. . . ."

Madeline leaned forward very slowly, as if giving Laura a chance to recoil, to deny what they now both knew was going to happen.

Laura accepted the fact that Madeline was going to kiss her, and only when she felt her breath against her face did she have a moment of panic. But it was too late then, and in a strange way she was filled with gratitude toward Madeline.

Her kiss was just long enough to show genuine interest, and gentle enough to show that she did not really expect any passionate return—that she understood what was bothering Laura even if she did not know the details.

Madeline placed her cheek softly against Laura's, then straightened up slowly as if any quick motion would send Laura away. She rested her hand on Laura's shoulder.

"Do you know why I did that?" she asked Laura.

"Yes." Laura could sense release coming up in her brain, feel it rise up in her throat. "So that I would know you're a *friend.* That I wasn't alone."

"Do you also know that I'm not pushing you into anything?" Madeline's tone was even, considerate, and calm.

Laura nodded. "I'm going to cry . . ." she managed to say.

"Good. Here, hold my hand. It'll make you feel better."

She sat down on the edge of Laura's chair and, putting her arm around her shoulder, pulled Laura's face to her breast and rocked her quietly while Laura sobbed out all her pent-up feelings. It was like lifting a floodgate in a dam that could always hold more.

Then, brokenly, she explained to Madeline what had happened in Los Angeles: her loneliness before she met Ginny; the swift but subtle love that had seemingly exploded in their faces; her unsure, confused reaction to Ginny's refusal to leave Saundra; and her hasty flight from Los Angeles . . . and Ginny.

"Sounds like a pretty bad script, doesn't it?" Laura said, her tears subsiding at last. But she didn't try to pull away from Madeline's breasts. She wanted to be comforted and secure right now—understood and not criticized. Tomorrow she would be an independent adult again, but right now it was almost beyond her.

"No, Laura. It doesn't—because it wasn't contrived beforehand." Madeline gave Laura a little hug. Then, laughing, she said, "The arm of this chair wasn't made for sitting. How about a break?"

Laura smiled and hoped Madeline hadn't thought her selfish and juvenile. "Yes . . . and I could use another drink now." Now that Madeline had moved over to the chair facing hers, Laura felt strangely awkward . . . lost. *Vulnerable,* that was it. As if she had drawn warmth from Madeline, and protection from the wind.

Well, she thought, that's just what I did, in a way. She wondered if she should feel ashamed, or embarrassed, or even a little scared. But she didn't, and for that she had to thank Madeline.

"Obviously you don't know anything about this kind of life, Laura. It's a very simple thing in a complicated sort of way. There are those who wear their guilt or their rebellion on their sleeves.

"And, like me, there are those who would rather not advertise our preference . . . if we actually have one. I'm lucky in that I'm not one of those dykes who always wanted to be a man—or, who hate men. But no matter what type we are, we're all neurotic as hell."

"I must sound like a whimpering adolescent to you. . . ." Laura joked, surprised that she *could* joke now.

Madeline looked at her quickly, seemed to take in everything about Laura, and then replied softly, "Hardly."

Laura flushed. She hoped it didn't show. She watched Madeline pour a fresh drink, and as she accepted it from her, Laura felt self-conscious and very naive.

"What do you want to do now?"

"What do you mean?" Laura asked.

"What are your plans? What do you hope to do with yourself?"

Something about the way Madeline said the word "hope" made Laura suddenly feel like a child who's been asked by an adult, "And what do you want to be when you grow up?"

"Do I have a choice?" Laura asked bitterly.

Madeline smiled. "You have a choice about what you *do*, but whether or not you have the same luxury about what you *feel* is something I couldn't answer. Only you can."

"I see." Laura sipped her drink, letting its coolness soothe her still-aching throat. "What is your considered opinion?"

"I can tell by your tone that you don't want to know." Madeline, too, became guarded.

Laura immediately felt contrite.

"I'm sorry—I had no right. I'm just so mixed up about everything right now . . ."

"I know," Madeline replied simply, without hidden implications or sarcasm.

There was a short silence between them. Yet it did not seem uncomfortable to Laura. She had faith in Madeline.

Faith. If love is a primary need for humans, Laura pondered, then trust surely runs a damned close second. She had never before appreciated the value of trusting someone. She had never had the occasion to give of herself, either.

Madeline smiled as she asked slowly, "I assume that you have resigned yourself to the homosexual aspect of this affair—it's a right church, wrong pew sort of thing?"

"Homosexual-heterosexual! I don't know and I don't even care right now." Laura's voice grew tight, bitter. "All I know is that I loved her and got the old married-man's stall. . . . Well, that wasn't good enough for me." Her own affair with Walter flashed through her mind, but somehow that seemed different.

"I didn't *want* to be queer," Laura added lamely.

"None of us do," Madeline laughed. "At least, none of the honest ones."

"But if I was going to get mixed up with something like this," Laura went on, "I at least wanted whatever satisfactions it had to offer." She glared resentfully at Madeline, as if everything were all at once her fault.

A strange expression crossed Madeline's face. "You wouldn't mind starving in a garret if you could be sure you were really a genius, is that it?" She gave a slight helpless gesture. "A guarantee of the future. Nice dream."

"No. Nothing like that. Not really, anyway. It's just that, well, I felt like since I was the one who was making the big conversion—or maybe I should say 'perversion'—the least she could do would be to give herself up to me, to our love . . . oh, I don't know."

"Self-sacrificing, aren't you?" Madeline chided gently.

"Well? Isn't it a sacrifice? To give up social acceptance just for love?"

"Just for love?" Madeline echoed half in dismay, half in amusement. "You talk as if love was some sort of a knickknack you picked up at a church bazaar or a summer cruise, or some other witless extravagance. It isn't, you know. And if you don't know it, you'd better—and fast."

Laura grinned wryly. "That's some bite you got there, lady. Okay, I deserved that. But I didn't mean it just that way."

"Besides," Madeline continued, "no one asked you to give up anything. You made up your own mind about that. True, discretion is imperative, but no one broke your arm to become a homosexual."

"In other words, I would have done it anyway sooner or later. Is that what you mean?"

"Who knows?" Madeline smiled. "But I do know that I certainly didn't *want* to be a lesbian. I would never have sat back and deliberately chosen this kind of life—there are no advantages, only disadvantages; our entire culture works against us, isolates us, punishes us in a thousand different ways. Frankly, I wouldn't even advise a purple cow to go out into the world and become queer."

"Why are you, then?" Laura could not bring herself to use the word "queer" at this point.

"Why am I what?" Madeline asked laughing. "A purple cow?"

"No," Laura answered, reddening, knowing that Madeline's bantering misinterpretation was really a jibe at her obvious embarrassment at "the word." "You know perfectly well what I meant."

"All right, then." Madeline nodded politely. "It's a compulsion, I suppose. An escape, a punishment. . . . I'm no analyst. It's more that I'm picking the lesser of two evils—emotional suicide or straws of happiness. I'd love to fall in love with a man and wear an apron and have bouncing babies. But so far . . . so far, I haven't."

"If you want a man so much, then aren't you cutting off your chances of ever meeting the right one this way? Aren't you crying uncle?"

"Sure!" Madeline conceded vehemently. "And that's just the way I feel. I'm tired. So goddamn tired of going out with this guy and that guy, getting felt up and listening to the same old pitches, being bored and having to pretend that I'm fascinated so his little ego doesn't get bruised. I'm not twenty-one, you know. I've done my stint, been on the hunt, made myself available—all for nothing. My husband was the closest thing to normal love I've ever known, and that wasn't enough." Madeline's words came rapidly, and the volume increased.

Laura sat stunned for a moment. It had been an unexpected outburst, and it had left her with a miserably helpless feeling. She couldn't really say that Madeline was bitter—at least, not in the accepted sense. It was her desperation, her cry against herself; there was self-pity, of course, but there was also pride and determination. It was a little frightening and awesome, this brutal awareness of one's own frailties, the drive to survive in spite of it.

"I'm sorry," Madeline said finally. "I didn't mean to take it out on you."

Laura made no reply but took a long swallow from her drink. She realized for the first time that one of the worst torments in this situation was the conversational taboos it imposed . . . except possibly to a bosom buddy, and even then it was chancy. All the important feelings had to be carried around inside you, had to be hidden carefully. Everything conspired to make you ashamed, and yet you knew that this was the only way for you.

Husbands and wives could bring each other along to social gatherings, talk about their arguments, their love, just each other . . . but a homosexual could not do this unless he or she moved in purely homosexual circles.

That this alternative had its own suffocating aspects was already obvious to Laura—she'd seen enough of it in Hollywood.

But could I do that? Laura asked herself. Could I give myself up to only this and nothing else? It had always seemed to her such a sterile and purposeless existence.

"Well," Madeline said, with her old cheer back, "let's not worry about it now. You're welcome to stay here as long as you wish. Dive into your work and get a hold on yourself. Then see how you feel."

Laura looked up from the glass still clenched in her hands, an uncertain expression crossing her face.

"No strings," Madeline smiled. "My kiss a while ago was just a kiss, Laura. Nothing more."

Laura couldn't help wondering if that was true, or if so, how long it would last.

"In any event, Laura, you won't find a place to live right away." She was right, and Laura knew it.

So she was attentive as Madeline showed her where everything was in the apartment, and ignored Madeline's discreet comment about the fact that the bedroom had twin beds.

They prepared for bed. Madeline considerately but obviously tried to make Laura feel at ease by asking her questions about *Fanfare*, about Walter, and about what she planned for the Special Features Department.

Laura gratefully climbed into the freshly made bed and allowed her body to sink into the soft mattress.

"Ah, bliss," Laura sighed.

Madeline laughed. "Eiderdown," she explained. "One of the whims my ex-husband indulged. . . ." She spread her feet firmly on the floor and bobbed over, touching her toes. "I'm not as young as you are," she laughed and grunted. "And money won't buy my figure."

Laura smiled with her. She could just make out Madeline's figure in the dimly lit room, pushing against her pajamas. It gave her a strange feeling to know that Madeline was a lesbian and that they were going to share the same room. She considered being on her guard but then realized it would be silly.

As she waited for her to finish her exercises, Laura went over the happenings of the evening, amazed at how she had blurted out the truth to Madeline. She tried to remember what she had felt—if anything—when Madeline had kissed her. It had been pleasant, she was sure of that. But it had not had that crazing, flesh-on-flesh sensation Ginny's kiss had given her.

Even so, she had to admit it was intriguing. In fact, she was almost disappointed that Madeline seemed to have no intentions of "seducing" her. If she's a lesbian and knows that I've been exposed to it, she told herself, why shouldn't she want me?

Then her mind went uncontrollably back to Ginny. What was she doing . . . ? What would she do? She thought of Ginny in the arms of another woman and immediately felt unreasonable rage and betrayal.

"And that does that!" Madeline declared, breathing heavily, breaking into Laura's unhappy preoccupation.

Laura smiled and watched her get into bed agilely. "Where do you get all your energy, Madeline?"

Madeline hesitated for a moment, then turned off the table lamp. "It's easy when you're not tearing yourself in too many directions at once."

Laura said nothing and lay staring up at the ceiling, watching the dancing reflection of the traffic lights from the street.

"Madeline."

"Uh-huh."

"You've known many lesbians, haven't you?"

"Uh-huh."

97

"And why are they the way they are?"

"No. Just their version."

"But is there any special set of circumstances—any particular type?" Laura turned over, leaning on one elbow, and faced Madeline's shadowed form.

"Looking for excuses, Laura?"

"Just trying to understand . . ." Laura laughed without humor. "Yes. I'm looking for excuses."

"You'll waste a lot of time that way . . . and a lot of heartache."

"But . . ."

"Look, Laura, I told you—this kind of life is just one step away from suicide!" Her voice was sober and full of warning.

"There are sick people bent on self-destruction who always get themselves into trouble and then wonder why; there are people who never allow themselves to use their potential—so many varying kinds of psychotics, it's beyond our comprehension. But don't kid yourself—being a homosexual is just as sick, just as psychotic. Maybe more so. Some people get that way in an effort to punish themselves; others, to avoid the responsibility of marriage and parenthood. Sometimes they're looking for a parental substitute . . . or any and all of those things combined. Nobody knows just exactly what is going on."

"What about analysis?" Laura finally asked. "Why don't people get help?"

Madeline sighed. "Many of them try; some succeed. The trouble is that most of them don't even want to change. There's more to this than just a sexual problem. It's environmental, sociological, and even involves economics. You don't walk into an analyst's office and say, 'Hey, Doc, give me a shot of hormones and a talking-to.' I suppose if people would go to an analyst before they are really physically exposed to this kind of thing, it might be easier . . . I don't know. Something like having to watch your weight or trying to lose fifty pounds—there's a lot of difference, you know."

"Maybe so," Laura replied. "But there's a flaw in that theory, too. I mean, even if I had never known about this side of myself, I might still never have been happy under any normal circumstances."

"Hm. Maybe," Madeline conceded. "But at least an analyst

might be able to help you without the struggle of a physical pull as well as an emotional one."

"It's none of my business, but why are you in this kind of thing? Why aren't you still married?"

"Ah, there's the rub! I don't think I can honestly answer that— my brain told me one thing and my emotions contradicted. I'd been gay long before I was married, and had become very bored and anxious about the kind of life and the people I met night after night. So I broke away from it. I wanted to see first if I could break away—most of them like to tell you it's impossible—but more than that, I wanted to try to build a real life for myself. I met my husband about eight months later. He was good, sweet, and intelligent—and believe it or not, I thought I honestly loved the guy."

"So?" Laura sat forward, wondering what kind of a man could let a woman like Madeline go.

Madeline snorted with secret knowledge. "Not too many months later, the old 'pull' began again. Don't ask me why; I don't know. But life became a hell of suppressed desires, fear of discovery, and the plain misery of feeling like an A-one heel."

"I suppose it would have been easier if you could have hated him," Laura offered sympathetically. "Why didn't you tell him about it, let him try to help you . . . or was he too selfish?" It was an unkind supposition and Laura knew it, but oddly enough, she felt a resentment against this man.

"Is it selfishness when you don't know what you're trying to hold on to? Some men could be told a thing like that, I suppose . . . but I'm afraid my husband was entirely too conventional. This was something that happened only in naughty books, or was hinted at in a night club—it didn't happen to people of good breeding. I'm sure he would have tried to understand, to help, but it was so outside his world that I would only have succeeded in destroying him, his image of himself, his masculinity. A man like him might accept the fact that his wife was attracted to another man—but to another woman?"

Laura could make out Madeline smoothing the blankets, almost compulsively.

"Anyway," Madeline continued in a monotone, "it would be an

area where he could not have competed. To a man like that, whose background was so proper, even the private knowledge of my tendencies would probably have shamed him into thinking he had married a freak. Consequently, my guilt grew and grew—my disposition suffered, of course, and eventually the marriage really began to fall apart. He began staying in town for dinner, and even though I hated myself I was glad not to have to face him."

"Divorce?" Laura asked quietly.

"It was funny," Madeline said with a wry laugh. "Just when I couldn't continue anymore and was about to suggest a divorce, he asked me for one—full of apologies and awkward embarrassment. He'd found someone else . . . a girl several years his junior who thought he was the greatest guy in the world—a girl who wanted babies and to keep house and to cook. All the things I couldn't bring myself to want."

Laura nodded. "And *his* guilt gives you a healthy alimony?"

"That's a crude way of putting it, but I suppose it's the natural way of looking at it. But just think what type of guy he was. I've a little money on my own, you know; I could have refused his support. But what for? This way he thinks he's doing the right thing and at the same time paying for his happiness—which, to such a morally proper man, seemed won by foul play."

Silence followed Madeline's softly spoken explanation. Laura thoughtfully tried to imagine herself in Madeline's position.

"Go to sleep, Laura. You won't come to any decisions tonight—or for many nights to come."

"I can't sleep. I feel strange and confused."

Madeline groaned and sat up in bed. "Women!"

She threw the blankets off and got out of bed. She crawled into bed with Laura, holding her protectively against her breast.

"Everybody's mother—nobody's husband," Madeline said sleepily.

Laura didn't think to protest. She felt like a little girl again, except that now there was somebody to "take care" of her. She was very comfortable and relaxed.

"Do you want to be somebody's husband, Madeline?" She could feel Madeline's body tense.

"No, baby. I just want to be able to love someone—man, woman, or grizzly bear. Go to sleep." She stroked Laura's hair slowly, lazily.

Little by little, Laura relaxed into sleep and was unaware when Madeline stopped stroking—or even if she ever did. . . .

Chapter 13

"Hey, Laura, where do you want these file cabinets?" Willy called from the hall, gesturing at the two burly men in white uniforms holding their awkward delivery.

"Anywhere, Willy."

He nodded and led the men into her office, then came out and stood nonchalantly by Laura in the receptionist's alcove. "How about dinner tonight? If Horn and Hardart isn't your speed we could give Nedick's a whirl."

She laughed and patted Willy on the cheek. She had met him before in Los Angeles when he had come there on business, but had never really had a chance to know him. Now she knew: if you weren't hugging him thirty minutes after meeting him, you weren't human. He was a kind, sweet guy. She would have been lost without him this past week.

Getting the office procedures and assigning furniture space had not been any problem, but knowing the shortcuts and getting some kind of service in a strange town like New York would have been a chore without his cheerful aid.

"Well?" he demanded lightly.

Laura had the feeling that if she ever accepted one of his offers he would pass out. "Sorry, Willy. Have a heavy date tonight."

"Going to see Walt off at the airport?"

She laughed. "Something like that."

"All right, all right. Just asking." He smiled, "Ye olde Friday night pitch." Willy tipped his hat jauntily over his eyes and stuck his hands in his pockets. "Have a nice time . . . see you Monday."

"Good night, Willy."

The two men came out of her office and stood waiting at the door. "That everything, lady?"

"Yes. Thank you," Laura said absently. She heard their heavy rubber-heeled shoes squealing on the polished hallway floor, the elevator doors open, and a faint voice say, "Down," and then the doors close.

It was quiet now.

She sat at the receptionist's desk and stared a moment at the clutter of back issues of *Fanfare* and opened and unopened cartons. On the desk were several frantic letters from Helen saying that somebody had to come back to Los Angeles at once or she would go mad. Then the little handwritten footnote to the letters saying that she hoped Laura was happy in "the big city" and that she was missed already.

The pile of galley sheets for proofing sat on one corner of the desk. Duplicates from Los Angeles Helen had sent as a joke. Laura's article about Saundra was in them. . . . What had been that little bit in the Press Time News section? Oh, yes, Saundra was going on tour . . .

That was an item, Laura thought. She wondered what Ginny knew about it, or had to do with it.

Laura leaned back in the chair and closed her eyes. It had rained all day, and now as the night sent the city into a defiant glittering, the rain was letting up. As if from planets away, she could hear an occasional car honking, or some particularly strong-lunged man calling for a taxi.

In her mind she could see Madison Avenue emptying out its tenants: ad men, TV wizards, and other familiar gray-flannel boys rushing to catch their trains to the suburbs, or walking swiftly toward some favorite bar to have a drink before going home, or meeting their wives or dates.

They all had someplace to go, something to do, and someone they wanted to do it with. Laura wished right now she could just go home to Madeline and talk, talk, talk.

But she wouldn't. She would meet Walter and, she knew, would probably go to bed with him. He had told everyone he was leaving that night for Los Angeles, but actually his reservation was for early Saturday morning. Laura knew she had been avoiding him—and he knew it, too.

She sighed and put on her coat, and headed for Walter's hotel, where she would dutifully meet him in the lounge.

The avenue had cleared considerably, and here and there she saw the "free" light on top of the cabs. The clouds were breaking and it was nice to see the top of the Empire State Building lighting up.

What was it Madeline had said? Oh, yes, if the top of the Empire State was enveloped in a cloud, it would either rain or snow. I'm growing too dependent upon Madeline, she thought without any intention of changing it.

Laura decided to walk to Walter's hotel and enjoy the rain-cleaned streets and the exhaust-free air. She had a sudden longing to be with Ginny—just to know that she was there. They could enjoy this rainy dusk together and walk along the same avenue and look in the same store windows. Maybe stop somewhere and have a cocktail or even a cup of coffee. The pang of loss still hit her occasionally. But then, she had missed Walter, too. It was becoming impossible to trust her emotions.

If it hadn't been for Madeline, Laura wondered if she would have stayed away from Ginny. Though Madeline had remained very discreet in her mentions of Ginny—or, for that matter, in all that might connect Laura with being a lesbian—it was as if she was waiting for Laura to make up her mind what she was and who she wanted to be with.

Thus far, their arrangement had worked out very well. For Laura, at least.

Madeline had not "pushed" her in any way. Except for the first night, when she had moved into Laura's bed to comfort her, Madeline had kept her part of the bargain.

The hotel doorman nodded politely to Laura as she passed through the heavy glass revolving door. Crossing the lobby, Laura wondered why she was bothering to meet Walter. Some hidden guilt-laden motive, no doubt. Have to prove myself as a woman or something equally Freudian, she concluded.

Walter was sitting at the piano bar when she entered. He rose when he saw her; his welcoming smile was strained and forced. It's lecture night, all right, she thought. He's worried about me.

"Hello, darling," he said brightly—a little too brightly.

She smiled in reply and let him lead her to a corner table "where they wouldn't be disturbed." Gallantly holding her chair, he kissed her on the cheek and sat down on her left, where he could keep an eye on everyone's movements.

"Haven't had a chance to talk to you alone since . . . in ages." He held her forearm affectionately. "How are you?"

"Fine. Fine, Walter. And you?" Laura answered, trying her best to sound sincere.

It was like Old Acquaintance Week, or Say Something Pleasant Day. She felt so disinterested, deceitful, and obligated. She knew Walter well enough to know that he was aware of something extra amiss, but the how and why and how much he could not possibly have guessed.

Walter cleared his throat, then hesitantly said, "You look rather tired, Laura. I suppose getting yourself oriented, and the department set up, and looking for an apartment, can be more than wearing."

It took all she could do not to laugh. He was being so transparent in his curiosity. "I haven't been looking for an apartment yet."

"Oh."

He paused as the waiter brought their drinks. "You and Madeline getting along all right?" He studied a faded Currier and Ives reproduction on the opposite wall.

"Yes." Laura suppressed a smile. "Is something troubling you, Walter?" she asked softly.

His eyes came back to her at once. Raising his thick eyebrows, he said, "Me? No. Not at all. I thought something was bothering you. . . ."

They both knew what they were skirting, and also that it couldn't be delayed any longer.

"I was wondering," Walter began, low-voiced, "if you'd decided yet how we stood together."

Immediately, Laura sensed the resentment that he himself did not seem fully aware of. She knew she would have to actually say the word "no," and she dreaded it.

"You're stalling me, you know," Walter said with a tight laugh. "Trying to have your cake and eat it, too?"

She looked at him swiftly. "Oh, no, Walter. I . . . well, I just haven't been able to really think it out."

He made the kind of smile the losing football team usually manages. "You're in love with someone else. Period. End romance."

She couldn't answer him for a moment, but after all, no matter what happened to her, now she could never marry him. Too much had happened already, which would be the third strike in a loveless marriage. "I . . ."

"Never mind. Just as long as I know that this was something which just happened and not a big deal behind my back."

"I feel like a rat," she said, unable to look at him.

Walter grinned. "The gentlemanly thing to do would be to protest, but I'm afraid I agree with you. You are a rat. Oh, intellectually, I know that that's life and my tough luck and all the other true-blue clichés."

"Don't be so bitter, Walter. . . . There would be no point in marrying you because of a guilty conscience."

"Spare me the excuses," Walter answered levelly.

"Well, what do you want me to say?"

He sighed heavily. "Nothing."

They remained silent for a few long seconds.

"Will you still get your divorce?"

Walter snorted. "You're goddamn right I will." He stared at her appraisingly. "And what are you going to do?"

"What do you mean?" Laura hedged.

"Is he going to meet you here?"

"No," she replied in a barely audible voice.

"Then you're running away from him?" Walter stressed the word "him." "Going to stay an old maid?"

The conversation was going the wrong way, she decided nervously.

"You've upset me enough lately; I'd like to not have to worry about you anymore," he added.

The coldness in his voice alarmed Laura, and she knew that he was not referring to their own breakup. "Why? What have you been upset about?" She immediately wished she hadn't asked.

Walter sat back in the polished captain's chair more comfortably. "I heard a few rumors, and well, I was worried."

"What kind of rumors, Walter?" Laura's heart began pounding in guilty terror, and she fought to keep her manner nonchalant.

"Oh, nothing really."

"Is that why you've stayed in New York so long? Rumors?"

"Not really. Although I'll admit I included it among the other reasons. The divorce hearing won't come up for another six months," he said in a hollow voice, changing the subject, "and I'm lucky it'll be that soon."

Laura raised her glass and looked deeply into Walter's concerned blue eyes. "To magazines, matrimony, and maligners," she toasted, only half joking.

"Nothing like that, Laura." Walter let his eyes pass over her as if expecting to find something unusual.

"Please don't lecture me tonight, Walter. I've had enough."

Walter placed his warm, big hand over her arm protectively. "Did I do the wrong thing when I asked you to come out here? To New York, I mean. Do you want to go back to the coast?"

Laura stared at him in surprise. Then she laughed lightly. "Of course not, darling," she said.

"You have been behaving strangely lately—avoiding me. Not your usual self at all." He cleared his throat again and, gulping down the last of his drink, signaled the waiter for another round. "Would you like to tell me what's bothering you? You can, you know."

She wished to Christ he would shut up, then felt even guiltier.

"Walter. For the last time, nothing of any importance is bothering me. I'm just tired."

"All right."

There was a brief silence, for which Laura was thankful enough, although she knew she shouldn't be. She felt Walter give her hand a resigned squeeze.

"How's Madeline?" He asked the question in such an offhand manner that it was quite plainly the reverse.

"Fine, thank you." Laura suppressed a smile.

"Oh." He smiled rather feebly. "So you two are hitting it off, are you?"

"Yes."

"Oh." He let go of her hand carefully. "You're not being very communicative."

Laura laughed kindly. "Walter, you dropped your little bomb about rumors, then clammed up as to their nature and then expect me to hand out information." She leaned over confidentially and whispered, "The very walls have ears!"

She waited a moment for him to comment, but when he didn't, she knew his worries were not superficial. "Do you think we're banding together and coming out with a competitive magazine?"

"No," he replied seriously. "It is not the kind of thing a gentleman repeats."

"Only implies and suggests, is that it?" she said coldly. "But Brutus is an honorable man."

"Now, see here, Laura. Stop playing cat-and-mouse with me."

"Aren't you getting your casting mixed up?" Then she stopped. "I'm sorry, Walter. That was harsh." She reached over and stroked his face gently.

He smiled and, taking her hand again, kissed the palm. "I'm sorry, too. I had no right to pry."

They said nothing for a moment, as if they each were organizing their mental reinforcements and clearing the wounded from the arena.

"I guess you may as well know," Walter said almost to himself, "what the rumors are, and then you'll perhaps see why I was so concerned."

Laura didn't answer. It was almost as if she knew what he was going to say, and had steeled herself to it.

"It's not pleasant." Walter stared at his glass.

Still Laura said nothing. What was there to say?

"When I first arrived and met Madeline, I thought she was charming and intelligent, besides still somewhat bitter from her recent divorce." He paused as if waiting for the words to reach their destination in Laura's brain and settle there.

"I don't want to imply that I wanted an affair between us; it's just that most women react at once to *safe* flattery and attention. I'm no gigolo, and Madeline's been around long enough to see that. But she almost ignored me—in a very friendly way, of course."

He looked over at Laura, who looked back at him. She found his male vanity amusing under ordinary circumstances, but this wasn't just vanity.

"It never dawned on me that there was something out of the way with her. I mean, she seemed all right and never said anything to seriously indicate . . ."

"Walter," Laura said in a low voice, "please get to the point."

"Well," he answered with a nervous smile, "it would appear that Madeline lives in that twilight world or whatever it is they call it."

And there it was. Target sighted—bombs away.

It didn't sound so bad. Of course, he had put it diplomatically, and it really wasn't an accusation against me, Laura thought, but still, one does feel on the defensive.

Shall I let on that I knew what the term means, or play dumb? she wondered. No. Playing dumb would tip him off, and as long as it's just a rumor, he can't be too sure yet.

"You mean she's supposed to be queer?" That was it—go him one better.

Walter started. "Well, I don't know how much truth there is in it. She has been married and all that."

That's better, Laura scolded him silently; back down.

"Look, Walter. You give me deep, searching looks all evening, let loose with a few little hints, and then decide there's nothing to anything. Did you think I was being seduced?"

"No. Of course not."

"Yes, you did, or you wouldn't have started all this. What were you looking for? Signs of acne? Loss of reason? Green hair?"

She had Walter on the defensive now, actually trying to convince her that the rumors were ridiculous.

"I . . . I just thought you should know. I felt guilty and responsible when I heard about her, because I more or less talked you into staying with her."

"You thought I should know what?" Laura asked sarcastically. "I haven't asked Madeline about her sex habits and she's allowed me the same privacy. I didn't even ask her if she'd been to bed with you. Although I'm surprised that she didn't at least try."

Laura threw in the last sentence to pacify him. And it worked.

"Let's forget about it, shall we? I wasn't accusing you of anything . . . perverted. Was I?" He smiled knowingly. "After all, I know your bed habits as well as your good," he punned.

Then Walter's face became serious again. "Just one more thing, Laura, and we'll drop the subject. I want you to know where I stand." He stared at the table, averting her eyes, and his voice took on a tone she had never noticed before.

"Even if you were seduced by her . . . I mean, no matter what you do or are or become"—he smiled and raised his eyes to hers—"I'm saying this badly, but I don't give a damn what you do. . . . I think you're one fine girl. My only objection to this . . . sort of thing . . . is the same as if you were to date a gangster or an alcoholic, or a Russian spy. You're too likely to get hurt, and I wouldn't want that for anything."

Laura wondered just how much Walter did know about Madeline, or if by some freak chance he had learned of her almost overnight friendship with Ginny, who was openly a friend of Saundra's. But then, how much did anyone know about Saundra?

He seemed very sincere, and Laura had no reason to disbelieve him. What a guy! she thought affectionately.

"Thank you, Walter."

"Well, now," he said with a humorous snort, "let's get off this auld lang syne kick and concentrate on us and enjoy this farewell party."

She could take it easy now. He was off the subject and satisfied that his virility had not been challenged. Now the rest of the conversation would be business, and in between he would work in one last seduction. But maybe he wouldn't even want to ask her now.

He suggested several places for dinner, but Laura wanted to stay where they were. Might as well eat here, she thought; we'd only have to come back to the hotel so Walter could ask me in for a nightcap.

She half listened to him as he talked on about the future of *Fanfare* magazine and her future with him—businesswise, of course. His whole attitude showed clearly—if not somewhat bitterly—that she needn't put into words that from now on they were simply "friends."

It seemed so silly, the protocol of male-female relations. There was no telling herself that she came anywhere near to loving him now the way she did before . . . before Ginny. Except that now that she felt closer to him, she could accept him better. Her feelings now were something else. The fact that she coldly planned to go to bed with him was another matter—she neither approved of it nor disapproved; she simply had to do it.

But why, she wondered, did they have to go through all the game of having dinner and idle chatter? She wasn't really hungry. Why didn't they skip dinner and just go upstairs? It would save so much time and money. Only it would never do; she knew that. *Nice* girls—and Walter certainly thought of her as a nice girl—don't have thoughts like that, much less act upon them. It would destroy a man's ego if he thought a girl was using him for the same thing he wanted from her.

Laura forced herself to listen to him and take an interest in what he was saying. It seemed to take forever for the dinner to be through and even longer for their cordial and coffee to arrive. She couldn't help thinking what a waste this evening was for both of them. To Walter, because it didn't really mean anything lasting to him, not anymore: he knew they were finished. And to Laura for even less sentimental reasons. It was more like a social debt she was repaying. She remembered what that night had been like with Ginny, and again attempted to understand what was motivating her now.

God! How it made her miss Ginny. Just to hold Ginny in her arms. Feel her soft, warm body pressed against her own, and feel Ginny's firm, young arms slowly reach up and pull Laura's head to hers in a long, probing kiss . . .

I suppose I really am queer, Laura told herself, and for an instant she wanted to cry. The acceptance of it was almost like realizing you were no longer a child and would have to meet life and deal with it as an adult now—no more finding solace in your mother's lap or hiding under the blanket so that nobody would find you. This was *it*.

She only wished she could really and completely get over her feeling for Ginny, whatever it was. It had lessened, naturally, except for moments like now. She pondered briefly if it was Ginny she missed or what Ginny stood for.

". . . Aren't you going to drink your coffee?" Walter's voice came through to her, and she was genuinely surprised to realize she again hadn't been paying any attention to him.

"I'm sorry, Walter," she offered apologetically. "I was just thinking that it might be a long time before I see you again," she lied.

His smile was unmistakably triumphant. "I don't know about that"—he touched his cup to hers—"I'll probably be back and forth a good deal just to keep you on your toes."

She smiled in reply and found herself dully waiting for him to suggest going up to his suite for a drink so that she could get the affair over with and go home.

Home. Where was that?

"How're you getting on with Willy?" Walter asked suddenly.

"He's a dear," Laura said genuinely. "I would have been tearing my hair out if he hadn't been around."

"Hmm," Walter said in a tone of mock petulance. "Don't become too fond of him."

"Well," Laura teased, "when the cat's away, and all that sort of jazz."

His smile faded slowly. "I'm going to miss you, darling. You know that." His voice was low and husky.

Somewhere in the back of Laura's mind came the thought "Here it comes," but she pushed it aside and gave herself up to the overture for act 2 this evening.

"And I'll miss you, too," she whispered. She sensed that Walter's breathing had quickened, and tried to lose herself in his passion, in his desire—so that tonight would mean something.

Odd, she thought. It's almost like raping myself.

"I know this sounds rather awkward"—Walter grinned his little-boy smile—"and even prearranged, but let's go upstairs so we can talk in comfort."

"Fresh out of etchings, Walter?" Laura laughed.

"We don't need them, do we?" he asked suddenly, very serious.

"No." Laura couldn't look into his eyes; she felt unforgivably hypocritical.

"As a matter of fact," Walter almost drawled, "I really don't know why I want you to come up. It was different when you were mine, but it's pretty damned selfish of me to expect you to . . . well, especially when your heart isn't in it." He thrust his hands into his pocket with plain frustration and confusion.

"You're under no obligation to me, Laura. Why don't I just put you in a cab and send you home before my male hormones ruin a good friendship?"

"No," Laura said without even realizing it. She couldn't stand the thought now of not going through with it. "No. I *want* to, Walter. Don't ask me why; I just do. Maybe it's because I trust you and need you despite . . . everything else. I'm not sure. I think I love you more right this minute than I ever did before—but it's different. Much different."

She knew that she only half meant what she had said, but it was now terribly important to go upstairs with him. As long as he knew that she wasn't offering herself with starry eyes, then nothing else seemed to matter but doing it and having done with it.

He slid his chair back and pulled the table out from the wall while Laura picked up her purse and coat. It was all so elaborately casual—so deliberate, so calculating. It was as if they had agreed to go window shopping.

Inside the elevator, Walter took her hand in his and held it tightly. His palm was moist and hot. She glanced at the operator of the car and wondered what he was thinking. Nothing, probably. Nobody ever thought anything in a hotel unless you left your shades up.

Laura controlled an impulse to look at her watch. Bad enough I'm so cold-blooded, she thought, without having to time it. Must be early, though. Maybe we'll be through in time for me to have a talk with Madeline—I need it.

But Walter doesn't think I'm cold-blooded, she reminded herself. He thinks I'm a torrid little broad who knows how to have an affair without mixing it up with business or babies—or the thousand other obstacles that flesh is heir to!

The elevator doors silently opened, and Walter led her down the hallway. She could tell by the way he held her arm that it wouldn't take long—he was almost hurting her, and that meant he was in a hurry.

She wished she could laugh, but knew in her heart that she didn't think it was very funny at all. It was sad. Two basically nice and intelligent people killing time, she thought, as he stopped in front of his door and pushed the key into the hole; just like filling in a story to cover a two-column shortage. That never did work out right. That was forced and awkward. So was this.

"I'll mix us a drink," Walter said softly, closing the door behind them.

His room smelled like a million other hotel rooms, and since he was such a meticulously tidy man, there was no indication that anyone was now inhabiting this room. How many girls, Laura wondered, have come into this room and, for one excuse or another, finished in bed . . . ?

She sighed and put her coat over the dumpy brown chair in the corner. "Ugly . . . ugly," she whispered to the chair, though she had to admire its defiant existence. "You wouldn't last ten minutes around me . . ." she said to it.

"What was that, darling? I didn't hear you," Walter asked, handing her a drink.

Laura laughed. "I was having an argument with that chair."

He glanced over at it and smiled. "Goddamn ugly, isn't it?"

Laura glanced up at him quickly and felt another surge of companionship and warmth toward Walter. She had expected him not to understand her comment—or to make fun of it. And there he sat, good, reliable Walter, agreeing with her. She wanted to thank him, to tell him she appreciated him, but knew the words would never come out or, if they did, would only embarrass them both.

"Walter," she said after a moment.

"Hmm?" He had taken off her shoes and was massaging her feet slowly, working up to her calves, taking the tension out of her muscles.

"How long have we known each other?"

He smiled without looking up. "Oh, I don't know. Several years, I guess."

She nodded and was pleased that he didn't know exactly. There was something so routine about people who remembered dates and hours. "Walter?"

"Yes?"

She felt his grip tighten around her calf as she stretched back against the arm of the divan. It felt cool on her neck, and she closed her eyes.

His hand slid up under her dress and pressed the inside of her exposed thigh. Walter was half lying on her now, and she could feel his hard body against her legs, and his face buried in her abdomen.

As if coming from far off she heard herself cry out in a desperate, frenzied voice, "Kiss me, Walter. Please . . . kiss me now!"

Chapter 14

The door was unlocked when Laura let herself into Madeline's apartment, feeling as tired as if she had built the apartment house by hand.

"Is that you, Laura?" Madeline's voice came from the kitchen.

"Yes." Laura slouched onto the divan.

Madeline walked into the living room. She stared openly at Laura's hastily put-on clothes and her disheveled hair.

"How's Walter?"

Laura sighed. "Probably sleeping by now."

Madeline laughed heartily. "Modest little tramp, aren't you?"

"No. Just a tired one." Laura stretched languidly.

"How's my investment doing these days? Selling a million issues?" Madeline sat down in the big armchair.

Laura laughed without humor. "Really want to know?"

"No. Just making conversation. Never talk about the war with battle-fatigued soldiers."

Laura snorted in appreciation. There was a silence that seemed very restful—but Laura was in a hurry. She didn't know why, but she felt that time was running out, that she had to hurry or it would be too late. Abruptly she asked, "Did you know you're a twilight lady?"

Madeline almost choked. "A what?"

"Twilight . . ."

"I heard you. Who says?" Her attitude was amused and tolerant. "Walter."

"Oh." She played with the catch on her wristwatch.

"Has he been reading Havelock Ellis again? I do wish he'd buy an up-to-date book. . . ."

"Did you know you've been seducing me?"

"That's nice. Did I enjoy it?"

"Suppose so—his source was rather vague on that." Laura frowned slightly. "Why haven't you?"

"Why haven't I what?"

"Seduced me."

"You've been busy."

"Oh."

Another short silence.

"Want a drink?" Madeline asked without making any attempt to rise.

Laura ignored her question. "What time is it?"

Glancing over her shoulder at the ornate wall clock, Madeline replied, "Little after midnight." Then she turned to Laura and asked impishly, "Which of us is going to turn into the pumpkin, and which of us will be the prince?"

"How can you make fun of it?" Laura asked without rancor.

"Being gay?" Madeline asked as a matter of routine. "Used to it, I guess. Might as well laugh at it . . . I'm stuck with it. Like a Siamese twin. It's always with me no matter what I do.

"Besides," Madeline went on, "I might as well accept it. Smarter brains than mine don't have any answers to offer. Some of my fondest memories are from the analyst's couch—also the most expensive."

"Do you like men? Sexually, I mean?"

She looked at Laura thoughtfully, and Laura watched her as she would a friendly Martian.

"Sexually? Yes. I like men—it, or they, satisfy my animal feelings, my libido. Or perhaps I enjoy punishing myself, or men, by using them. It's emotionally that we don't dig each other."

117

"I like you, Madeline. You're honest."

"So was Christ," Madeline joked, "and look what happened to him."

Time was running out again for Laura: she wanted to get to the point. "Are you interested in me physically?"

Madeline sat back in her chair, and Laura couldn't help thinking that Madeline should really smoke a pipe for effect.

"I'm interested, as you put it, but I've been around a long time, Laura, and I've learned a few things. One is, never make passes at anyone who is your friend—unless you plan to make it serious."

"Why?"

"Because people like me need friends more than we need a night's fun." Her voice was calm and sincere.

"And you wouldn't be serious about me?"

Madeline came to sit on the arm of Laura's chair. She leaned over and kissed her forehead gently. "Baby, I'd like very much to be serious about you. But you're carrying a torch big enough to make the Statue of Liberty green with envy, and you've got a lot of decisions to make."

"Ginny?" Laura asked softly. She could feel Madeline sigh and accepted her silence as confirmation.

"How do you know when you're a . . . lesbian?"

Madeline laughed sardonically. "You can talk to a million of them, and each one will believe she has the only answer. I personally think finding out is almost a matter of circumstance. Of course, there are many women with husbands and kids who are latent homosexuals but never know about themselves—perhaps they're better off."

Madeline broke off, stared at the opposite wall. Then she shrugged. "It's just something you feel . . ."

Laura sensed that Madeline was trying to be as impartial as possible, for her sake, and yet had not quite succeeded. She thought over Madeline's comments, weighing them as they might apply to her, and mumbled almost to herself, "No matter who the man is, I'll always feel that something's missing. I know that now," she smiled reminiscently. "But something will be missing either way. How do I know which is right?"

"Are you asking me to decide this for you?"

"Yes."

Madeline got up. She stood looking at Laura, deliberating. Finally, she asked, "Want to do the rounds and see what it's like?"

Laura suddenly felt excited and awake. She had to find out . . . had to know what she was. . . . Maybe the "rounds" would help, and they certainly couldn't harm her. She had to choose her way, and now. If this was going to be her life, she wanted to know everything about it that could be learned—firsthand.

And she could trust Madeline. She would not have to be alone in a strange new world that both fascinated and repulsed her.

Laura nodded.

"Just let me take a fast shower and I'll be right with you," she said slowly, trying to control her excitement.

"You may as well put on a pair of slacks, then." A few minutes later Madeline went into the bedroom. She watched Laura dress.

"One thing," Madeline said. "I don't want you to feel inhibited by me."

"What do you mean?" Laura asked, pulling on her Capri slacks, the same ones she had worn to Tijuana.

"I mean that if you want to make friends with someone you see, or if you get an invitation to leave, feel free to do so. No strings." Madeline studied Laura's body analytically. "I hope I'm doing the right thing."

Laura laughed suddenly, feeling young and . . . gay. "If *you're* doing the right thing!"

Just as unexpectedly, Madeline laughed, too.

When Laura was dressed, they walked to the front door. She paused, looked into Madeline's calm and patient eyes, then hugged her affectionately. "Thank you," she whispered.

They went out into the night air. Despite the late hour, there were still occasional strollers, and a few brave souls were sitting on the benches in Washington Square.

Laura kept pace with Madeline's quick step. She found herself peering into every window, noticing if the brownstone houses needed painting, noticing which streets were paved and which were cobblestone. Everything seemed to jump out at her for attention

119

and closer scrutiny. She didn't feel like a tourist now—more like a general inspecting a regiment, checking the supplies, listening to the men's troubles. Laura felt that the Village was her home now; it was her responsibility, her charge. She had to know everything about it, grow with it, feel it.

Madeline said nothing, but evidently she had a destination in mind. Finally, they arrived at a drugstore on MacDougal and Third. She stopped in front of the telephone booth outside.

"This is it, Laura. The heartbeat of the Village, although you would find many who would disagree with me. Let's say it's the Times Square."

Laura searched as if expecting to see some utterly distinctive characteristic that would set it apart from any other place in the world.

"Do you want to go on?" Madeline asked, half suggesting that Laura might have changed her mind.

"Yes." She couldn't stop now, and she knew it.

Madeline stared at her a moment, then began to walk again but more slowly. She paused in front of a stairway leading up to a bar. She glanced at Laura only once before climbing the steps. Laura followed her. She could hear the loud jukebox. Inside, the run-down, unimaginative-looking bar was jammed with people. Mostly girls.

Madeline took Laura's hand and tugged her through the crowd, murmuring "Excuse me," and "Pardon us," as she went elbowing to the rear.

Laura saw that the rear was a little better-looking, but the tables lining the walls were strewn with beer bottles, cocktail glasses, and twisted cigarette packages. And crowded with women. She couldn't help staring at the customers, the girls dancing together or standing close.

Madeline put her arm around Laura's waist and began to dance, quite nonchalantly. "Might as well," she explained, "there's no place to sit."

She led Laura quite smoothly and silently for about five bars; then she said, "Keep your eyes on that corner spot. I think they're leaving."

Laura nodded. But she wasn't really paying attention. She was torn between her own reactions and the fascination of just looking around. She was very conscious of Madeline's breath against her ear and found the softness of her cheek very pleasant. It seemed reasonable that Madeline's breasts were merged with her own, and that instead of a man's hard legs against hers, she found firm but rounded thighs.

Then she glanced at the corner table and saw a girl who wore a shirt and trousers standing next to the table, where two girls sat. The standing girl was talking and laughing with the younger of the two, who leaned toward her and seemed entranced. The third girl sat back rigidly in her chair; her pale mouth was compressed into a straight line.

"Fascinating, isn't it?" Madeline asked.

Laura knew she didn't expect an answer.

"C'mon," Madeline said. "I think they're getting up to go."

Laura followed her to the table. Madeline had been right. The table-hopper walked away with a smug expression as the other two silently put on their coats and left. Laura didn't envy them having to wade through the crowd of people in front.

She sat down at the table and really surveyed the room.

Madeline was apparently contented just to let her look her fill. She ordered two Scotches and then held Laura's hand. "Atmosphere," she said lightly.

There was a commotion at the door. A safari of girls, leather-jacketed and short-haired, marched in.

"It's a goddamn invasion," Laura said without meaning to be funny. "Occupation troops on leave . . ."

"You're not exactly a civilian," Madeline said flatly.

"Touché." Laura looked at Madeline for the first time since they had entered. "I just didn't know such places existed. . . . I wasn't being snide."

The tall, blasé waitress placed their glasses in front of them. "Hello, Georgie," Madeline said to her. "Who's here tonight?"

"Same crappy crowd, Del. Good to see you."

"This is a friend of mine, Georgie. If she ever comes in alone, take care of her for me, will you?"

"On her way in, out, or just shopping?" Georgie's voice was toneless, uninterested, and ageless. Laura decided that Georgie would be a good person to know, to have as a reserve.

"She's shopping," Madeline replied with a wink to Laura. Then to Georgie, "Got any bargains?"

The girl glared in a friendly way and grunted, "I'll keep an eye out for you."

"Thanks," Madeline said.

Georgie walked away with a lumbering precision. Laura would not have been surprised if she had pulled out a notebook and made a list of "bargains."

"Why did you tell her that?" she asked Madeline.

"You are, aren't you?"

Laura sat a moment considering it. "You're too goddamn smart," she told Madeline, yet she had to admit it was true. Still, it didn't seem as cold as all that, though her feelings didn't really enter into it at all. . . .

What difference is there, she thought, between picking up a girl and a man? A man doesn't expect love from a pickup. . . . Why should a girl?

And suddenly Laura knew her "bargain" had arrived.

Chapter 15

She came pushing through the front crowd with admirable determination. If someone had asked Laura to describe her, she would probably have said "average," and felt the description just short of eloquent.

Her hair, her face, her figure—everything about her—was average, including her coloring. The only distinctive or outstanding impression she gave was an aura of cleanliness.

Laura couldn't take her eyes off the girl. She had a quick surge of near terror followed by a strange resignation. It was almost like crossing the street and looking up to see a car coming right at her; there wasn't time to step aside, and knowing this, she could only hope the damage wasn't going to be too great. She wanted to close her eyes for an instant, to be sure it was happening to her, but the girl's eyes had found hers and it was settled.

She walked directly toward Laura with an air of calling Laura's bluff. Sassy, Laura thought—that's what she is. She's been to too many juvenile-delinquent movies.

The girl stopped at their table. Without taking her eyes from Laura, she said in a deep, well-modulated voice, "Hello, Del."

Madeline looked up from her surveillance of the patrons and, half laughing, said, "Edie! Where have you been all winter?"

Laura could tell by Madeline's tone that she had labeled this girl "bargain," too. Edie. Laura turned the name over in her mind. Well, it's better than Georgie.

"Away," Edie replied, still looking at Laura, "who's this?" She raised her chin toward Laura.

"Friend of mine. Edie, meet Laura."

"What kind of friend?"

Madeline laughed. "Just a friend. She's staying at my place until she gets settled here."

Laura sat quietly. Even though Edie wasn't particularly ingratiating, she did have a certain magnetism—a kind of primitiveness.

"Gay?" Edie asked without blinking.

Laura looked quickly at Madeline but said nothing. Madeline placed her hand on Laura's arm firmly. "Maybe, maybe not. We're waiting to find out."

When Laura looked back at Edie, she saw that something in the girl's expression had changed; she seemed softer, less antagonistic. For the first time she addressed Laura directly.

"Do you always stare at women when they enter a room?"

"No," Laura answered without hesitation.

Edie nodded as if the answer carried grave significance. "Would you like to dance?"

"Yes."

"Order me a beer, Del."

Laura felt Edie's hand on her waist as they took the two steps to the fringe of the dance floor, then let herself be taken into Edie's arms and walked to music, silently.

She's no dancer, Laura concluded.

She felt that one of them should say something.

"What do you do?" she asked. It sounded rather blunt and impolite. "I mean, do you have a job or go to school or . . ."

"Off-Broadway," Edie said, and brought Laura closer to her so that her lips were just even with Laura's neck. "Bit parts, mostly. One or two good roles with shows that close before they open, and the rest of the time unemployment lines."

"Are you a good actress?" Laura noticed that Edie's cheek was perspiring. The hand she had around Laura's waist was rubbing her lower back very gently. It was a strange sensation—it was a strange situation. Unlike her situation with Ginny, there was no love or tender exploration. This was sex. But how could sex be so important if they were both women . . . ? And yet, Laura admitted silently, it was stimulating in nearly the same way as with a man. The knowledge that she was attractive, physically desirable, and the feeling of power were there.

But there was no comparison to Ginny and what they had shared.

One jukebox song ended and another began. Edie gave no indication of tiring or wanting to sit down. A few times Laura glimpsed Madeline, visiting at various tables.

The place was beginning to clear out now. Lovers left, arm in arm or in grim silence; some girls were leaning over the table of another girl, making a last bid for company that night.

It was very like any ordinary corner bar except so terribly intensified . . . like living under a magnifying glass.

"Laura, baby," Madeline interrupted them on the floor. "It's almost three, and I'm pretty tired. Do you want to stay on or come home?"

Laura felt Edie's hand clutch at her back. Edie said, "I was thinking of asking Laura over to my pad for coffee, Del."

Madeline smiled with no expression in her eyes. She looked at Laura slowly. "There's Macy's and there's Lord and Taylor—but a bargain is a bargain."

Laura wished she could laugh or say something clever, but her mouth was suddenly very dry, and she couldn't think. They had stopped dancing and were walking toward their table. If I don't go with Edie, Laura reasoned, I'll never have the nerve again—I've got to stay.

Edie and Madeline stood by the table as Laura sat down and quickly gulped down the remainder of her watered Scotch. She knew it wasn't so much what she'd find out by going with Edie—after all, what could that show her? What would it prove? It was a compulsion—a Pandora's box that she had to open.

"Well . . ." Madeline stretched. "You two owls can stay up if you want to, but at my age I need my rest."

"You talk too much about your age," Edie said in a monotone. "What you need is somebody to shack up with."

"Uh-huh," Madeline laughed. "Take care of her for me, and if you're going to keep her up too late, then call me and let me know."

"Are you kidding?" Edie placed her hands on her hips defiantly.

"Hey, you two!" Laura found herself saying. "I'm over twenty-one."

Edie and Madeline looked at her, then at each other in mutual surprise.

"No one's even considered what I'd like to do," Laura continued, almost unable to stop herself.

Edie let out a thundering laugh and slapped Madeline heartily on the back. "It walks; it talks; it shimmys; it shakes . . ."

Laura could feel the color rising in her face and said nothing.

"All right," Edie said in mock seriousness. "What would you like to do?"

Confronted with the question, Laura felt foolish and awkward, but she managed to reply with some dignity, "I do want a cup of coffee, thank you. I would also like to be consulted in the future."

"Let's go, then," Edie said kindly, and took Laura's hand.

Madeline walked with them to the door and down the stairs into the fresh night air. She hailed a cab and threw Laura a kiss as she climbed in and was driven off.

Laura was slightly uncomfortable now that she was alone with Edie. But as they walked down MacDougal Street, she grew more excited and felt daring and wicked.

Edie carried the bulk of the conversation as they strolled on the nearly deserted street. She told Laura about various childhood experiences, not seeming to care if Laura was interested or not.

They walked up the well-kept stairs of a brownstone on Charlton Street.

"The apartment belongs to a friend of mine," Edie explained softly. "She's letting me stay here until I can find a place of my own. I gave up my pad in the fall."

"You did mention being away."

Edie smiled as she held the door open for Laura. "Anyway, she's gone for a vacation in Europe, and it's rent-free."

Inside, she took Laura's coat and hung it up neatly in a small closet. "We were madly in love for about twenty minutes once," Edie smiled reminiscently.

Laura laughed uncertainly. "What does that mean?"

"Nothing," Edie said, gesturing to Laura to take a chair. She watched Laura as she sat down on the sofa.

Edie crossed to the small kitchenette and put on water to boil. "Being gay can be pretty wild, you know. Most of us never really make out—for the long haul, that is. Just one-night stands, flings, passion, and arguments."

She shook her head sadly. "It's the drinking and always going out to bars; it's the kidding yourself that just because you've found somebody to take to bed that it's love. It's a lot of stupid things."

"Sounds more like fear of love," Laura said.

Edie sat down on the sofa next to Laura. She looked at her with unanticipated tenderness. "What do you expect from me?"

"I . . . I'm not sure," Laura answered. "Perhaps the same thing you expect from me—someone to help you get through the night, to fill the darkness, if only for a moment."

Edie asked, "Have you had any experience?"

Laura wanted to grab her coat and make a run for it, yet she knew she wouldn't "In a way . . ."

"Then that's what you really want, isn't it?" Edie leaned forward, pushing Laura back on the couch so that she was half lying, half sitting. Her face was inches from Laura's.

"Let's say I want to experience . . ."

Laura stopped as Edie's hand came to her throat and then moved down, unbuttoning her sweater.

"This is no time for semantics, honey. Don't think . . . feel."

Laura watched Edie's face come so near, she could no longer focus on it. She closed her eyes and opened her mouth to meet Edie's.

They both forgot the boiling water.

Chapter 16

At six P.M. exactly, Laura signaled a passing cab in front of the office. She couldn't bear the bus today—it was too nice a day. As she rode down Fifth Avenue, Laura sat pensively reviewing these past weeks and how much of a routine it had become for her to frequent the Village "rounds" almost nightly. The bartenders now knew her along with the other steady customers.

At the office she worked herself mercilessly each day, as her department took shape and more responsibility came. Then she ate a hurried dinner and lost herself in her new world.

It hadn't helped her to forget Ginny—she could never do that and accepted it now. But it did help her to find a place for herself in the world—a place that was both a sanctuary and a strange source of rebellion.

She knew that Madeline did not approve of what she was doing, and of the hours she kept. But Madeline had made it quite plain that she understood what was happening to Laura, that it was a phase of "coming out" and that it would pass. It annoyed Laura occasionally that Madeline seemed to take such a superior attitude, particularly when Madeline would make some comment about Laura going out "to punish yourself."

But it was also quite clear to Laura that she needed Madeline, needed a friend. . . .

She paid the driver and looked around the now familiar street before walking into the apartment building. It seems as if I've lived here all my life. Palm trees and freeways are a long way off. . . . It all happened to someone else—not me, she thought.

She looked up at the trees and saw the branches in their need to bud and grow. There was no doubt about it: spring had finally arrived in New York.

Sighing, she wondered if Ginny realized that spring had come. Or if Ginny knew she was thinking of her. She wondered how Ginny was doing and if she needed anything—or if she had found someone new.

It's strange, she thought, how you can numb your feelings about people yet can never really rid yourself of them. Some silly little incident or random association and . . . wham! . . . They were back, raw as ever. Instant amnesia—and anesthesia—for painful memories. That's what the world needed. Only it should be permanent as well. Liquor didn't really do the job. Not really.

"Just in time for soup," Madeline yelled as Laura let herself into the apartment.

Reliable, sweet Madeline, Laura thought with a comfortable sigh.

"I'm going with you tonight," Madeline announced. With a mischievous smile, she asked, "How do you like my drag outfit?"

Laura had to laugh. Madeline couldn't have looked masculine no matter what she did, and the jersey blouse with matching slacks she had on did very little to make her manly.

"You'll be the butch of the ball," Laura said.

"My. Aren't we learning the trade jargon!" Madeline laughed.

They sat down to a hurried dinner, and Laura speculated about what was making Madeline so chipper this evening. Not just the weather.

"Have you seen Edie lately?" Madeline asked.

"No," Laura answered. "Why?"

"She's doing a bit in some awful thing at Actor's Playhouse. Thought you might like to catch part of the rehearsal tonight."

"Why?" Laura asked cautiously.

"Friend of mine is in the show, too—kind of a friend, that is. Anyway, it won't kill you, and Edie does have quite a thing for you."

"Sure," Laura laughed. "She's loved me for twenty-five minutes. That's a five-minute edge over her old girlfriends." She stood up and walked into the kitchen, balancing her dishes. "All right. I'll be a sport. Do I have time to clean up?"

"Yes. But make it fast." Madeline began to wash the dishes, whistling merrily.

"Why don't you get a maid?" Laura called from the bedroom.

"How would I advertise? Gay and personable?"

Laura shrugged her shoulders in mock helplessness and took a shower, briefly enjoying the sheer luxury of the spray of water.

Drying herself, she looked at her reflection in the mirror impersonally and realized for the first time how tired she looked, and how much thinner.

"The wages of sin," she murmured to herself, and turned her back to the mirror. She dressed quickly and applied her makeup with hasty efficiency.

"You about ready, Laura?" Madeline called.

Laura went into the living room smiling. "In the flesh. What's your hurry?"

"You'll see."

They left the apartment just after dark and walked briskly to the small playhouse on Seventh Avenue.

A lanky youth with tight-fitting chino pants sat at a small table as they entered. He had the glazed look of the devout failure.

Madeline smiled at him benignly. "Max said it was all right for us to watch the rehearsal," she told him.

He looked at them both momentarily. "The producer?"

"Of course."

"Go on in," he said, as if he had a beer with old Maxie every evening. "You've missed about fifteen minutes of the first act."

Madeline walked down the narrow stairway and into the darkened theater. She paused by the refreshment stand inside the theater long enough for Laura to get accustomed to the dark, then led Laura to a seat in the last row.

Laura leaned over and whispered, "This better be good."

"You may never know how true that is," Madeline answered.

In the dim light from the stage, Laura could make out Madeline's expression. Gone was the mischievous look and the bright little smile. In their place were concern and speculation. Laura wondered if Madeline had sunk money into this show, but decided against it—Madeline knew better.

Laura settled back in the uncomfortable seat and wished she had a drink. Glancing around the room, she saw a cluster of people sitting off to the right and several leaning forward in the first row center.

"How does the audience see anything when there's no dais?" she heckled softly.

"Shh," Madeline ordered.

Laura shrugged and tried to listen to the gaunt young man on stage who was talking to a blue spotlight behind a blue sheer backdrop with modernistic foliage sewn on it.

She sat back and sniffed happily. Yes. It was there. That special, intoxicating smell of the theater—that kind of velvety, faintly perfumed, warm-dust aroma.

There was something curiously soothing about it all. Gradually Laura began to succumb to the wonderful mood a darkened theater always aroused in her. It struck her then that this was the first time she had ever really been in an honest-to-God New York theater, even though it was off-Broadway. She must come more often— she'd almost forgotten what a delicious experience it was.

Absently she watched the blue light dim and move to the edge of the stage. Somewhere music came through in a rhythmic, fragmented drumbeat. The figure of a woman began to emerge slowly from the offstage shadows. Laura found herself straining to see. She was barely conscious of Madeline, who had turned to watch her.

All Laura's attention was focused on that shadow figure that was now undulating to the center of the stage. There was something about it that sent a strange, warning thrill through her. She could not have said what it was exactly.

She wished they'd turn the damned spot up so she could see.

When it did happen, it was so swift Laura was unprepared.

"Ginny!" It was a full moment before Laura realized that the stifled gasp was her own. She stared in frozen realization at the crown of soft red hair that shimmered in the soft, ghostly light—at the pale, anxious face, the small, supple body that not even the ill-fitting costume could obliterate. So familiar, yet so unreal.

"Steady, old girl," whispered Madeline, closing her fingers around Laura's arm so tightly it was almost painful.

By this time Laura was almost standing up.

A thousand impressions and arguments flew through her mind, and the scene became a blur to her except for Ginny's small figure making stage gestures, walking upstage and, for some reason, into a man's arms.

The sight of her there was all too odd, too unexpected.

Laura picked up her purse mechanically and without a backward look left the theater. She was halfway out the street exit when she heard Madeline's voice calling her.

She turned on her heel and stopped. "That was a pretty cute trick," she said tightly.

"It wasn't meant as a cute trick," Madeline replied softly.

"What did you mean by it?"

"I . . . I just wanted you to know she was in town, and I thought this way you could see her without being discovered."

"You're lying." Laura said flatly.

Madeline took Laura by the shoulder gently. "You're not angry with me, are you?" She sighed. "I guess it was the actress in me—the dramatic approach. I'm genuinely sorry."

Laura felt the tears creeping into her eyes, and the back of her throat was aching. She fought them back and gained control of herself.

"No," she said finally. "I'm not really angry. It was just such a shock . . ."

They walked in silence past Sheridan Square. Laura wanted to get drunk, to just lose herself inside a bottle of Scotch until she drowned.

She paid no attention to Madeline. She tried to place the event in its proper perspective, tried to see the situation objectively. So what if Ginny was in town . . . Maybe she didn't know that Laura was here, too, or maybe she hated Laura after finding that she had run out. . . . Maybe many things.

But—what reason did Laura have for staying away from Ginny?

Laura led the way up the steps to the bar and, without even saying hello to Georgie, marched into the back and sat down. She half saw that Madeline paused to talk to Georgie, a terse conversation punctuated with stern expressions and lifted eyebrows. Then Madeline was walking toward her and sitting down at the table with Laura.

"How did you know who she was?" Laura asked.

Madeline smiled as if to admit that "she" could only be one person. "From your description, and knowing her name. When Max told me that she had been Saundra Simon's protégé, there could be no doubt." She sat silently a moment. "I talked with her yesterday."

Laura looked up at Madeline quickly.

"I was having lunch with Max." Madeline paused while Georgie set their drinks in front of them and walked silently away. "He was telling me about this girl in the show, and he said she was going to join us a little later. Seems he's taken a fancy to her and thought that with my new pull at *Fanfare* I might get a good plug in for both the show and her."

Laura nodded and, with a slightly shaking hand, took a deep swallow of her drink.

"The long arm of coincidence," she mumbled, savoring the harsh taste of the whisky.

"I didn't put two and two together until after she arrived and Max made some comment about Saundra and Ginny." Madeline laughed mirthlessly. "After that, my brain was going like a rampant IBM tabulator."

"And you concocted this little plot?"

"I'm afraid so. I thought the shock would stir you out of this waste of time in bars . . . and here we are."

Laura sat back and said nothing. She looked about the room at the few faceless girls coming in or already seated. Someone fed the jukebox, which glittered hungrily in its corner; an old Frank Sinatra ballad began. Too early for the rock'n'roll crowd, Laura thought.

"What are you going to do?" Madeline asked quietly.

"Probably nothing," Laura answered with a wry smile. "Did you tell her I was in town?"

"I didn't have to. She already knew."

"How do you know?"

"She asked if I knew you." Madeline stared at the lamp on the table, then reached out to straighten the shade.

"Stop playing with that thing, damn it," Laura commanded tersely. "What did you tell her?" She was sorry immediately; she hadn't meant to sound so harsh.

But Madeline accepted Laura's manner with calm understanding. "Only that I had met you," she said gravely. "And that was all. I changed the subject. There was no point in lying about it, was there?"

"No. I suppose not." Laura relaxed again.

"Why don't you call her? I'm sick of looking at you moping around."

"Would it do any good?" Laura signaled to Georgie for another round. "She probably hates me."

"You'll never find out at the rate you're going. If you do still love her, do something about it! Why are you building up such a 'thing' about it?"

"Shut up!" Laura demanded. She desperately wanted to call Ginny, and Madeline's urging didn't help. But Laura was afraid to—afraid of this emotion that Ginny aroused in her. She feared that if she called Ginny, somehow, in some mysterious way, she'd be "hooked" again and this time not able to break away. Laura felt trapped by her own desires—desires she didn't understand, much less control.

Later, Laura looked up and suddenly realized that the bar was full of people. There were several wet ring spots on the table, and Laura realized that she must have been drinking steadily, without thinking or keeping track of the drinks or the time.

Madeline was standing at the bar, talking to a very attractive blonde but keeping her eyes on Laura.

Laura looked at the clock over in the far corner of the bar. It was a quarter of eleven. She felt as if she had been unconscious and was awakening in some alien, bawdy place. But there was Madeline to remind her she was not alone, that she had a friend, someone who cared what happened to her and what went on inside her.

Madeline smiled at the blonde, touched her arm, and, circling the dancing couples, walked back toward Laura.

"How do you feel?" she asked, sitting down carefully.

"All right." Laura tried to clear her head as waves of fuzziness came at her. "Thank you, Madeline. Have I thanked you yet for being so wonderful? Have I?"

"Do you want me to take you home?"

"Be it ever so humble . . . but ours isn't. How come the words and the truth don't agree, Madeline?" She gripped the edge of the table with all her strength. "Yes . . . I want to go home. . . . I may as well . . ."

Laura's voice broke off as she looked over Madeline's shoulder. "Oh, no!" Laura whispered. She shook her head violently and looked again.

"What is it?" Madeline asked with real concern.

"Look . . ."

Madeline turned and sat motionless for a moment. "What's she doing here?"

She glanced at Laura sympathetically, then stood up effortlessly and walked away.

Madeline nodded as she passed Ginny.

Chapter 17

Ginny stood very still and stared at Laura with no visible expression on her face. Then, slowly, she walked to her.

In spite of herself Laura began to shake. She felt as if someone had hooked up her stomach to a vibrator. Her arms and legs were weak. She couldn't take her eyes away from Ginny's, yet she was unable to really look at her.

"May I sit down?" Ginny asked in a low, soft voice.

Laura said nothing, afraid that she would both cry and laugh if she tried to talk. She wished she had not drunk so much.

"I saw you leave the Playhouse," Ginny said. "One of the girls in the show knows you . . . Edie. She said you come here regularly."

Ginny sat down. It seemed to Laura that she had changed in some unfathomable way.

"I just wanted to say hello." Ginny smiled and carefully pushed her hair from her face. "It never occurred to me that you might be in a place like this." She seemed amused.

Laura still said nothing. A confusion of emotion swept over her, paralyzing all response. She had a maddening urge to throw her arms around Ginny, feel her warm, young body, hear Ginny tell her that they would never be apart again. . . . But the amusement in Ginny's voice chilled her, held her in check.

"How are you?" Laura managed to ask finally.

"Fine," Ginny said. "Shouldn't I be?"

Her coolness jolted Laura. The times when Laura had imagined their reunion, she had prepared herself for hurt accusations from Ginny, for tight-lipped fury, for scalding rejection—anything but this blankness, this indifference.

Laura leaned forward, her voice harsh with tension. "Are we going to make conversation like strangers on a train?"

"Are we anything else, really?" Ginny asked.

"We were plenty else!" Laura snapped, the drinks loosening her usual reserve. "Do you know what I've been through staying away from you?"

"Who asked you to?"

"My blind instinct for self-preservation," Laura muttered. "And my fears, my appalling ignorance."

"Perhaps it's just as well," Ginny replied levelly. "This would have been much more difficult if you had really fallen in love with me."

Laura's face seemed to freeze. "Really fallen in love? What in God's name did you think it was I felt for you?"

For an instant, Ginny's face softened. There was a flicker of compassion in her eyes as she raised them and looked directly at Laura.

"Not love, Laura. Not really."

Laura couldn't answer. She had known for some time that this was true. She was not sure just how she felt about Ginny. . . . There was a wild kind of craving to hold her, to breathe her in. Ginny made her feel so goddamn physical.

She must have loved Ginny in a rather special sort of way—certainly not everlasting, but intensely. Even now, with Ginny sitting so near to her, the old feelings . . .

"Besides," Ginny continued, "we got what we wanted from each other."

Laura wanted to ask Ginny what she meant by that, but just then Georgie walked up to the table and picked up the empty glass in front of Laura, depositing a fresh one. She wiped the top of the table with exceptional care, then, without looking at either of them, asked, "You Virginia Adams?"

"Yes."

Georgie gestured toward the bar. "Some dame on the phone for you. Says she's Saundra Simons," Georgie laughed. "I should've told her I was Rudolph Valentino."

Georgie walked away still chuckling, stopping to tell another couple the joke.

Saundra . . . Saundra . . . The name kept repeating in Laura's mind over and over. She could feel rage, hurt, resentment pyramiding inside her.

Ginny stood up slowly, wordlessly, and went to the phone near the bar.

Laura tried desperately to keep calm.

A moment later, Ginny came back and sat down on the edge of the chair. "I have to leave."

"Saundra?" Laura's voice was knife-edged.

Ginny nodded. "It's funny," she said with a slight curl on her lips, "but of all the times Saundra could have made a scene or been jealous of me, the only time she ever really gave any possessive signs was with you in the picture. She was jealous for the first time—of you."

"I'm laughing," Laura commented tightly. She could feel the heat rising inside her, strained to hold back the anger choking in her throat. "Why did you go back, Ginny? Why?"

"Why not?" Ginny answered resignedly. "Sure, I was attracted to you—no point in denying that. As a matter of fact, I felt a lot more for you than I ever did for Saundra. So when you left I was pretty hurt and pretty disappointed. But it was too damned frustrating lugging a torch around—getting circles under my eyes. After all, if I lose my looks, not only would Saundra not want me, but neither would any producer. It sure as hell wasn't any reason to ruin my career, was it? For what? No, Saundra, no career and no you. I just didn't see any point to it."

"So you went crawling back to Saundra? Only Saundra didn't know you'd ever been away; is that it?"

"More or less," Ginny answered. "Does it matter?"

"No. I guess it doesn't." Laura stared at her glass and lapsed into silence.

Ginny gave an irritated cluck. "Well? What would you have thought if I'd done it to you? Run away, I mean."

Laura just shook her head and shrugged.

"Actually," Ginny went on, "I didn't go back to Saundra—that way—for quite a while. It didn't seem to matter much to her at the time. She was on a kick of her own. That's the way it's been with her, anyway—she doesn't care what I do . . . as long as I'm there when she wants me. So I started dating an agent, remembering what you had said about making it on my own."

Numbly, Laura raised the fresh drink to her lips, unable to look at Ginny but listening to her with a kind of morbid fascination.

"The gang used to say he was a great lover and a big promoter. What did I have to lose? He took me to some parties and I got sick of him. Besides, he never did anything for me at all—not even one crummy bit part."

"Sorry I didn't bring my violin," Laura remarked bitterly.

Suddenly, with detached insight, she realized that Ginny was acting.

Watching her now, she wondered if Ginny was capable of just a plain unvarnished emotion—no spotlights, no Academy Awards. She didn't doubt that Ginny had been unhappy in her way, upset even, but she obviously was now milking this scene for all it was worth. She was giving Laura the four-star pitch. Laura's feelings toward Ginny at this point were a mixture of indifference and amused disbelief. She felt like asking, "So what else is new?" but didn't.

"Are you interested, or am I boring you?" Ginny asked sarcastically.

Laura smiled carefully. "Go right ahead," she answered. "This may save me a lot of research when I have to do a write-up on you someday."

"Oh, Laura, don't be this way. Try to see my side just for once. You didn't leave me much choice, you know."

"Go on, I said I'm listening," Laura replied, trying to sound sincere.

"Then I ran into Saundra one day, at one of those crazy parties up on Beechwood Drive. She was apologetic, understanding, charming—you know how she can be."

Laura nodded but found her attention wandering. She kept thinking what a fool she had been to let this girl take such a hold of her life and turn it upside down.

Suddenly she looked up to see that Ginny was watching her with tear-filled eyes. "Laura . . . could we . . . I mean, maybe we could still make it together. I've never forgotten you."

Laura was too startled to answer. Besides, she felt cold inside now, and tired.

"I was so glad," Ginny went on when Laura made no reply, "when Saundra got this chance to do a tour using New York as her base. And then when she got me this part on off-Broadway, I kind of figured I'd run into you again . . . somehow."

Still Laura said nothing. Even Ginny sat quietly now, and the silence between them grew visibly strained. It was amazing how very little they had to say to each other. It must be me, Laura thought, not just her. I'm the one who's changed, hardened. Good! She praised herself, maybe I'll know better next time. Next time what? Next time I fall in love . . .

She looked around the room and wondered how many of the people there were saying the same kind of desperate, hungry lies to cover an unbearable emptiness. She saw Ginny out of the corner of her eye and contemplated what they had been to each other, wondering what they had wanted from each other so urgently.

But it was too much to understand right now, and she searched for Madeline, hoping to draw reassurance from her, some measure of reality. That was it, Laura thought, this scene has no reality—it's just like a book or a movie. It's almost rehearsed.

Just as phony as what she had had with Ginny. It couldn't have been love—it had been too consuming, too sick, for love. It had been a compulsion, a springing loose of long-hidden fears and yearnings twisted and forged together into a mad kind of fascination . . . physical infatuation.

Ginny had been the one to touch the spring, and that was all.

As if out from nowhere Madeline appeared and stood behind Ginny's chair. "Am I intruding?" she asked hesitantly.

Madeline! Laura thought with relief. My better half . . . Then she immediately felt embarrassed, as if she had no right to such a thought. My best friend, she corrected herself.

Ginny twisted in her chair and looked, coldly at first, at Madeline; then her eyes brightened and she smiled. "Oh, hello again, Mrs. Van Norden."

She turned to Laura. "We met yesterday at lunch with Max Geisler. You know, the producer."

Laura cringed inwardly. That familiar, fawning tone of voice, she thought—the hopeful starlet.

Madeline sat down next to Laura. "Why don't you call me Madeline," she suggested.

Laura had a bristling response to Madeline's words. It was so out of keeping with her honest personality. It had that Hollywood quality of "Stick with me, baby, and we'll go places."

Ginny responded energetically to Madeline's presence. She sat forward and leaned on the table with calculated ease and began a conversation about the show she was appearing in, how Max had a great deal of confidence in her and, with lowered eyes, how she hoped she would fulfill his expectations.

Madeline came to her rescue gallantly with reassurances and told her that although she had not seen much of her rehearsal tonight, she thought Ginny showed real talent.

"Of course, I know I still have a lot to learn," Ginny commented with ritual modesty.

"Nothing that some real experience, and a little help, wouldn't take care of," Madeline replied sweetly.

Christ! Laura cursed silently, this isn't an interview! Madeline doesn't have the least intention of giving Ginny any help. Or does she? Suddenly Laura turned and scrutinized Madeline, searching for signs of sincere interest in Ginny's career. She was annoyed and confused by Madeline's behavior. It wasn't like the Madeline she knew, who was considerate, loyal, the Madeline who had kissed her that night long ago to show . . . to show what? This attitude toward Ginny didn't become her at all—it was beneath her! There was an excuse for Ginny. After all, she was looking to get ahead and she didn't care how—her behavior befitted her character.

But there sat Madeline, drinking it all up, playing straight man to Ginny's dialogue. *Don't tell me she's falling for Ginny's line!*

All at once, Saundra loomed over them, cloaked in vengeful wrath. Laura almost laughed, she looked so grotesquely menacing. Like the villain in a comic opera.

Saundra snapped, "Next time you intend to go slumming, Ginny, you might tell me. I don't enjoy having to smoke you out this way!" Saundra's voice was exquisitely acid.

With someone else the situation might have been honestly tragic, but Laura had the distinct impression that Saundra was enjoying herself—that she had summoned to this new role of the injured lover all the counterfeit passion of a summer stock celebrity playing to a packed house of adoring fans. Laura tried to feel resentment at the way Saundra spoke to Ginny, tried to feel protective, but couldn't—not even for old times' sake.

She looked at Madeline instinctively to share this amusing moment. Madeline had settled back in her seat and folded her hands neatly on top of the table. She looked up into Laura's eyes, and very swiftly an expression crossed her face that made it quite clear to Laura: Madeline had expected this meeting, had expected Ginny to show herself for what she was beyond any possible doubt. An impish curl came to Madeline's lips, and Laura was torn between wanting to burst out laughing and punching Madeline in the nose.

Ginny had simply shrugged her shoulders at Saundra's opening sentence. An empty look filled her large eyes, and Laura was appalled as she looked at her.

This is Ginny, she told herself; *this is the girl you once loved . . . the girl for whom you've been drowning your sorrows, the girl that made your flesh tingle whenever you thought of her. . . .*

Saundra glanced down at Laura icily. "I thought I'd find *you* here," she sneered. Her catlike stare had not failed to encompass Madeline. For a moment she seemed puzzled, faintly contemptuous.

Laura momentarily suspected that Saundra and Madeline might know each other, perhaps had met through Max, especially since Saundra's face held a rigid expression of not deigning to acknowledge Madeline. The woman's arrogance was infuriating.

Anger and liquor had robbed Laura of all caution. "What do you want, Saundra?" she heard herself ask. She wasn't quite sure why she bothered, unless it was just because of Saundra's nuisance value, or her own curiosity as to the outcome of this situation.

Saundra threw back her head and laughed coldly. "I think you know the answer to that. Let's not play games."

"Why not? Afraid you won't win this time?" Laura's quiet sarcasm shook Saundra's form-fitting composure ever so slightly.

"You *are* a miserable young snot, aren't you," she rasped.

"You're not so bad yourself," Laura parried.

Saundra stared at her with unblinking eyes.

For a moment Laura had the impression that she was a large, jeweled snake.

"I advise you to stay in your own backyard," the snake hissed softly. "With playmates more suited to your level." Her glance flicked over to Madeline, and the insult was unmistakable.

No one moved.

Saundra laughed maliciously and placed her hand on Ginny's shoulder possessively.

"Mrs. Van Norden is rather well known for her charity among lonely young women," Saundra baited venomously.

"You bitch!" Laura half rose from her chair. She found herself almost hypnotized by Saundra's dazzling viciousness—she could almost see the mechanism of that calculating brain making something sordid out of her relationship with Madeline.

"What would you know about charity, Saundra—or love, either, for that matter?"

"How clever you are." Saundra's reply was like the lash of a whip.

Laura ignored it. "What I might have felt for Ginny has nothing to do with my moving in with Madeline," Laura whispered hoarsely. "What happened between Ginny and me . . ." and suddenly Laura couldn't say anything more.

She could hear Saundra laughing, but she seemed miles away. It seemed to Laura that her brain had been turned inside out. She felt herself sit down, and she looked at Ginny, stared at her, tried to see through her.

But Ginny simply sat there and looked back at her. "You've been living with her ever since you arrived here?" Her tone was edged with reproof.

"There has been nothing between us," Laura said wearily, and felt as if she were lying. "Anyway, it's none of your business."

All at once Laura was struck by the peculiar paradox of her situation. In a way, there had been a great deal between her and Madeline. But nothing physical. It was only that she had needed Madeline, had needed her friendship, her understanding. Nothing more. What more could there have been? Nothing! Goddamn it, nothing!

Ginny stood up slowly. Laura watched her, unmoved. She was so filled with her own emotions that nothing else seemed to matter— she simply had to straighten herself out, had to put things back into some kind of order, some semblance of reality.

Reality. Madeline would give her that; she always had. Madeline could keep her in this world without making it impossible to endure . . .

"And to think that I chased you the way I did," Ginny pouted the way she would over a faulty purchase. "That I offered myself to you again because I thought you would be different, would have learned about yourself—I even kidded myself into thinking you would be everything I'd ever want or need." Tears welled up in her eyes. "You even sat there and let me . . . let me suggest we try again."

"That'll be enough, Ginny!" Laura snapped angrily. She wished to hell that Ginny would shut up and stop making an ass of herself. But that wasn't it, either. It was more that she herself felt like an even bigger ass for once having loved this shell of a human being. She wanted to get away from the sight of Ginny . . . and Saundra. Away from the sickness of it all.

It didn't seem to matter to Ginny that Saundra was there and heard all she said. Ginny sobbed, "All right, then. You keep your affair! I'll keep mine and we'll be square. But can't we see each other once in a while? Can't . . ."

"Oh, Christ!" Laura cursed aloud. "All of a sudden I'm the most wonderful thing that ever happened to you. How come? We'll double-date, Ginny. All right? On all the legal holidays—just the four of us."

"But, Laura . . ."

"But what?" Laura asked without expecting an answer. She stood up and hastily put on her coat, motioning to Madeline to do the same. It didn't occur to her to inquire if Madeline wanted to leave or not—she was leaving and that automatically meant that Madeline would leave, too.

She roughly pushed Madeline in front of her, and they exited, leaving Saundra and Ginny to complete their little drama alone.

Laura experienced an inexplicable sense of relief, as if a great, pressing weight had somehow been lifted from her. She no longer had to feel guilty for having run away, or think that she'd genuinely hurt Ginny. And she was no longer burdened with her love for Ginny.

There was a kind of justice in what had transpired. Laura had the fatalistic sensation that life had evened itself out. She was certain now that Saundra and Ginny deserved each other in some neurotic way. Saundra talked of love as if it were chattel to be bargained for—bought and sold and bought again. And Ginny made it sound like a necessary evil—a sexual and economic convenience that would last until the next conquest, a new sponsor for her aspirations and random passions.

She glanced over at Madeline, walking beside her. The look of concern and unhappiness on her face surprised Laura. It's been a rough night for her too, she thought, suddenly stricken with the cruelty of her own self-absorption. But she found Madeline's pained look oddly pleasing.

Let her suffer a little, Laura thought with a trace of sadism.

She wasn't sure why she wanted Madeline to suffer at all, unless it was because Laura believed that she had known all along that Laura's "torch" had been in vain, that what Laura had been going through was not really the agonies of denied love.

They walked silently and slowly. It was almost as if they would lose something if they walked too quickly or arrived too soon at the apartment. Something that was hanging, waiting to be said or understood . . . Something Laura was convinced she knew but couldn't think clearly enough to force into the open.

Arriving at the apartment, they entered wordlessly.

At last, Madeline broke the long silence.

"I'm sorry, Laura. Really sorry." Her voice was low and tender.

"Why?" Laura asked abruptly.

"If . . . if Ginny hadn't thought that there had been something between us, you might have . . . won her." Madeline said it as if there were no other way to describe Ginny.

Laura shook her head. "You might still," Madeline continued to soothe. "You could call her later, after . . . things cool off a little. . . ."

"But I don't want to," Laura interrupted vehemently. "Not now, not later . . . not ever!"

Madeline sat down and stared at Laura. "What do you mean? After all these weeks of . . . of denying yourself your big chance at happiness, and you don't want it any more?"

Laura turned and looked at Madeline, appraised her as if really seeing her for the first time.

"That's right."

"But . . ." Madeline protested.

Laura grinned. "All I want to know is how long you've known."

"Known? Known what?"

Laura didn't answer at once—she was glimpsing now what it was she had felt on the way home and had been unable to mask. "How long have you known that my torch had gone out?"

"Oh . . . that!" Madeline said. It seemed to Laura that she sounded both disappointed and relieved. "Does it matter, Laura?"

"Not really," Laura answered honestly. "Did you arrange for us all to meet tonight?"

"Of course not," Madeline replied indignantly. Then she laughed. "But the idea did occur to me."

Laura walked over to where Madeline sat, and perched on the arm of her chair. She could feel Madeline tense up. But she offered no comfort; she was enjoying her moment of revenge, of having Madeline in the position that Laura herself had occupied so many times herself.

"There is something else I'd like to know," she said with a half-amused tone, despite the fact that she was actually very serious and felt strangely elated.

Madeline didn't move, didn't even raise her head to look at Laura. "What's that?" she asked in a whisper.

"How long you've known that I would fall in love with you."

Laura's voice was low, and she could feel her temples throbbing. She leaned close toward Madeline, feeling her warmth and drawing a secure kind of comfort from it—a feeling of complete naturalness.

Calm, poised Madeline looked up with moist eyes. "I didn't know . . ." she said tightly. "I only hoped. Oh, God! How I hoped."

"And now—what happens now?"

"What do you want to happen now, Laura?"

She looked hard into Madeline's dark, questioning eyes. The love she saw there was so undemanding, so real and simple, that Laura felt herself filled, tranquilized with trust and security.

She took Madeline's face into her hands and kissed her forehead gently, then her eyes and the tip of her nose. "I'm going to let myself go and love you—and never lose you."

Laura touched her cheek to Madeline's, then reached for the slim, vibrant body. She could feel their bodies merge, their hearts pounding against each other. Their flesh leaped with the excitement that charged through them, intermingling.

Laura clung to her—motionless, savoring the painful sweetness.

"Are you going to kiss me, or are you going to torture me to death?" Madeline asked huskily.

"Both," whispered Laura.

She pulled Madeline's warm searching mouth to hers. The shock of pleasure was almost unbearable. All consciousness was blotted out in that first drowning moment.

The last thing Laura remembered before she went under was thinking how wonderful it was not to feel guilty anymore—or unwanted . . . or strange.

She was where she wanted to be at last.

She was home.

Love Is Where You Find It

Chapter 1

The late-afternoon sun sent shadows over the water, sprinkling it with glistening lights as the current passed under the East River Bridge to her left, sharp and clear.

Dee Sanders gazed absently through the grease-smudged window of the New Haven train as it crossed the trestle paralleling the Third Avenue Bridge.

It's just one of those days made for camera fiends, she thought, and silently cursed having left her Leica at the office. At least, she wouldn't have to go back anymore today. It was already past five, and she couldn't bear the thought of entering the massive Photo World building again. The July heat really didn't bother her nearly so much as the constant temperature changes from air-conditioned buildings to the steaming, soft tar streets and oppressive wind-blocking structures. She would just get used to one climate when she would have to enter another and feel like a human thermometer with berserk mercury.

Automatically she calculated that 150 at f:4 ought to do the trick, then gave a fatalistic shrug as the train took her into the rich, dark shadows of the approach to the 125th Street platform, throwing her mental reading completely out of kilter.

She caught a glimpse of herself in the window and was, as usual, surprised to realize it was she. So often she would suddenly see an attractive woman walking or sitting opposite her, with the uneasy feeling that she knew this person from someplace. It was a split-second reaction—and just as quickly she would realize it was her own image in a mirror. These were about the only times Dee ever blushed, when she had done or thought something utterly foolish or inane. After all, she had lived with herself for a long time and was generally aware of the fact that she was a carefully chic woman, her short brown hair brushed back from her face showing to advantage the strong line of her chin and the dramatic effect of her slim, arched nose.

With a start she glanced around to be sure no one had noticed her looking at herself; then she concentrated on watching the little milling knots on the platform thread out into lines of people getting off and on the train. Like automatons, she thought. Mindless like the armies of ants who moved about busily, pushed by instinct or nature, or whatever you wanted to call that mysterious force from which all life was drawn. Driven, she decided, recalling the line of a poem written by one of her college classmates years before: ". . . to their own extinction unaware."

Like me, like all of us, she mused bitterly.

Somehow trains always reminded her of the transiency and anonymity of life. They depressed her and she hated them. The chill of gloomy observation began to settle down over her mind like a mist. She tried to dispel it by focusing her attention elsewhere and found herself staring into the amused eyes of a young man standing just below her window. He winked at her, grinning broadly, and even though the bold invitation in his expression was unmistakable, she felt a sudden glow of pleasure.

My hard-lived twenty-seven years can't show too much if the boys are still winking, she thought. But she turned her head away with deliberate hauteur, feeling slightly guilty at having enjoyed the attention. It was exactly the sort of sly, flirtatious behavior that was so typical of Rita. The kind of thing that aroused her senseless jealousy and laid the groundwork for so many savage and futile quarrels.

Ah, Rita, she thought. That beautiful, impossible bitch.

There was a long squeak followed by a series of clanks and metallic groans, and the train began to move slowly forward.

She settled back in her seat and closed her eyes. Clear sailing now until Grand Central—unless the gods of New Haven decreed otherwise and there would be one of those frustrating halts in the tunnel. Well, she'd just not think about it. No use inviting trouble.

But as the train began to gather speed and move swiftly onward, her spirits lifted. A few minutes more, a quick walk up the ramp at Grand Central, then a cab, and finally . . . home.

It sounded good. She hoped she would get there before Rita. A few moments of peace and quiet was what she needed. For some inexplicable reason the thought of Rita made her feel uneasy again. Dee had to admit that her feelings about Rita had been growing increasingly confused. And this particular day was always trying. This was Rita's day to do the rounds of the agencies for work. She devoted one day a week to the ritual and spent the rest of the time recuperating and getting ready for the next assault.

It began to annoy Dee that Rita was so casual about accepting Dee's financial support. As though it were her due. Almost a kind of payment for the pleasure her beauty allowed Dee to experience.

Now, that's unfair, Dee scolded herself sharply. Rita loves me, and I love her. And their arrangement was perfectly natural under the circumstances. Or was it?

Dee's mood of confusion deepened. Part of her was so eager for Rita's embrace—eager to respond, to feel close and comfortable. But the other part. The other part longed desperately for time to be alone. How wonderful it would be if just one night she could be alone so that she could give herself up to her own thoughts, not have to keep Rita amused or be dragged against her will to one of those damned, noisy Village bars.

I should rent a place in the Village and save on cab fare, Dee contemplated without meaning it. Now, just stop it, she commanded, you're not starving anymore. You can afford it. It doesn't look right for one of New York's best-paid staff photographers to be so damn cheap. My, my. Look at the big conformist, she laughed mirthlessly to herself.

After a long, drawn-out halt, Dee mechanically left the train and walked with the crowd down the cement walkway, careful not to let anyone push her too close to the side, where she might fall. She wondered briefly if the train felt as relieved as she did.

Once outside, the early evening was too lovely to waste in a cab, and she began walking across Forty-third Street to Madison Avenue and uptown. The Empire State Building, proud and glittering, loomed over the city like a huge bird hatching her eggs.

Dee looked at it enviously, thinking that at least that huge hunk of steel, stone, glass and wires was closer to being a mother than she was . . . or probably ever would be.

This futile pondering left her so weary that at Fiftieth Street she gave up and took a cab to her apartment, even though it was only another six blocks up and one and a half blocks east.

She tipped the driver and climbed the five steps to the double red doors. The brass knob, polished as usual, and the gleaming windows—which had recently had their protective iron grill work painted a neat black—restored some of her usual optimistic disposition.

Her apartment was the only one on the floor, and the only one in the building with a yowling Siamese cat every time she came near it. "Hello, Cho-Cho," she whispered, and pushed her gently out of the doorway with her foot. "Anybody home?"

Cho-Cho-San glanced with imperial disdain, clearly indicating that as long as she was there, who else would Dee want. She raced in front of Dee into the bedroom on the first landing and leaped onto the king-size double bed to watch the routine of coming home from work. It didn't take Dee long to change into her slacks and blouse, and she quickly washed off the makeup from her face so as to let the air get into her pores.

She picked up her briefcase and carried it downstairs to the large living room, glancing briefly at Rita's potted plants on the windowsill overlooking their private garden-patio beyond. It *was* good to be home. Quiet. She stared a moment at the charred and dead fireplace and wondered if Rita had called the superintendent about getting a chimney sweep as she had asked. It would be fall soon, and Dee hated to wait until the last minute to do things. She wanted everything possible ready and waiting, or discarded.

Cho-Cho had situated herself—not lying nor sitting, but situated—in front of the low, dark oak cabinet that served as a room divider to the dining-kitchen area and also as a bar. Dee laughed aloud and crossed over to the cat, who was busily scratching her ear with her bare foot. "All right, Cho-Cho. A little one for you, too."

Dee poured a jigger of Scotch into a small dish for the cat and a healthy drink for herself.

"Hello, down there, anybody home?" Rita's familiar voice called down the staircase.

"Hi, darling. Just got in myself. Come down and keep me from feeling like a dipso, will you?" She anxiously waited for Rita to walk down the stairs and for that moment when her breath would catch, simply because Rita was so beautiful.

Rita had a way of walking down a staircase that made you think she was on an escalator. She didn't walk—she moved, her supple young body carrying her head like a priceless treasure.

Rita threw her bag and gloves on the chair by the bar and smiled sweetly to Dee. "I'd love a drink, thanks."

"It'll cost you a kiss," Dee said, playfully putting her arms around Rita, gently.

"Not now, darling." Rita pulled away. "I'm all sticky."

"I don't care. . . ."

"Now, darling, please," Rita said more firmly. "If you'd put on some lipstick you wouldn't feel so butch," she added with a falsely light voice.

"Sorry," Dee said, quickly bringing her hand to her mouth. The belittlement had killed any desire on her part. She brought Rita the already prepared drink and sat down on the long couch opposite the fireplace. "How was your day?"

Rita sighed dramatically. "The usual. Don't call us. We'll call you." She threw off her shoes and rubbed her feet. "Jesus! But it was hot today. Of course, you wouldn't know, being in an air-conditioned office, sitting on your behind. You really should get some exercise, darling. You'll get fat."

Dee ignored the bait. "Oh, I was out today. Had to go up to White Plains on business. It's like another world up there."

"Well, at least you get out once in a while . . . more than I get. I

155

hate New York in the summer. Why couldn't we go away for a month or so?"

"I work. Remember?"

"Is that a dig at me?" Rita's eyes narrowed and her voice became tight.

"No. It's not. Come on, let's not let the heat get us into an argument. We've both had a bad day and now we're home. Shall we forget about it?" Dee took a long swallow of her drink and hoped her tone had not been too conciliatory. Her eye landed on the fireplace again, but she caught herself just in time before asking Rita about the chimney sweep. It didn't seem a very prudent time in the event she hadn't called.

"What are you doing tonight?" Dee asked without thinking. "I mean, will you be home or do you have a business engagement?" In spite of herself, there was a note of sarcasm in her tone.

"I have a 'business engagement,' as you so tactfully put it. My hours aren't nine to five, you know. Job hunting doesn't give me that leisure."

"Honey," Dee said carefully, "it's not my fault you're not working. Please don't take it out on me."

"Well . . . you make everything sound so . . . so immoral."

If the shoe fits, wear it, honey, Dee thought, but said aloud, "I just miss you, that's all."

"Ha! When I am home you coop yourself up in that silly black room . . ."

"Darkroom," Dee amended.

". . . and I sit out here all by myself. Or how about all the time you spend working late?" Rita snorted. "At the office, dear," she mimicked. "I'd like to see what kind of work you do at the office."

"You're bound and determined to have an argument aren't you? If I said it was a sunny day, you'd argue that it looked like rain. All right, Rita. Let's fight."

"Quit the condescension," rasped Rita. "Maybe I didn't go to college, but I'm just as clever as you are."

Dee watched her, fascinated. Anger made Rita's eyes shine and her being so terribly vital that Dee was helpless against such loveliness, and the fury drained out of her. She looked at Rita with sudden tenderness and resignation.

"Cleverer," Dee said with a light smile. "I'm intelligent . . . but you're clever."

"What's that supposed to mean?"

"It means I love you—no matter how much you want to fight."

Rita tensed for a moment and then relaxed. She came over to Dee and sat in her lap. "I'm sorry," she murmured. "I've been acting like a real bitch. Forgive me?"

"Don't I always?"

Rita giggled. "Meaning I'm always a bitch?"

"That's why I love you."

"You're terrible . . . but kiss me anyway."

Chapter 2

It was late. Dee had been working steadily since dinner. She stretched, feeling happy and fulfilled despite the tight ache of her muscles. She pulled off her yellow rubber gloves, now stained with chemicals, stared at the neat row of capped brown bottles as if they were an alien army frozen into immobility, then slowly rubbed the small of her back.

Yawning lightly, she removed the roll of film from the developing reel carefully and, having placed a clamp at one end and a weighted clamp at the other, deftly dried the negative roll with the squeegee. It was the fourth roll of 620 she had developed tonight. No wonder she was tired.

Dee glanced at the stopwatch she kept on a pushpin in the converted darkroom, and then remembered she had changed the time to twelve o'clock for the sake of convenience.

Rita had given her the watch on their first anniversary. How long now? Going on four years . . . no, going on three. It was hard to tell—so much had happened and yet so little. Dee almost smiled, wondering if other people had the same feeling about their lives. Probably not. Most people were normal.

She hung the negatives up to dry and walked through the kitchen into the living room to switch on the radio. WPAT was already off the air; that meant it must be past three in the morning.

"Where is that child?" Dee muttered to herself, half in concern and half in anger.

Impatiently, Dee turned the dial on her FM tuner, trying to find something besides Lawrence Welk or the news. Finally, she simply turned the damn thing off, too irritable and tired to bother with putting on records.

She glanced around the room from habit, looking for dirty ashtrays. . . . Rita couldn't stand dirty ashtrays. And the condition Rita would probably be in when she came home would not be a tolerant one—it seldom was. Alcohol merely aggravated Rita's normal hostility.

Dee walked back into the small, compact kitchen and put the kettle on for tea. Somehow the idea of more coffee at that hour of the morning wasn't appetizing. She leaned against the drainboard and stretched again. Without looking she knew the sudden weight on her foot was Cho-Cho-San. Dee leaned over and scratched Cho-Cho behind her ear and under her collar, taking equal pleasure from the animal's diesel-like purring. "Silly, no-good, crummy cat," she said aloud and pulled her whiskers gently.

Cho-Cho's eyes blinked open, revealing round blue eyes full of mock scorn, then squinted as she yawned and feigned indifference.

"Where's your stepmother, Cho-Cho? Hmm?"

The cat raised herself elegantly and leaned against Dee's ankle.

Cho-Cho's ears went forward as the key on the latch sounded faintly downstairs while Rita obviously fumbled to fit it into the keyhole. Without hesitation, Cho-Cho bounded around the kitchen, through the living room, and up the stairs to the first floor and the front door, meowing as she went.

"Fickle creature," Dee chuckled. Well, guess my errant wife is home, Dee thought wryly. Errant husband? Errant wife!

The door opened as Dee poured the boiling water into her special cup, unanticipated anger swelling in her as she heard Rita thump against the open door.

A man's muffled voice drifted down to her. "It was fun, baby, really great."

A long silence. Then a soft moan from Rita. "Call me again . . . soon?" she heard Rita purr. Another long silence.

She stirred the sugar into her tea, her hands trembling slightly. Cho-Cho walked indolently back into the kitchen and crumpled on Dee's foot again.

Male and female murmurings for a minute or two more, and then the front door closed just loudly enough not to be considered "sneaking in."

Dee heard Rita's footsteps overhead in their bedroom, a closet door open and shut, a heavy sigh, and then the stocking-footed steps on the staircase.

"Darling?" Rita called softly. "Are you down there?"

Sure, Dee was tempted to reply, me and five Village dykes having an orgy. Sorry you missed it. "Yes," she said instead, her voice taut. "Having some tea. Want some?"

"No, thanks," Rita replied, and cautiously came up to Dee and encircled her around the waist from behind. She kissed the back of Dee's neck slowly.

"Cut it out," Dee ordered tightly. She couldn't stand to have Rita touch her after she'd been out on one of her dates. Nonetheless, she felt her blood rush to her temples, and an uncontrollable thrill through her body.

"You're so old-fashioned, darling." Rita pouted.

She preceded Dee into the living room, dropping into the easy chair she and Cho-Cho shared.

"Your hair is mussed and your lipstick is smeared," Dee said quietly. She sat down again opposite her on the sofa facing the fireplace.

"So what?" Rita said in a bored tone, but fussed with her shoulder-length black hair just the same. Automatically, she pressed her lips together in an effort to spread evenly what was left of her lipstick. "Really, Dee! You'd think I was going to bed with this guy, or something. You know it's just business."

"There's a name for *that* kind of business," Dee said harshly.

"You mean *whoring*?" Rita laughed. "And I suppose you don't? You've kissed plenty of asses to get where you are, and don't you forget it. Fat lot of nerve you've got calling me names."

"At least you're eating and warm because of it."

"There's all kinds of whoring," Rita said, reaching down to pick up Cho-Cho. "I suppose you think I enjoy dating these guys," Rita went on nuzzling the cat.

"I don't care whether you do or not—although I know damn well you do—but you don't have to stand in the hall necking with each and every one of them."

"Necking!" Rita snorted. "What's to neck? It's not as if I meant it or told them I loved them. It's *business.*"

It wouldn't have done any good to try to explain to Rita how she felt about their relationship. Rita could never understand Dee's feeling about being as much as "married"—that she loathed the idea of anyone else pawing Rita, taking her lips, even just holding her so that they, too, knew the wild hunger of wanting Rita's body. "How long have you been looking for a job?" Dee asked as calmly as she could.

"Why are we going into that now?" Rita countered, pretending heavy-lidded fogginess. "Which of my careers do you refer to—my modeling or my singing?"

"Careers! Plural?" Dee couldn't help laughing. "For a girl who hasn't worked in over a year, you're pretty lax with the language."

"You're beginning to bore me, darling." Rita's tone grew brittle.

"Pity," Dee replied levelly. "If you didn't enjoy dating these hoodlums, you'd be able to see that all your charms are getting you exactly nowhere."

"Hoodlums! They're agents, or executive producers."

"That little runt you were out with day before yesterday was right out of a Mafia movie."

"Oh, is that so! Well, for your information, he just happens to be the brother-in-law of one of Broadway's most influential personalities!"

"The sewer inspector, no doubt . . ."

Rita's lavender eyes flashed for an instant, and her face blanched with rage. Then, just as swiftly, her expression softened and the trace of a smile came to her lips as she pushed the cat off her lap and crossed over to where Dee sat. "Let's not argue. Please, Dee. Would you rather I took a job as an elevator operator somewhere?"

Dee stiffened imperceptibly, fearing the moment when Rita would bend forward and her perfume would wilt away all of her resolve. Yet her tone softened despite herself. "You know it's not the money, Rita. . . ."

"I know, baby," she said in that intimate voice she saved for moments like this, "but it's not easy to break in—you know that."

She leaned over and nuzzled her head against the nape of Dee's neck, letting her lips wander softly against her smooth skin.

Dee felt her hands go weak and a plaguing urgency creep into her lower abdomen. She half turned and pulled Rita over almost onto her lap, then clasped her head with her now hot hands. "You are beautiful, goddamn you."

"Of course, sweetie . . . but only to you."

Dee knew Rita didn't believe that for a moment, but didn't feel like arguing the point now. She watched Rita close her eyes in anticipation of her kiss, and the knowledge that this beautiful girl was not only willing but asking for her kiss sent a shiver of desire through Dee she could not dismiss. But still she could not let her anger go so quickly. "Do they kiss you like this, Rita?"

She savagely pushed her teeth against Rita's mouth, sinking into its softness with cruel passion. "Or like this . . . ?" she asked, catching Rita's full lips into her own and softly pulling at them. "Or like this . . . ?" She plied her tongue into her mouth as if savoring the rarest forbidden fruit.

Rita became tense immediately but could not pull out of Dee's grasp. Dee felt herself losing control of her emotions—anger became rage and rage became fury. Rita's eyes opened and she stared with fear into Dee's cold, smiling expression.

"Don't worry," Dee mouthed against Rita's lips, "I won't hurt your precious face. . . . I don't have the guts."

She pushed Rita over more and, placing all her weight on top of her, held her with a strength she didn't know she possessed. "Tell me about the men you date for 'business,' Rita. Tell me about how you hate their kisses. Come on, my little lover, you can tell me. I'm your soul mate, your spiritual companion—understanding, considerate, loving . . . "

"Nothing! Nothing!" Rita choked in fright. "They never touched me—ever!"

"You don't expect me to believe that when I can hear you time after time cooing at the door, letting their sloppy mouths run all over your face . . ."

"All right!" Rita screamed. "All right, you bitch! You want the truth?" Her body struggled against Dee's and finally threw her off balance.

"You're goddamn right I've gone to bed with some of them. Lots of them. Why not? Do you think I'm like you? Women aren't enough for me! *You're* not enough for me! I need men and I need their bodies and I need their attention. You think you can coop up someone with my looks in this apartment night after night?" Her eyes narrowed to pencil lines across her face. "And I'll tell you something, darling, I enjoyed every friggin' minute!"

The room was silent with deadly stillness except for Rita's hands rubbing her bruised wrists.

Dee let her head fall into her hands with such abject self-loathing, she couldn't look at Rita. She had never in her life felt such violent rage or allowed herself to behave so cruelly—in fact, it was almost as if she had not done this at all. Someone else had this sadistic streak, not Dee Sanders. Not the cool, self-possessed, kind and compassionate Mrs. Sanders to whom everyone came with their problems and whom they thought of as such a good-natured, affable gal—a woman of talent, breeding, and character.

"Oh, Christ," Dee moaned. "Rita . . ."

"Save it!"

"No . . . I want to tell you. . . . I don't know what came over me." She was sick with rage and jealousy. "I love you. . . ."

Suddenly, Rita came over to her and kneeled in front of her, kissing her lightly on her forehead and eyes. "I know, darling; I know. Don't torture yourself . . . you didn't mean it." She laughed lightly, and her eyes became purpled with sudden passion. "It's not as if you'd done this before . . ."

"I swear to you it'll never happen again, Rita. I swear it."

She pulled Dee's head to her breast and rocked gently. "Shh. I had it coming. I forget how hard it must be for you, waiting for me, not knowing . . ."

"I don't want to know, Rita. Don't tell me. Don't talk about it. Not now." She pressed her face closer to Rita's breasts, letting their warmth pass into her flesh, the contact draining her of any other thought.

"I love you, too, darling. I love you. . . ."

They clung to each other like frightened children in a witch-haunted fairy tale, like Hansel and Gretel. Dee wished to God she could forget that Rita was not always like this—close, sweet, womanly. They had good moments—rich moments filled with love and tenderness; precious moments with such complete understanding that Dee would almost cry with gratitude.

But not enough of them. Never enough.

"I had no right," Dee went on mumbling. "There was no excuse . . . *could* be no excuse for such sick violence no matter what you or anyone had ever done. It's just that I needed you so badly tonight. . . ."

"I'm here, darling; I'm here. Shh. It's all right. I belong to you. . . . You can do anything you want. As long as you let me stay with you—don't send me away."

"Away?" Dee smiled. "I couldn't. It would be like sentencing myself to hell. . . ."

Rita lifted Dee's head and gently laid her back on the couch. Slowly she began unbuttoning her blouse and looked into Dee's eyes with such desire that Dee felt she would burst. She sat down next to Dee, letting her hands touch her everywhere.

"Take my bra off, darling," she whispered. "You take it off as if you were discovering me for the first time. . . ."

"Christ," Dee said to herself. "Oh, Christ . . ."

Chapter 3

D on't open your eyes and you won't wake up, Dee thought. She
wanted to enjoy a leisurely Saturday morning for a change.
She tried not to think about the three undeveloped rolls of film in
the refrigerator, almost calling for her to get up. With a small sigh
of desperation, she rolled over and curled around Rita's warm flesh.
Rita slept nude no matter what the season.

But it was too hot to stay in bed. Heat prickles were already beginning up her back. Besides, there was that damned film. Actually,
she was pretty excited about it—a new formula for direct positives
she'd read about recently. But to avoid any possible arguments with
Rita she had said it was work for the office. Well, trying out new
methods was part of her job, wasn't it?

It was apparent from the beginning that Rita strongly resented
anything that took Dee's attention away from her. Even if they
weren't talking or really going to do anything, she just wanted Dee
there—on call. Particularly, Rita resented the time Dee spent in the
darkroom. It was an alien world to her and one which she had no
wish to learn about.

At first, Dee had been only too glad to surrender unconditionally
to the passion of their love. But she had to have an interest outside
of this; she couldn't go on and on, night after night, staring limpid-

eyed by candlelight into Rita's eyes. No one could—not constantly. She had her job and had to work hard at it—and her job was really her way of life because she loved it. But photography took time.

After almost a year of arguments about the time Dee spent working at home, she finally gave up and simply began staying late at the office.

Finally, Rita lost her job—or so she said—as a fashion model at one of the private, select dress shops on East 58th Street. Seemingly she couldn't work anywhere else except maybe a one-shot job here or there. She complained bitterly about being lonely and bored but didn't seem to want to do anything; she couldn't concentrate on a book, and the idea of school was evidently too humorous even to consider.

It was then Rita decided to pursue a singing career. She began taking lessons from some gin-soaked ex-opera star in the Village, a self-anointed genius who swore that without her the birds would only croak. Ever since then, Rita had been awaiting her "break" and making the agency rounds.

Strange, Dee half smiled, how lives twist and turn, emotions change, and attitudes shift without conscious awareness. She could not honestly say that her present resentment against Rita was really justified—perhaps it was she who had changed. . . . Or perhaps it was just that time had changed her more than Rita. Only now was she really aware of how much the physical had blinded her to their basic incompatibility, how the excitement of the moment had blurred the narrowness of their relationship. How dangerously she had misjudged the quality of Rita's attention. Rita's possessiveness had become suffocating.

Even so, Rita was the greater victim of this. Dee knew how deep and terrifying the fears and insecurities were that drove the girl to such destructive behavior.

Poor Rita . . .

With a sudden tender moment she bent down and brushed her lips against Rita's warm neck.

"Umm." Rita turned slightly and pulled away from her.

"Don't blame you," Dee whispered opening one eye into the shaded room. She sat up slowly, careful not to wake Rita, who liked to sleep late. The clock on the bed stand read nine. The heat had become more oppressive. Like an oven already, she thought, putting on her slippers. "Cremation: For Fun and Profit," she muttered aloud.

"What? What did you say?" Rita asked sleepily.

"Nothing, honey. Go back to sleep."

"Jesus! Must be dawn . . . it's so hot . . . Please try to be more quiet. . . ." She turned over onto her stomach, and her breathing became heavier and slower.

Must be quiet, must be quiet, Dee thought with mock anger. Stop that noise up there! She crept into the bathroom, dressed, and went downstairs to feed Cho-Cho and treat herself to her morning coffee.

She set to work in the converted downstairs bathroom and soon lost track of time. She coveted these precious hours alone with the challenge and excitement, which she had never lost over the years.

Later, as she was in the final stages of washing the last roll, she heard the kettle bang on the stove loudly.

"How long you been in there?" Rita called, her voice still husky with sleep.

"Morning, sunshine," Dee tried to make her voice sound cheerful and bright.

"Christ!" Rita's petulant tone scratched at Dee's taut nerves. "It's past one. You can at least come out and have coffee with me—if it isn't too inconvenient."

Dee's hands shook slightly as she held the hose inside the tank and kept an eye on the watch. "Ah . . . sure, honey," she said lightly. "Just a couple minutes and I'll be through. Okay?"

"I guess so. What difference would it make?"

Dee could hear Rita's furry slippers shuffle across the tile floor to the round table near the divider. "Good morning, Cho-Cho, baby. Come here, sweetie . . . *you* keep me company."

Good God! Dee cursed silently, but went on washing the film.

"I hope you didn't forget the party tonight," Rita yelled accusingly.

"No . . . 'course not! Babs's place, isn't it?" She threw in the name just to prove she hadn't forgotten.

"I'm not going to yell at you all morning. Come out here and talk."

Dee placed the clamps and hung the negatives from the line over the three-quarter tub. She quickly washed her hands and, still drying them, entered the kitchen and sat down.

"No kiss?"

"Sorry." Dee stood up again, performed the duty, then put the kettle on again and prepared her coffee.

"Get any interesting pictures?" Rita asked after a moment.

Dee nodded and smiled. It was Rita's way of apologizing for being so cranky. "A few. What time are we expected tonight?"

"Around eight, but I think it's silly to show up before ten. Everyone's so dull before they've had enough to drink. You know, if it hadn't been for me, all of Babs's parties would've been a flop. The way they all just sit around like friendly strangers—no action, no life."

"They all like to hear you sing, honey." Dee hoped she'd said the right thing.

"What about you?" Rita pouted playfully.

"I like anything you do."

Rita patted her hand across the table. "You're sweet."

Something in her tone embarrassed Dee, but she managed a modest smile nonetheless. "I was thinking about just the two of us going out for dinner tonight," she offered without having thought of it at all. "Someplace cozy in the Village, maybe."

"Wonderful. Could we go to Dino's? Oh, please, darling. Could we?"

That did it, Dee said to herself. There was only one other thing that melted her besides Rita's physical nearness, and that was her exuberant little-girl side. It undid her; that was a better description. "Is that the new place that just opened?" She tried to sound offhand, but her voice betrayed her consent.

"New place, old place—new management, new decor but the same crowd. It's mixed, so we won't really have to worry about being 'seen' there. Lots of off-Broadway people go there—you know the crowd. It would be such a wonderful thing to gloat over at Babs's later."

"Of course we can," Dee said. She had never been able to really understand or break Rita of the habit of having to gloat before her friends. She realized that it was probably a hangover from Rita's childhood. No wonder Rita coveted luxury and all things that meant status and prestige.

She'd driven by Rita's former home with her once. It was on a main truck route in New Jersey—dismal, depressing, and heavy with the odor of nearby factories. Her parents had died since then. Strange. Rita had often said they hated each other, but when her mother died it was only very shortly thereafter that her father died. No will to live, the doctor had said, plus a bad heart.

"Let me fix you some breakfast, darling," Rita said, jumping up with enthusiasm. She hummed softly as she pulled the bacon out of the refrigerator and broke the eggs into a shallow blue bowl. Suddenly, she turned, holding her wet hands up like a surgeon. "I do love you, Dee. Don't pay any attention to me when I'm bitchy. Just remember that I love you."

She walked over and kissed Dee gently on the mouth.

"I love you, too," said Dee, but she wondered silently, how can I not pay any attention to your moods, darling? All the compassion and understanding in the world doesn't make a situation any easier or more pleasant. A sharp, smokey aroma of burning food broke through her thoughts. "The bacon!" she cried aloud in dismay.

They laughed together and, after rescuing the imperiled breakfast, sat down to discuss what they would do and what they would wear that night. The afternoon passed swiftly, and they were delighted with each other. No arguments. Today Dee genuinely wanted to look dewy-eyed, into Rita's eyes. Today she could.

Dinner was good. The atmosphere was romantic. Time just seemed to evaporate. Before they knew it, Dee was following Rita into the elevator in the apartment on Seventy-eighth Street and West End, pushing the button for the fifth floor.

The muffled, discordant sounds of a party drifted through the door of the apartment. Dee hoped desperately she might meet someone to talk to at least. Babs's get-togethers were usually party-packed with assorted little swishes bustling, and a garden variety of bull dykes who looked as though they had just parked their trucks outside. Occasionally, Babs would invite some interesting-looking woman, and Dee would experience a flickering hope for salvation. But either Rita would manage to make the woman so uncomfortable she wouldn't talk to Dee, or the intelligent appearance was deceiving, and upon closer observation Dee would only encounter the nearsighted frown of some illiterate lovely too vain to wear glasses.

"Hi, kids, come on in. We'd about given you up." A short, dark girl—Babs's latest love—let them in as Babs herself came toward them, lumbering with her easy, boyish gait.

She shook hands firmly with Dee and then placed her arm around Rita's shoulder. "Okay, everybody, here they are. Dee . . . and Rita."

Some heads turned, nodding briefly, but most of the guests were too preoccupied with their drinks or their own trick for the evening.

"Sorry we're so late," Dee began in apologetic greeting.

"We were having such a divine time at Dino's," Rita interrupted, her voice shrill with forced gaiety. "The new place, you know. We just forgot what time it was."

Well, she got it in, Dee thought wryly. She watched a scrawny young man come swooping toward them. "Isn't she gorgeous! Do introduce me, Babs; I want her to tell me *all* her beauty secrets."

Babs roared with laughter, Rita tittered modestly, and Dee wished she were in her darkroom again. Rita waved merrily to a sallow-faced young girl at the other end of the room and glided toward her while the young man followed her with a frighteningly accurate imitation.

Babs slapped Dee lightly on the back. "Drive me nuts if I had to live with someone as beautiful as Rita."

"You get used to it." Dee smiled.

"Say, I'm glad you're here. One of the gals brought a friend from out of town and she's been sitting like a turtle all evening. Seems nice enough, but she won't talk to anyone. Would you help me out and see what you can do? Ask her to dance, or something? I'm a decorator, not a diplomat."

"Which one?" Dee asked warily.

Chapter 4

Babs nodded toward an imposing-looking woman who was somewhere between forty and forty-five. Or, as Dee guessed wryly—a very beat thirty-five or a well-preserved fifty. Hard to tell in this era of highly touted beauty aids, when even your hairdresser doesn't know. The woman looked up suddenly, and in that one unguarded moment Dee caught such an expression of loneliness and defeat that she turned away in embarrassment. She felt like an eavesdropper in a confessional. That look so nakedly revealing: I'm tired; this isn't what I wanted, but it's the only way to reach out to a life I don't really want . . . don't really understand. And it's too late to change.

Dee shuddered and blinked her eyes hard to shut out the oppressive vision. It was too close to home—and she didn't want to be reminded. She wanted to turn and run, but it was too late.

The woman had caught her glance, and the uncertain smile on her face was too vulnerable to refuse. Dee had always been a sucker for strays and underdogs.

She made her way slowly toward the stranger, unsure how she would approach her. But she smiled charmingly and extended her hand. "I'm Dee Sanders, ambassador of good will, pleasant tidings, bits of nonsense, or what-have-you. At least for the moment."

An uncertain flicker, then a slow, deliberate smile spread across the woman's face. "Hail. You speak English."

Dee bowed. "I try. I don't use double negatives, but I sometimes say 'ain't.' "

"You're entitled. *Noblesse oblige* . . . or something. My name's Eileen. I came with the blonde who *is* having a good time."

Her voice was warm and pleasant, and Dee found her earlier uneasiness dispelled. Dee sat down on the uncomfortable foam mattress placed on what should have been a door. "Blondes are supposed to have a good time, aren't they? At least, that's what the ads say."

"Madison Avenue hogwash," said Eileen, emphasizing the remark with an airy gesture. She turned to Dee with a look of confident intimacy. "Nobody else here does," she whispered.

"Nobody else here does what?"

"Speak English."

Dee nodded in grim appreciation as a young man tripped by, handing each of them a cocktail and going on to a cluster of three well-dressed older men.

"*They* say, 'Wasn't it a camp,' and 'Dish me, honey'—a cross between a Cub Scouts' outing and a short-order cooks' convention." Eileen raised her glass in a toast. "To fringe life—and benefits."

Dee shook her head and smiled. "I can't drink to that—it's an admission of defeat."

She wondered how much Eileen had had to drink.

"Then drink to roses and springtime and love. You go to your church and I'll go to mine. Do you think I'm drunk?"

"I've been considering it," Dee said lightly.

"You're right. First time in three years, too. I'm in A.A."

Oh, brother! Dee thought regretfully. Wonder if that's why no one would talk to her? But no. It wasn't that. Eileen wasn't the type to talk to just anyone this way. Besides, it was not uncommon to encounter A.A. members among the gay crowds. She was plainly miserable and had simply found someone who might possibly understand.

From the corner of her eye, Dee saw Rita making her way toward them. She dreaded what Rita's intrusion might do, but to stop her now would only be misunderstood and insulting to Eileen.

"Hello, sweetie. Having fun?" Rita's cool glance encompassed Eileen, categorized her, and dismissed her.

"Meet Eileen." Dee made the introduction as casual as she could without encouraging Rita to sit down and stay.

"Just checking up on you." Rita smiled, leaned over, and kissed Dee briefly on the forehead so that the perfume from her breasts floated seductively to Dee's face. "See you later, darling."

She knows every trick in the book, Dee thought as Rita walked away, leaving her with a twinge of excitement she could not deny.

"Yours?" Eileen's voice brought her back.

"Yes. As much as anyone ever is."

"A bitch?"

"Yes."

"Welcome to the club." Eileen finished off her drink carefully and set it down with a small sigh. "Why is it we always end up with bitches?"

Dee shrugged. "I don't know. Maybe some of us are just born asking for trouble. Misery hunters. Masochists."

"Christ! You sound like that damn head-shrinker who writes all those books about what's wrong with the homosexuals. Dr. Krugler, or somebody like that. *Injustice collectors*—that's what he calls us. *Garbage collectors* is more like it!" The drinks were obviously having an effect. She was slurring her words, but her focus was still sharp. "Ah, well, live and let live, I always say. Or do I?" She broke into a sudden bitter laugh. "Hell! Let's forget the unrespectable aspects of our lives. Let's talk shop. What do you do? Out there in the straight world, that is. I'm a respectable writer."

"I'm a photographer," Dee said briefly, not wishing to discuss herself more than necessary. It was safer to get Eileen to talk. "What do you write? Today, I thought, all writers were supposed to be respectable. Except the Beats, of course."

"Not so. Not so at all. Do you know"—she leaned forward whispering as though she were imparting a great and valuable secret, her pray eyes bright with mockery—"that at least half of them drink . . . and smoke . . . and that untold numbers of them are queer?"

"Shocking," agreed Dee with a wry grin. "Do go on."

"And I hear tell some of them even take dope. To say nothing of the awful influence they've had on suburbia. Minute a writer gets successful he heads for the country . . . and poof! There goes desecration."

She laughed hugely at her own joke, slapping Dee's shoulder for emphasis.

Dee winced under the force of the blow but smiled. "Well," she said carefully, "I suppose in this era of conformity some ritual must be observed to show distinction."

Eileen nodded. "You are so right. And you know how I achieve it? By being respectable. You can't hardly get that kind no more. In a world that's reeking with payola, Madison Avenue double-talk, expense account call girls, someone like me is a freak. What they call a square."

"It's nice to know there are a few left. I thought I was all alone. But you still haven't told me what you write."

"Okay. You asked for it. Children's stories."

Dee's eyebrows shot up.

"Don't laugh," said Eileen. "It's the truth, so help me. I've been doing it for fourteen years. Before that I was a teacher. Would you believe it?"

"Yes," Dee answered quickly. She began to warm to this tough-surfaced but strangely vulnerable woman. Almost automatically she began to analyze her face in terms of portrait angles. It was a good face, really. Intelligent, strong, yet somehow wistful. A low shot would be best. It would minimize the long nose without losing its dominating effect. "What kind of children's stories? Not fairy tales, I trust."

"No wisecracks, please. I write just plain children's stories. Sensible. Like English walking shoes."

The young man came back gingerly. "Another drink, girls?"

"Naturally. Do I look like a spy for A.A.?" Eileen raised one eyebrow and stared at him with exaggerated solemnity. "Martinis on the double."

The young man gave her a startled look and then giggled. "Oh, you are a camp!" He wiggled off toward the bar with a dexterity that would have made a burlesque dancer envious.

They watched him in silence for a few moments.

"I really can't stand them," Eileen said. "Faggots. Or the dykes either. They're just as bad. Guess it's because I really hate myself. But I'm not going to push it. I'm stuck with it and that's that."

The young man returned with the drinks just then, and Dee was spared the task of commenting. He deposited them somewhat nervously on the small coffee table beside them. "Here you are, dolls," he said in a sweet, girlish voice, and disappeared into the crowd.

Dee looked after him thoughtfully, wondering if he was really as swish as he appeared to be, or if it was part of an act. In a place like this it paid to swish.

She turned back to Eileen, wondering whether to encourage the confession that was about to spring forth. She had no choice. Eileen pinned her with a sardonic look and asked, "When do you intend to ask me how long I've been gay and how long my girl and I have been together?"

Dee opened her mouth to answer, but Eileen didn't bother to wait. "I've come to look upon such questions as standard procedure in a gay crowd. Funny, isn't it? Where else in the world do two strangers make idle conversation about their sex lives as a form of introduction? Almost like a password."

"Why not?" Dee asked lightly. "We are . . . well, underground, aren't we?"

"*Touché!*" cried Eileen. "And very diplomatically put, but I must say I detect a tone of definite resentment. Don't tell me you're giving in to respectability, too. Better watch out. The respectable ones—they're the worst kind."

"Why?"

"Because they're so damn guilty, that's why. Like you."

Dee suddenly felt irritated with the conversation. She didn't want anybody prying into raw spots, opening old confusions. It was painful enough to do it herself. "What makes you think I feel guilty?" she asked sharply.

Eileen took a long sip of her drink and measured Dee with a

long, shrewd look. "You simply ooze with the need for atone-ment—it sticks out all over you. You didn't walk through the door when you came in—you sneaked in." She grinned impishly. "Why don't you go straight?"

"Whatsa matter," Dee snapped back, deciding to make a joke of it, "you one of them religious fanatics or somethin' ?"

They both laughed uproariously. Dee was beginning to feel her drinks, too.

"Y'know, you just may have something there," Eileen remarked. "As a matter of fact, I'm beginning to think so." She laughed again, but this time there was a desperate quality to it. "I'm the reverse of what's-his-name in *The Rains Came*. You know what I did this week?"

Dee shook her head.

"I brought that young blond kid out . . . gave her a first-class in-troduction to the big wide, wonderful gay world." Her lips thinned to a bitter grin. "What do you think of an old dyke like me doing something like that?"

Dee's mind raced through a number of answers, frantically trying to pick out a reasonable and tactful response. But once again she was relieved of the responsibility by Eileen's compulsive need to unburden herself.

"She knew I was queer," she blurted without waiting for any comment from Dee. "She knew it and pushed and pushed and wheedled and seduced until I couldn't stand it anymore . . . until I thought I'd have a nervous breakdown if I didn't . . . until . . ."

She stopped abruptly and turned toward Dee. Her eyes were tear-less but glistening with backed-up misery. "Say something quick or I'll cry."

Dee took her hand and held it tightly. Eileen recited along with her:

> "*In winter I get up at night*
> *And dress by yellow candlelight*
> *In summer, quite the other way,*
> *I have to go to bed by day.*"

They went on that way for a few minutes, repeating half-remembered lines from old childhood poems, nursery rhymes, nonsense limericks. Dee wondered what people would think if they could overhear, but she didn't really care. It wasn't anyone's damn business. Slowly Eileen began to recover. Dee watched the muscles in her face relax; then she let go of her hand carefully.

"Thanks," Eileen whispered, flashing a grateful smile.

"Nothing at all," Dee said brightly. "Any friend of Robert Louis Stevenson or Old Mother Goose is a friend of mine."

"Dee!" Rita's voice shrilled toward them. "C'mon, darling. We're all going downtown for a nightcap."

She glided toward the table, then surveyed them with ill-concealed impatience. "You going to hide in a corner all night yakking?" She was being rude and she knew it, and didn't care.

Dee could see that she was quite drunk already, and had a sudden urge just to get up and slap her. But she sat quite still, looking at her with silent fury.

Rita ignored the warning in her eyes. "Hurry it up, will you? You can talk all night long some other time."

Dee glanced quickly at Eileen, half ashamed to leave her this way—yet honestly relieved. She had had enough of other people's traumas for one evening. Still, it was a hell of a thing to do.

As though sensing her conflict, Eileen waved her away with a smile. "Go ahead. I'm all right now. Besides, mine'll probably be along here any minute to drag me along, too."

Dee got up and tried to make as graceful an exit as possible, with Rita tugging at her sleeve.

When she turned at the door to wave good-bye, she saw Eileen dancing with her girl, laughing. If it hadn't been for the way Eileen was dancing, she might possibly have never thought of her again.

But there was something unforgettably touching in the way she managed to make a current rock-and-roll tune look like the Lindy.

Chapter 5

They hadn't been at the night club ten minutes when Rita stood up to dance with Bunny, Babs's girlfriend, and even from the table Dee could see she was knocking her brains out to be amusing. She would succeed. She always did. Dee briefly considered being jealous, but she just couldn't.

Jealousy. Such a peculiar and illogical emotion, Dee thought, despite the loud music and constant babble of voices. And in this kind of life, she had seen it take many faces—doubly frightening since every gay kid had to fear both sexes instead of one. She considered her own attitudes toward Rita with a momentary detachment. If she's out with a guy, I'm jealous. When we're out with gay kids, I'm not. At least, I don't think so. However, she had to admit that she did get angry when Rita flirted with girls . . . and sick, sometimes.

She signaled the waitress for another drink and looked around the filled room. It was too dark, really, to make out anything farther than ten feet away, but she tried anyhow. The young girls in tight pants with the trim boys' shirts and the inevitable cufflinks. There was something faintly obscene about wearing cufflinks; it was so nakedly symbolic of the homosexual confusion.

The women between twenty-five and forty varied the most from the traditional garb of the gay bar: a statuesque blonde wearing jodhpurs and carrying a riding crop; the petite brunette with the doe eyes wearing a frilly dress and a floppy hat. The costumes varied until the "past forty" stage.

Then, sprinkled in among them all were the subtle ones—the ones who would go unnoticed in the straight world except to the most discerning eye. Career women who, for social or economic reasons, needed to "pass"—the chameleonlike ones who took on the protective coloring of whatever group they were with.

And inevitably, the "bull dykes"—heavy, thin, tall, short; but all dedicated to the task of proving themselves just as good a man as any creature born a male.

"Dance?" A young girl suddenly appeared in front of Dee.

She looked up and immediately felt like taking the girl over her knee, spanking her, and sending her home . . . with a skirt on.

"Well? You can't sit there all night scowling." The girl grinned boyishly. "I've had my eye on you. But you wouldn't look back."

She was really quite pretty, Dee thought. "Sorry," she said. "I've been philosophizing."

"Here?" the girl laughed. "C'mon, honey. We'll chase your blues away."

The girl's laugh brought a smile to Dee's lips, and she stood up, feeling suddenly reckless. "No jitterbugging and no cha-cha-cha—understand?"

"You're the boss." She stood still a moment. "Tall broad, aren't you."

"No. Not at all. You're just standing in a hole." Dee took her hand and led her to the cramped dance floor. She pulled the girl close to her and was amused to realize that she felt no response to the girl's breasts pressed against hers. It was too much like her college days, when all the girls danced together and it didn't mean a thing . . . except for maybe one or two who would make Dee very nervous and she would always find a way to excuse herself without knowing why.

Being gay was something comparatively new to Dee. She had always known about such things, of course, but it had nothing to do with her. After all, she had fallen in love in her second year of college—with a musician, of all things. He was intense, brooding, dark, and treated her with an unbearable indifference. His thin face with the questioning eyes was intriguing and fiercely romantic—then. If she saw the same type of man on the street today, she'd think he was an overage juvenile delinquent.

She missed a step and quickly apologized to the girl.

"My fault," the girl replied. "You don't talk much, do you? I like that." She pushed closer so that her pelvic bones were jabbing Dee in the thighs.

Oh, God! Dee thought. What will I do with her?

"Actually, I talk a passion-purple streak when I get going. I'm just antisocial."

"Philosophizing again?" the girl asked coyly.

"Not really. The truth of the matter is that I have to count with the music or I can't dance. So conversation is out." Dee smiled.

"You're nice," she laughed. "What do you do for a living?"

"Secretary," Dee replied quickly with her standard answer. Bar frequenters had big mouths, and she needed her job. She glanced around the room again from her new vantage point. The decor was a sickly imitation of the plush Roman era, with flat black ceiling and wall panels. Off-white imitation candelabras clung to the center of each panel, and the same white-painted semicolumns separated them. The Formica bar tables seemingly grew from the floor like grotesque toadstools in a complete clash with the room decoration, and the jukebox was an unspeakable effrontery.

"May I break in?" Rita's voice chimed lyrically.

Dee turned quickly and smiled into Rita's eyes. "Hello, darling. Which of us do you want?"

The young girl's head plainly took in all of Rita with one motion, and a low "wow" sound came from deep inside her throat. "Yours?" she asked after a moment.

Dee smiled tolerantly. It was the second time tonight the question of possession had come up—but it was often asked, anyway—and she was beginning to feel like an art collector.

Rita bestowed a graceful pat on the girl's head and pushed herself between them, placing both her arms around Dee's neck with a soft caress. "Run along, darling. We haven't danced all evening . . . mind?"

"No. No, not at all." The girl took two steps back and then stopped at the bar.

"Hello, darling," Rita said softly. "I've missed you." She pulled Dee's face close to hers and nuzzled nearer to her.

"I thought you were having a good time . . ." Dee answered, with a light smile to show she wasn't picking an argument.

"I was," Rita answered with a thin sigh. "But they begin to bore me after a while. You know how it is." She kissed Dee on the lips softly. "How did you ever get stuck with that midget?"

It was the kind of comment Dee didn't appreciate, but she let it go. Rita seldom said anything kindly or with genuine humor.

"Guess who I have a chance to meet," Rita continued.

"Who?"

"Martie Thornton!" she said exuberantly.

"Who's he?"

Rita clucked with mild irritation. "Not *he. She!* One of the best nightclub singers in town. She's gay, of course. But Babs—dear old Babs who knows all and tells more—just happened to mention that her old high school chum was now a singer. You'd think she would have said something before now, wouldn't you? I mean, knowing how important it might be to me to know someone like Martie?"

Dee winced. It was "Martie" already. "Well, maybe they just re-discovered each other."

"Oh," Rita said with a condescending wave of her hand, "Babs gave me some silly story like that . . . just recently ran into her, or something. I don't believe her, of course."

"Why on earth not?" Dee asked sincerely.

Rita smiled to another girl on the floor.

"Because one simply doesn't lose track of someone as important as that!"

"For heaven's sake, Rita. Maybe singers aren't that important to Babs. It's a very plausible explanation."

"Oh! You'd stand up for anybody. I thought you didn't like Babs." Rita pouted.

"I'm not standing up for her, and I don't feel much of anything about Babs—either way. It's the principle. This habit of yours of always thinking people are out to do you in or purposely withholding information is dangerous. You're going to end up a paranoiac if you're not careful."

"Stop lecturing, Dee. I'm not in the mood. If you don't want me to have a career, just say so. Doesn't my happiness mean anything to you? Don't you want me to get ahead?"

"Of course I do, silly." Dee took a deep breath and, cautioning herself to go easy, asked, "So when's the audition?"

She wondered if she'd ever be free of having to watch every word she said.

"Oh, I haven't wrangled that part yet, but I will," Rita answered with secretive exhilaration. "Martie's doing a show at one of the East Side supper clubs, and Babs and I thought . . ."

I bet, "Babs and I thought," Dee exclaimed to herself.

". . . that we'd just sort of stop by one evening this week and invite her to the table. Cute?"

"Very cute," Dee answered. "What night?" She was already sure of the answer.

Rita smiled sweetly. "Like tomorrow . . . maybe?"

It was a trap and Dee knew it. "Sunday?" she asked anyway.

"People still eat on Sundays."

"Why not Monday?"

Rita sighed. "Everyone knows the right people never go to a supper club on a Monday—even if it's open."

"Well, why don't you and Babs go alone?"

"It just wouldn't look right. Besides, it's so impressive to introduce you as a big editor."

"Just a photography editor—there *is* a difference." It was a lost fight. She was just making a better show of it.

"Tomorrow!" Rita smiled sweetly.

"It seems I have no choice," Dee smiled back.

Rita's eyebrows lifted, and her lavender eyes glistened with twinkling triumph. "None whatsoever." She tightened her grasp around Dee's neck and clung closely to her every step. "Let's go home now, darling. Let's get to bed early," she whispered.

"Want to be pretty for tomorrow?" Dee asked huskily.

"Something like that," Rita replied, breathing in Dee's ear.

Dee smiled slowly. "It's a good thing I'm not a spy," she commented.

"Why?"

"I'd give away all my secrets to you. . . ."

Chapter 6

Martie Thornton was quite petite, actually, but her strapless sheath dress exposed the lean sinews in her arms and back, giving an impression of great physical strength. Dee watched her with rapt fascination, and for the first time in quite a while she was genuinely enjoying herself. Even though she had not really wanted to come tonight, the dinner had been very good, Babs and Rita had unintentionally brought her into their conversation by discussing the difficulties of getting good publicity pictures, and, best of all, the coffee had been delicious.

Dee felt a warm rapport with everything around her, and by the time Martie had walked up to the piano, Dee was prepared to relax and be entertained. The singer had come on with a perfectly blank expression, stood absolutely still for a suspenseful minute, and suddenly begun belting out a song in a voice that Dee was sure came from under the floorboards.

Martie Thornton wasn't just an entertainer—she was a way of life.

Some of her songs were bawdy, and she managed deftly to bring allusions about the gay kids into every conceivable tune. But when she sang a torch song, Dee felt that she had known Martie a long, long time and that she was singing it out for everyone who had ever been in love—or wished they could be. She had the kind of deep and sensitive approach to a song that many great ballad singers have—a sort of abandonment to the mood of the moment.

Dee knew she would like Martie, and she was glad when the last song was over and Martie was taking her bows. Finally, the lights in the club went on, and with a broad smile, Martie came toward them with surprisingly graceful movements.

"What is this?" she asked Babs with a throaty laugh. "I don't see you for a thousand years, and all of a sudden I can't get rid of you. Starting up a fan club?"

Dee was tempted to give Rita a significant I-told-you-so look, but let it go. She was trying to interpret Rita's facial expression. It was a mask of polite interest. But Dee was certain that underneath it Rita was asking herself how a woman like Martie got to the top when she couldn't even begin. A combination of jealousy and admiration—but the latter was grudging, Dee was sure.

Babs made the introductions with unconcealed pride, and Martie sat down at their table. She signaled the waiter.

"Joe"—she gestured a large circle—"once around on me."

"That's very nice of you," Rita said demurely.

Martie laughed. "It is, isn't it?"

Dee had difficulty not letting her smile become a guffaw. That took the wind out of Rita's sails, all right!

". . . and it'll just be a small group," Babs was saying. "I thought you might like to come by after the show. If we were all real nice to you, maybe you'd even sing a song for us."

Dee waited and watched Martie as she held their attention while she lit a cigarette. She exhaled the smoke carefully, inspected the end of the ash microscopically, and much to Dee's surprise, winked at her. "When did you say this party was going to be?"

"Soon," Rita answered for Babs hastily.

"Hm. Well now. Saturdays I have free and I'm usually home most of the day. Tell you what, Babs. You come by and decorate my apartment at no charge, and I'll sing at your party . . . gratis."

"What do you mean?" Babs spurted.

"Just that. I make my living with my voice—you with your decorating talents. If you wouldn't consider giving away your time in trade, why should I?" She smiled broadly, showing neat, white teeth. "Would you ask Miss Sanders here to take your picture for nothing?"

"How did you know . . . ?" Dee asked.

Martie's hand waved away the rest of her question. "One of my ex-girlfriends was a camera bug . . . used to yak constantly about the work you did with . . . buildings, wasn't it?"

"In a way. I specialize with architecture and city mood studies." She felt Rita's foot under the table.

"I didn't know you were so famous, darling," Rita said.

"Devil his due," Martie commented. "What do you do, Miss . . ."

Rita straightened up perceptibly. "Evans . . . but just call me Rita. I used to model, but now I'm studying voice. Of course, I'd never be able to compete with you, but I think I could develop my own style. . . ."

"But what about the party?" Babs interrupted.

Dee wouldn't have given odds on Babs's chance of survival if it were up to Rita at that moment. But she, too, was now interested in the outcome of this future event.

"I'll stop by, honey," Martie answered warmly, "if I can. I just don't like to be conned into anything. But don't rely on me to sing. If I feel like it, nothing would stop me. . . . If I don't, well, trying to make me is like trying to pull a stubborn mule out of a mudhole." She turned and took in Rita shrewdly. "But I'm sure you don't need me. Rita here looks like she would be entertaining even if she couldn't carry a tune in a bucket."

"Thank you," Rita said softly.

Dee wasn't so sure it had been a compliment, but didn't want to analyze it now, fearing she would miss one of Martie's marvelously unabashed comments.

Conversation stayed in high, with Martie asking Rita and Babs questions about themselves, showing a great interest in what they said. Suddenly, she stood up. "Well, kids, it's been nice. I've got a change to make, so if you're still around I'll see you later."

"I'm afraid I've got to be at work early tomorrow," Dee said. "But Rita can stay if she wants."

"No, no. I want to get a few things done tomorrow, too."

Dee recognized the maneuver of not seeming too anxious and briefly wondered if Martie recognized it, too. Babs mumbled something.

"It was nice meeting you two," Martie said warmly. "By the way," she added after a moment, "can I reach you at your office, Miss Sanders?"

"Usually," Dee answered, perplexed.

"I'd like you to recommend a good portrait photographer for me, if you would."

Dee smiled slowly. "That's not much of a bargain," she said lightly. "You can't recommend anything for me."

Martie grinned impishly. "Oh, yes, I can . . . but you're already taken." She vaguely saluted Rita. "About ten tomorrow morning? Fine."

She smiled once around the table again and walked off, leaving Dee feeling quite pleased with herself. She was rarely singled out that way. Usually Rita's beauty or her constant line of chatter forced Dee into the background, almost as a straight man for her. It was interesting, Dee thought, how Martie made her feel not so much feminine as womanly. She seemed to hit a responsive chord that by now Dee had decided must be out of tune from neglect.

Dee glanced over at Babs first to get a reaction estimate and, from her blank expression, knew that Rita was burning.

"Well!" Rita thrust coldly. "Aren't we the little impression maker!"

Babs cleared her throat carefully and picked up the check with unusual enthusiasm. "Okay, girls, check's on me tonight. Guess we might as well go home."

Rita smirked. " 'We might as well' is right!" Her smile was icy as she turned to Dee. "I'm glad you're not in the theater, darling. Your upstaging would get you a terrible reputation."

"I hardly said two words," Dee offered quietly. She didn't want to get into an argument in public but, on the other hand, could not allow herself to be completely trampled.

"That's right," Rita snickered. "I forgot how famous you are— everyone knows who Dee Sanders is. The photographer, you know. Not just everyone can do what she can with a box of tin and glass."

"C'mon, now, Rita. Martie talked most of the time with you, didn't she?" Babs asked in a consoling tone.

"But she didn't offer to call me!" Rita's eyes flashed as she spoke. "Or make any suggestive remarks."

"She was just trying to bolster my ego so that I wouldn't feel like a dud next to you," Dee said calmly.

It was evidently the correct thing to say; it shut Rita up. Dee knew Rita well enough to know that she only needed a thread to hang her rationalizations on, and her overactive vanity would carry her the rest of the way.

"Sure," Babs said. "And she's not likely to forget who you are this way, either." She looked quickly to Dee for confirmation.

That was one thing Dee could say on Babs's behalf: she couldn't stand to see anyone maligned.

"Are you two going to pat each other on the back all night or are we going home?" Rita said bitterly.

What's the use? Dee asked herself. To answer Rita's questions was like sticking your head in a hungry lion's mouth.

She picked up her purse and followed Rita and Babs past the small tables crowded with people talking and laughing. She wondered how many of them "knew" that they were gay as they walked by. Or maybe some of them were gay themselves, managing to "pass" somehow. It must be nice to be just plain ordinary people—straight and without self-consciousness.

As they stepped out of the cool restaurant into the hot, airless night, Dee glanced almost pitifully at Rita. This being gay is like being a dope addict, she thought: compulsive, cunning, destroying. You can't live with it—or without it.

Perhaps she should go see an analyst again. *Again*, she laughed mirthlessly. One consultation and I'm saying *again*. She remembered clearly the visit she had made four years before—the dark green walls of his office, the mahogany desk polished and unmarred, the wall of books: Jung, Adler, Freud, and many other names she was totally unfamiliar with. Big books, fat books, filled with one human's appraisal of other humans. She had sat waiting for him thinking, what would he say to her?

There, there, my dear . . . all you need is hormones.

Well, that would solve her problem nicely. Or perhaps he would simply suggest a little self-discipline. Nothing with her except that she'd fallen into a bad habit.

But she was unprepared when he turned, closed the door behind him, and sat down at his desk without a smile.

"How are you?" he had asked.

"Fine, thank you," she smiled uncertainly. "And you?"

Finally! A slow smile came across his face. She didn't like the smile. "You're not here to find out about me, are you." He hadn't asked it; he'd told her.

She'd shifted noisily in her chair—damn squeaking leather chairs. "In a way," she'd laughed. "After all, I understand it's important that I trust you." She was sorry as soon as it came out. It was so adolescently flip.

"I'm not a surgeon—I'm not going to cut into you. It is important that you trust yourself, your motives, and your desire to learn about yourself." He smiled again, and she was struck by what she thought to be the coldest blue eyes she'd ever seen.

"Well . . ." she began, "I'm not even really sure that I need take up your time this way, even though I am paying you for it. I mean, I'm not despondent or anything. I don't plan to kill myself. . . ."

"You don't think you should have to pay me?"

"Oh, well, of course you should get paid. It's your profession. I didn't mean . . ."

"Just what brought you to me?"

There was something so terribly unctuous about him. What right did he have—who the hell did he think he was, her father? "Are you trying to make me uncomfortable deliberately?" she asked self-righteously.

"Are you uncomfortable?"

Oh, Christ! Why had she bothered at all. "Perhaps . . . perhaps I made a mistake coming here at all." She started to stand up, clutching her purse as though he would take it from her and go through its contents.

"As long as you are paying me for a full fifty minutes, why don't you stick it out and get your money's worth?"

Well! That was better. He wasn't being so smug now.

He waited for her to sit down again, then asked, "Is there any special problem that's bothering you . . . or just general depression?"

"I suppose most of your patients are depressed," she stated.

"Mrs. Sanders, we're not here to discuss my health or the emotional state of my other patients. Shall we talk about you?"

Why did he have to make her feel so defensive? Perhaps this was part of the analytical process—bait you to see how you react. She suddenly realized that every muscle in her body was taut, and she forced herself to relax them.

"I'm sorry," she said after a moment. "I've never been to an analyst before. . . . I don't know what to expect or how to behave."

He leaned back in his chair slowly. "You're not in front of TV cameras . . . and I'm not here to judge you or make you follow any social patterns. You do as you please. Pace up and down, if you like . . . stare out the window . . . anything you like. But I'm not a magician. I can't begin to be of use to you until you tell me what's on your mind."

She sighed heavily. "Depression, as you put it. I just feel so damn lost most of the time, so completely out of pace with everything." She'd paused and taken a deep breath. "I think, I think part of it has to do with the fact that I'm a lesbian."

"Should that depress you?"

"Well," she said indignantly, "don't you think it should?"

"Only if you don't want to be one."

"I—I don't know. I'm not sure."

"How long have you considered yourself a lesbian?"

"That's a hell of a question to ask!"

"Really?"

"What is there to consider? You either are or you aren't. Isn't that right?"

"If you're so sure, why do you ask?" He sat forward and gazed at her intently.

"Well, if this is all there is to analysis—asking a lot of stupid questions and giving silly answers—then I really did make a mistake in coming."

He continued to gaze at her.

"I had my first experience about a year and a half ago!" She almost hurled the information at him. "I have been a practicing lesbian since then. I like it. I like women."

"You don't like men? But you were married?"

"To an idiot!"

"What about other men?"

"Oh . . ." She was so exasperated she was ready to cry. "I like men, too. But not the same way. Before I'd been introduced to this sort of thing, I thought I liked them fine."

"But since then?" He opened the desk drawer and peered into it, then pulled out a pad of paper and a dull pencil.

"I don't feel anything for them . . . other than as friends. I like them as companions . . . but physically they don't move me. I'd just as soon hug my pillow."

"You find women more appealing?" he asked.

"Infinitely. I can get stimulated by a woman . . . the fact that her skin is smooth and she smells of perfume . . . that she can be seductive and womanly . . ."

"Something a man cannot be?"

"Well . . . not very well, can he? I mean, he would have to be a woman."

"Why do you think you feel this way?"

"That's what I came to ask you." She smiled and for the first time began to feel more at ease. "After all, I came from a decent home; I've had no horrible experiences with men. . . . It was just sort of all-of-a-sudden."

"Many lesbians come from socially sound homes, had the usual advantages, and were spared any traumatic experiences with men . . . yet they became lesbians. Frankly, Mrs. Saunders"—he glanced at his watch and then smiled at her—"we don't really know that much about the subject yet. We don't know why these things happen in cases like yours. We don't even know if we can cure such cases . . . but we do the best we can. But the final outcome rests with you. It's your decision."

They had discussed a bit more what analysis could be expected to do and what it could not—a world of a person's hope held in a few sentences.

He glanced at his watch again and this time indicated the session was over. "I'd like to see you again and talk about this some more. Make the appointment with my nurse before you leave, will you?"

Dee sat very still now, as she had with those words. A little numb—not quite knowing what to do with herself. He had walked her to the door and opened it for her, a different door from the one through which she had come in.

Was it really only four years ago? she asked herself. It seemed like it was from another life altogether . . . about someone she knew intimately—but not herself. She'd made the appointment but never gone back. After all, she had told herself, she couldn't really afford it. It had been an impulsive thing to do. And since they didn't really know that much about it to begin with—well, then, why go back?

If she had to choose . . . Rita would win. Rita would always win. She needed Rita in a way she could never explain to anyone else, much less herself. Rita was just a part of her, good or bad.

But Lord! Rita could make her life a hell!

Chapter 7

Her office window was dirty with summer dust and exhaust fumes even though she was on the twenty-first floor. Dee could see the miragelike effect from the tops of the other buildings with heat distortion. New York. A hell or a haven. It was what your mood was, because all you had to do was cross the street to find a new world.

She wished she could feel the same about people. Dee could enjoy a city without any need to possess it. But she couldn't do this with people.

They frightened and bored her at the same time. All but a select few, and she could never tell how they had become her "select few," or why. Like Jerry Wilson, for instance, whom she was having lunch with today. She had not particularly liked him when they'd met seven years ago. He was just another one of her ex-husband's strange friends—a homosexual, and proud of it.

It was all so long ago, she thought. She was just a scrub-faced twenty-year-old whose arms and legs were always in the way.

Dee snorted silently. A newlywed! she thought wryly. Married a year already and just beginning to enjoy the love-turned-to-hatred she felt for her husband. The sweet joy of looking at him and thinking, "You're a nothing!" Why it was sweet, she was not too certain, except, perhaps, because it helped to bury the hurt she had covered up so many times when he had gone out of his way to be rude or sadistic. Because it helped to make her feel that when their marriage broke up—and it would—it was not going to be her fault. He would have done it to himself.

She had been ready to make a home for him, to have his children, and had oftentimes thought of them sitting around on a Saturday afternoon, out on the Island in their own tract home somewhere. Maybe Pete would be giving the oldest child piano lessons or something, and she would sit out on the porch on a hot day, keeping a motherly eye on the youngest of the brood, hearing the sounds of music, hesitant and awkward, as the lesson went on.

Dreams. Dreams that became nightmares in their mockery. But Jerry had somehow sensed her need for her dreams and had also known that Pete would never be the man to make them come true. Jerry Wilson had taken it upon himself to be a booby prize. He would help with the dishes after Pete would push his way from the table and stretch out on the couch to watch the fights. Jerry would take her to the theater, or to museums, or to the zoo, just to get her out of their West Side tenement apartment.

She had to work even then, of course, while finishing her college studies. Pete wouldn't. Pete was a musician, not an office slave. He was a composer, not an aspiring corporation idiot.

Dee had often wondered why Jerry put up with him . . . or her.

She smiled as she thought of those hot summers and freezing winters, of the many times they were happy to get one meal for the day from the pitiful savings in the sugar bowl. Pete had to have scored paper; she had to have film. He had to rent a practice studio; she had to rent a darkroom with enlarging facilities. What with the bare necessities for their respective fields plus what they needed in rent and clothes, money for food was a luxury. In fact, now as she thought about it, their closest moments after their first year together had been those occasions when they would pass a restaurant and the almost fablelike aromas of exotic cooking would taunt them in the street—then, a look would pass between them that held them in compassionate bondage.

It's strange, Dee thought, how a respect for hunger can keep two people together just a little while longer—even arguing helps to take the gnawing out of your stomach for a while.

The phone rang dully in the background, and Dee knew her reverie was over. She almost didn't want to let it go despite the unpleasantness of it. At least it was normal, she decided. I could talk about my depressions or have a loud fight with Pete and not worry about what the neighbors would "find out." I could confide in friends about our problems and know it was a part of their world, too—something they could honestly understand.

"Mrs. Sanders," Karen Lundquist's voice called her on the intercom.

"Yes, Karen." Dee smiled quietly at the sound of Karen's voice. It always had just a touch of awe about it, and Dee enjoyed the fact that even after almost two years, Karen still called her Mrs. Sanders.

"A Miss Thornton on the phone. Says you're expecting her call."

"Miss Thornton?" Dee searched her memory for a moment and then answered. "Oh, yes! Put her on, Karen. And go powder your nose or something . . . it's private."

A light laugh came from the other end. "I'm not now, nor have I ever been, a member of the FBI," Karen answered in mock reproof.

"I know you motherly types," Dee said. "Always wanting to keep us old maids out of trouble."

"You're hardly what I'd call the old-maid type! Besides, eavesdropping always gives me a headache."

Dee watched the intercom light go out in the button and come on again, signifying the transfer had been made.

"Martie! I'm glad you remembered to call."

"Hello, there." Martie's voice came over the line with such force that Dee had to hold the receiver away from her ear.

"I made up a pretty hasty list for you this morning," Dee said.

"List? What list?"

"You asked me for some portrait photographers. Remember?"

"Oh, that. Yeah. Tell you what, Dee. How about meeting me for lunch and we can discuss it. I know of a wild Armenian joint not too far from your office."

"You seem to know a lot about me and my surroundings," Dee

said, not a little unflattered. "Thanks, but no thanks. I have a luncheon date today."

"Tomorrow? C'mon, woman. I'm making a frantic pitch and I expect some cooperation." Martie's voice was hearty and good-natured.

"No. I really can't, Martie. But don't think I wouldn't love to."

"Your friend jealous? I'm trustworthy, you know. And I help old ladies across the street."

Dee laughed. "You know that and I know that. But my friend might misinterpret the situation. I'm sure you've been through it yourself."

"Man, I invented it! Okay. I get the message and I respect the fact that at least you play it square. I thought you would."

"Is there any other way?" Dee surprised herself with her own coyness.

"Not for people like you and me."

There was no doubt of her sincerity, and Dee felt a warm glow creep into her face. "Do you still want the list?"

Martie laughed. "Sure. Shall I say you sent me?"

"Would you understand if I asked you to leave my name out of it?"

"Yes."

Dee read off the six names she had gathered together, and she told Martie what each of them did best, so that she could choose. Dee couldn't shake the feeling that she was up to something terribly wicked as she talked. Actually, she felt as though she were flirting with a man, yet the knowledge that Martie was a woman made it doubly forbidden. It was, however, very safe and only a friendly admission of an immediate attraction between them. Nothing else.

"All right, kid. That should wrap it up. Hope I didn't put you to too much trouble."

"No. Of course not." Dee wanted to say something to let Martie know she really liked her . . . but she became embarrassed and couldn't.

"Well, guess I won't be able to see you for a while. I'm leaving for Europe next week . . . with a booking in London and Paris for sure. Lord knows what else will happen."

"Sounds great," Dee said, almost enviously. Even though she was going to Europe herself soon, she would never be able to have the inner sense of freedom and adventure that seemed so much a part of Martie's makeup.

"Can I call you when I get back?" Martie asked after a moment.

"Only if you want to talk to Rita, too." What else could she say?

"No. I don't have enough time to put up with her or to hang around waiting for you. But if you're ever free—or want a friend real bad—look me up. My agent can always find me."

Odd, Dee thought, I hardly know this woman and I almost feel like crying. "Thanks," she offered awkwardly.

"Well, so long, then. Good luck."

"Same to you, Martie. Same to you."

A short silence. "Bye, Dee."

"Bye," she answered almost in a whisper. The line went dead. She wanted to call Martie back and tell her something—anything. But she knew she wouldn't. She couldn't. What was there to say. Dee replaced the receiver, staring at her hand as she let it rest on it.

She didn't hear Karen's light rap in the open doorway connecting their offices. "I've got the August proofs for you, Mrs. Sanders. Production is all up in the air, claiming we're not going to have enough room for the ads if we don't cut some of the contest copy."

"Oh. Thanks, Karen." She turned and looked up at Karen's young, steady eyes and thought she saw a strange expression clouding the usually pansy, soft green color. "Problems?" she asked, turning back to her desk, with the proofs in her hand.

"No. Everything's fine . . . considering."

"Like what?"

"Oh. Nothing really serious, just several little things I'd like a chance to talk over with you, some time at lunch maybe. I'm having an awful time getting the right exposures with my flash . . . things like that."

"Who doesn't?" Dee smiled. But she knew that this wasn't quite true. She also knew Karen pretty well by now, and there was more on her mind than flash photography.

"How about lunch tomorrow?" she asked Karen. She tried to sound as offhand as possible.

"Swell. My treat."

"Oh, no. You'd just take me to Nedick's on your income. I'll put you on the expense account as Peter Basch or someone. We'll do it up right."

"Did I ever tell you that I'm very fond of you, Mrs. Sanders?"

"Write me a fan letter," Dee said. "Now get the hell out of the office and let me work."

Karen started to leave, then paused at the door. "I know what I wanted to ask you," she said. "Was that *the* Miss Thornton? I mean, it's none of my business but . . . *Martie* Thornton?"

There it was again. That sickening lump of lead in her stomach whenever she felt "caught," whenever there was any chance that someone might have guessed about her. Would she never get rid of it?

"Why, yes." It was better to tell the truth. Easier to lie about *why* she would be talking to a notorious lesbian than to be found out in a lie that she was talking to her at all.

"I thought so. You can't miss that voice, can you?" Karen smiled. "As my generation puts it, I dig that broad."

"Stop making me feel like an old woman and go oil your type-writer before it rusts." She didn't think Karen had really suspected anything. Not from the way she had asked. And actually, if she had suspected, Karen was too discreet to have brought it up uninvited.

"My typing is all done for this morning, madam. That's why I'm here. Efficiency is my motto."

"You're going to efficiency yourself out of a job if the old man sees you with nothing to do," Dee laughed.

"I'm also sneaky," Karen parried. "I'm doing back-issue research for you in case anyone asks."

"Beat it! Get out! Punk kids don't know any better than to take up an executive's time."

"I'm going, I'm going. Be nice to me or I'll organize a union."

Dee raised an arm as if to hit her, and she scampered off giggling. Damn fool kid, Dee thought kindly, and secretly complimented herself for having the best secretary on the floor. Not too long ago she'd brought in some of her still-life shots, and she was doing re-ally quite well. Like many beginners, Dee couldn't break her of using only color film, but the kid had a good eye for composition and a nice feel for texture. Qualities that could never be taught—you either had them or you didn't. She'd get someplace. That is, if she didn't marry the boy she was engaged to.

Dee guiltily changed the subject in her own mind. She didn't want to let herself think that way for fear it might show through in her conversations with Karen. Even if the girl never became a career woman, she'd have a creative hobby and a husband and a home. More than Dee could confess to.

Confess, Dee thought to herself. An interesting choice of words. Why would I have to *confess* to marriage? But the clock on the wall didn't allow for speculation right now. She had to meet Jerry Wilson in twenty minutes at the Plaza Hotel. Jerry always had lunch at the Plaza. Wouldn't be seen anywhere else.

She threw her cigarettes into her purse, glanced around the office, remembered that she had put aside a photo of a particularly handsome young man to tease Jerry with and stuck it in an envelope, then dashed out with a wave to Karen, who was proofreading some galleys for one of the other girls.

"Back by two," Dee said as she went out the door to the elevator. She stepped into the car seconds later, and as she turned, saw Karen look up at her and smile.

Chapter 8

The string ensemble played with a romantic desperation in a pathetic effort to preserve the elegance of a bygone day. Dee listened for a moment, trying to get a glimpse of the players, but couldn't see them with all the potted ferns around.

She shifted her attention to the patrons, who were seemingly oblivious of the contrived atmosphere. Women, dozens of them, expensively dressed, were all around—not too dissimilar from the potted ferns. They looked so much alike, it was almost like watching the chorus of a musical comedy. Their chic conformity exasperated Dee, who always felt that one of the privileges of being rich was to indulge one's individuality.

She sighed quietly, then turned and looked at Jerry, who was devouring his dessert with lustful glee. "It's funny," she said.

"What is?" Her comment didn't stop him from plopping another mouthful of pastry into its destination.

She laughed. "Stop eating a minute and listen to me."

"Don't be adolescent, dear. I need my strength to listen to your pedantic ravings." He nodded genteelly to her and smiled as best he could with his mouth full.

"You're impossible." She wrinkled her nose at him. "I was just thinking . . ."

"Oh, dear . . ." he interrupted.

". . . of my life's extremes, of the world we live in and how unpredictable everything is."

"Um." He waved his fork merrily at a lady seated at the far side of the room. "Smile," he whispered under his breath to Dee. "She's one of our angels."

"Oh, Christ!" Dee muttered through her clenched smile in the general direction of Jerry's gaze.

"All right, darling," he said, pushing his plate away from him and twisting the lemon peel into his coffee. "Now, what is all this soul-searching you re talking about?"

"Oh. I was just remembering the old days. Sort of lost myself this morning at the office, remembering how poor we were . . ."

"And what an ass Pete was!"

". . . and how no one would ever have guessed where I'd end up. Lunching at the Plaza with one of Broadway's most famous lyricists."

"*The* most famous. Actually, *notorious* would be more apropos." He snickered cheerfully.

"Why did you ever hang around in those days, Jerry? We weren't a part of your crowd."

Jerry stirred his coffee for a moment, and his expression became serious. Dee realized for the first time that he was beginning to show his age. His crew-cut steel gray hair helped to minimize the wrinkles around his steel gray eyes, but there was a sagging in his face—an almost visible deterioration of the skin tissues. But more than that, his expression these past few months had become genuinely weary. Oh, he still sparkled, all right. But it was a synthetic sparkle. The old spontaneity was gone. This was more a gleam of desperation.

"Are you going to answer me?" she asked gently.

"I was thinking." He turned and looked at her, a strange smile on his lips. "You promise you won't laugh at me?"

She couldn't help but smile yet promised not to laugh.

"It's been so long, I don't suppose it would matter anymore. Frankly, my dear, I was in love with you. No! Don't look so shocked. . . . I never intended to give up my precious young men.

But you were the only woman I'd ever known whom I genuinely respected and whose company and companionship I would prefer to any other person I knew. It had nothing to do with sex. It was love."

"Jerry! I . . ." Dee was stunned.

"Stop blubbering. I got exactly what I wanted from you. A home. A place to feel normal and at ease. Someone to talk to who took me as seriously as I did. A feeling of life and marriage. If you'd only had a child! My life would have been yours. Actually, darling, you've been a wonderful road sign in my life. I never wanted to marry you—I still don't. Good God! Copulate with a woman? It would be easier for me to become a lesbian!"

"It's crazy," Dee said with a choke in her voice. "But I think I'm going to cry."

"Don't you dare! Not in the Plaza!"

"Jerry? What's wrong with us? Why can't we be like other people? Happy in our married misery. Why couldn't you and I have been normal and married? Our interests are in common; we truly respect each other. You would have made a charming and attentive husband, and I could have given you the emotional security you want so much, and a family. Why? Why us? Why not that couple over there?"

Jerry looked at her a long moment, then smiled a little wistfully. He leaned over and kissed her on the cheek. "My name is Wilson—not Freud. Remember that. Besides," he added wryly, "at the rate we're multiplying, they probably *are* queer."

Dee laughed and caught a sob at the same time, but her control was back again.

"Now. Tell me all about that creature you're living with. I want to know every dreadful thing she's been up to. And when are you going to leave her so we can resume our wild, wicked ways?"

"You've got a nerve to talk about Rita!" Dee retorted, still a little breathless with emotion. "Look at the roster you've got!"

Jerry clucked irritably. "But I wouldn't dream of *living* with them."

Dee laughed again. "Well, let's just say I feel a moral responsibility to live with the person I'm loving."

"I can see higher education did you absolutely no good. Now

look. Rita is a lovely young thing, and I m sure she's quite cooperative in bed—but what else has she? Does she fill any of your needs?
Does she understand what you're talking about half the time?
Frankly, darling, she looks to me like a damned mannequin—or
one of those electronic creatures, except that she is power-driven.
Is this all you want from life? And, rumor has it she's being cooperative all over the town."

He was hitting low, but they were honest stabs from a friend who
really had her best interests at heart.

"She fills a certain kind of a need," Dee said slowly, unable to
look at him, almost ashamed. "How can I explain it to you? I simply
must have her."

"Oh, my sainted aunt!" Jerry snorted. "And I suppose you think
you would never find anyone else who could not only fill your deep,
dark needs but also your routine ones? Of course you would think
that! You're so corseted round with that damn Puritan conscience
of yours, you're scared to death to loosen the stays. I can see it
would be awful for you to be a human being, Dee. I mean, it leaves
one so subject to sin and frailty."

"Don't be sarcastic, Jerry. I can't turn myself inside out."

"Why not? Give you a much needed airing!"

Dee looked up at him suddenly. "Do I really seem so terribly unhappy to you?"

He nodded and met her troubled look with almost paternal compassion. She toyed nervously with her spoon. "I'll never understand
why you've taken such a dislike to Rita. What did she ever do to
you?"

"There's nothing she could do, m'love." He paused, and when he
spoke again, his voice was gentle and soft. "Did you know that she
came to see me about two months ago?"

Dee's head felt very heavy, and she anticipated what he was going
to say. She had had a faint hope that Jerry had been the one person
Rita had not tried to use as a "contact." "Yes. Of course I knew.
Afterwards," she lied. "I didn't send her."

His eyebrows went up, and he scrutinized Dee slowly. "It doesn't
matter. What does matter is that she's using you, Dee. And she'll
continue to use you until something better comes along and you're

going to get dumped. Think about it, Dee. I don't mind you throwing away your life so much as I mind that you're doing it stupidly."

"According to you."

"According to me."

She sat for a long moment, wondering what to say. In her mind she knew that what Jerry said was true—she was living on borrowed time with Rita. But her body . . . well, it was a different matter altogether. Even though Rita could drive her near to insanity with her moodiness and frightening lack of simple logic, Dee loved her—compulsively or not. Yet, whenever Dee tried to see into the future, tried to see herself in twenty years, Rita was never a part of the picture.

"Shall we change the subject?" Jerry asked kindly. "I didn't mean to ruin your day."

She smiled. "You didn't. You couldn't. I enjoy your company too much." Dee reached over and patted his hand. "Tell me," she asked, "will this new show run long?"

"Looks good. I certainly hope so . . . all those gorgeous male dancers—smorgasbord! They're simply beautiful. When are you coming to see it?"

"Never, I hope. The reviews were awful."

"Do you pay attention to that? Ridiculous! No one does anymore."

"The backers?"

"Dunderheads! Professional people do not back down because of a few sarcastic words from jealous, self-centered critics."

Dee laughed. "That's what I love about you, Jerry. Your charity, your openmindedness, your respect for others."

"The trouble with you, dear heart, is you can't stand genuine emotion. It embarrasses you. Right or wrong, you must admit I'm emphatic and sincere."

"It's funny," Dee said softly, "that you should say that about me."

"I don't think it funny at all. Just true."

"You may be right. Frightening, isn't it?"

"Good Lord, Dee. What has gotten into you? You sound like a teenager just learning about sex."

"Maybe I am," she answered slowly. "Maybe I am."

Chapter 9

All the way back in the cab, Dee kept trying to shake Jerry's words about Rita's being "cooperative." With whom? Agents? She'd already suspected that, but who else?

Even though she had been aware of it somewhere deep inside her, safely hidden to keep out the hurt, when Jerry had voiced it something inside her had gone numb—a coldness seeped through her even now, just thinking about it.

She would never understand what drove Rita to shack up with anyone. Especially those crude, gravel-voiced hoodlums who ran the music business. It wasn't nymphomania . . . at least, not the kind Dee had read about. It was some kind of compulsion, of course. Perhaps a means of offsetting her guilt about being a lesbian. But then, why bother to be gay? It would be easy to understand if Rita had fallen in love with any of them. At least she could understand that, even if she didn't like it. But this going from pillar to post, lying about looking for a job to cover up her affairs—it was almost too much.

What will be too much? she asked herself, staring out the cab window but not really seeing. What am I waiting for? For her to leave me so I won't have to make the decision? Am I really that gutless? Probably. Why can't I make up my mind?

"This is it, lady," the cabby's voice jolted her from her introspection with an unpleasant start. "Which side of the street?"

That's a hell of a question to ask, she thought wryly. "Right here'll be fine. Thanks."

She climbed out and stood for a moment on the sidewalk, looking up at her building. *Her* building. That more than a thousand people worked in it didn't matter in the least. It was hers.

Somewhere church bells rang faintly, and she was reminded of how much work she had to do and how little time she had to do it. She'd be leaving for Europe in a matter of days now. And just a short time ago it had seemed too remote even to get excited about. She hoped she wouldn't have any trouble getting film past customs, then decided it might be best to take it in bulk so that it wouldn't be so noticeable.

Christ! she swore to herself. I don't have enough things to worry about and a minor thing like that pops up. What devious mechanisms our minds set up.

She walked to the corner and dutifully waited for the light to change before crossing Forty-ninth Street. She wondered if all those people parading, rushing, loitering on Sixth Avenue had problems like hers. Worse, probably. Well, whatever they were, she'd keep her own. She was used to hers at least.

The nonstop elevator to the Photo World offices rose swiftly. She stood silently on the corner, her preoccupied glance refusing to meet the elevator boy's friendly look of curiosity. Usually, she liked to talk to Joe. But now his very presence seemed intrusive. Nice guy, Joe.

Everybody's nice. Wonder if there's someone somewhere saying, "Nice girl, Dee." More than likely. She could easily be considered a "nice girl."

She nodded to Joe on the way out and walked past the receptionist with a scowl on her face.

"Nice lunch, Mrs. Sanders?" the girl asked politely.

"No!" Dee answered curtly and then immediately felt guilty for being so rude.

"Hi, Mrs. Sanders. You're just in time," Karen said as Dee stormed past her desk into her own small office.

"Whatever it is, I don't want to know about it," Dee snapped, and as quickly said, "I'm sorry, Karen. What is it?"

"Whew! What kind of firecrackers did you have for lunch?" Karen laughed good-naturedly. "First, I need your okay on these layouts before I send out for stats."

Dee scrawled her initials on the layouts. Karen took them from her and smiled at her.

Dee stood a moment looking at her, saw her smooth white skin molded gently to her bones, and aesthetically enjoyed the contrast between Karen's green eyes and her long, black hair. She couldn't say that Karen was actually a pretty girl, but she had a wonderful face. Full of contour and shadows highlighting her bone structure, with just a little trace of the fullness of youth, and the healthy color of her flesh.

"How old are you, Karen?" she found herself asking suddenly.

Karen laughed. "I'm twenty-three. . . ." She patted under her chin rather proudly.

Dee grinned. "Well, just have a little respect for your elders today. I've had a hectic lunch and I'm in a foul mood."

"You?" Karen asked in genuine surprise.

"Me. Ogre Sanders." Dee laughed despite herself. "Now. What was this other pressing item I was just in time for?"

"Oh. Oh! A rush job. It seems everybody thought somebody else had gone through the contact prints for the August issue and it turns out there haven't even been any contacts made."

"And I'm elected?"

" 'Fraid so."

Dee took the negatives from Karen and leafed through them quickly. It meant working late again. She'd never get through them all. But in a way, she was relieved. She didn't really feel up to facing Rita tonight. She was afraid of what might come out of her mouth.

"If you want," Karen said quietly, "I can stay late tonight and help you."

Why was it people always managed to be nice to her whenever she felt like being unreasonable? "I hate to ask you," she said.

Karen waved aside any further comment. It's better than going back to that women's prison I live in. I hate that place more every day."

"Why don't you move?"

She looked at Dee a long moment before answering.

"I'm afraid if once I get on my own completely, I won't marry Phil."

That's a strange remark," Dee said. "Is that what's bothering you? Don't you want to marry him?" She fought a tremendous desire to hear Karen say no.

". . . I don't really know. I know I should. But there's something missing. Something I couldn't explain."

"Just premarriage jitters, Karen. Don't worry about it. Phil's a good boy and he loves you. He'll make a good provider and a good father for your children."

"I guess you're right," she answered, but without much enthusiasm. There was an awkward pause. "Shall I plan on staying?"

"If you don't mind. I'll pay for the sandwiches if you'll order them."

"Oh, I almost forgot. Mrs. Evans called. Wanted to know what time you were planning to leave. I told her I thought about five."

"Fine . . . thanks." She wished Rita would stop calling her at the office like a nagging wife. "Anything else?"

Karen shook her head. "That's all." She turned away and left Dee to settle down to the routine for the afternoon. The Paris representative had submitted some fine duplicates of entries for the international exhibit she was to help judge. There was so damn much to do.

For a moment she toyed with the idea of asking to take Karen along. The thought was strangely pleasant. But no. It would never work. The brass would never agree to the added expense. . . . perhaps it was just as well.

Dee busied herself in her work and shortly before five o'clock called home. Rita answered sleepily and Dee tried hard to keep the irritation out of her voice.

"Hi, Rita," she pitched her tone to just the right note of casual friendliness. "Thought I'd better let you know . . . I'm afraid I'll have to stay late tonight. No. Not too late. Well, I can't tell you for sure. No. I'll have a sandwich sent up. Oh? I guess I just won't be able to make it. Why don't you go alone? If I finish soon enough,

I'll meet you there. How was I supposed to know about it? You didn't tell me."

She heard steps outside the office and lowered her voice. Karen stood in the doorway with some papers in her hand. Dee looked up at her. "I'll be with you in a second, Karen."

The girl left as Dee grabbed a pencil. "What's the address? The Rendezvous Club. How late will you be there? All right, all right. I'm not promising but I'll try. Rita? Rita!" Dee stared at the dead phone in her hand.

Oh, Christ! Here we go again. She sighed and tossed the receiver into its holder.

"Ham or pastrami?" Karen yelled, sticking her head in the door.

Thank God for Karen, Dee thought, and smiled. My little stabilizer. "How about a drink first?" Dee asked her with a mischievous smile.

"You're kidding."

"I am not. C'mon. We'll run across the street, dip into a dry martini, grab a sandwich, and come back and go to work."

"You're out of your mind," Karen said half seriously.

"Yes. But it's fashionable these days. Analysts are coining money. Also, I do not like being challenged. If I instruct you to cut out paper dolls you will cut them out, and if I say let's have a drink, then you will have a drink!"

"Only on company time."

"Insolent! That's what you are," Dee scolded as she took Karen by the elbow and lightly pushed her out the door. As she turned to shut the office door, her face brushed past Karen's dark hair, and she noticed at once the wonderful clean smell of her. No deceitful perfume or synthetic essence of something or another, but honest soap and water.

Karen made no effort to pull her arm away. Dee suddenly became self-conscious with the awareness of her and let go abruptly. She smiled carefully when Karen twisted to give her a startled look that defied accurate interpretation.

It was almost nine o'clock before they finished. Dee offered to give Karen a lift, but once outside, Karen decided to walk.

Dee hailed a cab and waved good-bye to Karen as she gave the driver the address of the Rendezvous Club. She silently hoped Rita was not already drunk . . . unless it would prevent her from making a scene about her tardy arrival.

She climbed down from the cab wearily and pushed open the door of the club, painted white now, but the chips showed there were a few colors that had not been applied over the years. It was a heavy and stubborn door, and she cursed it as she walked into the smoke-filled room.

Couples huddled, heads touching, across the small round tables roped off leaving a square patch in the center for a dance floor. A heavy-set woman in slacks came up to Dee, taking her in from top to bottom. "Help you, miss?"

Good Lord! Dee thought. She thinks I'm straight! As tired as she was, Dee couldn't suppress a grin. Then, composing her face, she said in her throatiest voice, "I'm looking for some friends."

The woman stood stonily impassive.

"They arrived around seven-thirty." Dee let her have the old Vassar-type accent full force. A useful little device for just such occasions as these. "For dinner," she added. "Babs Whitaker's party . . ."

Stony-face cracked a bit.

"Oh. Why didn't you say so? You'll find them toward the rear. Biggest table in the house." She walked away as if disappointed, muttering, "Wish people would have their parties at home."

Dee looked uncertainly around the unfamiliar place and moved toward the rear of the room.

"Hello there," Babs called out even before Dee had seen them.

Dee threw her a quick smile, automatically looking for Rita as she stood uncomfortably by the table. She scanned all the unfamiliar-looking faces gazing up at her. "I finally made it," she said, offering her hand to Babs. Bright. Bright remark, ol' girl.

Babs quickly made a round of introductions, saving one effervescing blue-eyed, square-faced girl until last. "And my new friend, Brunhilde."

"You're joking," Dee said before she realized it.

"Nope," Babs laughed good-naturedly. "That's her real name. Just call her Hilda for short."

Dee pulled up a chair and sat down, trying to seem at home. She was mildly curious about what had happened to Babs's last girl-friend but decided it would be unforgivably tactless to make any mention of it. She wondered where old ex-girlfriends went when they were "through." Like, was there a pasture somewhere, or were they sent on a quota basis to alien ports, or what? She never seemed to see any of them again.

"Who's the bouncer?" Dee finally asked for lack of better conversation.

"Mac? The big butch at the door?"

Dee nodded. She might have guessed her name would be Mac.

"She's a real character. Been here a year, dying to bounce some-one and hasn't had a chance yet."

"I'm sure it's frustrating," Dee offered sympathetically.

"Yeh." Babs laughed and poked Hilda in the ribs. "Her real name's Patsy—isn't that a riot? I mean, with a build like hers? I think she'd kill the first person who called her that."

Hilda tittered.

Dee wished to hell she didn't feel so completely out of step with these women. Would it always be this way? Having to be friends with people you'd never pick in a hundred years? Probably. A homo-sexual's choice of friends was always very limited. Only with people like themselves could they let their hair down, act naturally. It was either join them or live under the constant pressure of fear of dis-covery. There had been several women Dee had met through her work whose friendships she would have enjoyed, but the lies and the petty deceits, the evasions, were too much of a strain. Require-ment: be gay. Big Brother says: be gay.

"Ah . . ." Dee said hesitantly, "anyone seen Rita?"

Babs's face flushed even in the dim light. She laughed nervously. "Sure. She's around someplace."

Hilda leaned forward rapturously. "Is she that gorgeous one that all the butches are falling over?"

Dee caught the swift movement of Babs's nudge under the table.

"I was only going to say she went to the powder room," Hilda added lamely, cringing under Babs's malevolent glare. The byplay was bitterly revealing.

Dee felt it before she knew it. She felt her hands grow hot and

211

clammy at the same time. And her head felt heavy, thick with fury—a sickening yellow clouded her vision.

"Excuse me," she muttered under her breath as she pushed her chair away from the table. She felt her limbs go stiff as she worked her way around the laughing patrons and the inconveniently placed tables. Dimly she made out the dark door adjoining another dark door. Two doors together. One had a badly worn picture of a top-hatted gentleman; the other of a cameolike lady. For a moment she thought she was going to be sick.

Somehow she managed to open the door, and the familiar sweet-sick sanitary odors hit her like a fist in the stomach. It was harshly bright—well lit so the butches could be sure their makeup didn't show.

And . . . there she was. Rita. Good God! Rita! Her blouse was unbuttoned and her bra almost off. She was leaning against the wallpapered partition, her head thrown back so that her long black hair hung down low across her shoulders. Her mouth was open slightly, showing just the tips of her white teeth, and her eyes were closed.

If anyone had come into the room before, she obviously wasn't paying attention or did not care.

Dee's shocked gaze shifted to the tall, slim figure bent over Rita. A remarkably handsome woman, Dee had to admit, even with the mannish haircut which set off her well-molded shoulders. As if she were someone else, Dee watched this woman's hands roam over Rita's shoulders, down to her breasts, and over her body with an air of ownership Dee almost believed. The woman's mouth clung hungrily to Rita's neck, then moved down . . . down.

"You whore!" The words tore through the small room like a jagged streak of lightning. She did not even realize she had uttered it. It was the voice of a stranger, not her own, surely. She stood there frozen, staring in mute horror at the incredible tableau before her. A sense of curious detachment swept over her.

Then, suddenly she began to laugh, wildly, bitterly.

Rita's head had come forward abruptly, and her eyes had snapped open with apparent surprise. "Dee!"

Dee wanted to throw up—to purge herself of the scene. She

wanted to run, but her legs wouldn't obey her. She could only stand there helplessly as the tall woman straightened up and glared at her as though she were an intruder, a light, sarcastic smile on her thin lips.

Rita fumbled at her buttons and at the same time tried to tidy her hair. Lipstick was smeared across her chin, and her mascara had spread a thin, dark circle beneath each eye.

"This isn't what it looks like, Dee . . . honest, Dee."

Dee turned her head away and stared at the lavatory doors beyond them. "In a place like this," she said, the words choking her with thick revulsion.

"But, Dee . . ." Rita interrupted, a frenzied look on her face.

Dee looked back at her. For a few seconds she wavered. Then, somehow she found the strength to stand steadily, and her self-command was returning. "I've had it, Rita," she said, her voice tight and hard with suppressed rage.

She walked back to the door, then paused with her hand on the smudged knob. "I'll spend the night in a hotel. Be out in the morning. I want nothing around the apartment to remind me. Just get out of my life."

In a daze she walked through the restaurant. She wondered vaguely if the woman had a "friend" sitting there in the room, waiting patiently, pretending not to be concerned.

Dee wished to God she were eighty so that she would never have to think of love or sex again.

Chapter 10

She sat at her desk the next morning, not really quite sure of where she was, much less why. She still felt sticky and dirty. The hotel accomodations had been spectacularly inferior; sleep even under the best conditions would have been difficult. In the morning she was too anxious to get out even to shower, and she threw on the same clothes she had worn the day before—something she hated to do.

But none of it mattered very much. Even if she'd slept beautifully, she would still have felt just as unkempt and sick. She didn't care. Not about anything. She just hoped to hell Rita was out of her apartment by the time she got home that night. She couldn't stand the thought of a scene or an argument. Not tonight. She was tired . . . so tired. All the years of pent-up hostilities, resentments, and fears had suddenly come cascading down around her head, and she was too immobilized to try to fight her way out.

And that was that. It was over. The torment, the passion, the excitement, the anguish, the ecstasy—all over. What of life was left? she wondered. Now what? Could she really live without Rita? Why had she done it? Oh, Christ! What had she hoped to get from it?

What did it matter now, anyway? It didn't, she supposed. Nothing mattered.

She put her head in her hands and pressed her palms against her aching eyes as if to blot out the turmoil of emotions that were pulling her toward that frightening inward center of unadmitted fear—the unknown. Like getting sucked into a whirlpool, she thought.

Stop it now. Just stop it! You keep on this way and you'll be signing in at Bellevue next.

"I thought," Karen said, softly placing a paper cup next to Dee's elbow, "you might like some coffee." She stood hesitantly by Dee's chair.

Dee looked up at her and fought with all her might not to cry. She wanted so badly to cry. And what was worse, Dee could tell that even Karen recognized this need. She didn't say it, but she could sense it. She showed it in her expression, in her tone of voice.

"Why don't you take the day off, Mrs. Sanders?" she suggested.

Dee shook her head slowly, half closing her eyes.

"Is there . . . is there anything I can do?"

She wanted to say, "Just stay near me; don't leave me alone," but instead managed what she hoped wasn't too pitiful a smile and replied, "No. No thanks, Karen. I'll be all right. Just a personal problem. I'll get over it."

Karen placed her hand lightly, maternally, on Dee's shoulder. "I don't like to see you this way. . . ." She smiled slowly, then turned and went back to her desk.

It was uncomfortable, this child being so concerned about her. Actually, the thought of anyone being really concerned about her was surprising. She wasn't used to it. Her friends had always taken an interest, of course, but their own lives were so busy and filled with their own problems, they didn't really have the time genuinely to give of themselves. Not that Dee expected it, or even really wanted it. Concern embarrassed her.

Her family life had certainly never given her much opportunity to feel wanted or loved, even though her parents were pretty average people—none of the more blatantly psychotic problems one so often heard about from other homosexuals. Her father had worked all day, hadn't he? Wasn't he entitled to a little leisure time without having to listen to his kids' problems? That was the mother's job! And her mother—well-meaning, certainly. Dee could say that for her. It's just that she became so overwhelmed with her duties as a wife that she forgot motherhood included anything over and above bearing the children. The kitchen floor had to be mopped. . . . Go put your own Band-Aid on. . . . What do you mean "have a picnic" when there's so much work to do? . . .

The intercom sounded harshly, and she hastily pushed down the switch. "Yes?"

"Sorry, Mrs. Sanders. The old man wants to talk to you in his office."

"Wouldn't you know it," Dee muttered under her breath. "He's been playing golf every day for a week, and the one day I can't stand the thought of him he wants to talk to me. All right, Karen," she said in a normal voice. "Tell him I'll be in. Give me about five minutes to clear my brain."

"Sure."

Dee pushed her chair back from the desk and took a deep breath, held it, and exhaled when she couldn't stand it any longer. It was an old trick of hers based on the stub-your-toe-when-your-head-aches principle.

She walked over to the water cooler outside her office, straightened her hair in front of the mirror, and poured herself two glasses of water.

"Hi, gorgeous," a young man in shirtsleeves called as he walked by.

She smiled in spite of herself. "Hello, Bill. How's the wife?"

"Beautiful! But it's you I really go for. How about it?" he flung teasingly over his shoulder.

Dee waved him away with a grin and felt her spirits suddenly lift. Amazing what a little male flattery will do, she thought, and happened to catch Karen's eye. She still looked worried.

Dee walked over to her and tugged at her hair playfully. "Don't worry, kitten. I'm really all right. What I need is a man, that's all." She wasn't so certain this wasn't true.

She sighed wearily and gathered herself for the approaching session as the elevator door slid open and she stepped onto the carpeted luxury of the penthouse.

"How was it?" Karen asked as Dee came toward her later.

"Well." Dee smiled slowly. "I'm not fired, anyway."

"I didn't mean that and you know it. What did he want?"

Dee stood pensively next to Karen's desk. "Nothing, really. Just checking. He wanted to talk over the European exhibit. He thinks I should leave a little earlier than we had planned. Can I get my work caught up? Will I be able to leave someone in charge here? Is the per diem satisfactory? Tune in tomorrow. . . ."

Karen stared at her a long moment, then shook her head. "You are nuts!" she muttered. "Aren't you excited about it? Don't you want to go?"

For a second, Dee had the feeling that Karen didn't want her to go, that she hated the whole idea and was just feigning enthusiasm. But it was probably just the idea of having to work with someone else that was bothering her. Of course, Karen would miss her. They worked together with almost uncanny perfection and, after all, they were friends.

"Sure. I want to go. In fact, I suppose it's a real pat on the back that they chose me to go."

"You're dern-tootin'!" Karen exclaimed, but the note of pride was quite evident. She was always after Dee to ask for a raise, or to make herself better known to the executive staff in general.

Sometimes Dee felt that Karen acted more like her mother than someone young enough to be—well, not her daughter, but maybe a kid sister.

On impulse, Dee swiftly bent over and kissed the top of Karen's head. "Just because you're such a nice kid."

She watched Karen turn crimson and suddenly busy herself with the yearbook paste-up. "You *are* in a funny mood today."

Dee nodded. "Think I'll go to Paris and find me a nice broken-down duke, or count, and settle down in some shabby but elegant villa in the north of France . . . or something equally historic. Or maybe I'll go to Spain and save a bullfighter from Ava Gardner."

"Doubt that any man would appreciate *that* much," Karen laughed.

"Maybe I'll even become a bullfighter myself."

"*That* I'd like to see," Karen giggled.

Dee stood pensively for a moment, thousands of wild thoughts running through her head. "Karen."

"Yes, Mrs. Sanders."

She looked down at Karen and wondered what it was she had been about to say. Her mind had gone blank. She couldn't remember . . . not even the general idea of her thoughts.

Laughing lightly, she said, "Never mind."

Chapter 11

The apartment had taken on a new life. It was a slow metamorphosis but a steady one. At first, Dee had been driven nearly insane without Rita around. She had wandered from one room to another aimlessly, half expecting to see some little personal article Rita might have left behind. Even if she'd found something she didn't know whether she would destroy it or kiss it.

Cho-Cho had spent a few listless days without Rita but now, too, had learned to accept the loss—in fact, seemed almost glad to be sole mistress of the apartment. Dee had found Cho-Cho an unbearable reminder those first few days—she kept seeing Rita curled in the armchair with Cho-Cho in her lap, or leaning over to pet the cat absentmindedly.

But now everything had taken on a settled look again. How long had it been? Dee thought. Only two weeks. Yet so much had happened: a passport to be obtained, visas, getting her immunization shots, clearing things up at the office, registering her Leica and Rollei with customs, arranging things so that Karen could assume a maximum of authority while she was gone. Thank heaven for Karen. She was going to miss her.

Even so, there was a new bounce to Dee's step as she left the Fifth Avenue bus to meet Jerry Wilson for lunch. She'd not talked to him since their last luncheon date and had not told him this morning over the phone about the breakup. She was almost afraid to tell him, although there was no real reason to be.

Yet she felt anxious, and her hands were moist as she walked into the hotel lobby. If Jerry sneered or belittled Rita, she was sure she would cry; yet if he was overjoyed she would probably get angry. There was no logic to her emotions; they were simply there. She wished now she hadn't made the appointment, and even briefly considered entering a phone booth and paging him to break the date with some wild excuse.

But it was too late for that. Besides, he was her friend. If she couldn't face him with the news, then her whole adjustment had been a farce. And she'd invested too much agony toward getting over Rita to waste it.

She worked hard, stayed late at the office, had had dinner with Karen a few times, and threw herself into a project of capturing the moods of Sixth Avenue and Forty-ninth Street. She was never without at least one of her cameras and spent every moment possible shooting just the northeast corner. She didn't know that she'd ever do anything with the shots she was getting, but it was something to do. She'd even gone into the building across the street and requested permission to shoot from the second-floor window and the top floor. They'd acted as if she were some intoxicated tourist, but allowed her the privilege. Few people could resist Dee's friendly candor.

She entered the restaurant and saw Jerry sitting at his usual table. He waved at her, half rising from the booth, looking dapper as ever, but with a special little smile on his face that betrayed secret knowledge.

When she reached him, he leaned over and pecked her on the cheek. "You get lovelier each time I see you."

Dee smiled. "You're sweet."

"But you look a little thinner," he admonished as they sat down. "Can't have that. Don't want you ruining that lovely body of yours."

"Going straight, Jerry?" Dee laughed.

He made a grimace. "Heaven forbid! You don't have to malign me, you know. What's the matter, can't you accept flattery?"

"Not from you. You're more the mother-hen type, always pecking away at me for my faults."

"That's unkind," he smiled slowly. "But true."

She sat back, crossing her legs carefully, placing her purse next to her on top of her camera. "What am I having for lunch today?" she asked him. Jerry never allowed her to order anything for herself.

"Ah," he pursed his lips appreciatively. "A feast! I decided to be nice to you today with a chateaubriand . . . but like you've never tasted before." He turned in his seat to face her. "When are you leaving for Paris?"

"Next week. Although there's a good chance I might leave the end of this week."

"What about passage? Haven't you made reservations?"

"Yes," Dee smiled. "For two separate dates. One of them will be canceled."

"Why? I'll never understand the publishing business. They're all so terribly, terribly intellectual, you know, and not an ounce of common sense in the lot."

"Now, now. Our Paris representative is away on business and isn't certain on which date he'll return. That's one reason. And then, we're putting an issue to bed right now and I am needed despite your low opinion of me, plus a lot of other miscellaneous reasons."

"Do you want me to give you a few addresses? Gay clubs, or something?"

She glanced at him sharply. He knew about her break with Rita, then. He would never have made that offer otherwise. Well. Just as well. It would save her a lot of trouble and embarrassment. But his question about gay addresses had stirred something within her. . . . A near panic seemed to grip her at the thought of being all alone in a foreign country and seeking out another lesbian. Didn't anything last? What did straight people do to stay married twenty, thirty years and longer?

Jerry's voice reached through her thoughts, asking her how long she planned to stay in Paris. "What? Oh. I'm not sure. A month, roughly."

"Look, darling. I don't mind your being preoccupied . . . but I don't feel like eating lunch alone. Do your daydreaming on company time if you don't mind."

"I'm sorry, Jerry. Really I am." She played with her fork a moment, hoping he would say something to catch her interest. For some reason the prospect of her trip was still unreal to her. But when several moments went by and he said nothing, she knew it was going to be up to her to carry the ball today.

She put her fork down carefully and sat back. "How long have you known and how did you find out?" She said it softly, tentatively.

Jerry frowned slightly. "Not the way you're thinking," he answered. "The word travels pretty fast about a girl like Rita. There was no mention of you . . . nor of your relationship with her. It was just that it became known she was 'available,' as it were."

"I see," Dee said lamely, not really knowing what to say or what she had expected him to say.

"It could only have meant one thing," he continued. "But if it's not too painful, I would like to be filled in on a few of the more important details. What finally made her leave you?"

Dee sighed silently, resigning herself to the answer. "I left her," she said bluntly. "That is, I requested her to leave."

Jerry snorted. "But that's marvelous! What miracle occurred to make you see the light about that . . . her?"

She bit her lower lip, severely trying to keep her emotions in check. She didn't want to feel anything—just the facts, ma'am. "It was rather sticky, Jerry. If you don't mind we'll let that part go until some other time."

It wasn't hard to tell he was controlling his curiosity, but she was still grateful for the attempt. "Let's just say I finally found out what an ass I'd been. Okay?"

"But look at you, darling," he said impatiently. "Just take a good look at yourself. Any imbecile could see you're still in love with her."

"Please, Jerry. Please. Not now."

"When? Five years from now when you're still dragging a long tragic face around? That wasn't love you felt for Rita—it was a morbid addiction."

"Jerry . . ." Dee interrupted, trying to keep calm.

"Don't 'Jerry' me. You're so in love with the idea of love that you invested in that conniving little broad a thousand virtues that she never even heard of. You—"

"Do you want me to cry?" she asked him in a whisper.

He stopped short, his mouth still open to speak. "Oh, I'm sorry, Dee. I hadn't meant to lecture you or rub things in. I was just reacting as an old friend and not really thinking about what you're going through. Forgive me. I know how painful it must be." He put his hand over hers for a moment and pressed it.

She looked at him a few minutes and felt herself filled with a strange kind of compassion. It was that rare feeling only the injured can have for the injurer—a private, special understanding. He looked so downcast, so remorseful. "Don't worry about me, Jerry. I'll be all right. But it's going to take time. This wasn't just a one-night stand. . . . A lot of my life and my emotions were tied up in this. I'll get over it, but right now I need the chance to feel sorry for myself."

"Of course . . ."

"And I'm not angry with you. You had every right . . ."

Jerry raised his well-manicured fingers to his lips. "Let's just drop the whole subject. We'll talk about it some other time, when you've regained your perspective. Maybe when you come back."

She smiled then and felt very much like hugging him. But any real demonstration of affection with Jerry was always difficult. He seemed to tense up and withdraw, as if anticipating some sort of maudlin scene. It was a side of his nature she'd learned to accept long ago.

He seemed to shrink from emotional displays of any sort, yet was always the first one to bawl her out for her own fears and reservations. But that was just Jerry. It was the least of her worries, certainly.

Their lunch arrived, and the conversation turned to Jerry's show and the doings at the theater, and his usual patter about people and events around town. Always witty, always sarcastic.

Recklessly she broke into his conversation. "What would happen, Jerry, if you really and truly fell in love with someone who loved you the same way?"

He sat very still for a moment, staring at her. Then a slow, deliberate smile crossed his face. "Happen?"

Dee shivered when the cold chuckle came up from his throat. "I'd probably die from the shock."

Chapter 12

The days that followed were marked by a merciful lack of leisure for Dee to give much thought to her own problems. By the time she reached her apartment, she was too tired to do anything but fall into bed after a hot bath. She had pushed herself and Karen at an incredible pace to have everything under control at her desk. They worked late almost every evening and yet managed somehow to show up at the office in the morning with the zest of people who were getting things done.

On several occasions Dee had caught herself wondering what she was going to do without Karen. She didn't want to feel that way. It wasn't safe—she couldn't trust her own motives anymore. But Karen had seemed to sense it indirectly, and more than once Dee had looked up to find Karen watching her. She would smile, and then they would both feel uneasy and self-conscious and return to their respective work.

It was a hot and humid day, the day before Dee was to leave. Even the sleeveless green sheath she had put on that morning offered no relief from the heat on her way to the office. She got off the elevator and saw Karen sitting at her desk with a paper cup of coffee on the right-hand side, wedged in between piles of correspondence and file copies of back issues.

" 'Morning, Mrs. Sanders," she said as cheerily as she could.

Dee smiled, secretly realizing how very tired Karen must be.

"How can you drink anything hot on a day like this?" she asked without expecting an answer.

"Air-conditioning . . ." Karen replied matter-of-factly.

Dee nodded appreciatively. "Any calls?"

Karen reached over and lifted some photographs from the top of her desk calendar. "Pan Am reconfirmed your flight tomorrow night. . . . The old man wishes you luck, and why aren't you at your desk? . . . And the boys in the stock room have smuggled in a bottle for a bon voyage drink after lunch." She put the photos back and glanced up at Dee with an inscrutable expression.

"All that so early in the morning?" Dee laughed.

Karen gave a noncommittal shrug.

Dee thought she sensed a certain holding-back on Karen's part, a reserve she did not usually have. She wondered if Karen's boyfriend was trying to press her for a marriage date again. "How about us treating ourselves to a decent place for dinner tonight?" Dee said suddenly. "Sort of a going-away spree."

Karen tensed almost imperceptibly, then looked up at Dee with a carefully blank gaze. "Sounds fine. Dutch treat, though. My folks sent me some money yesterday."

"Save it, then," Dee replied. "You'll need it to buy souvenirs in Indonesia, or wherever you end up with Phil."

"Dutch treat," Karen said again but more firmly. There was a strained look about her face that Dee had never seen before.

"All right. It's your money." She smiled a little uncertainly, then entered her own small office. She's tired, Dee reasoned, and a little edgy. And I suppose the prospect of having so much responsibility while I'm away is rather an awesome idea.

Johnny's Steak House was still comparatively empty at five-thirty. The dinner crowds wouldn't start until around six-thirty or seven. Dee and Karen sat in a yellow booth lining the wall, waiting for their drinks.

"We've really earned this," Dee said after a prolonged silence. "At least, you certainly have." She smiled, trying to draw Karen out of her strange mood, which had lasted all day.

226

"It was character-building," Karen said lightly, shifting uncomfortably. "Do you mind if I sit across from you? I like to look at people when I talk to them."

She made the move but instead of looking at Dee made a detailed survey of the large room, inquiring what kind of wood paneling was used, how many times Dee had been there.

The waiter arrived with their drinks, and for the first time since Dee had known Karen, she felt uncomfortable with her. They didn't have that much more to do when they returned to the office to make Karen feel apprehensive—in fact, there wasn't so much that it couldn't be finished up tomorrow morning in an hour. Karen's attitude was not only incomprehensible to Dee, it was a little frightening. She tried to think of what she might have done or said that perhaps had hurt Karen in some way.

What was worse, it left Dee unable to make conversation. She felt she was being shut out and didn't know why. Finally, no longer able to stand it, she blurted out the first thing that came to mind. "Want to tell me about it? Is there anything I can do?"

That was tactful, she scolded herself, like a bulldozer!

Karen's expression became veiled, defensive. It was as if she had had a reply on the tip of her tongue but had suddenly caught herself before letting it slip out. "Oh," Karen said nonchalantly, "nothing really. Just tired, I guess. And worried."

"About what?" Dee signaled the waiter for another round.

Karen sighed lightly. "The job . . . things like that."

"Like what?" Dee persisted.

She smiled slowly. "You writing a book or something?"

"If you don't want to tell me, then say so. But we've been pretty close friends up to now . . . don't get flip with me."

Karen sat quietly for a moment. She didn't appear to be thinking so much as forcing herself not to think. Her young face flushed for a second, and when she looked up there was just a trace of tears in her eyes. "I'm just a sentimental jerk," she said with a choke in her voice. "I'm going to miss you!"

Dee was so relieved that there wasn't anything else bothering Karen that she was speechless. Then the impact of what Karen was saying released her own feelings and brought tears to her eyes, too.

Without being very certain why, they both began to laugh as the tears rolled slowly down their cheeks.

When they regained control of themselves, Dee asked, "What do you plan to do while I'm gone?" She picked up the menu quickly and scrutinized it carefully. "Why not see more of Phil before you lose him?"

"Tell me," Karen began slowly, "why are you always trying so hard to get me to marry Phil? I mean, it just seems that every time I turn around, you've got another one of your subliminal plugs flashing by. If you think marriage is the only cure for all ills, then why haven't you remarried?"

Dee was torn between being amused at Karen's personality switch and fighting the awful fear that perhaps Karen knew more about her than she had let on. "That's a very good question," Dee answered with a light laugh. "Would you mind repeating it?"

It wasn't hard to tell that Karen found it difficult to be so blunt. Her usual approach to a difficult subject was one of circumlocution: mention it, then drop the whole topic, and eventually the "victim" would think he thought of it himself.

"Well," Karen said with a slightly embarrassed glance. "You're always telling me about security, babies, and the good, solid life. If it's so great why haven't you done it?"

Dee lighted a cigarette slowly, mindful of not letting any masculine gesture show. Pausing in her reply, she fleetingly considered how learning to be feminine while lighting a cigarette was one of the most difficult things she had accomplished. There should be no "evidence" of her lesbian tendencies. . . .

"I'm waiting, Mrs. Sanders," Karen said softly.

"I do wish you would call me Dee. . . ."

"Don't change the subject . . . Dee," Karen answered with a note of pleasure in her voice.

"Marriage. Home. Security. Hmm," she stated evasively.

"Why not?" Karen insisted.

Dee laughed. "That's a line from a TV show, isn't it?"

"Dee . . ."

"Oh, all right. I've not found the right guy for me. Period."

"That's not true. . . . I mean, I don't think you really mean that."

"Meaning?" Dee smiled, trying to appear casual. Yet strange flashes shot across her head, belying her conditioned calmness.

"You're an attractive, bright, and successful woman. I hear lots of the fellows around the office talk about how you've turned down dates with them."

Dee felt her hands grow cold. . . . Were they talking at the office—calling her queer? Oh, God! "I have outside friends," she said hastily.

"A lot of the editors around are good marriage material—you don't even give them a chance. If your 'outside friends' aren't panning out, then why don't you give the 'inside friends' a chance? Isn't it because you don't really want to get married?"

"Now, look here, Karen. What I plan to do with my life has very little to do with yours. . . . I've been married." Dee tried to keep her voice at its usual pitch. "You, however, have not. You are also a good deal younger than I am."

"Not that much!" Karen said with a grin.

"Enough. There's no big world of discovery left for me in marriage. And I'm in no big rush. For a while I dated so many guys I couldn't keep their names straight," she lied. "Now I'm putting my energies into my job, and if the right guy comes along, well and good. But I'm not actively looking anymore."

"What big world of discovery?" Karen asked. "Good heavens, Dee. I'm not some wide-eyed kid from Walla-Walla. I know all about the birds and the bees and have had some experience. . . ."

"Karen!" Dee was amazed to realize she was genuinely shocked. She had just never thought of Karen as having been to bed with a man. Or maybe she just didn't want to.

"Let's have another drink," Karen suggested mischievously.

"I think you're drunk already," Dee said, almost laughing with embarrassment, or discomfort, or for no reason at all. She was certain that if she were not leaving, Karen would never be talking this way.

"Really, Dee. Why do you insist on treating me like a crinoline-crocked—I mean frocked—little girl? Like why, man?" Karen giggled with obvious enjoyment of being able to shock the implacable Dee Sanders.

"Still waters," Dee mumbled, ordering their drinks "All right, Vampira, what other sordid details of your past are you going to reveal? Not that I believe you."

"None, really. But you want to know something?" She stared at Dee for a long moment. "I don't really *want* to get married, and least of all to Phil!"

"All right, all right," Dee said carefully, still reacting to Karen's confession of her love affairs. "Don't get married. What *do* you want to do?"

"Have a career . . . be wanton and wild . . . like the song 'I Want To Be Evil.' Then, when I've got it out of my system, I'll think about diapers and drudgery."

Dee shook her head disparagingly. "Karen. You crazy nut. Don't you see how foolish that would be? Wanton and wild," Dee mimicked. "It's like overeating. You'll stretch your stomach to the point that going on a diet is near to impossible. Once you've given marriage a chance, then you can always do what you want later if you must—but the reverse is rarely true."

"Well? What do women do who don't want to get married?"

Turn queer, Dee thought despite herself, and immediately hated herself for the notion. Oh, yes, Dee said silently. Turn queer and spend the rest of your life atoning for it, worrying about it, wondering what you would have been if you hadn't fallen into the convenience of a gay affair. Spend hours trying to rationalize your life after you've seen a mother in some simple little act like lifting a son to the water fountain with that special look of "This is mine; I made it; he came out of me." Just the expression that comes into a mother's eyes when she gazes at the back of her child's neck, or the surprised smile that comes to a mother's face when her child has said something genuinely amusing—even the moments of impatience and anger were to be envied.

"Make me a promise" Dee said suddenly.

"I'll try."

"Don't cut Phil off until I get back—please."

"But why?" Karen's frown was swiftly replaced with a smile. "You going to find me someone better?"

Dee ignored her comment with a sudden rush of thoughts whirl-winding scraps of conversation and ideas. "You once said you were afraid to take a place of your own because of what you thought you might do. Right?"

Karen nodded with an inquisitive, catlike tilt to her head.

"I'm going to be gone about a month. I have a pet and a paid-for apartment. . . ."

"You're not going to suggest . . ." Karen interrupted.

"You move in and stay until I get back. You feed the cat and keep out intruders. I think half of your problems are that you live in that woman's-prison residence and that you've not really given Phil a chance to be a man."

"Oh, we've made love before. . . ."

She felt herself tense at Karen's admission but managed to ask, "Where? In the backseat of his car? Oh, no, Karen. Give him a chance. Let him come up to the apartment; make dinner for him; do anything you want. But try. That's all I ask. Just try."

"Why is this so important to you?" Karen asked sincerely.

Dee didn't answer for a moment; she wasn't too certain herself. "Because . . ." she began, "because I'm very fond of you. And be-cause I don't want to see you make a tragic mistake."

"What's tragic? That I don't marry my high school sweetheart? There are other men."

Funny, Dee thought, taken aback. Of course there are other men. She had been projecting her own feelings—assuming that if she didn't marry Phil she wouldn't marry anyone. Dee felt foolish and presumptuous. She bit her lower lip lightly, then smiled.

"Of course there are. But"—she paused—"I still would appreci-ate it if you would move into my place while I'm gone. A change of scenery certainly wouldn't hurt you, and it won't hurt to give Phil one big chance."

Karen laughed suddenly. "As a matter of fact, I think I rather like the idea."

They ordered dinner and discussed the new arrangements with enthusiasm. Dee found herself vaguely considering asking Karen to stay on even after her return . . . but something stopped her.

Perhaps it was because each time she thought of it, the image of Phil and Karen making love followed immediately. She didn't understand the association, but she instinctively mistrusted it.

She was trying very hard to believe she was doing the right thing by asking Karen to stay at all.

Time would tell.

Chapter 13

Her landing at Orly Field a day and a half later was uneventful, and even the terminal was a bit of a disappointment. Dee didn't know what she had expected, but the lack of "foreign atmosphere" was surprising. It could have been any terminal in the States. She'd gone through customs with her fingers crossed and smilingly lied about the amount of film she had with her. Her Rollei and her Leica were properly inspected and registered with the usual warning about the dangers of trying to exchange them for new ones and smuggling out the replacements.

Even though newer models of each of her cameras were out on the market—indeed had been for several years—she had a foolish superstition about her two "eyes." They were a part of her. She might one day add to them but never replace them.

The porter was very attentive and personally selected a cab for her, haggling with the driver over the fare, then with a wonderfully candid smile informed her of the sum they had agreed upon and that she was not to pay him a cent more. Dee opened her purse to tip the porter, but he stepped back, dramatically shaking his finger at her.

"All France loves a beautiful woman," he said in broken English. "I welcome you for Frenchmen."

She was embarrassed yet terribly pleased. With a jolt the driver pulled away from the terminal and began the drive into Paris. As they passed the many vacant lots, run-down inns, remains of bombed buildings never rebuilt, and began to approach the city itself, Dee became more and more excited. She didn't care if the cabbie was taking her the long way around or not.

She was absorbing the texture and feel of her first moments in Paris. It was too good to worry about the fare. She hated even to blink lest she miss something.

Obviously she was going to need a lot more film than she had brought. They passed Notre Dame, continuing along the Seine, passed a railroad station on the left, then turned right over a bridge to the famous Place de la Concorde. They darted in and out of traffic like insane polo players, but she didn't care.

Dee was going to stay with Photo World's French representative. Monsieur Bizot had assured her office that he and his wife would be delighted to have her as their guest and that there was plenty of room for her, including a private entrance, since what had at one time been servants' quarters had been converted to a guest apartment.

All this and a per diem, too, Dee thought excitedly.

The cabbie stopped in front of a rather plain-looking building and thumbed to her that she had arrived. She carefully inspected the fare the meter indicated and compromised between what it said, what her porter had said, and the unhappy expression on the driver's face.

As she lifted her two valises, the high double doors opened and a short, round-faced man came rushing out to greet her and wrestled the bags from her hands. "How delightful," he said in a surprisingly low voice. "You are here and you are welcome. Please. Come inside. My wife, Renée (I call her Pepe, though, because she looks like a Spanish orphan boy—you call her Pepe, too) is so looking forward to your stay."

Dee liked him at once. He was sincere, frank, and had a wonderful enthusiasm.

"I want to thank you, M'sieur Bizot," she began as they entered the building.

"*Mais non!* Please. I am to call you Dee and you must call me Raoul. Please." He smiled as she paused inside the foyer. "It is impressive, yes? It is said that before Napoleon met Josephine he maintained a mistress in these apartments. And since I am not tall, I always feel that my wife perhaps is really my mistress. . . . It adds such flavor."

Dee laughed and followed him upstairs to the drawing room. She felt at home immediately. Raoul left her neither time nor silence to feel otherwise. Placing her valises at the side of the upstairs landing with a gesture that such mundane matters could wait, he led her into the drawing room with obvious pride and pleasure.

"Pepe, my beloved, this is our Dee Sanders from New York." He waved toward Dee, and from the tone in Raoul's voice she knew this man adored his wife more than anything else in the world.

Dee felt a surge of genuine pleasure and gratitude toward this man for giving her a renewed delight with romance. She looked across the long, narrow room to the Renaissance chair across from the rich blue velvet settee.

A medium-sized woman rose and came toward her with feline precision. Her tightly fitted slacks and wraparound white blouse showed a boyishness to her body, but when she reached Dee, her face held the history of the world. Angular, deep-set dark eyes and a full, sensitive mouth made her look like a statue that had seen mankind pass by for hundreds of years and now had suddenly come to life. She was ageless. She could have been fifteen or fifty—it was impossible to tell.

Pepe extended her hand to Dee, hesitantly at first, looking intently into Dee's eyes. There was a moment's silence.

Suddenly, Pepe laughed heartily and threw her arms open and embraced Dee like an old friend she had not seen in years. "But this is Paris!" she exclaimed in soft-voiced chastisement. "We are an affectionate people who find it difficult not to show our feelings. . . . You Americans are always so stiff."

Dee was a bit uncertain what she should do or say, but they were both so open, so demonstrative, that it didn't really worry her. "It is very kind of you. . . ."

"Feh!" Pepe said with another laugh. "I was dying of boredom.

Your visit is a vacation for me—besides, I love to shop for clothes but am too thin to look well in them. I will enjoy going with you . . . if you will allow."

Raoul had, in the meantime, mixed them all martinis in honor of Dee's visit. "Pepe, my darling," he said, handing her the drink, "Dee will think we have been imprisoned here the way we are both carrying on." He laughed at his own little joke and glanced sheepishly at Pepe.

She extended her hand to him and held it, looking all the while at Dee. "I think not, *mon cher*. Dee knows of life. . . . It is there in her eyes." She squeezed his hand briefly and let it go. "But now, Raoul, a toast. We must have a toast on this occasion."

He smiled and scratched his head slowly, plainly seeking something really original to say.

A thought came into Dee's mind, but she knew it was not her place to say anything, so instead she waited.

"Yes, Dee," Pepe smiled at her knowingly. "What were you to say. There are no formalities here—you are now family."

It surprised Dee, this immediate perceptiveness of Pepe's. Despite a lump that was rapidly forming in her throat, she asked, "May I suggest a toast?"

Raoul came over to her, clicked his heels without spilling a drop, and smiled patiently and approvingly at her.

Dee looked first from one to the other and took strength from their obvious zest for living. "To the birth of a lasting friendship . . . first," she hesitated.

"And second?" Pepe asked quietly.

"To the circumstances that allowed me to find a truly happily married couple who find that life is richer for the pleasure they find in each other." Dee felt a little melodramatic and foolish, but she meant it nonetheless.

"*Charmant!*" Raoul said, and took a long swallow from his drink as if to wash down the thought.

Chapter 14

As if in a dream, Dee filled the first few days with impressions and sensations. Then she discovered the shops. She hadn't ever been particularly enthused about clothes before, even though she always took great pains to dress simply and in taste. But Paris fashions! It had brought out a woman in her she did not know existed. It seemed to her that every smile she saw was directed personally at her, full of merry approval.

She also grew to adore Pepe and Raoul completely. All strangeness and reserve with them was gone—they wouldn't allow it.

In spite of all her tourist treks, she still found the necessary time to accomplish what she was there for. She arrived at Raoul's office around ten-thirty in the morning, worked furiously, to everyone's amazement, and left around three-thirty or four in the afternoon.

She knew no other city would ever hold her love as much as Paris did. Paris was her first European city. It had awakened her much as a lover might introduce a woman to sensations she never knew she could have. Dee wanted every moment to last as long as it could, to drink in her new sense of freedom.

She had never been so wide awake in the morning, never so grateful to breathe . . . French air had no distasteful associations for her. It was new, and it therefore had to be clean.

On the fifth evening, after a particularly grueling day sorting out hundreds of enlargements, Pepe had met Raoul and Dee in front of the office, waving mischievously from the small Renault parked at the curb. "So slow, you two! It is no one's funeral. Come, get in."

Pepe's dark eyes gleamed with secret knowledge, her short hair only slightly disarranged from the breeze as she slid into the driver's seat.

"We're coming, *ma petite*," Raoul called. It always sent a small wave of pleasure through Dee to see how he immediately straightened up and took on an air of "Now I am truly alive" whenever he was near Pepe.

He opened the rear door for Dee while she climbed in as gracefully as she could under the circumstances—foreign cars seemed to require the wearing of slacks—then hopped into the front seat next to Pepe, content to let her drive.

"What diabolical plan have you?" Dee laughed as they lurched off down the Boulevard de Courcelles.

"You have found me a mistress at last," Raoul teased.

Pepe's eyes darted in his direction with amused tolerance.

Dee would never fully understand how they could joke so openly about these things. To be sure of each other's love is fine . . . but joking sometimes too easily disguises the truth. "Don't listen to him, Pepe," Dee shouted over the traffic noise. "Even if he had a mistress he would spend all his time telling her she is not as marvelous as you."

Raoul laughed uproariously. "She's quite right, *ma cherie.*"

"C'mon, Pepe. Where are you taking us?" Dee asked. She caught Pepe's smiling glance in the rearview mirror.

"Tonight, my comrades . . ." She paused teasingly. "Tonight we let others amuse us. An intimate little dinner somewhere, perhaps the Folies-Bergère, or maybe the Lido later—perhaps even both. Then . . . ah . . ."

Raoul smiled and surreptitiously took out his large wallet and began counting the stiff francs quickly. "How much more 'then' are you planning?"

Pepe laughed. "I took the liberty of removing a few francs from our vacation savings—a loan to ourselves until you can put the whole evening down on your expense account."

Dee knew better than to offer to help pay for the evening, but she made a mental note to get them something specially nice before she left.

"I thought it would be fun," Pepe continued, "to take in the Pigalle clubs, just to round out the evening."

"Those . . . those cleep joints?" Raoul said in surprise.

Dee smiled at his pronunciation of the word but enjoyed it too much to correct him.

"Raoul, darling," Pepe said with an amused sternness. "Where is your patriotism? It is all in the name of saving France's national economy! So they charge too much money—but they in turn spend more money elsewhere, and the money goes to pay someone's bills, taxes . . ."

"*Halte!* Your point is clear—my duty lies before me."

They drove to a pleasant restaurant called Le Jour et Nuit, but it was hardly what Dee would have called intimate. Unless she wanted to consider the prostitutes sitting at the bar "atmosphere."

Over their coffee, Pepe observed that one of the girls seemed to have left and come back every fifteen to twenty minutes.

"That is because she must live nearby and does not bother to undress," Raoul explained.

Pepe shrugged her shoulders. "How unethical!"

Dee smiled. "It does seem that if the man is paying for the service he deserves more than a raised skirt. . . ."

"In your country this is not allowed, yes?" Pepe asked.

"Not legally," Dee answered. "But it goes on anyway."

"You Americans," Raoul said good-naturedly. "You deprive yourselves of everything except money and appliances!"

They discussed at length the advantages and disadvantages of organized prostitution, which somehow led to a discussion of homosexuality. Dee did her best to sound as if the subject were not foreign to her, yet that she had not really delved into it—a tactic she had long ago learned was the safest. It was an uncomfortable role, however.

And it reminded her of Rita. Where was she this minute? What was she doing? She wondered if Rita ever thought of her . . . if she had any idea of what she had done. Not likely, Dee concluded.

Pepe interrupted the conversation with the suggestion that they be on their way, admonishing them that she fully intended to get drunk that night.

They began a whirlwind of nightclub rounds, and it wasn't until they were sitting at the bar of the Lido, watching the floor show, that Dee became aware of how long it had been since she had been to bed with anyone.

Pepe commented on the ingenuity of the staging, or the scanty costumes . . . but Dee found herself staring at the loveliness of the dancers' exposed breasts. They were so very white under the stage lighting . . . and the nipples so innocently pink. One of the girls reminded her very much of Karen—she must send Karen a postcard or a letter. Karen would have breasts like that, Dee thought, and hated herself immediately. She's just a kid, a nice, sweet kid who's going to get married. Not some bull dyke you picked up in a gay nightclub downtown, Dee scolded herself.

Raoul poked her gently in the arm and whispered, "They are lovely, no?"

Her initial reaction was one of "He's guessed!" but she put it aside at once, cursing her uncontrollable guilt. She smiled at him slowly. "Very interesting," she whispered back.

What could she say? Of course they're lovely, and how does an American lesbian go about making a date with one of them?

"Come on," Raoul said after a moment. "The rest of the show is dull. Let's go on to Pigalle."

Dee was as entranced by Pigalle as she was by Times Square. Everything squirmed with life and pleasure seekers. The streets were never still, and she found the spiel of the cabaret barkers masterpieces of the hard-sell. They entered one place, downed a pony of brandy, then left for another. And Pepe was holding true to her threat—she was getting quite tight. Everything was cause for a deep, throaty giggle, which Dee could not help but laugh with even though she didn't know what Pepe was amused at.

"I know where we must go!" Pepe said, leaving no room for contradiction.

"Where?" Raoul asked suspiciously.

She patted him gently on the cheek, pursing her lips with maternal concern. "It is just a few doors down. But what is a trip to Pigalle without going to a lesbian club? Eh? Tell me . . ." she giggled again.

"Sometimes, darling, I become concerned about your background."

"Tsk!" she pouted, then turned to Dee. "Did you ever know such stuffiness? I am curious about everything which is life. . . . Even as a young girl I always looked on both sides of the street in search of something new, different, or exciting. I do not approve of people who close their eyes to anything which is outside their own small worlds—either out of snobbery or narrow-mindedness."

"Bravo!" Dee exclaimed with a smile.

"But a lesbian club?" Raoul protested.

"Why not? The club is very discreet and it is run by an internationally famous lesbian. They say she has been the lover of some of the world's most beautiful and famous women." Pepe sighed deeply. "To have such marvelous disregard for public opinion . . ."

"I don't know, Pepe," Dee said haltingly. She did not want to appear anxious or afraid about this. "It is getting rather late. . . ."

"Late! Late! Your life lies before you and you would sleep it away . . . like a bear! How frequently do you think you'll be coming to Paris? Perhaps never again. Live today."

"And what am I supposed to do in there?" Raoul objected. "Pretend I'm a transvestite?"

"Raoul . . ." Pepe scolded.

"And if one of those fish-eyed women makes a move toward you . . . what then?"

"Do not concern yourself, my darling. I can always pretend I came with Dee . . . that we are lovers . . ." She broke into a musical giggle that prevented both Raoul and Dee from arguing further.

They found the place, paid an exorbitant admission charge, climbed the carpeted stairs while the sounds of a small band made it clear that quality is no substitute for volume. At the landing, a short woman came forward and took them through the darkened room, weaving around the many tiny tables crowded with people. It was too dark for Dee to be able to tell what sex they were—if any.

A small stage stood illuminated at the far end of the room, with sparse props, and a young girl was doing her routine in an even sparser costume. Even without speaking French, Dee could tell it was a dance-skit about a girl talking to her lover on the telephone, placing the receiver at various points of her body as the lover's voice supposedly seduced her. Lurid—but effective.

The woman found them a tiny table to the far right of the stage, opposite the entrance. Pepe literally plopped into the spindly chair while Raoul almost slunk into his. Dee took the chair between them, careful to seem only mildly interested in her surroundings.

The girl finished her act and was followed immediately by a darkened stage while the noises of props being removed and re-placed scratched over the low murmur of voices.

"Isn't this exciting?" Pepe said gleefully.

"Hmph!" Raoul replied.

The band interrupted further comment with a few introductory chords of "Autumn in New York," and when the single blue spot-light shot out onto the entertainer on stage, Dee almost gagged.

It was Martie Thornton!

Chapter 15

She was very excited about finding Martie and watched her as she sang, feeling her pulse accelerate. Partly from homesickness, she assumed, and partly because she really had taken an instant liking to Martie and had regretted not being able to get to know her better.

Martie had evidently picked up enough French to be able to throw in some of her more "gay gags" to please the audience. She was enough of a showwoman to know that her accent didn't matter, just the fact that she was trying was all that counted. And the audience loved her. They kept applauding, and the more enthusiasm they showed, the more Martie threw herself into each song.

Finally, she finished her last song and walked down to the nearest table, grabbed the person closest to the stage, and kissed her on the forehead. The place very nearly went wild.

As beer bottles banged on the tables and everyone hooted, Pepe partially stood up—not too steadily—and exclaimed, "I must meet her! *C'est magnifique!*"

Before Raoul could stop her, she had run over to Martie, pointed eloquently at their table, and had obviously talked her into coming over for a drink. As Martie drew near, her expression changed from one of professional good humor to one of genuine surprise and pleasure.

Dee hoped it would not prove to be an embarrassing meeting and that Martie would not say something including Dee in her circle of lesbian friends.

Martie was close enough to her now that Dee could hear Martie ask Pepe, "This is your friend from America?"

"Why, yes . . ." Pepe answered hesitantly.

Martie smiled broadly. She strode up to the table and stood before Dee with a diabolical smile.

"Mrs. Sanders, I presume?" she said evenly.

Dee felt like a teenager at her first prom. She didn't quite know what to do. Delighted though she was at seeing Martie, at the same time she didn't want Pepe and Raoul to get any ideas.

"What a pleasant surprise," she managed to say. "You've met Madame Bizot. . . . This is M'sieu Bizot, my company's French representative." She said it calmly but hoped to hell that Martie got the idea this was business, so that she wouldn't make any slips. Why did she always end up in these impossible situations?

"Sit down, please," Raoul said, bringing another chair from an adjacent table. "What will you drink?" He carefully avoided Dee's eyes, but Pepe was unable to control her curiosity.

"But you already know each other? How marvelous!"

Martie glanced at Pepe, yet directed her reply toward Raoul. "Mrs. Sanders was once kind enough to recommend some competent photographers for my publicity pictures in New York."

Thank God! Dee thought with relief. "We met at one of those dreadful little 'intimate' parties downtown," she cued.

Martie laughed as if remembering a real party. "What a night!" She sat back and lit a cigarette. "Those parties are all the same. They invite one left-wing writer, one off-Broadway actor, one beatnik, and one homosexual . . . then everyone gets drunk and thinks he is really being terribly democratic and intellectual."

Raoul seemed to accept this explanation, and his expression softened considerably. He smiled for the first time since they'd entered the place, and put a protective arm around Dee's shoulder. "But you forgot someone, Miss Thornton. They invited one excellent photographer."

"Doesn't count, M'sieur Bizot. Too normal."

Pepe clapped her hands lightly. "What you call in America, too 'in.' . . ."

"They should have invited you, Pepe," Dee said, laughing.

"I should have arrived barefooted with a long cigarette holder. But no! A cigar would have been better."

It was plain to Dee that Martie was controlling herself admirably yet was bursting to ask her many questions. How could she explain it to Raoul?

She only half listened as Martie drew Raoul out with conversation about his work and photography in general. Martie told him she'd always been interested in the subject and absolutely marveled at anyone who could figure out all the settings on a camera. Raoul promptly offered to explain it to her and proceeded to give her a rough breakdown of the principles involved.

Poor Martie, Dee thought. She watched Martie's face intently— mindful to shift her gaze occasionally—and once again was intrigued by her. She certainly was not pretty, but her face was so mobile, so rich with life, that it more than compensated for lack of physical beauty. She looked over to Pepe, who sat in rapt fascination with Martie.

She's got it, all right, Dee decided. Raoul is eating out of her hand, Pepe adores her . . . and me? It was a good question, she told herself. Just how did she feel about Martie? She liked her; that much she knew. But how far was she willing to go with Martie?

You pompous egotist! she exclaimed silently. Why should Martie want to 'go' anywhere with you? She's probably got dozens of girlfriends, and if tonight's audience is any indication, thousands of propositions.

Pepe was, surprisingly enough, the one to break it all up. "Raoul, darling, you have bored Miss Thornton enough with your talk about cameras."

"On the contrary, madame, it's been very interesting, and I intend to go out tomorrow and buy a camera."

Raoul laughed. "You see?" He nodded smugly to Pepe. "If it

were not for an important appointment, I would gladly go with you and help you select one."

Martie said nothing but smiled pleasantly at Pepe.

"But, Dee, you could help Miss Thornton, could you not?" Pepe asked enthusiastically.

"Oh, I wouldn't want to put you to that trouble," Martie answered quickly.

"There's nothing too pressing for you tomorrow, Dee," Raoul collaborated. "You could take off during the afternoon."

It's fate, Dee decided. Don't fight it.

"It's no trouble, Miss Thornton . . . if you really would like me to tag along." Signed, sealed, and delivered. Amen.

"In that case," Martie grinned broadly, "why not meet me for lunch? There's a crazy little place on the Rue Bassano."

"No need for that," Dee smiled. "Besides, I thought perhaps Pepe might like to come along." She mentally crossed her fingers and waited.

"Ah . . . I would have loved to, Dee. You are sweet. But I could not. My sister-in-law is coming in from Saint Ouen tomorrow, and I must have lunch with her and take her shopping." She threw a mildly reproaching glance at Raoul.

"Then I insist!" Martie said politely. "It's the least I can do to repay you."

Dee decided she had put up enough of a display battle, and agreed. The appointment was arranged, Martie excused herself, and shortly after, they left the club and headed for home, accompanied by the constant chatter from Pepe praising Martie.

They arrived home tired but in good spirits. Raoul opened the front door, followed by Pepe, who stopped to bend over and pick up a white envelope.

"Dee, it is for you," she said, and handed it to her.

The Photo World address had been crossed out, and Dee's home address was written below it in Karen's neat handwriting. "Thank you," Dee muttered, and put the letter nonchalantly in her purse.

"I will never understand the diabolical mind that can receive a letter and not open it immediately," Pepe laughed as they proceeded up the stairs. "Would you like a nightcap?"

"No," Dee answered quickly. "No, thank you anyway."

She headed for her room only half hearing Raoul's comment to Pepe that Martie did not seem as offensive as most of the lesbians one sees on the street.

Dee let her hand rest for a moment on the chest-high door handle to her room, then opened it and went in. There were this morning's flowers, arranged carefully in a slim blue vase on her chiffonier. Every morning Pepe put fresh flowers in her room—in almost every room, in fact. It was her firm belief that a home without flowers was a home without love.

Dee threw her purse on the high four-poster bed, crossed over to the louvered windows, and opened them wider. She could just make out the illuminated tip of the Obélisque from her room in between the night-shadowed Paris rooftops and chimney stacks. Street sounds drifted faintly up to her over the dull, constant hum of the city at night.

She had to admit she did not want to open Karen's letter. She didn't know why—just a premonition. She stood for a long while at the window.

Instead of feeling elated, the drinks of the evening had left her very depressed. Her feelings were disturbingly mixed about meeting Martie the next day. She didn't know how wise it was to have agreed—after all, Martie was a notorious lesbian. She didn't want any gossip starting when she was the houseguest of the Bizots.

Open the letter, Dee! she told herself aloud.

Sighing, she walked back to the bed and picked up her purse from the white chenille spread. The letter lay on top, the contents folded in quarters. Dee had the feeling of timelessness as she took it out, the stiff paper making the only sound in the room.

She tore the envelope across its side and pulled out three neatly folded sheets of company paper. Karen's familiar script began with *Dearest Dee*.

One or two paragraphs about how everyone missed her and the office was the same and it was hotter than blazes in good old New York and hoping she was having a good time and why hadn't she dropped her a card.

Cho-Cho-San and she had become good friends after the cat had become drunk one night when she had left a glass of vodka and tomato juice in the living room while she had gone to check how her dinner was doing. She had been worried the next morning when Cho-Cho had overslept, but everything was fine now.

Phil had come by several times. They were having some difficulty, though. She didn't know how to say it, but one night the previous week, while Phil was there, Mrs. Evans had shown up unexpectedly. Quite drunk—and quite upset.

Dee put the letter down for a moment and lighted a cigarette with trembling hands. What had Rita said to them?

There was a smudge on the next line, which read: *Please believe me when I say nothing will ever be repeated about what was said.* She cut short the events, but it was sordid enough for Dee to know the occasion had not been pleasant.

Rita had asked who Karen was, and when Karen replied, she had thrown back her head with laughter, saying she had figured Dee was having a side affair with her. Then she had looked intently at Phil and, with a cruel smile, commented on how she was pleased to see that she had not been the only one unfaithful to Dee.

Phil asked her what she meant, but Rita refused to reply. She had simply laughed—yet the way she laughed had been more revealing than any words could have been.

As a parting shot, Rita leaned against the door dramatically and exclaimed in front of Phil that if Karen ever got tired of Dee, Rita might find time for her . . . show her some educational variations.

Poor Karen! Dee thought, what must she think? Karen closed the letter telling Dee not to worry and that she would write again as soon as she could get things straightened out in her own mind. She had been more than mildly shocked . . . and Phil had made quite a scene of his own, demanding that she move immediately.

P.S.: she wasn't going to move until Dee got back.

P.S.S.: something should be done about Mrs. Evans before she really got Dee into trouble.

The wages of perversion are fear, Dee mumbled and threw the letter on the bed.

Chapter 16

Dee picked a table in the shade the next day and ordered an extra-dry martini while she waited for Martie to show up. She glanced around furtively and hated herself for being such a hypocrite. She could "pass" easily—if she weren't seen with an obvious lesbian.

If word got around about her, she would probably lose her job. And more than likely not get another in the same field. It was stupid, of course, but that's the way the world was. People at the office who had been her friends would turn their backs, or titter, or worse yet, try to be understanding when they didn't understand at all.

It certainly would be Rita's fault—it takes two to have an affair—but Rita didn't have to be such a blabbermouth. Of course, there was no indication that Rita would say anything to anyone else—no real reason for her to. Rita had been drunk and shocked to find Karen there, had naturally jumped to the conclusion that Karen was her new love, and had behaved with illogical jealousy and spite.

Dee fished the onion from the bottom of her glass and carefully placed it in her mouth. The day was uncomfortably warm. She wished she had worn something lighter.

She looked up to see Martie walking toward her—wearing a

dress, thank heaven. Actually, Dee considered, if one didn't know better or recognize Martie, one might think she was simply the athletic type.

Martie weaved between the tables and extended her hand to Dee before she sat down. "Mrs. Sanders, I'm glad you could make it," she said loud enough for a one-mile radius of eavesdroppers.

A conspiratorial curl came to her lips as she sat down gracefully. Unlike her nightclub personality, she was careful to wait for the waiter to come up to the table rather than simply signal him. She gave him her order through a pleasant, feminine smile. "Another?" she asked Dee, pointing demurely to her empty glass.

Dee hesitated.

"Please," Martie suggested. "I so hate to drink alone."

Dee hid a smile at the feminine use of the word "so" coming from Martie. She was sure Martie would have preferred to use four-letter words in a positive command. "All right."

The waiter nodded and walked away. Dee wasn't too sure what she should say now that Martie was facing her. But Martie took the lead.

Without changing her expression she said softly, "You're a no-good bitch! Why didn't you tell me you were coming?"

"How? You didn't give me an address," Dee laughed.

"Come off it! I told you that you could reach me through my agent."

"Who the hell thought you meant it?" Dee asked, still smiling.

"I don't exactly have a reputation for making idle polite suggestions." She sat back in her chair as the last remaining couple seated near them stood up and left. "Where's your friend, Miss Professional Torrid, or whatever her name was. She come with you?"

"No," Dee said slowly. "We . . . split up." She was under no obligation to tell Martie, and it did place her on the "open market" list and she knew it. But why not? She was tired of being so damn careful about everything, worrying lest someone find out or see her in a gay bar. She was thousands of miles away, and Paris was a city large enough for anyone to get lost in.

"I see. . . ." Martie said and fell silent.

Dee waited and watched her. Martie's short blond hair was

combed with a slight wave—in Dee's behalf, she was sure—and softened with tiny bouquetlike earrings. She was really very touched by Martie's pain not to cause her embarrassment and appreciated it.

"I suppose I should say I'm sorry. But to be frank, I didn't like her looks."

Dee had to laugh. "Not many people had *that* complaint."

"You know what I meant; don't be facetious. She looked like a first-class selfish, egomaniacal shrew."

"Your vocabulary is slipping," Dee said with a broad smile. She didn't know Martie well enough to use poker-face humor yet.

Martie grinned. "You won't believe it, but I have an M.A. from NYU. I put myself through singing in clubs in the Village."

"You're full of surprises, aren't you?" Dee said it in an offhand way, but she really was surprised. She'd never thought of Martie as being particularly literate or academic—more in the school-of-hard-knocks way. "What was your major?"

"Music," she answered with an *of course!* nod. But I minored in English."

Their drinks arrived, leaving Dee an opportunity to change the subject. "How long are you going to stay in Paris?"

"That depends on you," Martie said cautiously, sipping her drink. "I've another four days at this club and then a week before my next engagement in Munich. I had planned on leaving right away, but . . ."

"You're putting me on the spot," Dee said slowly.

"Are you tied up with anyone?"

Dee ignored the sudden flash of excitement in her body. She suddenly realized that she was just a little afraid of Martie . . . but she wasn't sure why, unless perhaps it was the meeting of a new challenge. "I'm not tied up . . . but I'm not looking to be, either. And I do have some obligations while I'm here."

"Certainly. So do I. But is there any reason why we couldn't get together a few times and enjoy a couple of drinks? I'm not officially on the make, you know. It'll just be for kicks."

"You know," Dee said, feeling terribly adventurous, "I believe you."

"Shall I plan on staying, then?"

251

"If you think you can stand me . . . yes."

"Well, then," Martie laughed, "let's stop jawing and order something to eat. I'm famished." She picked up the huge menu, glanced at it, and put it down. "Can't make head or tail of all that jazz there. Even if I could read French, the handwriting is always so damn fancy you couldn't make it out anyway. But I can recommend their duckling here. They put it in a casserole and do something absolutely perverse to it."

"So be it," Dee smiled. They placed their order along with one for another drink, and Dee felt the martinis relaxing her—even though they only made her feel warmer.

"Do you really want to buy a camera today?" Dee said. "Raoul will never know the difference, you know."

"Of course I want to. Whoever went to Europe without a camera? But I expect private instruction from you," she said with a wicked glint. "Purely an educational advance, you understand."

"Certainly," Dee smiled. "We can start this afternoon. I've got my Leica in my purse and I've been dying to go to the top of the Eiffel Tower. Are you game?"

"Only if we can have dinner together . . ."

"I'll have to make a phone call and give some excuse to the Bizots."

"Phone . . ."

"After lunch," Dee replied. She couldn't remember ever meeting anyone like Martie before. This was going to be quite an experience.

Dee called the office from the restaurant after lunch and wrote down the name of the closest camera store where they would give her a discount. She picked out a Petri 2:8 for Martie; an inexpensive but adequate light meter; and three rolls of black-and-white film.

They stopped at a sidewalk café and sipped Cinzano while Dee explained how to operate the camera and meter and supervised Martie while she loaded it. Then they began to walk and walk and walk, stopping frequently as something would catch their eye as being typical of the area, laughing at Martie's initial clumsiness with the camera, comparing light meter readings, or discussing the best approach to the picture.

Dee honestly forgot for most of the time that she was a lesbian on a date with another lesbian. It was just two women friends enjoying a foreign country and a common interest. She had relaxed considerably since lunch; her first mixed reactions to Martie had been calmed.

They didn't reach the Eiffel Tower until late afternoon and enjoyed a cocktail in the Tower restaurant, watching the warm sun surrender to night, speeding long shadows across the twisted, fascinating Paris streets and long-ago-turned-green copper roofs everywhere.

"I think I will always remember Paris," Martie said softly, "as a horizon of rooftops and chimneys."

Dee looked up at her quickly. Her own thoughts had not been too dissimilar. It was strange to be with someone she could actually communicate with. So unlike Rita, who usually replied with an undisguised "Huh?" or a bored "Uh-huh." Of course, she was always able to talk with Karen, but it was a strain to be careful not to say something that would give her away. There had been many times when she had felt so at ease with Karen she had almost slipped and said something incriminating. But Rita had solved that little problem for her.

She hoped Karen would not recoil from her now, and that she would not lose her friendship. It was going to be such a goddamn relief not to have to be constantly on guard.

They finished their drinks, and Martie led her away from the Tower grounds, down a quiet, narrow street through which even the French cars would not have been able to maneuver. She refused to tell Dee where they were going.

An inconspicuous doorway with a small wooden sign overhead was their destination. Dee only knew she was somewhere on the Left Bank, but had long ago lost track of their exact direction now that the sun was gone. Dee's navigational attempts ended with the fact that the sun always set in the west.

Martie led the way through the Dutch door, obviously hundreds of years old, into a dark, wood-paneled oblong room. A marvelous room. Dee could feel the spirit of the Three Musketeers, Madame Defarge, Napoleon . . . the history of the entire city within its four walls dank with the smell of serving as a pub throughout the centuries. She doubted that the bar had changed in all the years it had stood, initials carved upon initials. The plank floor was worn hollow where it had received the most use, and polished brass spittoons still sat lined against the bar rail. There was only one small difference.

It was a gay bar now. There were no chairs or stools. Clusters of women stood separated from the boys, with rare exception. Draught beer or red wine seemed to be the order of the day despite the fact that the cabinet behind the bar was lined with a complete stock of liquor. But here there was no pretense of a caste system, separating the fems from the butches. They could have been shop girls or university students belonging to a mutual club.

Dee delighted in the unevenness of the room, the ceiling high with beams at one end, then sloping to an uncomfortable low for anyone over five feet six. Electricity had been added, Dee noted sadly, but at least it had been done without removing the old fixtures. The owners at the time had simply converted the glass-covered gas jets to preserve the atmosphere, or perhaps to save money.

"I thought you'd be intrigued," Martie grinned. "Your eyes have turned into a goddamn twin reflex."

Dee laughed. "Listen to the amateur! But you're right. I'm fascinated. Where did you ever find this place?"

"Ah, the advantages of being a successful lesbian. The gal that owns the club where I'm working clued me in about this crazy pad." Martie waved to an old woman across the bar. "That's Madame Journet. Her family has owned this joint for the last four generations—but I doubt that it was gay all that time," she snickered.

"Is she a member of the clan?" Dee asked curiously.

"No," Martie replied simply.

Dee was pleased that Martie had not made any of the common guesses like, "She says no, but I think . . ." or, "She must have been at one time. . . ." Looking at her, the woman was probably in her sixties—bent over with rheumatism. She wore a drab ankle-length dress with a faded green, loose-knit shawl around her shoulders tied in a knot at her breast.

Madame Journet's unkempt hair was a dull brown, hastily pulled back in a bun with enormous hairpins hanging perilously from all sides. Her face was relatively unlined, and she had a bright expression despite the fact she didn't seem to have a tooth in her mouth. She waved them to approach closer and, as she did, placed two glasses of Cinzano on the bar for them, her hands a light brown with thousands of freckles, the knuckles swollen with years of work.

"Mademoiselle Thornton, how glad I am to see you, and not alone." Her voice half lilted and half croaked out the words.

Martie pulled Dee closer to the bar. "My friend from New York. She has just arrived in Paris, and I couldn't let her go another minute without meeting you . . . and certainly not without tasting your wonderful food."

Madame almost blushed with pleasure, then leaned forward secretively. "Tonight . . . *boeuf a la Bourguignonne.*" She rolled her eyes heavenward and pursed her lips. "If this pleases you?" she added hastily.

"Anything you cook pleases me," Martie answered promptly.

"I make onion soup this morning, also. My father's recipe—not like this city's *avortement*. He learned it from his mama, who was from the provinces."

Dee's mouth was beginning to water. She felt as if she were about to be introduced into a ceremonial rite rather than simply have dinner.

"Is the dining room crowded, Madame, or can we go up now?"

"No, no. It is still too early for the French to eat. All the better for you—the food has not been overheated."

"Then if you will make up a pitcher of six martinis, I will carry them upstairs for you. We will finish our Cinzano while you make them."

Madame smiled broadly. She looked at Dee a long time. "Always considerate, this one. Always a way to save me work." She winked merrily, then turned back to Martie. "I like your friend. Strong, good face."

Dee, having felt like a first-class tongue-tied fool, decided it was time to open her mouth. But everything that came to mind seemed trite or superficial. It was better to wait until she was spoken to directly.

Madame ambled down the long bar to mix the martinis, leaving them alone.

"The dining room is upstairs," Martie explained, "and a narrow stairway it is. But you'll like it. At one time, it was probably the living quarters. There are two sections now. One has a series of long picnic-like tables with regular menus. We can sit at either—whichever you prefer. The most expensive item on the menu is pretty reasonably priced, so it doesn't matter much unless the budget is really cramped."

"What do you mean, family-style?" Dee asked.

"As many people as will fit sit down at one table, and there's no choice of menu. You have whatever is the dinner for the day. It's brought out on a big platter and you help yourself, then pass it down to the next person." Martie smiled knowingly. "It's a great way to make friends if you're normally a little bashful . . . but that's never been my problem. I occasionally sit there anyhow when I come in alone, so I don't have to eat all by myself. A pretty nice bunch of kids come in here. Madame doesn't allow any monkey business, and in order to be admitted you have to be introduced by someone already known here as well-behaved and able to hold her liquor. No cruising—no brawls."

Madame returned carrying a tankard of martinis. Dee suppressed a smile, thinking of what all the self-appointed martini experts would say about their being mixed in a metal container.

She followed Martie up the poorly lit stairway, fully expecting secret passages. The dining room was even more than she had imagined. A walk-in fireplace with a huge black kettle suspended over the unlit logs took up almost one whole wall. The room was painted in an off-white with French blue on the woodwork and the one paneled wall. Orange-print café curtains added warmth and privacy for the customers. And, of course, each table had a wine bottle with a candle. Heavy sliding doors separated the kitchen but could not keep out the delicious aroma of the food.

They decided on a private table, and their waiter turned out to be Madame's nephew—a courtly gay boy who would inherit the place when she died.

Dee couldn't remember when she had had a more wonderful day. The dinner was perfect, and she was comfortably tired from all the walking and the drinks.

If she never moved from her chair, she felt as if she could be happy the rest of her life.

Chapter 17

Dee saw quite a bit of Martie—every day, in fact. The Bizots did not question her about the mysterious "man" she had invented to account for her activities.

But her time was running short now, and Dee found herself having off moments of near panic at the thought of returning to New York. She didn't want to go back. . . . What for? To face Karen? To the prospect of the approaching fall and winter with its slush and bleak, naked buildings? To an empty apartment filled with the echo of her vacuum-sealed life—work, eat, and sleep . . . alone.

Yet here in Paris she had a childlike, clinging belief that things might be different, that her prince would come and wake her. It was silly and she knew it. But in her current mood the whole routine process of living seemed just as silly.

And even if her prince never showed up, at least she had a pseudo-prince in Martie. Martie had been a perfect gentleman. There was no other way to put it. If the circumstances allowed, she would place a light kiss on Dee's lips at the private entrance to her rooms—otherwise, a cheery wave of her hand and back into the cab she would go. They had gone dancing in some of the more discreet clubs, and Dee had enjoyed it—Martie was an excellent dancer.

In fact, Dee had to admit she was really enjoying the role of femme for a change. But if Martie was thinking of her in a sexual way, she was controlling it admirably. So much so that Dee sometimes wondered if she was slipping. Yet she was so happy to have found a friend in Martie that it overshadowed any other thoughts she might have.

She had a way of pulling Dee out of her depressed moods without prying into their cause, and when Dee already felt elated, Martie was a genius at making the most of them. It was like having an alter ego at her beck and call, especially when Martie had finished her engagement at the club and was completely free.

She made no demands upon Dee's office time, and actually took advantage of those hours to take pictures of everything she came across. Her enthusiasm for photography was growing, and she listened carefully to anything Dee said about it. And Dee was oddly pleased that Martie was quick to learn and had ideas of her own.

Occasionally, Dee had the feeling that Martie was doing all this only to ingratiate herself. But it was a ridiculous idea—Martie didn't have to. And she certainly wasn't the type to go to that much trouble unless she really wanted to.

Two days before Martie had to leave for her Munich engagement, they had agreed to have dinner, then return to the office so that Dee could develop the first three rolls she had taken. Martie's curiosity had finally overcome her, and she couldn't wait for them to be processed regularly by a store. Besides, she claimed, she really was interested to see how the processing was done.

Only the night light was on when they approached the building. Dee had her own key and felt terribly conspiritorial when they entered the dim hallway, senselessly whispering.

"I don't trust those flimsy elevators," Dee said, "and it's only one flight up to the darkroom. Do you mind the walk?"

Martie shook her head. "I'm not *that* old," she answered, and followed Dee up the marble stairway, which wound around the elevator in the shape of a cocoon.

Dee led the way into the empty workroom, deftly maneuvering around the desks and equipment. Not until they were inside did she turn on the light and quickly close the door.

"There," she said in a hushed tone. "Now the light won't be visible to the street." She pointed to the black curtain covering the only window in the rectangular room.

"Worried someone might see us?" Martie laughed.

Dee guiltily mumbled yes, but busied herself setting up the reel tank and solutions. "It would be hard to explain . . . you and me here . . ."

"Jesus! Dee, these aren't pornographic, you know. Just buildings and scenery. You know that."

Dee felt her face reddening. She hated to do this to Martie and didn't really expect her to understand. "Sure," she said quietly. "But if Mr. Bizot—unlikely though it is—or someone else who would recognize you comes into this office at this late hour, and sees us . . . how do I explain it?"

Martie looked at her seriously. "Are you really that guilty about being gay?"

"I'm *that* guilty about being caught!" A slow smile crossed her face. "Unlike you," she said kindly, "I cannot afford to be a professional lesbian. I live in a different world from you, Martie. You can capitalize on it, exploit it, stamp on it and scuff it and still lose nothing. In my world, they want to know about everything which is considered par for the sophisticated mind, photograph it or write about it—but they don't want it to touch their lives."

"Just one question, Dee. If my life weren't open to the public—if no one would ever recognize me—would you still hide me or be afraid to be seen with me?"

Dee returned her stare calmly. "In that case, I'd only be afraid of being spotted myself coming out of a gay bar."

"You're sure?"

"Have I ever tried to hide you anywhere but around the office or places where it's probable I'd meet someone I know?"

"You win. But you had me worried. . . . I hadn't taken you for being gutless." Martie turned and began to inspect the room.

"I don't believe it has anything to do with guts," Dee replied, a little angry. "It's just plain common sense not to lie down in the middle of the street just to see if you'll get run over."

"All right, all right," Martie laughed. "Let's develop these French postcards and get out of here before you make me nervous, too."

Dee relaxed and managed a light laugh. "I'm sorry."

She put on a smock and a rubber apron to protect her dress, told Martie to put out her cigarette or she'd clobber her, and started to work.

Martie remained right behind her throughout and watched every step carefully, occasionally expressing complete awe or asking a question. Finally, Dee hung up the film to dry and pulled off her gloves.

"So tiny?" Martie asked, staring at the negative strips.

"How big do you think thirty-five millimeters is?" Dee answered.

Martie snorted. "Even a Brownie makes bigger pictures than that!"

Dee laughed. "Want your money back?"

"No. I'm tired. What happens next?" She stretched to emphasize the point.

"We can take a break if you want. Then come back, and make contact prints later. I could use a drink myself."

"Ah," Martie said hesitantly, "I have some cognac in my place."

The suggestion had been so unexpected that it took a moment to register in Dee's mind. She felt the old mixture of panic and excitement Martie had first brought out in her, then told herself she was being juvenile. It was a perfectly natural suggestion—it didn't have to have hidden meanings or contain lecherous undertones. Martie had certainly never given her any reason to think she was "on the make."

"How far is your place?" Dee heard herself ask, half hoping it would be too far.

"Walking distance," Martie smiled.

Silence.

Dee laughed nervously. "It's a deal. Just let me tag these negatives so they don't get thrown out."

"Aren't you planning to steal back tonight?" Martie asked softly with gentle reproach in her voice.

"Certainly. But the best-laid plans of mice and men . . ."

"Uh-huh." Martie helped her remove the apron and put things back.

Dee took a fast look around as she turned off the light and opened the door. "Okay. Let's go, Karen."

"Who?" Martie asked.

"Now, why did I call you that?" she smiled uncertainly. "It was silly."

They left the building and walked briskly to Martie's hotel on the Rue Laugier, and said nothing going up the elevator or walking down the carpeted hallway.

Martie opened the door and ushered Dee into the room almost awkwardly. "Not bad for a hotel suite, is it? The bedroom's in there . . . I mean, the bathroom is, too."

Dee sat down in the armchair and lit a cigarette while Martie poured the cognac. She felt almost sorry for Martie now. . . . She was behaving like a young boy with his first woman. Martie was all nerves, and every one of them was showing.

It was then she realized she had every intention of having an affair with Martie; not tomorrow or next year, but tonight, in this room. Dee wasn't certain of why she should be so adamant about it; she simply recognized that she was going to, wanted to, and had to. No rationalizations, no deep probings. Freud could go to hell! She needed the affair the way some people need a drink. And she was fully prepared to be the seductress if necessary.

The acceptance of this situation filled Dee with a sense of superior position, humor, and tenderness. Had Martie been a man, Dee would have been bored with the entire play. Men were so predictable! But she was very amused that the "tough, been-around gal" was no longer the master of the scene.

"What's that silly-ass grin on your face for?" Martie asked gruffly as she handed Dee the glass.

"You."

Martie stood before her, swishing the amber liquid around in the glass. "Me?" she laughed. "Why?"

"I'm speculating about what's going on in your busy head at this moment."

"I was just wondering," Martie began slowly, "who this Karen is and how she figures into your life."

"Oh." Dee put her glass down on the small round table next to her. "She's my secretary in New York. A very young kid and I'm quite fond of her . . . She's staying in my apartment while I'm gone."

She wondered if she should mention the incident with Rita and decided against it. "Has my name-slip bothered you that much?"

"Are you playing coy with me?"

Dee smiled. "A little."

"Bitch!" Martie laughed again. "All right. So I was feeling a little jealous. Don't worry, your concern this evening about being seen with me tells me just where I stand. I'm not turning possessive or anything."

"I didn't think you would . . . and even if you felt it I'm sure you'd never show it."

Martie faltered a moment, then took a long drink. "You bug me," she said at last.

"While I'm bugging you," Dee said, "would you mind telling me something you don't have to?"

"Like?"

"Like, why did you suggest our coming here?"

Martie sighed quietly. "You see? That's just what I mean about you! Sometimes you're kind of shy and sweet; then sometimes you knock a person down with some absolutely blunt, aggressive statement."

"My question wasn't blunt—your reaction was."

Dee lifted her glass in a toast and drank it all down. "So why aren't you following through?"

"Jesus! What a perverse creature you are!"

"D'you want me to go home?"

"No," Martie answered petulantly. "What did you expect? I'd open the door, trip you, then beat you to the floor?"

"I'm not so sure what I expected." Dee stood up and crossed the room to where the bottle of cognac sat, then filled her glass again.

"You think I'm stalling? Or that I've changed my mind?"

"Yes." Dee was taunting her and she knew it. I *am* a bitch, she agreed silently.

"It's not that at all," Martie mumbled. "It's just that I'm not so sure it would be a good idea. Naturally, I've thought about it a lot . . . going to bed with you. But something like that could ruin our friendship; it might open the door for me to fall in love with you. I could, you know. Very easily."

"I hadn't thought of that," Dee admitted.

"You haven't thought of the possibility of love. . . ."

Dee looked at her sharply. "How do you mean that?"

Martie shook her head patiently. "How many women have you been to bed with?"

"Several." Other than Rita, Dee had never really been able to remember her previous relationships with women. They had usually occurred after a lot of drinking and were accompanied by furtive passes, never being too sure of herself or them. But she'd learned a lot from Rita—Rita had been used to the best and meant to continue having it.

"If you can still count them . . ." Her voice trailed off. "I don't know why you make me feel so goddamn protective. You're a big girl and able to take care of yourself. I'm not bringing you out, exactly."

"Hardly," Dee smiled. She was more than well aware of the routine performances in bed—she'd witnessed Rita's practiced reactions when she was not "really in the mood." Dee was only too sensitive to the knotted feeling in her stomach whenever this happened—the self-loathing and hatred she felt when she knew she was forcing Rita . . . but couldn't help herself.

Dee walked back over to Martie. "Would it help you to decide if I told you I'd like to go to bed with you?"

"Not much."

Dee was too surprised to let her female vanity be offended. "Why not?"

"Because that's not the problem. You wouldn't have agreed to come up here if you hadn't already made up your mind. But you're going to be able to get up and walk away with just a nice little episode tucked into your brain for handy reference. You don't want love right now—and least of all from me. You only want romance—"

"And you think I'm being selfish?"

"No. Not at all. You put me straight from the start. I thought I could take care of myself. . . . I'm not so sure now. It has nothing to do with anyone being at fault or selfish. It's life. But as things are now, I can still rationalize that you're probably a cold turkey, a precision lay, or that you've got warts on your belly. Anything to make you less appealing."

"That's putting things on a rather primitive level, isn't it?"

"Just honest. I don't want just cow eyes and mush notes. I want someone real, someone I can talk to, laugh with, and enjoy physically. I'm not one of these anxious-poodle lesbians waiting to get thrown a few small bones of attention."

"Neither am I . . ."

"Goddamn it, Dee! I've not felt this way about anyone in almost ten years. I'm scared of it."

"I don't know why," Dee said carefully, "but you're making me feel terribly guilty and responsible."

Martie sighed. She took her own and Dee's glasses and placed them on the table. Then she turned, placed her hands on Dee's arms, and with unexpected strength pulled her against her. "I'm a fool . . . a fool," she whispered into Dee's hair.

"Never . . ." Dee managed to say, but already she could feel the blood beginning to pound in her head. It had been safest just to forget what it was like to make love . . . not to think about it. But now . . .

"And if I should tell you I love you, don't pay any attention to me," Martie breathed against Dee's closed eyes. She let her mouth linger a moment, then slowly kissed her way down to meet Dee's lips.

It was so good—so damn good! Dee let her mind go blank and give in to the feel of Martie's body against hers. No awkward sensations because of too great a difference in height, no fumbling or sloppiness. They fit in each other's arms securely, their mouths molded into each other like lovers of long standing who knew just how the other wants to be kissed.

"Oh, Dee, Jesus! Dee . . ."

"Shh," she whispered back and pulled away just enough to lead Martie, with pauses and gentle kisses, into the bedroom.

It was sweet and tender, urgent yet savoring . . . It was too many things to waste her time interpreting, rationalizing. And it was so apparent that Martie really wanted her that Dee almost cried from gratitude—wanted to love her, to feel her, to touch her.

It was an emotional restoration for Dee.

She didn't dare think what it might be to Martie.

And just before she completely lost all other thought she wondered why Karen hadn't written. . . .

Chapter 18

Dee was aware of the fact that she was dreaming but couldn't wake up. All she knew was that Karen lay humped up on the floor at her feet, crying—crying until the sobs themselves could no longer be heard over the torrential roar of the tears that were flooding the room. She began to feel herself pulled under as if she were being sucked down into a whirlpool. And she knew, somehow, that it was all her fault.

Then, suddenly it seemed as if the heap on the floor were not Karen at all but someone else. Someone she knew, not a stranger. She forgot about being drowned, because she had to find out who this someone was. Maybe Karen knew. Of course. Karen would know. Karen would save her.

"Karen!" she screamed. Her own voice awakened her.

She was trembling, beads of perspiration all over her body. She opened her eyes in bewilderment, disturbingly aware of the strangeness of her surroundings. Then she heard the shower in the bathroom being turned off, and memory flooded back.

A door opened nearby, and Martie's voice boomed at her. "Did you call me, baby?"

Dee closed her eyes quickly.

Firm footsteps came to the side of the bed when Dee did not answer immediately. "Hey," she said, gently touching Dee's shoulder. "Wake up in there."

Dee knew she would have to acknowledge consciousness. She didn't want to. "Okay, okay," she mumbled.

"You were yelling in your sleep," Martie laughed. "I've called for coffee and toast to be sent up," she added after a moment. "That all right by you?"

Dee nodded, still groggy from the dream. "Light me a cigarette, will you, please?"

"Sure." The mattress only slightly rose when she stood up and crossed the room to the dresser. "Have a nightmare?"

Dee lifted herself up on her elbows and propped herself against the headboard.

"Sorta," she said finally. "I was drowning . . ."

Martie laughed. "Sex dream, huh?"

Dee opened her eyes into the sun-filled room. She smiled slowly at Martie. "If there's anything I can't stand first thing in the morning, it's an amateur psychoanalyst."

"Hah," began Martie, gathering herself for one of her usual spitball retorts. But a light rap on the outside door interrupted her. She threw a disdainful look at Dee and pulled her robe about her, knotting the cord with exaggerated flourish.

"Saved by the bell," she chuckled, turning away. "Be right back. I'll tend to you later."

Martie had pulled the bedroom door shut behind her, leaving Dee free to stretch leisurely in the huge bed. She turned over and sprawled across the bed sideways with her arms hanging over the side. Except for the fading sensations from her dream, Dee felt wonderful—better than she had in too long a time.

She heard the outer door close and the cart clanking across the carpet. She sat up as Martie opened the door, then pulled the cart to the side of the bed. "Breakfast," Martie proclaimed happily.

"You sound chipper this morning," Dee smiled.

"Why not?" Martie replied. "I've had a marvelous stay in Paris, enjoyed the company of a fascinating woman—you—and am leaving for Munich tonight with nothing but pleasant memories. . . ." Her voice trailed off for a moment, belying the airy dismissal in her tone. "I hope," she said more seriously, "that there are no, well, shall we say, regrets."

Dee lifted the coffee to her lips and took a slow sip. "About last night, you mean . . ."

Martie nodded.

"I should be the one to ask *you*—you didn't stand much of a chance, you know."

Martie stared at her a moment. "No. No regrets," she laughed suddenly. "It's pretty damn hard to tell who's seducing whom when two women are involved, isn't it?"

Dee smiled. She didn't like the timbre of Martie's joviality; it sounded forced and theatrical. She put her cup on the tray carefully. "Do you remember," she began softly, "what you said last night . . . before we came in here?"

Martie nodded again. There was a quality about her that reminded Dee of the little boy who's been told he can't go to summer camp this year and is trying to be brave about it. Dee knew she would have to tread very carefully—if she behaved as if she expected Martie to be in love with her, she risked sounding like the worst kind of egotist. On the other hand, if she acted on the assumption that their relationship was completely casual, then she might hurt her terribly.

"Martie . . . come here. Closer." She opened her arms out to her and, when Martie had edged right next to her, enfolded Martie against her breasts. "Last night was something pretty special for me. I don't mean that it was the culmination of any grand passion or forever-and-ever love . . . but it wasn't curiosity or just the old biological urge, either. I like you, Martie . . . very much. If you had turned me down, I don't know what would have happened. I needed you, you as a person, not just a one-night-stand affair. I needed someone I could trust, someone gentle and sweet." She stroked Martie's hair and kissed the top of her head. "I just needed you . . . and you were there for me. I know it sounds cold and calculating, but thank you."

"I could fall in love with you—you know damn well I could!" Martie's voice was choked and muffled.

Dee could feel warm tears on her breasts and held Martie even closer to her. "Don't let yourself, Martie. I would only make your life a hell," Dee almost whispered now. "I'm in no shape to return your love, or even accept it, with the tenderness it deserves. You saw that last night. . . ." Dee paused. "Do you still see it this morning?"

Martie pressed her face closer and kissed the soft roundness of Dee's body. "I know, I know. . . ."

"You don't think I'm awful . . ."

Martie hugged her firmly. "No, baby. I only wish I did." She gave a short laugh.

They stayed like that, in each other's arms, for a few moments without saying a word—each privately guarding her own thoughts. Then Martie pulled away slowly and sat up, kissing Dee lightly on her lips. "C'mon, this breakfast is getting cold and it set me back four hundred and fifty francs plus tip."

"Just like a man!" Dee teased, and they both laughed. They finished their coffee and Dee showered quickly. The mood now was one of good-natured kidding, and they did not come near enough to each other to touch. Martie called the airline office while Dee finished dressing.

Martie came back into the bedroom with an expression of something settled, irrevocable. "Lufthansa at five-fifteen this afternoon. Doesn't give me much time to pack."

Dee turned around, indicating that Martie should zip her dress. "I'll be out of your way in fifteen minutes; don't worry."

"Guess I won't see you again today . . ."

"Not likely," Dee answered deliberately. "Will you be in Munich long?" She turned and faced Martie. Her expression was carefully blank.

Martie stepped back a pace, looking intently at her. A slow, almost wistful smile crossed her face. "It's a one-week engagement. . . . I could make it longer—or shorter. Depends how well they like me."

"Of course they'll like you," Dee assured her. "You're terrific."

Martie gave her a quick, grateful grin and walked over to the luggage rack at the foot of the bed and opened her suitcase. She kept her back to Dee and said, "It's going to seem strange not to see you every day . . . to be way the hell the other side of the ocean from you . . . once you return."

"Yes," Dee sighed suddenly. "Most of the work is done here. I hate to think about going back so soon."

"You might take a leave of absence and take a short vacation . . . in Munich, for instance."

The suggestion was both frightening and gratifying. Dee felt like putting her arms around Martie then, but was afraid of how Martie would take the gesture—she didn't want to encourage her any more than she already had.

"I'd like to, Martie . . . I really would. But it's out of the question. There'll be so much work to do back in New York . . . work that only I can cover. And then," Dee paused pensively, "there's a personal matter I have to take up with Karen. It's going to be difficult . . ." she said almost to herself.

"She's in love with you, isn't she," Martie said simply.

Dee was startled. "No. Of course not! In fact, until just recently, she didn't even know I was gay. It's a long and complicated situation. . . ."

"But you'd like it if she were in love with you?"

"Don't be childish!" Dee snapped. Then, contritely she walked up to Martie and placed her hand on her arm "I'm sorry, I didn't mean to bark at you like that. I'd be lying if I said I wasn't very fond of Karen. But if I'm in love with her . . . oh no. It would be impossible. Really quite impossible."

Martie's voice was low and controlled. "But you would like it if she loved you, wouldn't you?"

"None of that, now, Martie! I don't know and I don't want to think about it. Sometimes it's better not to let your conscious know what your subconscious is doing. All this damn psychological probing—like playing war with live ammunition . . . you could get killed that way!" It was an old joke punch line that she knew Martie would recognize and hoped would take the edge out of her own voice.

Martie shook her head patiently. "All right, all right. Don't get your dandruff up again. Let's drop it. Let's discuss something that isn't impossible."

Dee leaned across the bed to the tray and picked up her cup, finishing the now cold coffee. She tried not to let her hand shake. She didn't want to show how much Martie's question had affected her.

"Let's talk about us and when we'll meet again. Now that your friend Chloe—"

"Rita," Dee corrected with a smile.

"Now that *she* has departed, may I call you at home when I get back?"

"Certainly," Dee answered quickly. "I'll even cook you a TV dinner."

"Reluctantly accepted. What's your home phone?" Martie grabbed a pencil and in a boyish scrawl wrote down the number Dee gave her on the inside of her passport. "If you don't hear from me right away," she advised Dee, "don't think I've forgotten. It would only be because I'm still on this side of the world."

Dee smiled. "I trust your motives. . . ."

"Well," Martie gave a wry chuckle, "at least I fooled you that much." The tone was joking, but the swift shadow of pain that crossed her face did not escape Dee.

She stood a moment without comment. She wished she could reassure Martie, tell her that perhaps her present feelings would turn into love with time . . . but what for? Even if she did fall in love with Martie, what would the future hold for them? She considered the advantages of living with someone who adored her but whom she was only fond of. There were many advantages, she knew. But she just wasn't ready to accept life on those terms yet. Somewhere there was someone who was exactly what she wanted.

"Well," Dee began finally, "guess I'll be off. Have a good trip."

"Sure, sure. And I'll give you a call as soon as I get back."

They walked side by side to the front door, carefully formal. Martie opened the door for her and stood, uneasily twisting the handle up and down.

"Martie . . ." Dee was suddenly reminded of the telephone conversation she had had with Martie so long ago in New York—of that terrible feeling of losing something, of needing to say more and not knowing how or what.

"Go on," Martie laughed nervously. "Don't prolong the agony. Never saw such a ham in all my life, always milking your scene."

Dee smiled slowly, then leaned forward and despite the open door quickly kissed Martie on the lips. "Please do call . . . I mean that," she whispered.

Martie only nodded, and Dee left swiftly when she saw the tears coming into Martie's eyes. She couldn't stand the thought of having made Martie cry. Even though she knew it wasn't really her fault or her responsibility, she felt guilty.

She hailed a cab in front of the hotel and gave the driver Bizot's address. The last few days began to seem incredible to her—that all of this was happening in Paris, that she had run into Martie. And last night seemed the most unreal of it all.

She felt a sudden need to see Karen, just to know she was around. If Karen was still talking to her. Dee wouldn't blame Karen at all if she had pulled up stakes and gone back to the hotel—even if she'd quit her job rather than look at Dee again. It had been stupid of her to place the girl in a situation that could expose her to Rita. And then not having the courage to answer Karen's letter after what Rita had put her through . . . simply trusting that Karen would come out of it unscathed, without jeopardizing their friendship. What a gutless, shallow, and selfish thing to do!

Dee tried to visualize Karen in the apartment, using her things, sleeping in her bed. . . .

Stop it now, Dee warned herself. Some friend I've been, she thought ruefully. Just leaving her there to sweat it out while I've been having a wild time myself.

She did not know then that she had already made up her mind to leave. It never formed actual words in Dee's mind—it simply went from intuitive recognition into purposeful decision. She would call the airline when she got back to the Bizots' and try to set up the date for her departure. As soon as possible. Preferably tomorrow.

Chapter 19

The small Renault bounced and swerved at a moderate speed through the traffic down the Boulevard Raspail heading toward Orly Field. Raoul had attached the luggage rack to the top of the car and strapped Dee's valises to it carefully.

Dee sat up in front with him, perched in a sideways position so she could also talk with Pepe. However, they had driven mostly in silence thus far. Dee wished now she were the clever type, with a running line of jokes and puns, something witty forever at the tip of her tongue. She hated to say good-bye—she always felt so damn inadequate.

The headlights of the oncoming traffic illuminated each of their faces just enough for her to make out their expressions, yet not enough to be able to interpret them.

Raoul broke the silence, cursing a car in front of them, which had made a sudden decision to pull into his lane.

"I wish one of you would say something," he said a moment later. "This silence is making me nervous."

Dee smiled. "I feel the same way, Raoul, but what can I say? That you've been wonderful, that I'll never forget how perfect you both made my visit? It sounds so synthetic."

"Oh, no!" Pepe interrupted. "Those are things for polite strangers.

We were friends the moment we saw you, and it grew deeper each day like a love affair of the minds. Had you not been at home, do you think we would not have sensed it? Please. Let us not waste time with this kind of nonsense. Let us speak plainly like friends."

"This is true, darling," Raoul agreed. "We are going to miss you very much, Dee. It is not as if you were simply going to be gone on a vacation—we may never see you again."

Dee felt the warm sting of tears coming into her eyes and blinked to hold them back. The same thought had been going through her mind, too. She glanced at Pepe in the backseat and wondered what, if anything, she thought about the time Dee had spent away from them. Pepe had not actually asked *why* Dee was suddenly so anxious to get back to New York . . . but the question was obviously bursting to come out.

Yet she didn't want to say anything—it was better to let them use their own imaginations than to try to make up a story. Let them think she'd been jilted, or was afraid of falling in love, or anything they wanted. If she lied and they were able to see through it, things would be much worse. She wished to hell she could find a man and get married. . . . If she could be just half as happy as Pepe and Raoul, it would be worth any sacrifice. But that's the trouble, Dee thought. Marriage for me *is* a sacrifice!

As if by some kind of telepathy, Pepe brightened up a bit and said, "Perhaps Dee will marry and come to Paris for a honeymoon."

Dee shook her head with a slow smile. "Don't count on it. But there's no reason why you couldn't come to New York on a vacation or business trip—then you would be my guests! Pepe would love New York, Raoul. Why don't you plan it?"

"We have often talked about it," Pepe said thoughtfully.

"Well, then. Why not?"

"Perhaps . . . who knows?"

Suddenly they all fell silent again as if each of them had tired of the game of making gracious noises at one another.

"Raoul," Dee said suddenly as he turned into the approach to the terminal, "don't park."

"What?" Pepe said, not a little confused.

"No . . . please," Dee continued. "Just let me off in front and the porter will take my things inside."

Raoul glanced in the mirror for a moment, then shrugged his shoulders. "Women . . ." he commented to no one.

"You wish to leave alone?" Pepe asked.

She nodded. "I just can't stand the thought of us all standing around, nervous and uncomfortable, and then having to say good-bye. I—I don't think I could take it."

Raoul pulled up to the terminal and, with a barely noticeable choke in his voice, said, "I think perhaps Dee is right."

Pepe was beginning to cry herself. "I intend to go home and get drunk."

"I'm not exactly being shot off to the moon, you know," Dee said, keeping her voice in control, "and the mails are still running."

"And we might really go to New York," Pepe said.

"Or Dee might come back," Raoul offered.

The porter walked up to the car and began removing the luggage from the top. None of them said anything for a few moments.

Suddenly, Pepe leaned forward and grasped Dee gently by the head and kissed her on both cheeks. The taste of her tears was still on Dee's face when Pepe whispered, "We will meet again, *chérie*. . . ."

"I know."

Dee hesitated a moment, looked at them both, then quickly opened the door and kissed them swiftly before stepping out. "*Adieu*," she managed to say, and shut the door firmly.

She almost ran into the terminal, the porter following her more slowly. She didn't dare look back and focused only on the Pan Am counter ahead of her—she hoped she would not have to wait too long before takeoff.

Dee used her briefcase as a lap desk inside the lounge of the Strato-cruiser. She tried to keep her mind on her notes, to compile them before she got back to the office. She had slept for several hours after the first part of the trip between Shannon and Gander, but now it was impossible.

It was a little foolish, she realized, to be working now. No one at the office expected her back before Thursday or Friday—and she still had a vacation coming to her despite the trip to Paris.

But just sitting in her seat had been unbearable. She kept turning over and over in her mind what she would say to Karen. Karen would have received her cable by now and would know she was coming in sooner.

"Sir," she called suddenly, and her voice sounded strange, "how much farther now?"

"Let's see," the flight attendant said, looking at his watch. "About another two hours, Miss."

For no apparent reason, Dee felt tears welling up and wondered what Martie was doing just now. She would have to write Martie a long letter. Why was it she always felt as if she had so much to say to Martie until it came time to say it? She could talk to Karen . . . Karen.

Am I falling in love with her? Dee asked herself. Could I be that big a fool? But it wouldn't matter much now. . . . Karen had probably cleared out. She had never sent that second letter she'd promised. Christ! Dee realized, I'm falling in love with someone who practically can't stand me, and moreover, I've lost a damn good secretary!

Chapter 20

The morning was cool and nippy with the preview of fall as she stepped onto the aluminum ramp and walked down to the metal-covered passageway leading to the terminal. She trailed behind the other passengers, letting them rush on ahead. She had nothing to rush for.

As she came around the first bend in the walkway, she saw a girl standing against the wall. At first she thought it was just a girl . . . but as she drew nearer, she recognized Karen. In a moment of guilty panic, she wanted to turn and go back. But Karen had already spotted her and came running to meet her.

"What on earth are you doing here?" Dee asked, shocked, pleased, and unsure of herself.

They began to walk together, and as Karen talked and explained all that had gone on at the office, or asked questions about her trip, Dee couldn't help but realize how happy she was to see Karen again. How easily everything fell into place when Karen was near. Or how Karen made her feel that she could handle any situation gracefully, intelligently.

Naturally, neither of them said a word about Rita—or Karen's letter. The airport was hardly a place to discuss something as delicate as that.

Dee cleared customs and met Karen next to the car-rental counter, and then they went outside to the cab stand. "How'd you get out here?" Dee asked, her as she held the door open for Karen.

"Cab," she answered simply.

"That's pretty expensive."

"My rent has been pretty cheap of late," Karen smiled. It was the first reference she'd made to something besides work or the trip.

"How's Cho-Cho?" Dee asked, feeling stupidly introverted.

Karen looked at her pensively. "She's missed you. She wouldn't be bothered with me during the day, but in the evening, around five-thirty or six she begins to yowl and rub against my legs."

Suddenly, Karen stopped. It was as if the reference to her legs were forbidden conversation. Of course, Dee knew from long experience, the moment someone finds out you're gay, they conclude immediately that you're on the make for them. So naturally, certain topics become taboo.

"Anyhow," she went on, "I finally got across to her that I wasn't trying to replace you or . . ." Karen laughed nervously.

You or Rita, Dee finished the sentence for her silently.

"But we get along fine—it's understood that I'm better than nothing and Cho-Cho allows me to stay. But she sure does want her little nip in the morning," Karen laughed.

"Well, at least you accept Cho-Cho as a personality and not just an animal. . . ." She wondered how long they were going to discuss banalities.

Nothing of particular importance was said until they came to the Queensborough Bridge. Somehow this link with Manhattan jolted them into present problems.

"I . . . I guess you'll want me to move out as soon as I can now that you're back," Karen said softly.

Dee felt her blood turn hot and wanted time to think out her reply. Unlike their previous relationship, if she asked Karen to stay on now, it would sound like a pass. The tires of the cab thumped and swished across the bridge like water-soaked galoshes on a dry rug.

"Actually, Karen," Dee began, "my plans are rather vague. I'd not really . . . expected you still to be in my place . . . that is . . ."

"Did you think I'd run out on you?" Karen asked in obvious surprise.

"No! No, of course not," Dee lied.

Karen twisted in her seat and stared at her for a moment, then covered Dee's hand with her own. "You must have been hurt many times by stupid people."

There was no reply to that one, so Dee let it go. "I was rather hoping that since this is Sunday you might not be committed elsewhere and be able to help me go over my notes from the trip. We could whip them into order and get them ready for the old man before the end of the week."

"Sure," Karen said.

"Look, Karen," Dee said falteringly. "I don't want you to get out or anything. I'm damn grateful for the company . . . particularly yours." She could feel her face flush, and she hated herself. "But I know how complicated these things can be—I mean, maybe Phil would rather . . ."

"Oh Dee! For heaven's sake! Will you stop acting like Emily Brontë. . . . It's my life—not Phil's."

"Sorry!" Dee said, mindful to have a broad smile on her face.

"Forgive me," Karen said after a pause. "I didn't mean to snap at you. But you can be awfully stuffy sometimes."

The cab pulled up in front of her apartment, and they got out in silence. The apartment house looked like something out of a childhood remembrance as they walked to the door of her place. They both fumbled for the door key in their purses, grinning inanely now that they were about to be alone, without outside interference.

"I didn't realize," Karen said as Dee fitted her key into the latch, "how much I'd come to accept your apartment as my home. I mean . . ." She blushed slightly. The door pushed open, and Cho-Cho came bounding from the bedroom and in one motion leaped onto Dee's shoulder, crying and purring at the same time. "Hello, sweetie," Dee said softly, nuzzling her cheek against the cat's soft face.

Karen helped her carry the baggage in and put it in the bedroom. Cho-Cho wouldn't stop yowling her vindictive reproaches while following Dee about the room.

"Oh, stop it, Cho-Cho," Dee said in false anger, "you don't look as if you suffered so much."

"That animal will outlive us all," Karen laughed.

There was something frighteningly domestic about the scene, and as if they had both sensed it simultaneously, the conversation ended.

Dee hung up her dresses and coats but decided to leave the rest until later when she had rested. She picked up her bulging briefcase and led the way downstairs like a mother hen followed by her chicks.

"Place looks great," she said to Karen almost too cheerfully.

"I'm a good housekeeper . . . if it's someone else's home."

"Did you do any darkroom work at all?" She didn't really care if Karen had or not. It was the last thing she wanted to ask her.

"I started to . . ." Karen replied. "But, I don't know, it just didn't seem right . . . using your chemicals and your things. It made me feel kind of lonely."

Dee put on some water for coffee. She wondered if Karen expected her to say something, but decided to let it go. She didn't really understand why using her things would bother Karen, but didn't want to go into it now.

They spent a few silent moments setting up the cups and pulling out the instant coffee.

"I hope your briefcase isn't all work—it looks like there's enough there for three secretaries." Karen smiled slowly.

"The bulge is due to a duty-free bottle of Drambuie I bought in Shannon. . . . The rest is work, and lots of it."

"Well," Karen said slowly, "let's get to it. Might as well get it out of the way so we can get to the bottle. I should think you'd like to relax a little."

Dee nodded. "It's a little chilly in here. How about a fire before we start? Make the work seem less tedious." She walked over to the fireplace and laid the pressed sawdust logs carefully over the kindling. Then she lit it and crossed the room to the divan, placing her briefcase on top of the coffee table on her left. Dee pulled out the bottle and set it on the floor.

Cho-Cho jumped up on the couch and sat down next to Dee

with her front paws resting on Dee's thigh. "There's a steno pad in the drawer over there," she said absently to Karen. "Pencils, too."

"Stealing company property, eh?" Karen said, laughing.

"Uh-huh," Dee said, her mind already at work on her notes and how to dictate them into memos. Without even trying too hard, she was again Karen's boss, and they might as well have been in the office.

The fire had burned down to an occasional tongue of flame darting out of the embers. Dee stood up, threw the papers in her hand into the fireplace, and placed another log on top.

"Please, Dee," Karen said in a tired voice, "I'm getting writer's cramp."

Dee laughed sympathetically. "Sorry. But that's all we'll do for now. You can type them up tomorrow at the office."

"Are you coming in?"

"I doubt it. . . . I'd like a day or two to catch my breath." She stared at the log as it began to burn. "How about a martini? I could use one."

"You must be exhausted. Sure. I'll have one with you."

In a few minutes, Dee returned from the kitchen, carefully balancing the two glasses.

"I'll have to get you a tray for Christmas," Karen smiled as she accepted her glass.

"That's worse," Dee grinned. "They slide all over the tray then."

Karen lit a cigarette and blew the smoke into the air with a heavy sigh. "Well, at least the old man will know you weren't just goofing off in Paris—not once he sees these memos."

"No. I was plenty busy," Dee managed to answer. She felt her throat constrict and, for no particular reason, wanted to cry at the mention of Paris. "You'd like the French rep, Mr. Bizot," she said after a moment.

"I'd like Paris!" Karen raised her glass and smiled. "To better understanding . . ." There was a knowing look in her eyes.

Dee said nothing but took a long swallow from her drink. She felt its effects at once. She was much more tired than she had been willing to admit.

Karen pulled her legs up under her and sipped her drink quietly. "You know," she said finally, "I've done a lot of reading in the past few weeks."

"Anything worthwhile?"

"Depends on what you're trying to learn," Karen said evasively. "I . . . well, I found your private reserve of nondisplayable literature."

"Oh?" Dee stalled.

"I couldn't sleep one night after your . . . friend stopped by. I'd looked down here but didn't see anything I really wanted to begin . . . so I looked upstairs. I'd remembered some books in that shelf next to the radiator in the bedroom." She stood up carefully and went into the kitchen, then brought the decanter of martinis back with her and poured them each some more.

Dee knew she should have thrown away those lesbian novels ages ago, but for some reason never was quite able to do it. "I'm afraid," she said slowly after a prolonged and pregnant silence, "that those novels are not very indicative of anything but a desire to exploit for money."

"Oh, I don't know," Karen said carefully. "I learned a good deal from them."

"Like what?" She knew she shouldn't have the second drink.

"Like, this sort of thing is not nearly so shocking or so rare as I had thought . . . that it's really quite a social problem, and yet sort of romantic at the same time."

"Yes to the first, no to the second," Dee said guardedly. Here it comes. "These martinis are pretty potent," she added, pushing Cho-Cho off the couch just for something to do.

"And how lots of women are . . . *gay* and sometimes never know it, or learn about it too late to find themselves the right companion."

"Why should they want to find the right companion?" Dee asked her, wondering what the hell Karen was leading up to. Some sort of excuse for her?

"Love . . . romance . . . the whole bit."

"And do the books tell you that they never really find it?"

"No . . . the women are usually cowards and throw themselves out of windows, or marry the first guy who asks them rather than face what they really are. . . ."

"And this sounds romantic to you?"

Karen stood up and crossed over to Dee, sitting down next to her. "But I'm not a coward, Dee. . . ."

Dee could feel her pulse beat throughout her body, and she was afraid to think more than one sentence ahead. She could feel the warmth from Karen's thigh against hers, was aware of her heavy breathing and the change in Karen's voice. Christ! how she would love to take Karen in her arms and kiss her.

"It's beginning to rain," Dee stated, feeling idiotic.

Karen smiled slowly. "Rain, fireplace, martinis . . . and marvelous company. What more could I hope for?"

"Karen," Dee said slowly, "just what do you want?"

"That's a difficult question to answer, Mrs. Sanders." Her grin was absolutely evil.

"But answerable nonetheless," Dee countered.

Karen smiled seductively. "Who was it who said something about the emptiness of words?"

Whatever question that had lingered in Dee's mind about whether or not Karen's closeness was unintentional was completely gone now.

"And then," Karen continued, "there's the man who decided that action speaks louder than words."

Dee just had time to put down her drink, phrasing a reply in her mind, when Karen leaned across her and kissed her softly—yet purposefully—on the lips.

"Are you out of your mind?" Dee asked, her emotions turning into a tornado of reactions.

"It always surprises me that I seem to shock you—what kind of a hermit do you think I am?" Karen's face grew serious again. She raised one hand to Dee's cheek and ran her fingers over it, then across her lips. "I've never kissed a woman before. . . . It seems so strange."

"Why on earth do you want to now?" Dee asked, trying to make sense out of Karen's actions, wanting to hold her close, and yet trying to keep in mind that this was Karen's first experience. But what for? If Karen was just "experimenting," she was taking a big risk fooling around with Dee. . . .

But she did want Karen! And here was Karen, making it so damn easy for her. She had not really realized before how very much she wanted Karen . . . wanted to love her, but had never had the guts to admit it—even when Martie had thrown the facts to her.

Dee felt awful. Sure, the kid wanted to play around. But hell! She didn't want this to be some kind of a "steam bath club" affair—just grab someone who's willing. . . . Just because Karen was curious didn't mean that Dee had to go along with it—what kind of an animal was she?

"I love you," Karen whispered without warning.

Dee was so startled, she could only stare at her.

"I guess I've loved you for a long time . . . but this kind of love never occurred to me. I always thought you had to be some kind of nut, but now . . ."

This fantastic admission was more than Dee had figured on. She didn't know what to do now. Karen placed her cheek against Dee's, and the sweet scent of her youth and femininity was an irresistible temptation. Dee could feel her young, firm breasts pushing against her arm, then slide past to her own breasts as Karen shifted her position so that Dee could hold her near, could caress her, could love her.

When Dee did not immediately kiss her, Karen again took the initiative and sought out Dee's lips with her own. This time it was not a gentle, curious kiss—this time she meant it, and the blood rushed to Dee's head until she thought she would explode.

Dee could not control her warning mind any longer. She let her lips pass over Karen's face and down to Karen's throat . . . letting her teeth sink lightly into her soft flesh. Dee could feel every pressure point in her body throbbing wildly.

Karen sat up slowly. "You look so tired, darling," she mouthed against Dee's forehead. "Why not lie back and rest?"

I shouldn't; I shouldn't, Dee told herself, but knew she would.

Karen maternally placed the throw pillows under her head. Yet why shouldn't I? Dee thought. Karen's an adult . . . she knows what she's letting herself in for . . . she can take care of herself . . . I didn't go after her. . . .

She saw Karen's face coming closer and closer to her own. . . . She lifted her hands and put them on Karen's young face—so young and smooth. She pulled Karen against her, enjoying her weight as reassurance that it really was Karen and not a dream. She let her hands wander over Karen slowly, almost like someone blind trying to feel what a person looks like.

Rita and Martie were as unreal as a science-fiction story to her now. . . . Karen's response to her was neither forced nor proficient. It was warm, ingenuous, and beautifully candid.

The softness of Karen's arms wrapped around the back of Dee's neck, the touch of her hand on Dee's shoulder, the sweetness of Karen's body resting against hers at once urgent and tender. . . .

Chapter 21

Later, as she pretended to sleep, she could hear Karen's footsteps padding softly up to her and covering her with a warm blanket. Then she felt Karen's light breath as she leaned over and kissed Dee very gently on the mouth, then softly made her way upstairs.

It took every ounce of her strength not to pull Karen down on her and engulf her with the sudden rush of love and tenderness Dee felt. But the years of self-discipline helped her now, helped her to keep her eyelids from making a move and to keep her breathing slow and heavy.

As if Dee's hands had a built-in memory of their own, she could still sense the feel of Karen's body, the soft, womanly ripeness of the girl's breasts. It still amazed Dee how her ego could work independently of her libido. She had wanted—still wanted—nothing more than to give in to her passion, to take this girl who met her desire with the same intensity. But she had stopped.

Dee smiled, mentally recalling that it had been rather ludicrous for the experienced lesbian to recoil from physical love, rather than the novice. But it was true. When Karen had begun to undo the buttons of her blouse, Dee had panicked.

It would have been so easy to let Karen plunge into this gay life, bedazzled by shocking and nonconforming souls who "only needed a little love and understanding." Knowing Karen, she would have thrown herself into gay life with all the fervor of a suffragette. And then?

Then the possessiveness would begin, the jealousies, and the self-doubt, and worse, the self-deceit. Dee had never met a lesbian yet who didn't think she could "go straight" if she really wanted to. But it wasn't true. What these women were really saying was that they could "pass for straight"—play the role, pretend, even get married and fool their husbands as so many other lesbians did.

Christ, no! This wasn't what she wanted for Karen. And she'd be goddamned if she would be the means to Karen's destruction, no matter how she might hurt her now. There was no farm in Kentucky for lesbians who wanted to kick the habit.

Dee lay quietly until she heard the light go off upstairs and the sound of Karen getting into bed overhead. Then she sat up and lit a cigarette in the dark.

"All right, smartie," she barely whispered to the night, "you succeeded with the passing-out bit—now what do you do?"

She began to swear in mutters, but a stir from the other direction stopped her. Dee looked up to see Karen standing at the foot of the stairs. She could barely make out a light smile playing across Karen's face.

It was a moment Dee was not likely ever to forget. She felt caught, frightened, exhilarated, and excited all at once. There was nothing to say. All she knew was that in what seemed to be a matter of seconds, Karen was on her knees before her with her arms wrapped around Dee's legs, her head resting on her lap, and her tears falling on Dee's thighs.

Dee held her that way and just gave up to the warmth and love of this girl. She lifted Karen's face gently, her own hands trembling and warm, and kissed her very carefully, very slowly; kissed her as if this were going to be the last time. Then she lifted Karen up to the couch and lay down beside her, enjoying the feel of her young body, the slope from hip to shoulder, the full roundness just beneath Dee's palm as she passed Karen's breasts. She had never wanted anyone so much in all her life—never wanted to give someone pleasure so much . . . or to use love-making as a means of communicating her emotional love.

There was nothing left in her to fight. Her thighs had grown tense and hard with anticipation, and her own breasts seemed to loom with wanting to give. The first articulate sound since Karen had come downstairs was the chuckle in Dee's throat.

Chapter 22

It was a pity, Dee had often thought in the following weeks, that emotions could not be put into any kind of time equation. If she had had to describe those weeks, looking back over them, the only way to have done so would be to reply: Eternity divided between damnation and ecstasy.

Karen filled her every thought. At work, she would glimpse someone going into an elevator and think it was Karen; or spend extra time away from her desk so that she wouldn't be tempted to talk to her, or touch her. She was in a constant state of fear that someone would recognize the way she looked at Karen and figure out the whole picture.

Karen had not let it escape her notice, either. She had become morose about it at times. Other times, she would simply tease Dee. To Karen it was all very simple: let 'em find out—who cares? It was love, and what was love had to be good. Who cared about what people thought?

At first, Dee was unable to make Karen understand the importance of keeping their relationship a secret. Since Karen had never thought much one way or another about homosexuality, she had had no real prejudice against it. She did not seem to realize that most people found homosexuals disgusting.

Then a very ordinary thing happened at the office that had made further argument unnecessary. One of the mail boys had asked Karen for a date, and when Karen had refused, he had laughed, then joked about her being careful of turning queer.

Dee overheard it and had felt the slap for Karen, but said nothing. Nothing, that is, until that evening, some time after dinner. Dee was loading film cartridges and marking them with their ASA ratings and number of exposures.

Karen had just washed her hair and came downstairs towel-drying it. "All through?" she asked cheerfully. Too cheerfully, Dee thought.

"Um-hum, just about." She glanced up at Karen and saw her, like a fourteen-year-old getting ready to go to her first school dance the next day. She seemed so very young at the moment. It was silly, Dee knew; there wasn't that much of an age difference— and yet Dee always felt so much older, so lived-out compared to Karen.

"Can I bum a roll of Adox from you if you've plenty?"

"Sure." Dee smiled at her casually. "Noticed the mail room has discovered your charm today." She said it lightly, keeping the smile on her face.

Karen sat down next to her very slowly. "I—I wanted to talk to you about it . . . but I didn't know how to bring it up." She gave a small, nervous laugh. "I learned something today."

"That you're attractive?" Dee teased. "I think you're beautiful."

"No . . . something much deeper. I wanted to . . . apologize to you."

"Apologize? For what? You didn't ask him for the date."

"Please, Dee, it's hard enough to explain. Let me get it out."

"Okay," she answered softly, and brought Karen against her breasts, holding her loosely.

"All the times I've kidded you about how you worried about getting found out, y'know? Well . . . I got my first taste of it today."

"I thought that might have happened."

"It wasn't that I couldn't accept the date, but the knowledge that I couldn't explain why. I couldn't tell him, 'Sorry, I've got a date,' or 'I'm going steady' . . . because that would lead to explanations which I'd have to make up. But then, when he made that crack about being queer . . . Dee, I crawled inside. I felt my hands go cold and clammy . . . felt myself tighten up. I'd never gone through anything like that before. Never really knew what you meant. In that moment, I realized real *fear!*"

"Poor baby," Dee said into Karen's still-damp hair.

"But *why*, Dee? Why should I be afraid? I'm not doing anything wrong. . . . I know it. I'm not hurting anyone. Why should I care about what he—or anyone else—thinks?"

Dee stood up then and walked over to the bar and poured them both a stiff drink. "Conditioning, I suppose," Dee answered finally. "It's just that it goes against everything around us, from movies to toothpaste—you're no longer a part of the same world anymore."

"That's not enough of a reason."

"That's all I've got on hand right now."

Karen sat pensively for a long moment. "Will it always be like this?" she said finally.

Dee took a deep breath. "Yes. And it will get worse. Much worse as you grow older and have more responsibilities, begin to wonder what you missed, have a better job, where your moral character might be sufficient grounds for being fired."

"But good God, it's none of their business!"

"Am I my brother's keeper?" Dee's tone was gently sardonic. "Yes! Think of what the general attitude toward alcoholism was just a few years back—even being a dope addict is received more favorably than being queer. It's something people cannot accept, because there's no tangible cause—or because of their own subconscious fears." She lifted her glass to her lips and thoughtfully added, "Or, perhaps, because they're part of the society against which you're rebelling—it's an attack against them personally."

"I accepted it!" Karen shouted.

"Sweetie, I can't answer it for you. I just know that that's the way it is. There are some people who wouldn't give a damn; there are some people who think it's terribly sophisticated and urbane or intellectual or some-other idiotic notion . . . but most people just don't buy it! What do you want me to do about it?"

Karen's eyes filled with tears, and she rushed over to Dee and put her arms around her tightly like a frightened little girl. "I don't know . . . I don't know."

Well, Dee thought, here goes nothing. "Which brings up something I've been wanting to say for a long time."

Karen nodded against Dee's neck—a gesture she used to show she was listening.

"It just isn't wise for us to continue working together, darling."

Karen pulled away brusquely and stared at Dee, as if she didn't understand. "What?"

Dee's heart felt like someone had thrown an anchor out and it had sunk with it. "Please try to understand. It's an awful strain having to be with you so near all day, watching every gesture, careful that no one might overhear us talking and notice the change in voice. One slip of the tongue, one *darling* might mean both our jobs. . . ."

"You mean just because some of the gang at the office know I'm living with you?"

"Well? What would you think?"

"Oh, Christ! Dee, is it all worth it?" Karen's face screwed into immediate repentance at her words. "Oh, darling, I didn't mean it that way—you know that."

"Sure, sure," she answered, but her throat was a hard knot keeping the tears from choking her. That had hurt . . . and what was worse, Dee knew that Karen *had* meant it that way—but that Karen didn't know it. She's beginning to learn, Dee thought. She's beginning to discover the price of this great love. There is no way, Dee suddenly found, to test gay love, because none of the tests are fair.

Dee put her head back a moment as if to stretch her neck muscles, but it was just to get her control back. She couldn't let Karen know what she knew—that their relationship was not going to last. It couldn't.

"Let's have a refresher and sit down," she suggested, trying to get back to the subject of the job. "I think I've found a good deal for you. . . . A friend of mine has a public relations office on Park Avenue."

"You mean you've made up your mind about my leaving. I

haven't any choice." She said it passively, without resentment or accusation.

"Oh, I know you're probably right," she continued. "It'll just take me a little while to get used to the idea." Karen laughed sarcastically, "I've had a great job up till now, a really swell boss—the kind you just *love.*"

"I'm honestly sorry, Karen. Do you think I wanted this? In fact," Dee said, "on the way home from Paris I had a similar thought . . . about how much harder it was to find a good secretary than a lover."

Karen grinned impishly, all kitten now. "Oh-ho! So, you were just holding out on me when you got back . . . just playing hard to get. Making me do all the work."

"Well," she smiled back foolishly, "a secretary's a secretary, but a—"

Karen pulled at her hand and drew her to the living room, onto the couch. "Were you really in love with me even then? How long had you known? Come on, tell me." She wrapped her arms around Dee and began nuzzling, tracing lines across the length of Dee's thighs with her nails.

Dee looked at her for a long time. Love seemed to fill her so much, she wondered how so much emotion could fill one person. But she couldn't let herself go this way; it was dangerous. She knew very well that her relationship with Karen would not last—that she had to keep her feelings strapped down, keep a part of herself to herself so that when the breakup came she would be able to pick up the pieces and keep going. Otherwise . . . She shuddered at what might happen if she didn't keep her control. Even thinking about it was a kind of self-torture.

"Cold?" Karen asked, still lying in Dee's arms. "Shall I light the fire?"

"I'll do it," Dee answered. She needed the chance to stand up and collect her thoughts.

The flames spread quickly, and she took the long-handled broom and brushed the ashes back into a neat pile under the logs. She knew by the sounds behind her that Karen was mixing them another drink. It was snug and comfortable living with Karen. She simply sensed things—Dee didn't have to spell out every need, every emotion.

Dee suddenly became aware of the fact that right now, at this very moment, she had more peace—real, genuine, honest peace—than she had ever had in her life . . . or was ever likely to have. Sure, she knew it would not last—but then, what did?

"Tell me," Karen said, interrupting Dee's thoughts, "about this grand new job you've lined up for me." She sat down cross-legged in front of the fire, twirling the ice in her glass.

"I told you, public relations," Dee said, marveling at the way the flames reflected in Karen's eyes. "You'd be secretary, girl Friday, assistant to a man named Seth Barron."

"Sounds like some romantic hero out of an old English movie," she laughed.

"You're not too far off. I know Seth—not too well. Met him at several cocktail parties. He seems very nice, and he's bright. A very sharp guy indeed, but without that consuming Madison Avenue drive-or-die. You'd like him. It's a growing agency and you'd have a good chance to grow with it."

"Park Avenue, you said?"

"Uh-huh."

"Well, that's a help." She grinned impishly. "So, why am I quitting my present employ?"

Dee sat down next to her. "How about no future? Or, not enough pay?"

"You mean I can't say that my boss is chasing me around the desk all day?"

"Sure, baby, sure. You just do that," Dee laughed.

"How do you know I'll get the job?"

"Are you kidding . . .?" Dee smiled and stroked the side of Karen's face nearer the fireplace . . . enjoying the unnatural warmth, making her especially aware of the very existence of this girl.

"Thank you, darling," Dee said very softly.

Karen looked at her, tilting her head slightly with a slow smile. "For what?"

"Just for being."

"Oh, darling!" Karen leaned forward and kissed Dee sweetly on the lips. "I feel the same way about you . . . only, it's hard for me to say it."

"You've not waited as long as I have. . . ."

"When you want something," Karen said slowly, keeping her lips against Dee's, "getting there is half the fun."

"Hey! Watch out. You're pushing me over!"

"Am I?'"

"I adore you," Dee said, feeling desire rise up beyond control. "Show me. . . ."

Chapter 23

D ee couldn't help but note the subtle metamorphosis in Karen. It seemed to be one that took several directions and yet left the exterior unchanged—so far. She sensed how Karen seemed to need her demonstration of love more and more . . . her terrible dependency upon Dee. As if she needed to prove that love was all that was necessary and she mustn't let go of it for a second—mustn't let it out of her sight.

She had apparently adjusted very well to her new job, and perhaps this was having some effect in making her feel guilty . . . or whatever it was that was making her so demanding of Dee's attention.

One of the problems, Dee knew, was that Karen would not go anywhere. The gay clubs depressed and repelled her. And it wasn't any fun going to the straight places, because she couldn't relax.

Dee shared every discomfort of Karen's experience with gay life. She knew the girl was quietly suffering, the confinement turning her into a recluse. It was as if only Dee's devotion made any part of life worthwhile. Except, perhaps, for Karen's new job.

She spoke in an offhand way about her job, and any mention of Seth was particularly brief. Dee would have liked it better if Karen could have let out some of her feelings—she didn't approve of this keeping everything in. It was changing Karen into someone Dee now had difficulty reaching. Even Karen's interest in photography had grown dim and sporadic. The crispness in Karen's personality that Dee had found so attractive was gone. In its place was a kind of limp resignation.

Dee knew it, watched it grow worse, but there didn't seem to be anything she could do about it. If she tried to mention it, to bring it up for discussion, Karen withdrew and shrugged it off as a temporary mood, or that she was just too tired, or something else equally evasive.

There was no real point in pressing the matter—it only created a greater bridge between them. It was impossible for Dee to try to phrase to herself what it had been like to watch the decay of Karen's spirit, of her zest for life.

Karen couldn't admit how guilty she was about her "new life," couldn't even begin to understand that this was most of her problem. That angry statement she'd made so many weeks ago was truer and truer: it just wasn't *worth* it!

But she had received a really indisputably clear picture of Karen's problem when one day she had had to call Seth Barron about getting a release for pictures from one of his accounts. Naturally, the conversation eventually turned to Karen.

"How's she working out?" Dee had asked, knowing full well he would be more than pleased with her.

"Great," his rich, deep voice boomed with enthusiasm and sincerity. "I owe you a dozen martinis for sending her over."

"I'll take you up on that," Dee laughed. "Believe me, I hated to lose her. But you know how it is over here. There's just no room to grow for a gal like Karen. Either you come into the job at the top, or just forget about it. They've already lost several good people because they wouldn't promote anyone from within the company. . . . They'll learn someday."

The voice on the other end of the line hummed deeply. "Well, she won't have that problem here. She's a real bright kid, and we've got plans for her."

"I'm really happy to hear that, Seth. I'm rather fond of that girl."

"So am I."

"You should be! Two more months and you'll wonder what the hell you ever did without her. She'll get you so organized, you'll start thinking in triplicate."

Seth chuckled. "She's already started . . . cleared off my desk yesterday—went over umpteen piles of memos and notes like a goddamn vacuum cleaner with an electronic brain. Everything where it should be. Now I'm so organized I don't want to move—just want to sit here and admire this miracle of efficiency."

"Which miracle? Karen or the desk?"

"Both. Now that you mention it, she's a damned attractive girl. Which reminds me . . ." There was a note of hesitancy in his voice.

"Yes," Dee prodded.

"Well, I know this is not the sort of thing to be asking . . . like telling tales out of school, you know—but would you know if Karen is tied up with anyone? Engaged, or anything like that?"

Dee tried to make her voice light and teasing. "Aha! The big question: will she or won't she? You damn men are all alike."

"I didn't mean it that way." Seth sounded genuinely hurt. "I like her, that's all. Just want to keep the vital statistics in mind . . . in case of emergency, you know."

"Now, what do you mean by that?"

"Well, hell! It's just good to know what the competition is even if you're not planning to campaign. Now, stop being such a goddamn mother hen and tell me. You know what I mean."

Dee knew very well what he meant. But facing it this way was something of a shock. It shouldn't be. After all, she practically planned that it would happen this way. And Seth was a nice guy. If he just wanted to fool around, he wouldn't pick Karen. No, the way he was asking questions indicated he was serious. More serious than perhaps even he knew. It gave her a sudden sick feeling of panic, but she managed to keep her voice even.

"Seth, stop being coy. She's free, a delight, and over twenty-one. She was engaged to some hometown shmo a while back, but that's all over. Now, you take it from here."

There were a few more light exchanges; then, almost before she knew it, the conversation had ended. She sat there absently rubbing the phone, trying not to fall apart. She was going to have to do a lot of thinking. . . . Somehow, she managed to stand up and close the door to her office so the new girl wouldn't be able to see her.

"No calls," she called out to her . . . just in time. The door closed, and the tears came to Dee's eyes, and the sobs choked out of her like some great release she had denied herself. Dee just stood by the window, looking out and sobbing, looking at the world before her going on its way—not knowing she existed. The tears came and they came and she didn't care—she just didn't care.

She'd earned the cry . . . oh, God! how she'd earned it!

Dinner had passed very quietly that night. It seemed as if both of them were too filled with their own unsorted thoughts to be able to verbalize.

Dee offered to do the dishes, thinking perhaps they might go out afterward just to get into the world and mix a bit.

"I don't really feel like going out, honey," Karen said, looking into her cup as intensely as a fortune teller. She sighed heavily. "I'm rather tired . . . and besides, where the hell would we go?"

"Christ! Karen, we're not lepers, you know. We can go anywhere we want to." Dee just had to break through this blasé withdrawal of Karen's.

"So we go. Then what? It's either a bar where we get funny looks because we're unescorted and then the guys begin to try to pick us up, or we have to go to a gay bar, and I'm just not up to the Nellies tonight."

"Or any other night," Dee added. "What's the matter, think you're too good for them?"

Karen looked up instantly with a flashing hurt expression, which turned immediately into self-righteous rage. "You know goddamn well that has nothing to do with it. You've admitted plenty of times you don't like those places either!"

"Sure, but I don't just crawl into a hole and sulk because of it. Refuse to do anything or go anywhere, with that breast-beating self-sacrificing resignation you seem to love so much. You and I used to enjoy ourselves in bars alone before all this happened." Dee gestured widely, encompassing the apartment and themselves. "It never seemed to bother you then that we were two girls alone, or that some poor jerk with too many drinks decided we were gorgeous."

"I didn't know then I was in love with you. . . ."

"Oh, come off it, Karen! It isn't being in love that has changed anything—admit it. It's *this* kind of love and the guilt about it."

"All right, so what if that's true?" Karen's voice became tighter and louder.

"Do you think anyone in a bar knows it? Neither of us is exactly Miss Butch of the twentieth century—we don't look or act any differently from any other two women, or from the way we used to when it never bothered you."

"So make your point. . . . What are you building up to?"

"Do I have to draw pictures for you? Do I have to take you by the hand to the mirror to make you see what you're becoming?"

"For God's sake, Dee, will you leave me alone! You want to go out? Okay. Let's go. But I don't feel like being lectured or analyzed about it." Karen stood up abruptly and started taking the dishes to the sink with angry determination.

Dee followed her to the drain board and gently turned Karen's stiff body around to face her. She took Karen's face in her hands and kissed her eyes softly, then held her close. "It isn't that I'm just picking on you, darling. I don't want you to get hurt, or hurt yourself. . . . Don't you see how you've changed?"

"Oh, Dee, I'm sorry . . . so sorry." Karen began to cry. "I don't know what's wrong with me anymore. I'm fine while I'm at work; you know what I mean? Like everything is great and I honestly look forward to coming home and talking to you and being with you. . . ." The words spilled out of her in a rush of remorse and release.

"But then," she added more thoughtfully, "when I'm actually here, I don't know; something just happens to me and I get to feeling all alone inside—almost like a watch that's been wound too tight and I'm just going to bust my springs if I get jarred. . . ."

"Can't you tell me about it when it happens?" Dee asked softly.

"I'm so afraid of hurting you. . . ."

"You hurt me much more by not telling me. How do you think that makes me feel—to know you're disturbed but won't trust me to be your friend? We were friends long before we were lovers, Karen, and no matter what happens, I'd rather keep our friendship than our love life."

Karen relaxed somewhat in Dee's arms. "I must really know that—somewhere deep inside me. But I never understand enough about what's going on inside my head to be able to say it. I just feel it coming on, and then I begin to think that whatever it is, it would be better not to bother you with it since I can't describe it, or that I'm just being foolish and it's probably an early change of life or something."

Dee laughed. "Not likely—but I'm glad to see you've still got your humor left."

"I do love you, Dee. I love you so very much."

"I know . . . I love you, too. But shutting me out is the best way I know of to kill love, slowly to strangle it."

Dee held her closer, thinking it would not be too long before Karen finally realized that she just wasn't homosexual. Then this love would not strangle—nothing so drawn out as that—it would just be put back where it belonged. And that would be the end of that. Dee knew, too, that Karen would have to suffer a great deal more before she could come to this—that they would both be hurt, and often. She only hoped that when the time came they would not destroy each other—that enough of their real love would be left for each of them to get a new start without bitterness. . . .

Chapter 24

Things were much better after that night—the air had been cleared enough so that Karen was able to admit her depressions, and even able to discuss them if Dee didn't probe too much. Karen seemed to feel that her cheerfulness at the office, in contrast to her moods at home, was some kind of disloyalty toward Dee.

But at least, Karen began coming home in the evening and could now talk about some event in the office; and she was able to open up quite a bit about Seth. "He's such a doll," she would say, and in the next breath somehow mention what she thought would seem to be a fault in him. Especially if Seth happened to ask Karen to join him and a client for lunch, or suggest her coming along for a drink after work. Then Karen was in her glory with accusations about Seth being just another Madison Avenue hot-pants.

"But that's part of your job," Dee would argue. "How do you expect to get promoted if you don't know how to handle the clients?"

Karen would smirk sardonically and answer, "It's probably a setup . . . he thinks that afterwards he'll have a chance to make the scene."

"After lunch?" Dee would laugh. "Be reasonable, honey. I told you I know Seth. . . ."

"Not that well. You said so yourself."

"But you like him, too. You're always saying that he did this, or was so sweet about that—what kind of a Jekyll-and-Hyde do you think he is?"

And then Karen would get very defensive, and Dee would have to drop the subject before she lost contact altogether.

But this week he had managed to maneuver Karen into accepting a luncheon—business, of course. A couple of movie moguls were in town with their wives. The temptation to meet them was just too great for Karen—and then, by this time she had talked out enough of her suspicions about Seth to test him.

She came home that night with an air of near disappointment.

"How'd the big luncheon go?" Dee asked as she began getting dinner ready. "Did they offer you a movie contract?"

Karen smiled and dropped into the chair nearest Dee. "I'm dead; that's all."

"How come?"

"I never realized what a strain it is to have to watch every word and action . . . knowing the business depends on good personal relations . . . and then, too, martinis at lunch are murder!"

"That they are. It's known as the creeping gin blues—an occupational hazard for all executives." Dee placed the dishes on the table and gestured to Karen to sit still while she brought out the silverware. "Ah . . ." she said slowly, "how was Seth?"

Karen didn't reply at first; then she smiled rather sheepishly. "He hardly even knew I was there . . . just sort of left me to manage for myself."

Dee grinned. "Disappointed?"

Karen glanced at her quizzically. "I'm not sure how I feel about it. I mean, he was so very clinical about the things I said, or how I got along with them. As if testing me to see if I had the stuff needed for a PR gal."

"You mean," Dee said melodramatically, "he didn't suggest anything vulgar to you after lunch? Tsk, tsk."

"I feel silly enough," Karen laughed lightly. "Don't make it worse." She paused pensively. "You know, he really is very nice."

Dee waited for the qualifying "but" she usually threw in and was both pleased and a little jealous when none came.

"Ready for dinner?" Dee asked finally.

The following days were ones of agonizing ambivalence for Dee. Karen could talk of only one thing: Seth.

Seth did this, Seth did that, a stroke of genius Seth had had, the cleverest thing. Dee grudgingly admitted that Seth was not in his business for nothing—he'd certainly promoted himself with Karen.

But then, she had known this would come. She had held her own feelings in check because of this knowledge, hadn't she? And if it had to be, then Seth was probably the best guy to lose Karen to. Lose? she would question. How can you lose what you never really had . . . what had simply been borrowed?

Dee had moments of wanting to fight for Karen—strong urges of what she now sarcastically called love-survival. Then she would look at Karen, at how she was beginning to come alive again, losing that foggy, confused gaze in her eyes that Dee had learned to accept. Sure, she could probably hold on to Karen—but what for? To make her life miserable again? It only made Dee miserable, too.

She had suggested several times that Karen ask Seth to have cocktails after work with them somewhere in between their offices. But the reaction had been so guiltily refused that Dee almost gave up. The following Sunday evening, though, while Karen was helping Dee sort out and decide on the October issue's photo spread, Dee tried once more.

Karen actually introduced the suggestion herself by mentioning that she wanted to see a certain musical currently on Broadway.

"That's Jerry's show—maybe he could get us passes."

"What for?"

"You can't buy a ticket to save your life—everything's sold out for the next six months. Besides, it's high time you two met; I'm having lunch with him tomorrow. . . . I'll ask him."

Karen laughed. "Have you ever missed your one lunch a week with Jerry?"

"Sure," Dee smiled. "But not very many. Why don't you join us . . . in fact, why not ask Seth to join, too? It wouldn't hurt Seth's business to have Jerry's friendship."

"Oh, I don't know . . . I mean, don't you think it would be a little awkward?"

"Why on earth would it?"

"Well, Jerry being gay and all."

"So what?" Dee exclaimed. "He's no flying faggot, you know. And what makes you think Seth would care anyway? I'm sure a lot of his clients are gay. All of a sudden Seth's going around making moral judgments? Since when?"

"Even if he didn't care . . . I would," Karen pouted.

"But *why?*"

"For Christ's sake, Dee, if Seth knows you and Jerry are good friends, and I'm friends with you . . ."

Instead of being hurt or resentful, Dee began to laugh. "Well, well . . . what happened to the little girl who kept making fun of me worrying about appearances?"

"I don't think that's very funny!" Karen stood up and opened a fresh pack of cigarettes. "Besides, Seth and I are having lunch elsewhere tomorrow." She walked over to the windows and stared out at the small garden, where the fall colors were already in command.

"Well, it doesn't have to be the Plaza. . . . We could go someplace else for a change. I'm a little tired of the place anyhow."

"Dee," Karen said stubbornly, "I'm having lunch with Seth alone. I—I wanted to talk to him about my future there."

Dee put down the enlargements in her hand and glanced over at Karen's rigid back. "Oh. Well, why didn't you say so instead of going through all the business about gay and the rest?" She crossed over to the bar, stood before it hesitantly, then decided she really didn't want a drink.

"It was just that I thought you might think . . . well, that it was a date or something. It wasn't a secret or anything."

There was an awkward silence between them. For some reason, it hadn't occurred to Dee to think it might be a date. But now that Karen had mentioned it . . . well, of course. Karen might not be prepared to accept the idea as such—not with her strong streak of loyalty—but Dee could see it clearly. Why else would she be afraid to tell her that she was having lunch with Seth?

Dee walked over to her, started to hold her, then changed her mind. "Shall we have a drink?" she asked slowly.

Karen's eyes filled with tears, and Dee knew how the girl must have been torturing herself. "You aren't angry with me, are you?" she asked, a barely noticeable trembling in her voice.

"No," Dee answered quickly. "Why should I be, honey? You yourself said it wasn't a date—why should you have to apologize about it?"

"I don't know. I just felt . . . that you might misunderstand." Karen stared at her for a long time; then a slow, grateful smile came to her lips. "I'll join you in that drink, if the offer still holds."

"Sure," Dee grinned, and walked around the pictures on the floor to the bar. "We really should think about cutting down on booze," she called idly.

"Dee?" Karen said hesitantly.

"Um-hum," Dee replied, already bracing herself.

"I may as well tell you now, I suppose," Karen mumbled. "I'm supposed to have dinner tomorrow night with a client and Seth. I . . . uh, I probably won't get home until rather late."

Dee put the decanter down carefully. She was suddenly filled with outraged anger. "But why the hell do you feel so goddamn guilty about it! Have I ever beaten you? Do I send you to bed without your supper like a naughty little girl? Why the hell do you have to behave like I'm going to take your 'fix' away from you?" Her hands were shaking with the violent emotions inside her. "I *expect* you to have to go out, to have to work late on occasion, to be a human being living up to a human being's obligations! Why do you act as if you were some kind of Judas?"

"Dee . . ." Karen mouthed, her eyes large with confusion.

"I assume you tell me the truth; I assume you trust me; I assume you realize that I trust you. . . . The only reason you can possibly have for being so afraid to tell me is that you are *not* telling the truth—either to me or to yourself."

"That's not true!"

"Then what is?"

"It's just that I feel as if I'm deserting you, like . . ."

"Like you shouldn't have a good time unless it's with me?" Dee offered Karen the out, waiting to see if she'd be able to be honest enough with herself not to need it.

"Something like that . . ."

"But that's idiotic!" She wished Karen could have admitted that she enjoyed being with a man—with Seth. But she argued it Karen's way. "I have good times without you. . . . I don't feel guilty about it. Why should you?"

The unexpected ringing of the phone stopped them both up short. They looked at each other in stubborn contest as to which one should answer it.

Finally, Dee walked over and lifted the receiver.

"Yes?" She tried to sound calm.

"Dee? Seth. I'm trying to reach Karen. . . ."

Dee fought the greatest urge to tell him to take the telephone and give it an anatomical thrust. "She's . . . she's here, as a matter of fact," Dee said at last, not knowing exactly what Karen had told him about where she lived or with whom.

"Hold on a second," she said slowly, and thought, I'm trying to reach her, too.

She handed the receiver to Karen and finished pouring the drinks.

Karen's voice sounded restrained and embarrassed. "Hello?"

The ice in Dee's glass clinked loudly.

"What? Oh, sure, Seth. No . . . no, I'll be there tomorrow night. My . . . my aunt isn't coming into town after all. . . ."

So that's what she had stalled him with, Dee thought bitterly. She had to check first before she could give him a definite answer—I'm an aunt again. Oh, Christ!

"No. I think the Algonquin is better for someone like him. You can always fill in the conversation lags with the history of the place. . . ." Her voice was muffled somewhat, but Dee could hear enough.

Dee snickered. The Algonquin. Well, that was innocuous enough. She drank down her drink in one gulp and refilled the glass despite Karen's disapproving glare.

Finally, Karen hung up.

"I didn't ask him to call, you know," she threw out defensively. It *was* about business. . . . You don't have go into an alcoholic stupor as if I'm setting up an appointment to whore!"

Dee downed the second drink and glared back at her. "I don't like you to talk that way—it doesn't become you." She suddenly thought of Rita and couldn't help wondering if somehow, one day, Karen would turn out the same way if they stayed on together.

"Are you kidding? You don't know enough about what I really think to know what does or doesn't become me. All you can do is dissect and analyze and read in meanings I've never even thought of."

"Oh, hell!" Dee muttered, and started up the stairs

"Where are you going!" Karen demanded.

"Out!" Dee screamed back. "I'm going out and getting drunk. I'm not so goddamn afraid to admit I'm human."

"You're not going to walk out of here and leave me like this . . ."

"Why not? All we're doing is fighting anyway. You do whatever you goddamn well please!" Dee slammed the front door behind her and ran down the hall, out onto the street as quickly as she could.

She hailed a cab, climbed in, gave him Jerry's address, and began to cry.

"This is really it," she said to herself. "This is the beginning of the end. . . ."

Chapter 25

Dee sat down along the wall just next to the doorway so that anyone coming in would not see her immediately. Jerry would be along soon. She smiled to herself, knowing how much he would disapprove if he knew why she had insisted on the Algonquin—and on a Monday night of all nights.

Karen was in bed and asleep—or pretending to be—when she had come home last night. They had not spoken to each other this morning at all. Dee knew she shouldn't be doing this tonight, knew that Karen was going to be very angry and upset. But at this point, Dee had decided it was best to bring the whole problem to a head. She couldn't go through all these fights with Karen, couldn't keep holding herself in or watch Karen tearing herself apart with her own intolerable conflicts. She just had to do something to force this goddamn, miserable situation to some sort of conclusion. Either Karen was going to face facts or they were both going to have a nervous breakdown.

It was a cheap, low-down trick she was pulling tonight, and she knew it. She couldn't even rationalize her feline action into a deed on Karen's behalf, for her own good. She was doing this simply because she wanted to see her competition flesh to flesh—wanted to test them both together, to see just how Karen behaved with Seth.

Even Jerry had said last night that the whole thing was just too complicated to last. What did she hope to gain, he had asked, by clinging to Karen this way? When she had tried to explain that she wasn't really clinging, he had only laughed and said, "You push with one hand and pull with the other."

Well, he was right. She couldn't deny it. But now she was going to use both hands—in one direction.

Jerry came in looking miffed and questioning. He had not seen her yet, but finally spotted her. It was a small bar but a dark one. Unless you were looking for someone, you might never notice who was there. "Why are you crouching in the corner like that?" he asked, sitting down next to her.

"I'm not crouching—I'm sitting."

He gave the waiter their order and then turned toward her asking, "Why on earth did you insist I meet you here, and so very mysteriously?"

"I just wanted to thank you for holding my hand last night," she said lightly.

"Here?"

"Well . . . I'll admit this isn't exactly a friendship club, but it happened to be in the neighborhood when I called you."

"All right," he muttered. "we'll have one drink. You've thanked me. You're welcome."

"Whew! You must have had a bad day." She smiled.

"I'm sorry, baby. It's just that last-minute whirlwind decisions like this always throw me off balance. I like things to be organized and prearranged. Neat and orderly."

She asked him questions about the new show he was being sought for, and this seemed to calm him considerably. He told her how he felt sort of "in between" himself and how he didn't feel like getting involved in another show right now. He was tired of the same mediocre junk year after year and wanted to work on something with a little challenge . . . maybe even off Broadway if the right thing came along. That, or take off for a while to his farm in New Hampshire.

It wasn't too long before she saw Seth and Karen come in. Dee felt strangely detached. Not disinterested, just uninvolved. She managed to keep out of view, and fortunately, they took a table along the wall, where they would not see Jerry and Dee.

Dee deliberately avoided mentioning their entrance to Jerry. He would guess at once that he had been set up, become furious, and insist they leave. She went on being interested in what Jerry said instead, asking questions when he seemed to pause. In between, she was able to catch glimpses of Karen and Seth.

She had almost forgotten how wonderfully virile Seth was. Not because he was muscular, or necessarily square-jawed . . . It was just in his manner. He had that lusty, cleft-chin, green-eyed hero look.

She found herself hating him momentarily—for his maleness, his casual confidence, and mostly for the way he sat next to Karen. His attitude made it very evident that this was his woman and don't let anybody forget it!

But what was even more striking was Karen herself. Dee could understand Seth's masculine confidence, but it shocked her how comfortable and at ease Karen was with him. She had suddenly become a woman who knew how to hold her man . . . and not only wanted to but enjoyed it. This was a Karen she didn't know. This was the woman Dee had always sensed was there, but had never revealed itself before Dee. Self-assured, graceful, womanly. In fact, Dee had to admit, Karen was actually very sophisticated.

If Dee were to meet her now for the first time . . . she would think that here was a woman who had never known a questioning moment about her own femininity, where homosexuality was never a part of her world except perhaps among a few amusing friends.

Jerry's voice rang in on her. ". . . Why don't you, dear? You really look rather peaked these days."

"What?" Dee glanced at him quickly. "I'm sorry, Jerry, I didn't quite hear you," she apologized.

"Now look, Dee, let's not go through that bit again. You dragged me here, the least you can do is listen to me. I asked you why you don't come up to the farm with me."

"Oh, I can't get away right now, Jerry. You know that."

"I'm sure Karen would understand, at least from what you've said about her. And she is old enough to take care of herself."

"Yes, but I think it's more important—"

She was interrupted by a shadow falling across the table. It was Seth.

"Dee Sanders, I presume?" his deep voice asked in pleasant mockery.

For the first time that evening, she felt panic. Now that the planned moment had come, she wasn't so sure she wanted to go through with it. But she succeeded in looking up, looking surprised, smiling, and answering, "Seth! Seth Barron. How are you?" She extended her hand and introduced him to Jerry.

"Seth's a public relations man, Jerry. And a damned good one." She matched Seth's smile . . . she hoped.

"Don't tell me you've arranged this little meeting," Jerry said, not sure whether to be amused or irritated.

"I swear to you, Mr. Wilson, this was not prearranged." He looked over at Dee and winked. "Actually, I'm here with my secretary tonight . . . waiting for one of my accounts to come in. A night for 'finalizing'—as the boys in Washington say."

"Well, we won't keep you," Dee said coyly. "And be sure to say hello to Karen for me."

Jerry shot a suspicious look at Dee, then glanced back at Seth, towering over them. It wasn't hard for Dee to see he now had the whole plot firmly in his mind.

"Please," insisted Seth, "you'd be doing me a favor if you'd join us. My client won't be here for at least another half hour and . . ."

"Well, if you're sure we won't bother you . . ." Dee began to get up from her chair. She wanted to get into motion before Jerry could ruin the whole setup.

"Really, now, Dee," protested Jerry.

"But she's quite right, Mr. Wilson. It would be a favor. And I'd appreciate the chance to meet you socially rather than like some sort of a salesman. I'm really quite a fan of yours."

"But no business, please," Jerry said with practiced weariness. "My hours with Dee are for pleasure. . . ."

Bless his evil little heart, Dee thought, smiling inwardly. Jerry certainly knew how to play the gentleman.

"Guaranteed," Seth grinned.

"Kismet," Jerry sighed good-naturedly, and stood up, pulling the table back for Dee.

So far, Dee hadn't dared to look at Karen sitting alone. She knew that Karen was going to be furious.

They crossed the small room, and Dee suddenly had to steady herself a bit on Jerry's arm—she hadn't realized how much she had had to drink. . . . Better watch it, she cautioned herself.

Seth introduced Jerry to Karen. She smiled at him, extended her hand, and asked him to sit next to her on the booth rather than in the hard chairs. She gave a rather blanket nod of recognition to Dee and devoted herself to Jerry.

Her tactic so surprised Dee that she sat absolutely quiet, just watching Karen. She was maneuvering Jerry perfectly, showing some interest in his career but working mostly on him as a person. Out of sheer desperation, Dee turned toward Seth and said, "I can see she's invaluable to you—she has Jerry completely wound around her little finger."

"He's not the only one," Seth whispered back, then said more loudly, "You'll never know what a favor you did me by sending her over."

"Dee couldn't help but notice the deep comradeship, or perhaps, closeness between the exchange of glances. Like a husband and wife who know each other's moods and nuances so well they can afford to play with them.

This wasn't going the way Dee had thought at all. And she was beginning to get annoyed at Karen's attitude. After all, she could have admitted more than the nodding acquaintance with Dee that she had implied. Christ! Everyone knew they were close friends, if not roommates. Why the cold shoulder . . . ? It was going to look stranger than if she had just played it straight. Even last night's argument didn't warrant this.

Dee found herself suddenly leaning across toward Seth, in open amusement at all he said. But she was being mindful of every motion Karen made. She just wished she hadn't drunk so much, so she could be more clearheaded!

Seth had a wonderfully fresh way of telling stories and had a collection of them—many from personal dealings with clients with whom he had blundered somehow and had to get back on firm ground again. Always he described them with amusing facial gestures or a keen ear for mimicry.

Dee laughed with him, perhaps forcing a little too much, and keeping one hand on her lap so that her low-cut dress would show her breasts to advantage. She leaned forward again and softly touched Seth's arm. "You know," she whispered conspiratorially, "I'd forgotten how very amusing you can be."

"Now that I think of it," he replied, "it does seem a waste of time that we haven't gotten to be better friends."

"It's something easily repaired." She looked into his eyes with a promise in her own.

He seemed a little surprised, which she had not expected. "Do I embarrass you?" she asked, plunging into the situation.

"Not at all," he answered with a wry grin. "I find you"—his glance wandered from her eyes to her mouth and swiftly to her breasts then back again—"very stimulating, to say the least."

"I had rather hoped so," Dee said, watching his mouth carefully. So I'm feeling my liquor, she thought to herself with rare abandon, enjoying the male-female game of seduction in the civilized world. Goddamn it! she swore silently, if Karen wants this guy, I'm going to make her fight for him.

It was one of those occasions when Dee felt white-skinned, desirable, and full-breasted . . . on stage with the best makeup artist and the best lighting technicians helping her.

Karen broke into the conversation—clever broad, Dee allowed— saying, "I wonder what's holding up Mr. Reither? He's a little late."

Never hit a man where he works, Dee thought. . . . It'll catch him every time. Seth glanced at his watch immediately, and Dee noticed the very fine, dark hairs on his hands and wrists. She was attracted to the maleness of him—yet, for some reason, she couldn't help but recognize that she would rather look at Karen's smooth, soft arm. At the sweeping gentle line of her that made her a woman— a creature warm and to be desired and loved.

Someone long ago had once said that men were for going to bed with, and women were to love. She had laughed then. But now . . .

She suddenly felt very dizzy.

She wanted to cry; she wanted Karen to love her, to look at her the way she looked at Seth. But this would never be, and Dee knew it. *This* was Karen's world. Oh, she loved Dee in her way, and Dee knew that, too. But it wasn't the same kind of love. Karen had just added the physical to the emotional. But it wasn't really a physical love. . . . It had just become that because she had nothing else. If Phil had turned out to be any kind of a man, or if Rita had never shown up to create doubts in Karen's mind . . . then none of this would ever have occurred to Karen.

Karen could put this behind her if she had the right guy. Dee couldn't . . . not now, at least—maybe never.

Then Jerry was holding on to her arm, and from far away she could hear him saying, "She's been under a heavy strain lately. . . . I'll take her home."

Dee wanted to be embarrassed but couldn't. She just had the most awful feeling that none of it mattered. That Seth had been flirting, yes . . . sure, but it hadn't meant anything . . . he'd kept looking back at Karen. Oh, he thought Dee hadn't noticed—but she had.

Karen, baby, Dee thought, trying to stand up with some degree of dignity. Karen, I love you; I love you . . . You may never know just how much I love you. . . .

Her last semiclear thought was the way that Karen had looked at her. Like some drunken old sot who had to be taken away, some over-age matron trying to act twenty years younger.

Karen . . .

Chapter 26

It was ten-thirty the next morning when Dee decided she should go into the office, hangover or not. Jerry had taken her to his apartment and let her sleep it off there. Just before he'd left in the morning for an early appointment, he had explained that he thought it was better than risking the scene she'd have had to face at home for the Algonquin fiasco last night. Also, he'd decided to go to his farm for a month—strongly urging her to come with him.

But he'd kissed her before he left, so Dee knew he had already forgiven her. She had wandered around his Park Avenue apartment carrying a cup of coffee with her. She began to get her bearings again, and called the office to say she'd be late. Dee liked Jerry's apartment, but she was glad she didn't have to live in it. It was so terribly ornate, with gilt-edged furniture, purple velvet settees, and statues on pedestals. Heavy, embroidered drapes lined one whole wall and continued across the ceiling in waves. It made her feel as if she had just been purchased and brought to the sheik's tent for a test run or whatever you'd call it.

The whole atmosphere made her nervous after a while, especially now, with a hangover. "So," she muttered aloud, "guess I'll go home and change and go to work."

Karen certainly would not be home at this hour. She didn't want to face her right now. She went into the compact kitchen and started to wash out her cup until she remembered Jerry had a maid come in every afternoon.

Dee found herself staring at the faucet for a moment and realized she wasn't thinking about anything—just a blank moment in her mind. She smiled foolishly to herself, went back into the living room, and, picking up her coat and purse, left the apartment.

The doorman hailed a cab for her, tipping his hat politely, and the ride home was fast and without incident. She paused before her front door, trying to decide what she would say if Karen should be home.

"I'll just play it by ear," she said helplessly, and opened the door. There was something wrong immediately. The place had that abandoned feeling: stale cigarette smoke and closed windows. Then she heard Cho-Cho downstairs, meowing to herself.

Dee went into the bedroom. It seemed quite evident that Karen hadn't been home last night, either.

She was too numb to have any immediate reaction. Instead, she went downstairs and stood staring at Cho-Cho who was leaning against the refrigerator now and purring.

Mechanically she fed the cat and made herself some breakfast. She wasn't really hungry, but she had to do something to keep her hands busy. In her mind, Dee kept thinking of where Karen could be, or perhaps that she had had an accident on the way home . . . probably in some hospital, unconscious. "But . . . if she was with Seth last night . . ." Dee said aloud and amazed herself with the vehemence in her voice.

Christ! Dee thought, her anger and jealousy mounting, so what if *I* didn't come home last night. She knows damn well I'm not having an affair with *Jerry!* What a spiteful goddamn bitch of a thing to do. . . . So I made a stupid but human mistake, and she goes running off with Seth like an anxious puppy! And I suppose she thinks I'm just going to sit back and take it . . . just be grateful for the fact that she comes back home at all. . . .

But what if she doesn't come home . . . ?

Oh, stop it! Dee ordered herself. You don't know what happened or didn't happen. It's a good thing you're not a lawyer, she argued silently.

Dee walked over to the telephone and lifted the receiver slowly, her right index finger poised over the dial. "I'll have to talk to her eventually," she rationalized.

"Harper and Barron," a cheerful voice announced as soon as the second ring finished.

"Uh, yes," Dee said, trying to sound businesslike. "Miss Lundquist, please."

"One moment, please."

Dee fought the contradictory panic and jealousy raging inside her. If Karen was there, what would she say? And if Karen wasn't . . . then?

"Mr. Barron's office," Karen's voice said efficiently.

Dee hung up. She hated herself afterward. In fact, she didn't even really know why she had hung up. Why hadn't she gone through with the call . . . ?

The phone rang seconds later, and Dee automatically answered it.

"Why did you hang up?" Karen's voice said in a weary tone.

"How the hell'd you know it was me?" Dee asked before she remembered she was jealous or embarrassed.

A short silence ensued before Karen replied, "I don't know that many people who ask for me by name at the switchboard, then hang up. Dee . . . what's the *matter* with you?"

"With me! It's you, not me. But . . . it was stupid of me to call. I—I wanted to apologize," she lied, and again hated herself for not being able to come out and ask, *Just where the hell were you last night?*

"I won't kid you, Dee, I was plenty mad. First, that idiotic argument the night before, and then that juvenile trick you pulled at the Algonquin, and then not coming home all night . . ."

"How would you know!" Her anger was taking over again now. She didn't feel quite so inept.

"Oh, Dee, for God's sake! I waited up until three-thirty for you . . . and only half slept on the couch the rest of the time, ready to give you hell when you walked in that door. You never did."

"You what?"

"You heard me. What are you trying to pull?"

Dee felt like a first-class idiot.

Karen sounded as if she was working up into a full-size rage now, "Do you mean to tell me you thought I wasn't home all night, so you were going to pull a martyr scene? Listen here, Dee, I think you'd better see a head-shrinker; you're really cracking up!"

"No. It wasn't that." Dee tried to keep her voice from showing how relieved she was. "It's just that the place looked so, so unlived in when I got in this morning. You knew where I was. . . . I just didn't know . . ."

"Dee," Karen interrupted patiently, "I don't mind if you want to build up a jealousy case, but why not come out and say it? That's what you're always telling me to do! How do you think I feel when your old girlfriends call up in the middle of the night?"

"*What* old girlfriend?" Dee blurted.

Karen snickered. "Not Rita," she held on to the "i" in mimicry. "She's done her bit for the season."

"Then who?"

"That singer, you know . . . Martie Thornton. Gave me some song-and-dance about having run into you in Paris and that you had taken some pictures or something." Karen sighed. "I wrote down the number she left and put it on the nightstand in the bedroom—be sure you call her. I wouldn't want you to miss out on anything. . . ."

"Now who's jealous?"

"Frankly, Dee, at this point I really no longer care."

Dee wondered just how she really meant that. Perhaps she would come to her decision alone. But then, she always had about everything else—why shouldn't she now?

"Dee, I've got to go now. Do you suppose you could manage to be home this evening? I'd like to have a talk with you."

"I suppose I had that coming. . . ."

"Oh, Dee," Karen said tiredly, "I don't care anymore who has what coming—just answer me."

Dee knew she was going to cry and hoped she could hold out

until Karen had hung up. "Yes, damn it! I'll be here. Don't let your personal life interfere with the office, Karen, by all means."

Well, Dee thought, that does that! She was surprised that she didn't feel the need to cry anymore. It was as if she had been purged already with Karen's "I no longer care" in that tight, barely civil voice.

It was true that Dee had behaved badly . . . but Karen had some growing up of her own to do, also. Only, now as Dee knew with certainty, it was not going to be with her. In spite of her anger, she experienced a strange kind of relief. . . . She could feel guilt falling off her the way bark cracks, then falls off a tree. The responsibility for Karen's life was no longer hanging over her, pulling at her in opposite directions . . . no more of the wrenching confusion of wanting her and knowing she would have to let her go.

Dee didn't go into the office at all that day. She'd puttered around the apartment, and when she came across Martie's phone number written in Karen's neat writing, she had even taken it downstairs and placed it by the telephone as a reminder to call. Several times she'd meant to call "right then and there," but each time she became busy with something else.

She went into the shower about five o'clock and wondered what she should wear for their "talk" tonight. Black, of course. Black slacks and a black blouse. Despite the emotional strain of the past two days, she looked exceptionally well tonight. She was careful to put on makeup and to look like a friend expecting another friend to come by for dinner.

She was chilling the martinis when Karen came in. For some reason, Dee felt completely in control of the situation—devoid of any personal involvement.

"Martini?" Dee asked calmly when Karen came downstairs.

She nodded.

"You look tired," Dee offered, knowing it was the wrong thing to say. She brought the drink over to her.

"I should. . . ." Karen answered sarcastically but without enthusiasm.

They raised their glasses to each other almost in silent understanding of what was to come.

"Um . . . good," Karen sighed. "It's a little chilly; how about
some atmosphere?"

She's made up her mind, all right, Dee decided by the tone of
Karen's voice, but said instead, "I'm getting a bit superstitious
about the fireplace."

Karen smiled. "Life goes on one way or another."

Not exactly brilliant repartee, Dee smiled inwardly, but logical.
She crossed over and lit it, waited for the flames to spread, then
scratched Cho-Cho absently.

"I'd become very fond of Cho-Cho," Karen said at last.

"That sounds ominous," Dee answered. "Planning to do the old
girl in?"

"Dee, please . . . I don't feel much like jolly jokes."

Dee shrugged her shoulders and crossed over to the bar and refilled her glass. "More?" she asked indifferently.

"I suppose so . . . may as well."

There was a long silence. "For someone who was so insistent
that I be home for a talk, you're not saying much."

Karen looked at her quizzically. "I don't understand you, Dee. I
really don't. . . . I'm just beginning to realize it."

Dee laughed lightly. "You will . . . in time. Or maybe not. It
doesn't matter."

"Are you really so indifferent to what happened last night? Are
you proud of yourself for the trick you pulled with Seth?" Karen
paused a moment, lighting a cigarette. "At least, if Seth noticed
anything, he was gentleman enough not to say it."

"Are you implying," Dee said levelly, "that you are more concerned with Seth's reaction than you are about what motivated me
in the first place?"

"Oh, stop it!" Karen replied in that same tired tone she'd used
earlier. "It was unforgivable. . . ."

"So is murder unless it's self-defense. You do allow for self-defense
in your orderly little world, don't you?"

"The comparison is too idiotic to answer. I think you need a long
vacation. . . . I think I do, too."

Dee watched Cho-Cho wash herself in front of the fireplace. "Is this the point of our little 'talk'? A vacation from each other?"

"Something like that . . ." Karen said defensively.

Dee grinned sardonically. "We've not even been together six months—a vacation? What kind of a punch-drunk fool do you take me for, Karen? Are you trying to spare my feelings . . . be civilized about the whole thing?"

Karen didn't answer—she couldn't even look at Dee.

"Look, baby . . ."

"Don't call me that!" Karen snapped.

Dee laughed. "I'll call you any damn thing I please, and you'll listen to me." She had trouble believing she was really saying all these things. She felt positively giddy with control and power.

"Why are you acting this way?" Karen pleaded.

"Because I think you're making a big thing out of a . . . very small thing." Dee quavered a moment, but it didn't last. "You were at loose ends . . . you developed a crush which was both forbidden and exciting . . ."

"You *know*, then?" Karen asked, taken by surprise.

"I always knew, baby. I tried and tried to make you understand, but you wouldn't. And, forgive the expression, I'm just human. I've got desires, too."

"Didn't this mean anything to you?" Karen cried. "Were you just laughing at me behind my back?"

Dee sat down next to her on the couch but didn't touch her. She took a deep breath, then said, "How can I explain it to you . . . ?" she looked intently into Karen's eyes.

"It's like when you've been to an emotionally exhausting movie—when you've lived the part of the heroine, felt all her hurts and joys. For the duration of the movie, you *are* the heroine."

Karen placed her hand in Dee's, and they both knew it was simply a gesture of understanding and friendship.

"But now," Dee continued with a tender smile on her lips, "the movie is over and everybody's picking up their purses, umbrellas, hats, and coats and going home—to where they belong. To their real lives."

"It's too pat, too corny," Karen whispered.

"That's the biggest lesson to learn in life, Karen. It is corny—everything we all yearn for has been so over-commercialized that it's almost embarrassing to admit love, or the spring in your step on a beautiful day. Name me something that makes you feel *good* that the world doesn't consider corny today."

"But then, what was all this we had?"

"For you?" Dee carefully avoided her own emotions, "For you it was a crutch till you got well, or something to hold on to during the hurricane. . . . It was, well, just a phase."

"But I thought you'd be crushed . . . hurt . . ."

"I'd be hurt if I thought you'd taken me for a ride, or if you had been playing both ends against the middle—but I already told you, I expected this to happen. I'm only glad it was now, before too much damage could be done."

"And you don't hate me?"

"What for? Sure, I'll be lonely for a while, and I'll miss you. . . ."

"Couldn't we stay friends, though?" Karen asked. Gone was the determined, bitter young woman.

Dee winced at the question. "Not for a while," she said quickly. "Get back on your own two feet . . . begin a real life for yourself. Once you're on your way . . . well, then we'll see."

The phone rang suddenly, and Dee felt as if she had never had so many phone calls in her life. She stood up and answered it.

"Martie!" she answered with genuine pleasure, turning her back to Karen.

"No . . . I've just not had the time—honest—to develop them. I didn't know you'd be back so soon. But now, I'll simply make the time."

She heard Karen fidget in her seat, then walk over to get them both a refill.

"Tonight?" she paused dramatically. "I don't know . . ." Dee glanced over at Karen. She was biting her lip lightly but met Dee's glance evenly. Karen nodded slowly.

"I'll tell you, Martie, why I hesitated. I've a very good friend here right now and we're having a few martinis—no . . . not a party. But my friend just said she couldn't stay very late. Why not come by for a late supper . . . like around nine?"

Dee was beginning to lose her control again but held on with everything in her. "Sure, sure. And listen, bring the pictures you took. . . . I'd like to see how you've improved." She laughed a little too falsely but hoped Martie hadn't noticed. "All right, nine o'clock, then. S'long."

She replaced the receiver and stood still a moment, not wanting to turn around.

Karen's voice broke through her thoughts, and she was reminded that she wasn't the only one with problems.

"I . . . I don't know why it should be," Karen said, "but I feel like crying and running over to you to hold me close."

Dee felt herself just sag inside. "Then do," she said, turning around slowly.

Karen stood for a second, then ran to her, sobbing.

Dee stroked her hair gently, felt Karen's body against hers, and knew this would be the last time. "You're crying because you're both relieved and guilty about leaving me, that's all. But if you didn't, we'd have grown to despise each other and then the destruction would have begun. . . . Even very good friends cry when they know they won't see each other for a long time. . . ."

"I feel," Karen said now that her crying was subsiding, "like the person I was six months ago no longer exists."

Dee nodded. "She doesn't. At least, not in an emotional sense— she's evolved, to be disgustingly clinical about the whole thing."

Karen laughed.

Dee could feel her body tense up again and knew that Karen wanted to be let go, knew that Karen needed to be on her own. She released her slowly . . . regretfully. Dee went cold all over as Karen smiled nervously at her, took a step back, then handed Dee her drink.

It would be awkward now. . . . She should get Karen out of here. Get her started on her new world before they both called the whole thing off because of one tender moment.

"Jerry's going away for a month," Dee said absently, sitting down near the fire. "Would you like to use his place till you find one of your own?"

"I . . . I suppose so. When's he leaving?" Karen stood in front of the fire, looking like some displaced waif.

"This weekend, I think he said. You could go to a hotel tonight and stay until then . . . in fact, you should leave right away."

"Before we change our minds?" Karen smiled weakly.

Dee looked at her a moment. "People should hate each other before they try to break up. . . . It's so much easier that way."

"I'll . . . I'll start packing." She finished her drink and went upstairs.

As if out of compassion, Cho-Cho followed her up the stairs and stayed with her. Dee listened to the sounds of doors opening and closing and Karen's footsteps.

"Here we go again," she whispered to herself, thinking of that period after Rita. But this was going to be different. She didn't know why—she just knew it would. She still loved Karen, deeply . . . but not in the same way. She'd done a little growing up, too, perhaps.

She stood up and took a look in the refrigerator to see what she was going to make for dinner. The telephone rang again. Damn thing! Dee thought, but answered, "Hello?"

"It's Karen. . . . I left straight from upstairs."

"You what?"

"I'm . . . I'm down the street. The cab's waiting for me."

"But Karen . . . good God, why?"

"I, well, I couldn't face you to say good-bye—even for just a little while. I feel like a rat to be such a coward, Dee, but if I'd had to say good-bye . . . well, I don't think I could have gone."

Dee felt the tears come into her eyes. "I understand.` Will you let me know tomorrow where you're staying?"

"I'll write it to you. . . . I don't think I'll be able to talk to you for a while yet—you were right about not seeing each other. It . . . it's all beginning to hit me now."

"All right, Karen, but you know where I am if you need . . . anything."

"Don't cry. . . ."

"Hell! Who's crying? You promise to let me know?"

"Yes . . ."

"That's it, then. Have a good life, baby."

"You, too . . ."

Neither of them said good-bye—they simply put the receiver back on the hook. Dee smiled a little uncertainly, then went back into the kitchen and started dinner—tears or no tears.

Martie would be arriving soon.